REIGN OF NIGHT

SARA C. ROETHLE

CHAPTER ONE

I wiped the blood from my blade on the dead vampire's loose white shirt. Vampires share a penchant for fine fabrics and lace, don't ask me why. I'm not a scholar, I have no interest in studying the undead. My only purpose is to kill them.

I stood, taking in the stone walls mostly covered with tapestries, the heavy wooden furniture, and the sconces casting firelight across the dead vampire's body. I sheathed my sword across my back, wincing at the protesting bruising lining my shoulder blades. Even through a tough leather cuirass, getting thrown into a wall by a thousand-year-old being took its toll.

I froze at the sound of footsteps behind me, then relaxed as I caught his scent. "Hello Steifan, you're late." This was only our second hunt together, but it didn't take me long to memorize a scent.

"Alright Lyssandra, how do you do that?" He stepped into the room, then stood at my side, looking down at the corpse. His armor matched mine, bearing the flaming crossed-swords insignia of the Helius Order. His jet black

1

hair, hanging loose to his chin, framed questioning hazel eyes.

"Do what? Kill vampires?"

"Know it's me approaching when I haven't spoken a word."

I shrugged as I unbraided my fiery red hair. "Trade secret." Unfortunately, I couldn't tell him I could recognize his scent. It would lead to other questions, the answers to which would guarantee excommunication from the very order to which I'd sworn fealty. The red hair, an uncommon trait in the Ebon Province, had already caused me enough trouble within the Order. Lesser hunters thought me a witch. They were wrong, but the accusation was better than the truth.

"Did you cut out the heart?"

I smiled. "No, that's your punishment for being late." Cut out the heart and burn it. Just to be sure. I turned and strode out of the chamber, leaving Steifan cursing behind me.

I hated cutting out the hearts, though there was one vampire for whom I'd make an exception. I'd hoped tonight's hunt would lead me to him, but it seemed I'd been wrong again. Years of hunting across the continent, and still he eluded me.

Sometimes I could swear he watched me from the shadows, laughing at my ineptitude. Or maybe all that haunted me were the memories of what he'd done. Maybe he no longer cared at all.

I walked through the quiet estate, wondering what had happened to its true owners, though my imagination didn't have to stretch far. The vampire I'd just slain had likely killed them. The blood-drained bodies were probably buried in the wilting gardens.

I pushed open the heavy oak and iron door, taking a

deep inhale of cool night air, tinged with the scent of swamp water. I wrinkled my nose at the after-scent. I hated hunting in the mires.

I waited outside until Steifan joined me. We untethered our horses and began our long ride. We wouldn't reach Castle Helius until the following night, if we were lucky and did not run afoul of any beasts. Or the dead vampire's flock.

I was an experienced hunter, and Steifan had made it far enough to be my trainee, but facing an entire flock would be the death of us.

We rode on through the night until morning's light graced us. The dawn was always a sigh of relief for a hunter. During daylight we could rest easy.

Steifan dismounted first. We weren't far from the road, but in these parts, bandits were less of a worry than the creatures which dwelt deep in the mires. Still atop my mount, I searched for a flat area to sleep for the first time in three nights. Yet another thing I couldn't tell Steifan. Going so long without sleep was . . . unnatural.

Finding a suitable spot, I dismounted, unfurling a rough woolen blanket from my saddlebag. The covering was more to keep out the light than for warmth. I hated sleeping in daylight.

With our horses tethered to a nearby tree, we both lay down to rest. Steifan was too close to me, but I didn't chastise him. It was only his second hunt, after all. Though most hunters trained from birth, actually going on a hunt was always unnerving. We came from family lines resistant to vampire trickery, not from lines impervious to the emotional effects of cutting out someone's heart.

"Lyssandra?"

"Call me Lyss," I sighed, hoping whatever he needed to say would be brief. I was desperately in need of sleep.

"What if something sneaks up on us while we rest? Shouldn't one of us stand guard?"

"I'm a light sleeper."

This seemed to comfort him, for soon he snored as loud as a bear.

I sighed, tugging my blanket further over my face, willing myself to rest. I focused my senses on our surroundings. The horses gently grazing. A stream running somewhere far off. Birds carrying on a conversation in the oaks overhead.

I had almost drifted off when a new sound joined the cadence. Soft steps. Human. More than one.

If I woke Steifan I'd give myself away. I moved my fingers toward the sword at my side, under the blanket. I had just sealed my grip around the hilt when they charged.

I leapt from the ground, striking at a man who'd been ready to plunge a dagger into my chest. He jumped back out of reach. I knew instantly what he was, what they all were. I could sense them, just like I could sense vampires.

"Human servants!" I shouted, hoping Steifan was already awake behind me.

I glanced back to see him standing with his sword out. The three human servants, two males and a female, circled us. Their clothing was little more than rags, their forms thin, but appearances could be deceiving. Servants were almost as strong as vampires, and almost as fast, though they lacked vampire mind tricks and a thirst for blood.

"Watch my back," I growled to Steifan. I hefted my sword, looking at the man who'd tried to impale me in my sleep. "Well, are you going to avenge your fallen master, or are we going to stare at each other all day?"

They attacked. The man with the dagger fell easily to my blade. The second man went for Steifan, and I could only hope he'd be alright. The woman wielded her blade like she knew how to use it, and her rage-filled eyes were on me. Her brown hair hung limp and loose down to her waist, adding to the feral appearance provided by her tattered clothing.

We charged as one, our blades meeting with a deafening *clang*. Her eyes widened at my strength. I sensed what she was, but it was clear she did not share such gifts.

She let out a guttural cry and charged again. I could hear Steifan fighting the other man behind us, but couldn't look. I had to quickly disable my opponent so I could help him. The woman sliced her sword toward my belly. I spun away, then rammed my blade's tip into her back. I shoved the blade upward, then pulled it out. Before she could drop, I turned toward Steifan.

The man had him on the ground. Steifan's hands patted about him for his sword, lost somewhere in the yellow grass. They were ten paces away, too far for me to reach him in time. But I couldn't let Steifan die so young.

I threw my heavy sword, aimed with precision, and it thunked into the remaining man's back. He toppled over, dead.

Human servants weren't nearly as hardy as their masters, though these had not belonged to the vampire we killed. Servants died with their masters. Kill a vampire, kill its servants. These belonged to someone else in the dead vampire's flock.

With a final glance around to ensure no one else approached, I walked toward Steifan and retrieved my blade.

Steifan stared up at me, his hazel eyes wide. "How did you do that?" he panted.

I knelt to wipe my blade on the man's grimy clothing. "I've been with the Order a long time."

"No." He was still sitting in the grass, looking at me all

5

horrified. "No, I've seen the greatest fighters perform, none move as fast as you. None could throw a heavy sword like that. A dagger, maybe, but not a sword."

I grimaced, rising as I sheathed my clean blade. It would need to be oiled later to prevent rust. "I don't know what you want me to tell you."

Finally, he stood, his eyes scanning the grass for his sword. "I want you to tell me the truth."

I looked down at the three dead servants, debating my options. What would he say if I told him the truth? Would he tell the Order? My cynicism set in. That would be some way to thank me for saving his life. But if I didn't tell him, would he speak of what happened here today? Would he tell others I moved too fast for a human? Would they begin to question what I was?

The Potentate had made it very clear Steifan was to be my trainee until he was ready to hunt on his own. It would take at least a year. Could I really keep my secret from him when our lives might depend on my skills?

I sighed heavily. Better to catch him off guard and know his reaction now. If he seemed too horrified, I could always kill him. I didn't like the idea, but if I thought it necessary, I'd do it to protect myself.

I met his waiting gaze. "I will tell you this, and your secrecy will be my payment for saving your life."

My gut churned. Maybe I should just let him talk, let him tell others his suspicions about me. Then again, if he told them what I was about to divulge, would they even believe it? Not likely, but . . .

"I am a vampire's human servant," I breathed. "Every hunt, I hope he will be my quarry."

Steifan blinked at me for several heartbeats, then burst out laughing, sounding a bit shrill and hysterical, probably because of the three dead bodies at our feet. It took him a moment to calm himself. "Thanks for that, I needed a laugh, and thanks for saving my life."

He searched around, finally finding his sword. He picked it up and sheathed it, then turned back toward me. "Perhaps we'll find better rest at an inn."

I nodded hesitantly, schooling my expression to not give too much away. It was probably for the best that he didn't believe me. He now seemed to have dismissed my speed as a trick of his frantic mind.

I took one last look at the bodies before we moved toward our battle-hardened horses. Poor sots. Most human servants were entirely devout to their masters, they would die for them. But not me. I wasn't sure if it was because hunter blood ran through my veins, or some other trick of fate, but I hadn't been besotted with my master. He'd been the one besotted with me.

Though neither of us would die for each other, we'd eventually die together. Taking his life would in effect take my own. I quite literally couldn't live without him.

What price, freedom?

CHAPTER TWO

Castle Helius was a grand sight for sore eyes. Its high stone walls and heavy portcullis meant safety. They meant sleeping in the night without fear of losing all one's blood. It also meant hiding what I truly was, but nothing in life is perfect.

The portcullis was raised now in the safe light of day. No mortals would dare lay siege to the castle, not with so many skilled fighters within. And why would they want to? We protected them from the monsters.

As we ventured within the castle walls, a young stable hand came to take away our tired horses. With a wave to Steifan, I headed toward my chambers. I'd report to the Potentate later. For now, I needed rest.

Alright, what I really needed was to peruse my research. My boots slid across cobblestones with nary a sound as I reached the first of the hunter residences. I had been so sure this hunt would lead me to the one I sought, Asher. I'd been tracing the movements of vampire flocks, figuring out territory lines. The mires were Asher's territory. It should have been him.

9

But it wasn't, and there was no time to question the vampire before killing him. If you left time for questions, you left time for them to entrance you. It was important to catch vampires off guard. Hunters wouldn't stand a chance otherwise.

Reaching my heavy oaken door, I took a moment to survey the locks for signs of tampering. Call me paranoid, but if any other hunters discovered my research, I'd be stuck on stable duty for a month. We were prohibited from hunting specific vampires. Emotions could not play a part in our work. Neither could a long-lived thirst for vengeance.

The locks were fine. They always were. No one had any reason to suspect me of anything. I was a respected huntress obeying my vows, and nothing more.

I withdrew a set of heavy iron keys from my belt pouch, unlocked each lock, then went inside.

My chambers were like any other hunter's chambers, bare bones. A one-person bed with a heavy oak frame and simple cream-colored bedding took up the center of the cold stone floor. To its left was the fireplace, always swept free of ash with fresh logs waiting. To the right was the stuffed bookcase, adjacent to the room's single small window. At the foot of the bed was a weapon's trunk etched with ancient symbols of protection. My clothing lived in a neat stack beside the washbasin.

Shutting the door behind me, I tossed my weapons on the bed. They'd need to be cleaned and oiled before I could put them away. I knelt low, wedging my hands behind one bottom edge of the bookcase so I could scoot it outward without moving all the books. Behind the case there was a cubby-hole formed by a missing stone, a convenient place to hide my research.

I froze for a moment at a knock on the door, then shoved the bookcase back in place and stood.

The door opened before I could answer, and in walked Tholdri Radran. He grinned, showcasing straight white teeth, then raked nimble fingers through his golden hair. "Steifan said I'd find you here. You know, you're supposed to report to the Potentate as soon as you return from a hunt. Just because you're from the illustrious Yonvrode family, doesn't mean the rules don't apply to you."

I narrowed my eyes, reaching one hand behind me toward the bookcase. "Don't think just because we grew up together, I won't throw a book at your head. What do you want? I'm tired."

Without an invitation, he stepped further into the room and shut the door behind him. "How did Steifan do? The Potentate thinks him too squeamish."

I shrugged, then sat on the bed. Tholdri would leave me alone when he was good and ready. For now, it would take less time to simply humor him. "The vampire was dead by the time he finished tethering the horses. But he did cut out the heart without fainting." I thought back, realizing I'd left the room instead of ensuring Steifan completed his task. It was my job to train the new hunter. If I slacked off, he could get killed.

Tholdri watched my thoughts play across my face, then sat beside me on the bed. "He's never going to learn if you kill the vampires before he arrives. Cutting out the heart is the easy part."

I didn't know what to say. I couldn't tell him I'd rushed ahead, believing the vampire within the estate was Asher. He would have recognized me instantly, and I didn't want Steifan to be present.

"You're too soft," Tholdri taunted, misinterpreting my worry. "You can't protect him forever."

"I don't know why the Potentate wants me to train him to begin with. Other hunters are far better suited to the task."

Tholdri lifted a golden brow. "You're the best, Lyss. And Steifan is a Syvise. His family's gold keeps Castle Helius up and running. The Potentate wants him skilled enough to become captain."

I frowned. I couldn't care less that Steifan was from the wealthy Syvise family. I came from one of the oldest hunter lines in existence. Survivability was more valuable than gold. You couldn't spend coin if you were dead.

Unless you were a vampire.

"I'm tired," I sighed. "If Steifan wants to be a hunter, it's up to him to gain the needed skills. If he wants to become a captain . . . " I shook my head. "Well, he will have to become a might more dangerous than he is now. He was unarmed by a single human servant on our return journey."

"He mentioned that," Tholdri laughed. "He gushed about how skilled you were, how you tossed a greatsword like it was a dagger."

I fought the urge to wince. Tholdri would have noticed, and he would have held on to my reaction. If anyone eventually figured out my secret, it would be Tholdri. He was far too clever for his own good.

"Did he mention anything else?" Why in the light had I told him the truth? I could have found another excuse for my inhuman strength and speed.

Tholdri shook his head. "No, but it's clear he worships you." He stood. "I'll let you get some rest, but don't forget to report to the Potentate. Next time you're sent to muck the stables, I won't be down there helping you."

I waved him off. He'd help me, and he knew it.

He went for the door, but paused with it partially ajar.

"Oh, I almost forgot. There was a killing in Bordtham last night. The Potentate has asked that we both journey to speak with the family before the hunt."

I blinked at him. "Both of us? Why? How many were killed?"

"Just one, but apparently some of the details are quite strange. You'll be told everything once you report to the Potentate." He winked at me. "Pleasant dreams, Lyss."

I glared at the door as it shut behind him. He knew very well that I wouldn't be resting now. What could be strange enough about a killing that it would require two highly skilled hunters to attend? And so close in Bordtham? If the killing occurred last night, Tholdri could have already gone to question the family, and could hunt the monster responsible as soon as night fell.

I glanced at my bookcase, then at my weapons. Both could wait. It was time to see the Potentate.

CHAPTER THREE

The double doors to the Potentate's chambers were thrice my height, and I'm not short. Tall for a woman, but not as tall as many of the men around Castle Helius. Those with hunter's blood tended to be tall and built for strength. I had no idea why. Perhaps because the weak died young. Their smaller stature ended up weeded out of the bloodlines.

That wasn't to say that we solely intermarried with other hunter lines, we could marry any we chose, but I had no intention of marrying regardless.

I silenced my thoughts, realizing I was stalling, because the Potentate would be irate if he knew Steifan had almost been killed by a human servant. He was my charge, for better or worse, and it was my task to keep him alive. Not to mention that I'd killed the vampire before he arrived. I was supposed to be training him, and he'd never learn if he never saw a vampire while it was alive. Though I supposed alive wasn't exactly the right word to describe what vampires were before hunters killed them for good.

I knocked on the chamber door and waited. Some

might think there'd be guards outside such an important man's door, but the Potentate was dangerous in his own right. He didn't climb to his rank through politics. He got there through bloodshed.

One side of the double doors opened, seemingly of its own accord, and I stepped into the room. I didn't know how the Potentate made the door open like that—some claimed he had magic—but if that were the case, we saw few other signs of it.

The Potentate rested by the fire in a cushioned chair. Though his short hair and beard were silver, and his face deeply lined, his blue eyes radiated youth, strength, and a cunning wit. A leather tome rested open across his thin but strong legs, clad in simple gray woolen breeches two shades darker than his shirt.

He lifted one hand, gesturing me toward the adjacent seat near the fire.

I walked into the room and sat, anxious to get through whatever lecture was about to occur.

"Steifan had fine things to say about your hunt. I'm pleased it went better than the first."

My brow furrowed before I could stop it, but the Potentate was staring into the fire. "This case in Bordtham worries me."

I sat a little straighter, hiding my relief. Had Steifan lied to protect me, or was he simply embarrassed to have been of so little use on the hunt? "Why?" I asked.

His hand caressed the open tome in his lap like it was an old friend or lover, then he lifted it toward me.

I took the book, looking down at the open page. It was an old hunter's journal. With quarry so long-lived, we kept track of any who eluded us. The information might be useful to future generations.

On the page, an artful hand had sketched a murder. The

woman's blouse was torn around a bloody hole near her heart. Inside that hole was placed a single rose.

The page lacked color, but I knew the rose was red. I knew, because I'd witnessed this particular scene back when I'd been a young and naïve hunter, not understanding how truly monstrous vampires were.

My heart beat slower and slower as I stared at the page. My blood turned to ice. Or at least it felt that way. "Karpov." I raised my eyes to the Potentate. "He has returned?"

He gave a slight nod. "I believe so. The woman killed last night was left in such a state."

My gut twisted as I looked back down to the scene on the page. Karpov was old, positively ancient. His victims popped up here and there over the years, but few had managed to track him down and face him. Those who did never returned.

Except for me.

"Can you do this, Lyssandra?" He watched me intently, searching for what, fear?

I did feel the fear, but it was a quiet quaking thing compared to the fire burning in my heart. I met his gaze solidly. "I will depart at once."

He nodded, a small smile on his lips. "You will bring Tholdri to guard your back, and Steifan, to learn."

My jaw dropped. "Steifan is not ready for something like this. He will be a distraction."

"His father wants him to go, so he will go, and if he dies, I recommend you die with him."

My mouth twisted in distaste. Karpov was the hunt I wanted, second only to Asher. Or perhaps I wanted it more. My guardian, my beloved uncle Isaac, had trained me since I was a girl. When we'd hunted Karpov, I'd stood by helplessly while he tore out Isaac's heart. I had no idea why Karpov let me live, perhaps Asher had already laid claim to me by that time, though I wouldn't meet him until roughly a year after my uncle's death.

I could still picture my uncle's death fresh in my mind. The gushing blood, the fear in his eyes moments before his features went slack.

I stood. "We will depart for Bordtham immediately. I will return with Karpov's head."

He nodded. "Good." His gaze crept back to the fire. I was dismissed.

Halfway to the door, I turned. "Thank you, Potentate, for giving me a second chance at this hunt."

"Do not disgrace us again."

His words made my skin itch. I exited his chambers, then hurried down the hall. My weariness disappeared with thoughts of preparation. I may have disgraced myself once by not dying with my uncle, but it wouldn't happen again. I'd only been seventeen, but it had been my duty to either avenge him or die trying. Return with the head as proof that the fallen hunter was avenged. It was our way, and it was law.

I'd only been spared because the Potentate had stepped in. I still didn't know why he'd saved me, but now he was giving me the opportunity to repay him.

I still longed to slay Asher, but it would have to wait. Karpov had been deep in hiding since my uncle's death. If I didn't claim him now, I might never lift the shame from my shoulders.

And there was one thing different now than when I last faced him. It wasn't that I was a few years older, a few years wiser. It was that I was a human servant. I was strong enough, and fast enough, to stand a chance against a being so ancient. The only issue was that Tholdri and Steifan would both be there to witness my true capabilities. Hard to convince two men seeing the same thing that their eyes were playing tricks on them.

But that was a problem for later. I needed to prepare for the hunt. If I succeeded, Karpov would not make it to see the dawn.

Metaphorically speaking, of course, since he hadn't seen the dawn in centuries.

CHAPTER FOUR

It was nearly dusk by the time we reached Bordtham, and I could only hope we wouldn't be too late. If Karpov had already moved his flock to a new lair, we might not find him.

Tholdri rode to my left, and Steifan to my right, the latter glancing around the small village like Karpov might jump out at any moment.

He wouldn't. Though some of the old ones could walk around during daylight hours, they couldn't in the direct sun. We still had an hour or two before we had to worry.

The few people in the streets watched us curiously. It was clear who we were. We all bore the flaming double sword insignia of the Helius Order. I received more long looks than my two male companions. It was commonly thought that women couldn't be hunters, and my red hair didn't help matters.

I stared down any who watched me for too long. Most of the time I delighted in disproving common thought, but not today. Today there was a cold pit of fear in my stomach. Self-doubt had set in. When I faced Karpov once more, would I be able to act? It was a nightmare which had plagued me for years.

"The house should be over there." Tholdri pointed. "They were instructed to leave the body where it lay."

Steifan leaned over in his saddle to whisper, "Aren't they worried she'll rise as a vampire?"

I rolled my eyes. "Karpov took her heart. This was a murder, not a conversion."

Woodsmoke tickled my senses, tinged with the scent of manure and baking bread. Underneath that was the scent of blood. Tholdri and Steifan wouldn't be able to smell it, but I could. The scent of congealing blood and fear turned my stomach.

We reached the house, a modest dwelling with a thatched roof. The wooden siding was in dire need of fresh whitewash, but the exterior was tidy. Whoever lived here was poor, but took pride in their home.

I dismounted, followed by Steifan and Tholdri. I extended my reins toward Tholdri.

He shook his head, tossing golden hair back and forth. "Oh no, I'm not going to be the one waiting with the horses." He hiked a thumb toward Steifan. "Make him do it."

My reins remained extended. "He needs to learn. Seeing the scene will do you no good."

He took the reins reluctantly. "You know, I might find something that would lead us to Karpov. Something you may overlook."

I turned away. "Then you can take a look after us if that is your desire." I knew it wasn't, he just didn't want to be left outside. "Come, Steifan."

A few villagers had followed us, keeping their distance as they watched me move forward to knock on the door. Steifan stood too close to me, but I didn't tell him to move.

Never dress down another hunter when there's an audience.

The door opened, revealing an older woman with red-rimmed eyes. Her skin was deeply tanned—probably a field worker or shepherdess—with lines that showed she laughed more than she cried.

"Are you here about Mela?" her voice cracked.

Mela. I hadn't known the name. It was always somehow worse when you knew the name. I nodded. "May we come in?"

She stood back, opening the door further.

The interior of the home was dark and cold, with only a few half-melted candles to chase away the darkness. Normally there would be a fire in the hearth, but not tonight. When you had to leave a body lying around, cold was better. Steifan closed the door behind us, sealing out the gawkers now brave enough to approach Tholdri.

The woman, Mela's mother I assumed, stepped back into the corner near a cupboard, as far from the bed as she could get.

I looked around. Just one bed in a single-roomed home. The mother and daughter must have lived here alone. I briefly wondered where the father was, then decided it didn't matter.

Ignoring the mother, I approached the bed. The girl wore white nightclothes stained rusty brown with dried blood. The rose sticking out of the gaping hole in her chest was crimson. When the kill was fresh, the petals would have matched the blood.

I glanced at Steifan a couple steps back. His hand was clasped over his mouth, his eyes filled with horror. His skin had gone so pale, his black hair made him look like a phantom.

I peered past him to the hollow-eyed mother. "Where were you when this happened?"

Her face seemed to crumple in on itself as all the grief concealed just beneath the surface poured out. She pawed her graying braid like it was a comforting pet. "I was here —I don't know what happened. It's like my memories have been wiped clean. One moment, we had gone to bed after a long day of work, and the next, the bedding was warm and soaked with blood."

I looked her over, seeing no signs of blood, though she'd had plenty of time to clean herself while she waited with her dead daughter. I felt a brief wash of rage that the Potentate had made her wait for so long—then guilt, because she'd been waiting for me.

"The vampire must have bespelled you," I explained. *I'm surprised he didn't kill you*, I added silently, though I had a feeling I knew why.

I walked around the bed, looking more closely at the girl, and I realized something peculiar. She had red hair, as rich and ruby-colored as mine. I hadn't initially noticed it in the room's darkness. My heart sputtered in my chest, and I had to force myself to breathe.

It couldn't be—

My eyes darted down to the rose in her chest, Karpov's signature. This was no thoughtless murder, and it wasn't even a message for the Helius Order as I'd initially assumed.

This was a message for me. The red hair told me that. The mother had been left alive so that the death would be reported quickly. Otherwise, it might have taken days before the body was discovered. Karpov wanted me to hunt him, but why?

"What do we do now?" Steifan whispered.

I paced around the bed, ignoring him as I turned back to the mother. "What time did you wake?"

She clutched her throat, her eyes on her daughter, though distant as if recalling the new memory. "Close to dawn. I remember the sun just rising as I rushed out into the street for help."

Close to dawn, and she'd woken while the blood was still warm. That meant his resting place couldn't be far. Vampires were fast, but there was only so much distance they could cover when the sun threatened to burn them to ash.

I saw nothing else about the scene that could tell me where he was. We couldn't track him, vampires leave no tracks, but if he was close, I might sense him.

All hunters could sense vampires to a certain degree, but my abilities were akin to a hound's. I could feel a vampire's presence in a place long after it had passed through. Though how I could explain that to Steifan and Tholdri, I wasn't sure.

I left the corpse behind and approached the mother. "You may prepare her for her rites now. I've seen all that I need."

She wiped a fresh tear from her eye, then steadily met my gaze. The first hints of anger showed in her expression, and in the way she stood. Grief comes first, but the anger always finds its way in. It was hard not to be angry when a monster had taken someone you love. I knew the emotion better than most.

"I will find him," I promised, "and I will cut out his heart."

She gave one quick nod. "See that you do. Now, I must tend to my daughter."

I nodded to Steifan, then we exited the home. I didn't want to be there to watch the mother washing her daughter's corpse. Would she remove the rose, or would she be burned with it? All bodies were burned in the Ebon Province, just to make sure they didn't come back as vampires or some other form of undead.

Tholdri was waiting outside with our three horses and a flock of young girls around him.

"How many vampires have you killed?" one asked.

"Do you hunt other monsters?" asked another.

"Are you married?" asked a third.

They all fell silent as Steifan and I approached.

"Time to go," I said, retrieving my reins. I glared at a young girl standing too close to me.

Her eyes widened, then she scurried away, followed by her friends, all chattering excitedly.

"You don't have to be so rude," Tholdri lectured. "Was it him?"

I nodded. "No mistaking the rose sticking out of her chest. It was either him, or someone trying to replicate one of his kills. Whoever did this was powerful enough to bespell the mother while he killed her daughter." I climbed into my saddle.

Tholdri looked up at me. "It could have been more than one. One to bespell, and one to kill."

I lifted a brow. "Do you really believe that?"

He sighed. "No, I think it was Karpov, as much as I'd like that to not be the case."

Still on his feet, but with reins in hand, Steifan was glancing back and forth between the two of us. "I don't understand. Why don't we want it to be him?"

Tholdri put one foot in his stirrup, then tossed his right leg over the saddle, settling in. "Because if it's him, we're probably all going to die tonight."

Steifan clutched his reins so hard his knuckles turned

white. "But isn't that why the Potentate sent both of you together? Surely with two of you he will stand no chance."

I laughed. "If you believe the Potentate values our lives above our task, you still have much to learn." I winked at him. "Here's hoping you survive past tonight to learn it."

I kicked my horse forward, leaving the men with little choice but to follow. Perhaps I could convince them I'd found a hint to lead me in the right direction. Because I now knew which direction to go. Just as darkness fell, I could feel it, that peculiar, neck-ruffling sensation in the air that said *vampire*. Karpov was near, no longer confined to his resting place.

I could only move forward into the dark, and hope fate intended for me to live long enough to see the sun.

CHAPTER FIVE

The small hairs on my neck prickled as we left behind the last lights of Bordtham. Soon we would be truly alone in the dark. Steifan and Tholdri had followed me this far without question, but I knew soon the suggestions would come on how best to track our quarry.

The scent of rain carried on a warm breeze from the direction of the mires. The swamplands weren't far from Bordtham. Had I been wrong about the territory lines? Was Karpov part of Asher's flock? Normally, two such powerful vampires wouldn't hunt together, but if Asher's territory was the mires, Karpov was way too close.

Unless the one I was hunting wasn't Karpov at all, but Asher, luring me out the best way he knew how.

"We should split up," Tholdri suggested, his horse just a few paces behind mine. "We'll cover more ground. Else we may not find him."

I halted my horse, taking a deep inhale, searching for that particular scent of vampire. "No," I breathed with my exhale. "We cannot be left vulnerable when facing one as old as Karpov. I have an idea of where he may be."

Tholdri moved his horse beside mine. "How?"

Steifan watched us from my other side, not offering any suggestions or arguments. I liked the lad better and better.

I looked out toward the sliver of moon visible amongst thick, black clouds. "Trust me, Tholdri. I have faced him before."

I felt him watching me for a moment longer. "Fine, but if he eludes us, you get to tell the Potentate."

"Fine," I agreed. I didn't bother to explain that whomever had lured us out here, whether it was Karpov, Asher, or someone else, we'd find them. They'd sent me a message, and I was here to reply.

Goosebumps erupted up my arms beneath my shirt and leather vambraces. My breath caught in the back of my throat, my senses overwhelmed by the smell of the dead. Not rot, vampires didn't stink. It was a scent of dark hidden places, rich and damp like turned earth.

"Lyss?" Tholdri whispered. "What is it?"

I tilted my head, waiting for the tell-tale swish of air preceding inhumanely fast movement.

I felt it only seconds before I shouted, "Down!"

Steifan screamed as something dark and large as a man leapt and knocked him from his saddle.

I was on my feet in a heartbeat, slashing at the thing on top of Steifan.

The vampire rolled, evading my blade with a hiss before scurrying into the darkness.

Tholdri moved to my back, both our blades drawn as we stood over Steifan. I had a crossbow strapped to my saddle, but it would do little good now in the darkness.

"Are you hurt?" I asked, not daring to look down. I trained my eyes on the night, waiting for the next attack.

"It bit me!" Steifan panted.

"It can be cleansed," I assured, "but only if we survive the night. Can you stand?"

He stood without replying, clutching his left hand to his bleeding throat as he unsheathed the blade strapped across his back. He moved into formation, creating a triangle with us, our swords at the ready. "Where did it go?"

I scanned the darkness. Our well-trained horses huffed hot breath, but did not flee. They'd faced vampires before. My skin prickled. "They are near."

"They?" Steifan's voice strained.

"They. The first was just testing us."

There was no warning before the next attack. The creature was simply upon us, forcing Tholdri to break formation as he swung his sword in a well-practiced arc. He sliced the creature across its abdomen, filling the path with the scent of fresh blood spilling onto dry earth.

I stepped in front of Steifan as something moved to my right. The vampire rushed us and received my blade in its belly. I shoved my sword upward, searching for its heart, but the creature back-peddled and fled before I could make the killing blow.

I glanced back, seeing that the vampire Tholdri had faced was dead.

"Were either of them Karpov?" he huffed, the whites of his eyes shining in the sparse moonlight.

I shook my head. "When Karpov comes, we'll know it."

Although, I was no longer sure of my deductions. The vampires who'd attacked thus far were young and inexperienced. Why would Karpov lure us out here, only to throw his lackies at us? It wasn't his style. He'd want to kill us himself.

Unless he wanted Tholdri and Steifan out of the way first. Even young vampires were formidable foes. They'd wear us down eventually.

"We should flee," I said evenly. No use whispering. The creatures waiting in the darkness would hear us no matter what. That thought gave me an idea. I raised my voice, "If Karpov is too cowardly to face us, I'd rather not waste our time with such weaklings."

Tholdri caught on quickly. "Perhaps he is frightened. Maybe he spends so much of his existence in hiding because *he* is the weakling. He only likes to kill young defenseless girls in their beds."

The night air felt heavy. I couldn't be sure, but I felt power nearby, and it had to be Karpov or whoever owned the fledgling vampires. It would take someone ancient to control so many.

"It's been a long time, Lyssandra." Karpov's voice was deep and rich like aged honey.

I spun, sighting him further down the path we'd been following. He was taller than Tholdri, taller than most men, and painfully thin. But the thinness was deceiving. He could lift any of our horses and toss them as if they were tiny stones.

"Karpov," I said, keeping my voice steady. "I have waited long for this night."

Dim moonlight caught his gaunt face as he grinned, showing delicate fangs. His dark brown hair was pulled back from his forehead in a tight braid. His loose black clothing seemed to meld with the night.

"This is not a night for killing," he explained. "I only hoped to speak with you. Alone."

I snorted. "If you had something to say, you could have written a letter. Now will you face me bravely, or will you cower behind your lackies?"

His throaty laugh seemed to infect the night around us, echoed by his chortling fledglings.

"Take her," he ordered. "Feed on the others."

The surrounding darkness seemed to move, only it wasn't the darkness, it was an entire flock of vampires circling their prey, too many to count. Had I known there would be so many, I wouldn't have come. Karpov normally traveled on his own, or with just a single companion, and most flocks only consisted of three or four vampires, along with their human servants.

I pressed my back against Steifan's. "Always keep your back to us. Stay as close as you can. And don't look into their eyes. Try to kill at least a few."

Steifan's words came out in a panicked rush. "At least a few?"

"Yes," Tholdri answered for me. "If we must die, we'll at least see that many of them die with us."

And then they attacked, and the world was nothing but blood, screams, and darkness.

CHAPTER SIX

I woke with a pounding in my skull, though I was surprised to be waking at all. Tholdri and Steifan must have dragged me out of there. The last thing I remembered was a pile of dead vampires at my feet, then something slammed into my head from behind.

I blinked my eyes, but the surrounding darkness was so complete I couldn't tell where I was.

I tried to sit up, but a silky cushion loomed above me. What in the light could that be? I extended my arms. Cushions on both sides, same as the one beneath me.

My pulse raced. I had a sneaking suspicion where I was, and it wasn't somewhere Tholdri or Steifan would put me.

Fear snaked through my stomach, but I managed to bring my knees toward my chest. I pressed my boots into the soft cushion above me, then pushed. The lid of the coffin groaned with the pressure, then the latches tore free from their hinges, showering me with splintering wood as the lid swung outward.

I sat up, straining to hear. White candles flickered in the candelabras lining a heavy oak table. The light cast dancing shadows on the stone walls. Three more coffins were in a row next to mine. The rest of the corpses in the old crypt were bricked into the walls, likely long dead before vampires infested this land. Unless the other visible coffins held Tholdri and Steifan, they were empty. No one buried their dead these days. Coffins held corpses during the death rites, then they were burned.

Some legends spoke of vampires sleeping in coffins. I had never seen it, but there was a first time for everything. Even with the lack of windows, I could sense it was still night.

From within a darkened hall emerged Karpov. I instinctively reached for my sword, but it wasn't there.

Karpov splayed his hands outward. "Welcome back to the land of the living." He chuckled at his jest, though I didn't get why it was funny.

My eyes flicked around the room, but as far as I could tell, we were alone. "Where am I? Where are the others?"

"I told you, I wanted to speak with you. You could have simply come willingly."

My legs felt shaky and weak, but I climbed out of the coffin. If I was going to die here tonight, I wanted to face my enemy standing. "You murdered that girl simply because you wanted to speak with me?"

He inclined his pointy chin. "Would you have truly responded had I written you a letter?"

"No."

He shrugged. "Then you gave me little choice. I knew killing a girl with hair such as yours would draw you out into the night. Your extra gifts make you bold. You thought I'd be alone, and that you would stand some chance of defeating me."

If my weapons hadn't been stripped from me, I would

have challenged him. Instead, I asked, "Where are Tholdri and Steifan?"

He arched one thin brow. "The other hunters? I left them with my children. It will be interesting to see who comes out victorious."

I clenched my fists, wondering how long I'd been unconscious. Did the battle rage on, or was it already over? His children were all young, newly dead. Tholdri and Steifan might yet stand a chance. Well, Tholdri anyway. Steifan might survive on pure dumb luck. "Tell me what you want."

He took a step further into the room, then leaned against the candle-lined table. "We share a common enemy, Lyssandra. I brought you here tonight on the presumption that you hate him more than you hate me."

I didn't have to ask who he was talking about. He could only mean Asher, which meant he knew he was my master. Had Asher told him, or had Karpov been keeping an eye on me? "I hate you both, and I will see you both dead, truly dead."

"So bold," he laughed. "But you are in no position to make threats. You are not strong enough to defeat me, and if you think you can defeat him on your own," he tsked, "then you are a fool."

I narrowed my eyes. "So you want to help me kill Asher?"

He nodded.

"Why?"

He pushed away from the table and paced. "Have you noticed more vampire killings of late? More tales of dark creatures lurking in the mires?"

I had, but I saw no reason to confirm it. I waited for him to continue.

He rolled his eyes. "You mortals have no sense of

drama. Too short-lived to ever be clever. Fine," he returned to his spot and leaned against the table, "I will tell you. The vampire clans will soon be at war. Some have grown too quickly, the lines of territory have blurred. There are those of us who would like to see our old laws overturned."

My heart tapped against my throat. A vampire . . . war? It was unheard of. They were mostly solitary creatures, but even when they traveled in flocks, they kept to themselves, never causing too great a disturbance lest the hunters of the Helius Order mark them as targets.

He steepled his fingers in front of his chest. "I see you realize the weight of the situation."

"That's why you had so many young vampires with you tonight," I observed. "You're bringing them over, to what, secure your territory?"

He nodded. "Indeed. And Asher has stood in my way too many times."

"So kill him yourself. You're older than him."

"Am I?"

I shook my head slowly. I really wasn't sure. Karpov had a lengthy reputation, so I'd assumed he was the eldest of the two, but I really didn't know what year Asher was born, nor when he died.

I watched Karpov for a long moment, glad I could meet his eyes, unlike other humans. You could find a lot of secrets hidden in one's eyes.

And yet, his dark eyes gave nothing away. All I could think to do was circle back around. "So you want me to help you kill Asher, knowing full well it will kill me too? It seems a better plan for me to kill you first."

His eyes narrowed, showing the first hints of irritation. "You could never kill either of us on your own. You could not even find us unless we willed it. You have been searching for years, have you not?"

I hesitated, then nodded.

"I can find Asher for you. I can lead you right to his lair, and you may have your vengeance. In fact, I will ensure it. Better to have that than spend eternity hunting us, is it not?"

Was it better? I wasn't sure. My palms itched for a sword at the mere thought of finally locating Asher. I was ready to die to defeat him, but could I do it if it meant leaving a monster like Karpov alive? Could I truly march to my death, knowing my uncle Isaac would remain unavenged? I had been prepared to do just that, but now, with Karpov standing right in front of me, I wasn't sure.

Karpov seemed to read my thoughts. "You know, if you do not agree to help me, I will still defeat Asher. Once he dies, you will die. It can either be by your hand, or someone else's. You do not have the time nor the resources to kill me before this occurs."

He had a point, and I needed to get away from him to find Steifan and Tholdri, if they even still lived.

"I'll think about it."

"See that you do. Come to this place three nights from now, alone, and give me your answer. Bring any others, and they will be killed." I barely saw him move, he was just suddenly gone, and I was alone in an unusually furnished crypt.

I would not accept his offer, at least not in full. I'd told the girl's mother I'd cut out Karpov's heart, and I meant it. But his heart could wait. He knew where Asher was. I could use Karpov to lead me to Asher, then I'd kill him before confronting my master. Asher would be next. Once both vampires were dead, I would finally be free.

I journeyed down the hall where Karpov had first appeared, hoping to find a door out of the crypt. If he'd locked it behind him I was going to be angry.

CHAPTER SEVEN

Tholdri and Steifan awaited me with our three horses at the road leading into Bordtham. Though I was feeling cantankerous after the long walk, my feet felt light with relief upon seeing them, each standing with a torch in hand to ward away the darkness.

They wouldn't need the torches for long, dawn was not far off. I could feel it like a comforting hand on my shoulder.

"I told you she'd make it." Tholdri grinned. Blood caked his golden hair to one side of his face. His light brown eyes seemed to glitter in the yellow torchlight.

Steifan shook his head, his jaw slightly agape. "When Karpov took you, I thought you were lost to us."

The bite on his neck had begun to bruise. Deep purple extended up the side to his ear, but at least it had stopped bleeding. It would need to be cleansed with special herbs before night fell, which meant we needed to return to Castle Helius.

I rubbed my aching head, feeling oddly light, yet vulnerable without my weapons. "Who hit me?"

Steifan winced. His eyes flicked to Tholdri, then down to the ground.

"Tell her," Tholdri ordered.

Steifan's gaze remained on his blood-spattered boots. "Me, by accident, I assure you. It was the pommel of my blade. I was trying to remain in formation, but I guess I got too close."

Irritation flushed my cheeks. This idiot could have easily gotten us all killed. What was the Potentate thinking sending him on hunts so early in his training? I was good, but I wasn't good enough to defend myself from his stupidity while facing vampires.

My next words showed a massive amount of restraint and maturity . . . or they just showed that I was bone-tired, and more irritated with Karpov than I was with Steifan. "It's fine. Let's return to Castle Helius."

Tholdri withheld my reins as I reached for them. "Uh uh, Lyss. You were taken by Karpov, and judging by your lack of weapons, you did not kill him, he let you go. We've waited here all night to hear your tale."

I lifted my brows. "And here I thought you cared only for my well-being."

He smiled, but didn't move.

"Fine," I sighed. "Give me my damn horse and I'll tell you what happened. We've a long ride ahead. May as well fill it with my tale."

Looking smug, he offered me my reins.

Steifan watched us warily. "Should we really travel away from Bordtham again while it's still dark?"

I climbed into my saddle, gazing at the yellow warmth of the nearby village. "It's almost dawn." I turned my horse so I could look down at him. "And even the largest city will not protect us from a creature like Karpov." I thought for a moment, then added, "I'll need you to tell the Potentate why I'm returning with no weapons, lest he make me purchase the new ones myself."

Steifan scrambled into his saddle. Tholdri had already mounted.

I cast a wary glance behind us, wondering if Karpov was watching, or if he'd fled to whatever dark hole he'd come out of. He wasn't living in the crypt—he'd never take me to the place he actually slept—but he was somewhere nearby.

I almost debated searching for him while he was weakened by the sun, but quickly dismissed the idea. Finding a vampire while he rested was like searching for a grain of sand in a well. They didn't need to breathe and could hide their bodies anywhere. They could literally hide at the bottom of the aforementioned well, and we'd never find them. It was why we faced vampires at night, even though they were at their most dangerous. They had to come out into our world to hunt.

I turned back to Tholdri and Steifan, both awaiting my command. With a sigh, I kicked my horse forward, quickly piecing together a believable tale in my mind.

We were silent as we rode through Bordtham, though there was no one awake to hear our words. I felt uneasy as we passed the murdered girl's home, imagining her mother's questioning eyes when she found out I was yet to kill Karpov.

She wouldn't find out, other hunters wouldn't tell her, but it still felt somehow dishonest. She should have a surety of vengeance for her daughter.

We reached the end of the village and started down the long road toward Castle Helius just as the pink hues of dawn seeped up from the distant mountainside. I felt I had come up with a decent lie, but Tholdri was incredibly perceptive. He'd be a difficult one to fool.

"Karpov wanted me to betray the Order," I explained, my voice seeming loud after the drawn out silence, filled only with the sound of horses and creaking leather saddles. "He offered me a great deal of riches and protection. I lied and agreed to his terms in order to escape."

Tholdri's furrowed brow told me what I already knew. I was a terrible liar. "Why would he choose you? You, the only hunter with a particular vendetta against him?"

"He would have taken any of us. I was simply the one who fell first." There, that made sense.

Steifan shifted in his saddle. "The murdered girl had hair just like yours, a rare color."

He wasn't exactly accusing me of lying, but it was close enough. Tholdri was watching me with lips pursed. He hadn't seen the girl's hair, and I hadn't thought Steifan would have made note of it.

"Why are you lying, Lyss?" Tholdri asked. "What could Karpov have possibly done to you that would make you lie to us?"

I chewed my lip, feeling a fool. I should have come up with a better lie. "I don't know what you're talking about."

"Then let me explain it to you," he said caustically. "We were lured into the darkness by a murdered girl, a girl who unbeknownst to me, was killed as a direct message to *you*. We were attacked by an unusually large flock of vampires, all young and inexperienced—lest we never would have survived. Then, one of the most ancient vampires on record, the vampire who killed your uncle, takes you. You return to us with no weapons, but also with no further harm than what you suffered during the initial battle."

I looked down at my lap, wishing my tired horse would walk faster so Tholdri couldn't see the indecision on my face.

"How do you explain it, Lyss?" he pressed.

I glared at him, anger filling the uncertain void in my gut. All of this because of stupid Asher. I'd kept this secret for years, made excuses, lied to my friends, all because he had to go and make me his human servant. All because I'd gotten stupidly drunk while mourning my uncle's death, and had been brazen enough to have a night-long conversation with a vampire.

"He wants to kill another ancient vampire," I grumbled, "one I would like to kill very much. He knows this, and can lead me to him."

His eyes widened. "Who?"

I lowered my chin, draping the loose red locks of hair framing my face in front of my eyes. "You would not know him."

"Who?" he demanded again. "Who could you want to kill more than Karpov himself?"

I looked past him to Steifan. His expression had shifted to one of wonder. "You really are a vampire's human servant, aren't you?"

I was quite sure my heart stopped beating.

Tholdri whipped his head toward Steifan. "What in the light are you going on about? Do you realize the grave accusation you've just made?"

My heart seemed to reanimate, suddenly thundering in my chest so violently I thought I might faint. Why had I told Steifan of all people? *Because you needed to tell someone,* a tiny voice echoed in my head. I'd been alone with my secret for so long, wanting to tell someone for so long that it had come tumbling out to the wrong person.

I realized too late that Tholdri was watching me with a stunned expression. "Why aren't you arguing, Lyss? Did you hear what he just called you?"

Steifan watched me from behind Tholdri's turned back, offering an apologetic shrug.

I met Tholdri's gaze and lifted my nose. There was no going back. Now that the thought was in his mind, Tholdri would figure it out eventually. It was better if I told him first. "He speaks the truth. I am a vampire's human servant. I have hunted the one who turned me for years to no avail. Karpov has agreed to lead me to him."

Tholdri blinked rapidly, as if he couldn't quite comprehend my words. "Lyss," he began, "do you realize how utterly mad that sounds? I've seen human servants, killed them, and they don't act like you. They are loyal dogs to their masters."

"Perhaps it is because I'm a hunter, I don't know," I explained. "All I know is that I've never felt a shred of devotion toward him. I hate him for what he's done to me. And I will kill him."

He watched me for a long moment as our horses ambled peacefully down the wide dirt road. Slowly, he shook his head. "Lyss, if you kill him, it will kill you too."

It was my turn to blink at him. "You find out I'm a human servant, and that's all that you have to say?"

"I've known you my entire life, you idiot. I would not turn on you so easily."

Steifan was grinning at Tholdri's back.

"You're both utterly mad," I scoffed. "You should be trying to kill me while I'm still unarmed."

Tholdri shook his head. "I would never kill you, Lyss. You did not have to keep this secret from me."

I scowled. "Well I know that now. How was I supposed to know that from the start?"

He sighed, glancing both ways at the surrounding meadows slowly filling with pink and yellow light. The wildflowers had recently bloomed, echoing the colors of sunrise. "We must think of what to tell the Potentate. He cannot know about any of this."

"You want us to lie to him?" Steifan balked.

We both looked at him, and he raised his hands in surrender. "Alright, alright, we'll lie." He fidgeted in his saddle. "Stop looking at me like you're a pair of wolves wondering which parts of me are the tastiest. Lyssandra had already told me her secret, and I didn't tell a soul."

He had a point, though I'd just assumed it was because he didn't believe me. He hadn't believed me, not really, but it was clear now he hadn't fully dismissed the idea either. He'd been thinking upon it, and now he'd figured it out.

Yet, he hadn't told. He hadn't exposed me, nor the fact that I'd killed the vampire before he got there, or that I almost let him get killed by a human servant. Well he'd told the latter to Tholdri, of course, but hadn't breathed a word to the Potentate.

"He won't tell," I said to Tholdri. "I trust him."

Tholdri nodded, then spoke about Steifan as if he were no longer riding beside us. "If you trust him, then I trust him. But what do we tell the Potentate?"

"Tell him we faced a flock of vampires," Steifan suggested. "We killed them, but Karpov never showed himself. One of them admitted, under torture, to mimicking Karpov's signature."

I raised a brow. As far as lies went, it wasn't a bad one. Best to keep things simple. "And my lost weapons?"

"You'll take mine. My father will have new ones forged for me without question."

My jaw fell agape. I stared at him past Tholdri for several heartbeats. "Why would you do all of this for me?"

He grinned. "You saved my life, and I imagine it will not be the last time. Because of my cushioned upbringing, I have not endured proper hunter training. I know I am a liability to you. So help me train, help me stay alive, and I will keep your secret and guard your back."

Suddenly I felt horrible about all the mean thoughts I'd had about him. He was truly an idiot. This latest offer was proof of that. But he was a kind idiot, and a loyal one.

"It's settled then," Tholdri agreed. "We will both keep Lyss' secret." He turned to me. "But Lyss, I will not let you end your life just to kill the one who made you his servant. If you want me to keep your secret, you must promise me at least that much. Instead, we will hunt Karpov. We will avenge your uncle, and that will have to be good enough for you."

I hesitated, then nodded. He would never understand. Asher had to die. I could not give up on my hunt, but for now . . .

For now, both Asher and I could live a little longer, because Karpov must die first. And if Tholdri wanted to help me do it, I would not turn him away.

After all, I'd spent years trying on my own, and all it had gotten me was trapped in a crypt with my enemy, at his mercy, just like I'd been so many years prior. Apparently I needed help, and finally, finally I had it.

CHAPTER EIGHT

I resisted the urge to squirm. The Potentate's unwavering gaze told me nothing. He had not countered our lie, but something told me he didn't quite believe it.

He looked at Tholdri. "Take Steifan and cleanse his bite. I will speak with Lyssandra privately."

Tholdri gave me an apologetic smile, then led Steifan toward the door of the Potentate's chamber. Neither looked back at me, which was good, because it concealed our worry. Worry would make the Potentate suspicious.

Once we were alone, the Potentate strode toward a long desk with its back to an open expanse of windows. The windows were glass, large enough for a vampire to break through, but it wasn't an issue considering we were several stories up in the main keep. Despite popular belief, vampires couldn't fly. At least, I'd never seen it.

The Potentate's bony shoulders sagged beneath his loose black shirt. I wished his back wasn't toward me. I had no idea what he was about to say.

"Come here, Lyssandra."

I approached, keeping my steps light. Steifan's borrowed sword felt like a weighty imposter riding my shoulder. The pommel was slightly different from my own. Would the Potentate notice?

He walked around the desk, pushed aside the wooden chair, then knelt.

Curiosity swallowed my worry. I stepped around the desk, watching over his shoulder. He pushed aside a well-worn rug, revealing an oblong hatch long enough to fit a man, but the width fell short. It was a hatch made for hiding items, not people.

The Potentate withdrew a keyring from his belt, then unlocked the hatch, lifting it with a look of reverence on his aged features.

I stepped back. What in the light was going on?

He reached into the hatch and withdrew something wrapped in heavy canvas. The canvas fell away as he stood, revealing a greatsword.

The sheath's leather was so ancient it looked black. The inlaid designs were shiny, all texture rubbed off the leather long ago.

He placed the sword on the desk, then unsheathed it, handing me the ancient leather casing to hold.

I looked down at the sword. The finely crafted blade was plain, except for a steel rain guard near the hilt. The grip was wrapped in the same hard leather as the sheath, contrasting with the pommel and cross-guard, composed of finely worked steel, the edges twisting ornately outward like frozen flames. The most interesting part was the engraved sleeping eye in the center of the cross-guard, so realistic I almost expected it to open.

"Take the blade," the Potentate instructed. "Hold it in your bare hand. I'd like to test something."

I set the sheath on the desk, then removed my right

glove, hesitating for a moment before wiping my sweaty palm on my breeches. With my gaze locked on the lovely sword, I wrapped my fingers around the hilt and lifted.

It was well-weighted, perhaps a bit long for my stature, but I knew I was strong enough to wield it effectively. I took a moment to admire the fine cross-guard, captivated by the artistry of the closed eye. The eye snapped open. I gasped, unnerved by the blue orb staring back at me.

Cold sweat erupted on my skin. I wanted to toss the blade away, but the Potentate's presence kept me immobile. "What is going on?" My voice was steadier than I'd expected it to be.

The Potentate smiled as he stepped nearer. "This is the *Voir L'épée*, the Seeing Sword. An ancient relic of our order."

I was still staring at the open eye, and it was still staring back. "The Helius Order isn't ancient. Old, but not ancient."

"Perhaps not in its current form," he explained, "nor with its current name, but as long as there have been vampires, there have been hunters. This blade was crafted with old magics to aid the most devout of hunters in their quest."

I shook my head, watching the blade. "I don't understand."

"It has awoken for you, Lyssandra. It finds you worthy."

I wanted more than anything to sheathe the blade, wrap it back in the canvas, and lock it away, but not in front of the Potentate. In front of him, I'd sooner die than show my fear. "What does it do?"

"It sees," he said. "It senses predators when they are near. It will guard your back better than any fellow hunter ever could. You'll learn the truth of this soon."

I turned wide eyes to him. "You want me to use this blade?"

He nodded. "The last hunter it woke for was me, but I am too old now to hunt. I have been waiting many years for a successor. I've had others hold it, but it did not awaken."

"Tholdri?" I questioned, knowing he was one of the few young hunters in the Order as skilled as I.

"No, I'm quite sure it would not awaken for him. You must trust me on this."

I just stared at him, wondering if this was all a test. He couldn't truly intend for me to use the strange, magical sword.

He lifted the sheath from the desk and extended it toward me. "Give Steifan back his sword. You will not be needing it. Hunt only with this blade henceforth. Use it when you find Karpov."

So, he had noticed my sword was missing. And he knew we were still hunting Karpov. I looked down at my boots, too afraid of what he might read in my eyes. The sheath remained extended toward me.

His laugh was a harsh, bitter sound. "You should know better than to lie to me, Lyssandra. You will hunt Karpov, and do not return to Castle Helius unless you have his head. I will not save you from your failure a second time."

He really was putting a great deal of faith in me to let me leave with the valuable blade. If I couldn't kill Karpov, I'd not return to the Order. Shame would kill me if the Potentate didn't.

I finally took the offered sheath, forcing my gaze upward. "I will kill him."

"I know. Now leave me. Gather supplies and rest. You'll depart at dusk."

I sheathed the blade, turned on my heel, and went for

the door. I could feel the Potentate's eyes on my back the entire way.

Once I was out in the hall, alone, the itching between my shoulder blades continued. There was something the Potentate wasn't telling me. He knew more than he was letting on. Did he know about the brewing vampire war?

I swallowed the lump in my throat and started walking. That had to be it, because surely he didn't know about me. He couldn't know what I truly was, else he'd have never entrusted me with the Seeing Sword.

He didn't know, or I'd already be dead, so there was no reason for me to worry. At least, not about that.

What I had to worry about now was killing Karpov. Fortunately, I already knew where he'd be in three days' time. Now I just needed to convince him I intended to kill Asher, and only Asher. Once I knew where he was, I'd confront them both. I would kill two ancient vampires, or I would die trying.

THE NIGHT WAS dark as pitch. I had my horse, a week's worth of supplies, a crossbow, extra blades, and the Seeing Sword. I hadn't sought Tholdri and Steifan to say farewell. They were probably still cleansing Steifan's bite. A thorough cleaning was imperative. Even though the vampire who'd bit him had likely died with the others, he could not risk the creature returning and messing with his mind.

That's how vampire bites worked, they made even hunters vulnerable to bespellment.

Asher had never bitten me. The ritual to make someone a human servant was far more painful, especially when it was against the person's will.

I cast a final glance back at Castle Helius' high walls,

wondering if I'd ever return. Asher and Karpov had both lived so long for a reason. They would not be easy to kill. Once I had their locations, I would enlist Tholdri if I was able.

I turned back toward the road and tensed, noticing movement in the darkness. Two people rode toward me on horseback.

I lifted my hand to the hilt of the Seeing Sword strapped across my back, though it hadn't alerted me of any predators. I wasn't sure how a sword was supposed to alert me of anything.

The riders neared, and I lowered my hand with a sigh.

"Did you really think you'd sneak off without us?" Tholdri asked.

I nudged my horse's sides with my boots, riding forward to meet them. "The Potentate assigned this task to me alone." My horse stopped near theirs. "How did you know?"

I could just make out Tholdri's smug smile in the darkness. "I knew you might run off. I paid the stable hand to tell me if your horse was to be readied. I'm not letting you hunt Karpov alone. And I am most certainly not letting you go after . . . I'm not sure what to call him, your master?"

I whipped my gaze back toward the castle, worried someone would hear, but the high walls were far off now. No one was listening. I turned back to Tholdri. "Refer to him as my master ever again, and I'll cut out your tongue. His name is Asher." I looked past him toward Steifan. "And you? What are you doing here?"

He shrugged. "I sort of figured we're all in this together." The hilt of a new sword peeked over his shoulder. I hadn't had the time to return the one he'd lent me yet. I was glad he'd replaced it. Having wealthy parents did seem to have its advantages.

I shook my head, but couldn't help my smile. "You're both fools. I can't bring you when I meet Karpov, you do know that, right? He's making baby vampires to protect his lands. You were lucky to escape last time."

"We'll be fine, Lyss," Tholdri assured. "Now let's start riding. I'd like the comfort of an inn before sunrise."

I didn't argue. The Potentate expected me to begin my hunt tonight, but it would be a waste of time. Karpov would meet me in three night's time. I assumed tonight was the first night, leaving two more full days to wait. I had nothing but time to kill until then. An inn sounded nice, and a hot meal even better. It might be the last one I'd ever have.

CHAPTER NINE

My dream woke me, leaving me dazed and sweating on my stiff straw mattress. We'd found an inn in the village of Charmant, west of Bordtham. We'd eaten and drank our fill while discussing our mission ahead. Tholdri and Steifan had retired to the next room over. I had a small room to myself.

I blinked in the darkness, tilting my head in the hearth's direction. Only a few barely glowing embers remained. I shouldn't have been sweating, but the memory of my dream still burned across my skin.

I sat up, rubbing my eyes, wondering why the dream had come tonight of all nights. It wasn't like I hadn't dreamed of Asher before—we were bonded whether I liked it or not—but this dream was different. I'd been in a warm room by a roaring fire, seated on a plush fur rug next to the vampire of my nightmares. His white-blond hair, the color leeched away by centuries living in the dark, hung nearly to his trim waist. His gray eyes watched me intently, reflecting yellow flames from the fire. He was dressed casually, gray linen shirt half-unbuttoned, black breeches, no stockings. One leg curled up against his chest with an arm wrapped loosely around it.

We sat together like old friends, or lovers. Nothing could be further from the truth.

"Would you truly kill me?" he'd asked. "Even though it would mean your death?"

I wasn't quite able to meet his eyes, so I stared into the fire instead. "Yes, but only after I kill Karpov." I didn't ask how he knew I would soon hunt him. This was my dream, after all, my imagination. Or was it? I hoped it was.

He watched me for a moment before answering. "Karpov, I understand. I know what he did to your uncle. But me? You truly hate me that much?"

Anger washed through my body, granting me the boldness to meet his eyes. But the look stole my breath. Did I find him so heartbreakingly handsome because of our bond, or was it just him? My eyes drifted down to the top open buttons of his shirt, following the line of his chest, wishing there was less fabric to cover it.

I inhaled sharply and closed my eyes, shaking away the image. This wasn't like me. He had done something to make me more attracted to him. But this was just a dream . . . wasn't it?

I swallowed the lump in my throat, ignoring the warm, pulsing feeling in my belly, then opened my eyes. "Karpov may have stolen my uncle, but you stole my life."

With one arm still looped around his knee, he gestured toward me with the other. "You are still alive, Lyssandra. Still healthy, and stronger than ever."

I scowled. My mouth was too dry, my chest tight. "You know what I mean. You did this against my will."

"You would have died otherwise."

I'd wanted to stand then, to run away, but my dream-self held me immobile. In truth, I didn't *want* to be away from him. It felt good having him near. "Do not pretend to care if I lived or died. That was only an excuse."

He lifted one pale brow. "Was it? Are you sure?"

"You wanted a strong human servant, but you got more than you bargained for."

He smiled softly, like he found me terribly amusing. My eyes lingered on his soft lips. Curse it all, I needed to wake up.

The fire suddenly felt too hot, stifling. I lifted my fingers toward my throat, tugging at the collar of my shirt. "Why is it so hot in here?"

He stared at me, and the fire grew larger until flames were licking out of the hearth toward Asher's bare feet. He seemed unfazed.

"What are you doing?" I gasped, wanting to move away from the fire, but yet unable to stand.

"I will not let you kill me for saving you, Lyssandra. I have granted you freedom. It is more than I would grant any other."

I shook my head. My face felt like it was melting. "I *took* my freedom. You couldn't have controlled me if you'd tried."

He inclined his head. "Perhaps. But still, I let you live with my gifts, and did not require you to serve me."

"It's a curse," I growled, "not a gift." I fought with every muscle in my body to stand. Finally, I staggered to my feet, breaking free of whatever spell I was under.

But he was right there, matching me step for step as I backed away. My shoulders hit the wall. He stood too close, invading my personal space. The fire grew larger, licking across the floor.

He smiled at my horrified expression. "You know little of curses, young one. If you did, you would not say such a thing."

Even with his threatening tone, and the fire inching ever closer, it was like there was a cord between us, pulled taut. I pressed my palms against my sides to keep myself from touching him. The bond was a *curse*. I had free will unlike any other servant, but I was still unnaturally drawn to him.

He leaned close like he might kiss me, his mouth hovering near mine.

I couldn't help my flinch. I wanted him, yes, but I was also afraid.

With a sad smile, he stepped back, leaving me alone by the sweltering fire. "Hunt me if you must, Lyssandra, but I will not let you kill me."

"Then I shall die trying," I rasped, but I was suddenly alone in the room. The fire went out, and that was when I woke.

I lowered my legs to the floor, knowing I'd had all the sleep I would get for the night. As the dream faded, my sweaty skin grew chill. It was actually freezing in the room, not hot.

My bare feet padded across the well-worn wood, carrying me to the hearth where I threw a fresh log on the smoldering embers. Once the log took, I moved to the room's sole small window. I peered out through the glass, searching for the sliver of moon that should be out, but the sky was too dark with clouds. The clouds had been threatening for days, but now there was a heaviness in the air. It was fortunate we wouldn't be traveling tomorrow. We'd be drenched, and the horses might break an ankle in the slick mud.

I narrowed my eyes, noticing a figure out in the darkness, a male judging by his stature. He was coming toward the inn. It was too dark to see his features. I could only see his movements because his clothing was light colored. All I could think was that the dream had been a warning, and Asher had finally come for me.

I watched, barely breathing as the figure neared the inn. Then I blinked, and suddenly, he was gone.

I had to stifle a scream at a knock on the door. With my heart fluttering in my throat like a frantic moth, I turned, eyes on the key protruding from the lock. Who was on the other side? Certainly not Steifan or Tholdri. Aside from consuming too much ale, neither should be awake at this hour. It wouldn't be Asher. My heart pounded. Would it?

The fire roared in a sudden blaze, casting an eerie flicker about the room. I walked lightly across the floorboards, retrieving the Seeing Sword from where it leaned against my bed. Once again, it had not warned me of predators. *Useless sword.*

I reached the door, my hand hovering near the key in the lock.

"It's me."

I let out a huff of breath. Only Tholdri. And here I'd thought Asher was knocking at my door. Foolish, considering he hadn't come for me all these years.

I turned the key, then opened the door. There stood Tholdri, his golden hair neatly framing his handsome face. He looked tired.

"What do you want?"

He pushed his way inside. "An opportunity to speak with you without Steifan present."

My eyes followed his movements as he walked across the room. His leather armor was off, but he was fully dressed in a burgundy linen shirt, breeches, and boots. It seemed he hadn't been to bed yet. With a heavy sigh, he sat on the bed, gesturing with a slight jerk of the head for me to join him.

I shut and locked the door with my free hand, then

headed his way. "You waited until Steifan was asleep to come speak with me?"

He nodded, though his gaze now lingered on the Seeing Sword in my grasp. "So does the eye really open? You weren't telling tales?"

I joined him on the bed, leaning the sword near my knee. "Yes, it opens. The sword awoke for me. The Potentate believes it chooses who it will work for."

"That seems a little too close to magic."

It *was* too close to magic, and hunters didn't like magic, but, "The Potentate requested I wield it. I could not say no."

"I suppose I cannot argue with you," he muttered.

With Tholdri's shoulder so near mine, sitting on the bed in the near dark felt somehow intimate, and I wished I hadn't sat so close to his side. There'd never been much sexual tension between Tholdri and me, though I knew he liked women as well as men, and there was a first time for everything. I shifted, putting just a hair's extra distance between us. "What do you want, Tholdri?"

His brow furrowed as he angled his body toward me. "I want to talk to you about your vampire master. When did you first meet?"

I gnawed my lip. In truth, I'd expected this inquiry, but I'd hoped to push it off until after I killed Asher. At that point, I'd be dead, and I'd never have to answer any embarrassing questions.

Tholdri's light brown eyes bore into me. He wasn't going to let this go.

A cold pit of old fear settled into my stomach as I gave in. "It was nearly a year after my uncle was killed," I sighed. "I was struggling to deal with his death, and the other hunters had not made it easy on me for failing to slay Karpov."

He seemed almost surprised I was agreeing to tell him,

then quickly nodded. "Many thought you should be put to death, or at the very least, exiled."

I glared at him. "Yes, thank you for reminding me."

He smiled. "I wasn't one of them."

I rolled my eyes. "Do you want to hear the story, or not?"

He bowed his head. "Please continue."

"I had gone out to hunt," I recalled, unable to suppress flashes of the memory flitting through my mind. "But my prey was elusive that night. I ended up at a small tavern in the mires. That's where I met Asher."

"Could you not tell what he was?"

I glared at him, and he made a soothing gesture with his hands. "I'm sorry, no more interruptions."

"I could tell what he was. I knew he'd come to the tavern to hunt, at least, that's what I thought. The few other patrons couldn't tell he was a vampire, else they would have fled."

"The old ones are good at hiding what they are."

I nodded, ignoring the fact that he'd interrupted me once again. Tholdri had always struggled to keep his mouth shut. "I believe Asher knew what I was too, yet he approached my table and asked if he could sit."

I eyed Tholdri sharply before he could say anything. "Yes, I allowed him to sit. I agreed to converse with a vampire, and it was the biggest mistake of my life, so I'd not like to hear whatever lecture your mind is brewing."

I was pretty sure Tholdri was counting to ten in his head to stay quiet. Once the shock had faded from his expression, he gestured for me to continue.

"We talked all night," I said, feeling my eyes go distant. "We even spoke of my uncle, and I told him of my vendetta against Karpov. He didn't seem to mind that I intended to kill another vampire, though he cautioned that Karpov would not be easy to kill." I shrugged. "And that was it. That's how we met."

Tholdri's brows raised. "And what, he waited for you to go outside, kidnapped you, and made you his human servant?"

"You asked when we first met, not how I became his servant."

He lowered his chin, peering at me from behind a golden lock. I wished the hearth had cast a dimmer light, so he couldn't see me blush.

"Fine," I huffed, my cheeks burning. "I left while it was still dark, and I admit, I'd had a bit too much wine. I'd stumbled to my horse just in time to find it surrounded by a pack of ghouls. I fought them, killed most of them, but there were too many and my senses were dulled."

I shivered, recalling the memory like it was still fresh. "They tore me apart. Then I remember being carried, then horrible burning pain. Pain worse than having my flesh ripped by ghouls. I don't remember what happened after that, but I woke in an unfamiliar place, though I could tell it was a room at an inn. It was daylight, and I was alone."

"And not dead?"

"Not dead. My horse wasn't dead either. Asher had gotten there in time to save us both."

Realization twisted Tholdri's expression. "He made you his servant to save you. He gave you a bit of his immortality so that you would not die."

I looked down at my lap. "He did it against my will. Given a choice, I would have chosen death over being tied to a vampire."

"Did you ever see him again after that?"

I nodded. "A few times. A vampire does not simply make a human servant, then set them free. He wanted me to stay with him. He offered me protection. I refused. I told him if he ever approached me again, I'd kill him. I should have killed him then and there, but I'd needed time to come to terms with my own death."

"And you returned to the Order," Tholdri finished for me. "And you hid what you were. But why hunt him now?"

I eyed him sharply. "He stole my life, and he is a vampire. Both are reason enough."

He shrugged. "I suppose, but neither is worth dying over."

"Perhaps not to you, but I shudder to consider what my uncle would think if he knew this about me, or the Potentate for that matter. A vampire slayer who is a vampire's servant? They'd probably kill me themselves. I should have died that day in the mires, a victim of my own stupidity."

He patted my leg. "Thank you for telling me, Lyss. I understand. But I won't let you kill him."

I pushed his hand off my leg. "Regardless of what I intend to do about Asher, I will kill Karpov first. For now, we focus on that."

He met my gaze. "Only if you agree that you won't kill Asher without telling me first. No rushing toward death until you discuss it with me."

I wanted to say I owed him no such consideration, but in truth, I did. After my uncle was killed, Tholdri had defended me against the other hunters. He'd been a good friend. I at least owed him a warning if I was to perish.

"Fine," I grumbled. "I promise, I will discuss it with you first."

He patted my leg again. "Good, now let's get some rest. You take the side by the window."

My eyes flew wide. "You're not sleeping in here, you fiend!"

He laughed. "I trust you, Lyss, but that trust only goes

so far. Just in case you get any irrational ideas, I must be nearby to save you from yourself."

I wanted to shove him out the door, but with a heavy sigh, gave in. He'd pester me until I agreed, and it wasn't like we hadn't slept in the same bed before. We'd traveled on many long hunts together.

"Fine," I hissed, "but if you steal the blankets like last time, you'll wake up on the floor."

He laughed, then shooed me to my side of the bed. Tholdri was a thorn in my side, but he *had* made me feel better. He deserved a far better friend than I could ever be to him.

CHAPTER TEN

I woke to find Tholdri with the blankets tightly bundled around him. My nose and feet felt numb with cold. I sat up and glared down at him. *Greedy little hoglet.*

I poked his arm. "Get up. I'm hungry."

He groaned and rolled over, tightening the blankets around his shoulders.

With the remnants of some dark dream—thankfully unremembered—clinging to me, I stomped out of bed. I grasped the edges of the blanket near his feet and gave a sudden tug. The blanket flew free, and Tholdri sat up with a huff.

He squinted his eyes toward the window, only now showing the first hints of dawn. "You're up rather early for someone with nothing to do."

Still holding the blanket in one hand, I crossed my arms. "We can search for other information. If a vampire war is brewing, folk will have stories to tell. Perhaps we can find something to use against Karpov."

He rolled his eyes. "Fine, but you're buying breakfast."

I didn't argue. I had, after all, gotten him into this mess. "Leave so I can get dressed."

He looked at me, knowing it was an excuse. I'd slept in my shirt and breeches. I'd only need to don my armor, weapons, and boots. Or perhaps I'd delay those things and head to the baths. After the night I'd had, getting clean sounded divine.

With a final speculating look, Tholdri ambled toward the door and let himself out. I wondered how Steifan might judge us sleeping together. Then I wondered if I cared.

Shaking my head, I readied myself for the day, opting for the washbasin and chamber pot instead of heading to the baths. Finally, I twined my fiery hair into a neat braid that fell down the center of my back. I felt better with my armor on, though in truth it could only do so much against ancient vampires. I inhaled deeply, then let it out, feeling like a bird settling its feathers. My dream, the one I actually remembered, still had me shaken. The conversation with Asher had almost made me doubt my ability to kill him. I might just fall into bed with him.

It wasn't a conflict of conscience, but if the meeting had somehow been real, and what he'd done with the fire . . .

He was powerful, more powerful than Karpov given the latter seemed incapable of killing him. What if I put a blade through Asher's heart, but it killed me first? Asher might pull the blade out and recover, and I'd still be dead. It was an issue I'd take the next two days to think about. For now, my internal debate had entirely stolen my appetite. Hard to eat on a belly filled with icy fear.

I observed the Seeing Sword lying against the bed, and almost didn't want to put it on. It had done me little good thus far, but if the Potentate believed in its power, I couldn't ignore the fact that it might help me in the coming nights. I walked across the room, picked it up, and strapped it across my shoulder. I drew it, then resheathed it, making sure my braid wouldn't get in the way.

When I could delay no longer, I left my room and headed downstairs. Tholdri and Steifan already had steaming plates of boiled eggs, cured pork, and lentils in front of them. I must have taken longer to get ready than I'd thought.

There were few others in the common room. Just a lone barmaid, and a handful of quiet patrons focused on their morning meals.

I ignored them and moved toward Tholdri and Steifan.

"We have a plea for help." Tholdri hiked his thumb over his shoulder, gesturing to a young man seated near the door.

The youth stared at me blatantly, his dark eyes imploring. Though his clothing was shabby, and dark hair unkempt, well-honed muscles showed in his arms and the way he held himself. Blacksmith's apprentice would be my guess, or perhaps a farrier.

I glanced down at Tholdri. "Why is he waiting over there?"

Tholdri waggled his eyebrows. "I told him you're our leader, and that he must wait patiently to speak with you."

I sighed. "You're such a pain." I strode away from Tholdri and Steifan, leaving them to their meals. In truth, I was glad for the distraction, and my stomach was too twisted in knots to leave any room for food.

I reached the youth, then sat across the table from him. "What has happened?"

The young man blinked, shifting uneasily in his seat. "What makes you think something has happened?"

I fought to keep the glare off my face. Didn't want to scare the lad away. "You've asked for an audience with three hunters. People only do that when something has happened."

His shoulders slumped. "Forgive me, I'm nervous. If I'm wrong about this, our father will see my sister whipped. But if I'm right," he shook his head. "I cannot risk keeping Nina's secret if she's in danger."

I leaned in a little closer, wondering if he meant to speak of this secret so blatantly in public. A faint prickling had started between my shoulder blades, making me uneasy, though I wasn't sure why speaking to this young man would inspire wariness.

He seemed to take my hint and leaned in. His eyes were too wide, like a horse ready to bolt. "Nina has been seeing the fletcher's son," he whispered. "She sneaks out almost every night to meet with him, so when she left last night, I thought nothing of it. Only Nina never returned. The fletcher's son, Thom, is missing too."

I lifted a brow. "And what makes you believe your sister and this boy didn't simply run off together?"

He looked down at his hands splayed across the smooth wooden tabletop, then shook his head. "If Nina was leaving for good, she would have told me. She knew I wouldn't have stopped her." He lifted his gaze. "Something happened to them. After the recent killing in Bordtham, I can't help but fear the worst."

Word certainly did travel fast. I leaned back in my seat, thinking. I could feel Tholdri's eyes on me, surely curious about the issue, but I wasn't about to bring him in now. He'd had his fun, now he could just wait and wonder.

"Do you know where Nina and Thom would meet?" I asked softly, still half in thought.

The youth nodded. "I do. Thom's father has a workshop separate from their home. Thom and Nina would go there after it was closed for the night. That was the first place I went this morning, but Thom's dad didn't know where his son had gone. Said he wasn't home when he woke."

I nodded. "We'll check there first, but I may need to visit your home as well. If I find nothing amiss at the fletcher's, I will try to find Nina's trail."

He chewed his lip, seeming to debate this idea, then finally nodded. "I understand. I don't know what I'll tell my father. He starts work before dawn, so he doesn't yet know Nina is missing."

I stood. "We'll do our best for you, but we have other matters to tend to while we're here. If I can find no sign of her, we'll have to move on."

He stood, towering over me. He was much taller than he seemed, though I'd probably just based the assumption on his demeanor. "Thank you. I cannot thank you enough." He reached for his belt pouch.

I lifted a hand. "If you can afford it, send a donation to the Order. We do not take coin directly." I didn't explain that the measure had been put in place to cut down on corruption. Folk were wary of hunters enough as it was.

He bowed his head, then stepped away.

"Wait."

He froze, watching me warily.

I still had an uneasy feeling prickling up my back. With a start, I realized it was coming from the Seeing Sword. Perhaps there was a predator nearby. For a moment, staring at the young man, I found myself at a lack for words. I cleared my throat. "I need to know where you live."

His mouth fell open, then he snapped it shut. "Oh, of course. Our house is just behind the smithy where my father works." He hesitated. "If you can, avoid the forge and come straight back to the house. Maybe we can have you in and out without my father noticing."

Despite my nerves, I couldn't help my smile. It was nice seeing a brother looking out for his sister. "What of your mother?"

"Dead."

"Alright, if we find nothing at the fletcher's, we'll see you soon."

He gave a final nod, then hurried out the door, almost as if relieved to escape me.

He probably was. I wasn't well known for making people comfortable. I realized I'd never asked his name, but it was too late now.

I heard Tholdri approach as I stared at the closed door. He hovered over my shoulder. "Do we have more vampires to hunt?"

I shrugged. "Perhaps. Or perhaps the girl and her forbidden love have simply run off together."

"Oh, I do love a good intrigue."

I rolled my eyes. In all likelihood, the girl had just run off to escape her father and be with the man she loved. But maybe not. Maybe she'd been killed, or maybe Karpov had taken her to replace the baby vampires he'd lost.

Either way, at least I had something to occupy my day.

CHAPTER ELEVEN

The fletcher's shop stunk of blood, but no one else seemed to notice. An effort had been made to clean things up. Nothing in the shop seemed amiss . . . except that smell. To me, it was unmistakable.

Tholdri spoke with the fletcher, a man with a thin face and hair gone gray early. His worry over his son seemed genuine. I didn't place him for a man to grow violent upon discovering his son with a lover in his shop.

Steifan followed me around the small space, mirroring my every step. The creak of his boots on the floorboards made me twitch. I glared over my shoulder at him, and he backed up.

I looked across slats of ash and yew leaned up against one wall next to a rack used to shape bows. The fletcher's tools were neatly placed. Nothing was disturbed.

Tholdri said his final words to the fletcher, then walked across the shop toward us. "He knows nothing," he muttered under his breath. "It doesn't seem like the girl and boy were taken from here."

I glanced at the fletcher, now stringing a bow,

pretending he wasn't trying to listen to our hushed conversation. "This is where they were taken," I whispered, "but there will be nothing for us to find. Let us go to the house behind the smithy."

Steifan watched us liked he'd memorize every word. Perhaps he would learn enough to stay alive after all.

Tholdri waved to the fletcher as we went through the door. I felt better once we were outside, away from the fletcher's nervous energy. Nervous about the hunters in his shop and his missing son, I thought, but I could be wrong.

There was a first time for everything.

"Anyone know where the smithy is?" I asked as we started walking. If it was far enough, we'd fetch our horses from the inn's stables.

Tholdri pointed to black smoke pumping up from a building in the distance. "I asked the fletcher. He claims the smith will be at work from dawn 'till dusk. The man never seems to tire, even with age. Works his son just as hard."

I snorted, aiming my feet toward the smithy. "I'm surprised the boy managed to slip away and find us." I stopped walking and looked at Tholdri. "How *did* he find us? How did he know we'd be at the inn?"

I hadn't asked Steifan, but he answered to my back. "Perhaps that was the first place he thought to go for help. Makes sense."

I nodded with my eyes again on the distant smithy. "Perhaps, but let us be wary, just in case."

Tholdri fell into step at my side as I started walking. "You think this is another trap?"

I shook my head, watching as a young lady batted her eyelashes at Steifan walking on my other side. I glared at her, then regretted it as she hurried off. I had no excuse to take my bad mood out on others.

"Karpov sent his message," I said as we neared the

smithy. I could smell fresh pastries baking somewhere nearby and glanced around for the source. After we searched the smith's home, I'd need something to eat.

"Could it be your master?" Steifan blurted.

I whirled on him. "Keep your voice down!" I hissed. "And I told you not to call him that. If this was a message for me, the blood wouldn't have been cleaned up."

"What blood?" Tholdri asked to my back.

My shoulders slumped. I would rather not have explained it. Foolish of me. "I don't want to hear a word from either of you about this." I stepped back with a warning finger raised so I could waggle it at both of them. I glanced around, but no one else was near. People avoided us in the streets if they could. "I could smell the blood," I whispered. "The girl and boy were taken from there, or perhaps killed and their bodies dragged away. There was enough blood to account for at least one death."

Steifan's eyes tightened, and he seemed to swallow a lump in his throat.

Tholdri stroked his chin, thoughtful. "If they were taken from the fletcher's, why check the house behind the smithy?"

I shrugged. "It's the only other place to look. I saw no trail from the fletcher's. Plus, I want to know how the girl's brother knew to find us at the inn, and why he asked us to sneak around to avoid his father."

Tholdri's eyebrows shot up. "You failed to mention that part."

I shrugged again. "He claimed the girl would be whipped if her father found out she'd been sneaking around. It seemed a legitimate excuse at the time. Now let's get this over with."

I continued on toward the smithy before they could ask

any more questions. Talking about my ability to smell blood had been uncomfortable enough.

Soon we reached the aged wooden building adorned with a large window to let out the furnace heat required to melt and mold metal. A well-muscled man was near the forge, absorbed enough in his work to not see the three hunters walking past his window.

We skirted around the building, then approached the home behind it. The boy we'd met at the inn opened the front door. His forehead beneath a flop of dark hair shone with sweat, and he gripped the door a bit too tightly. He was nervous, but why? What would his father do if he came back to the house and found us inside?

I reached the door first. "Nothing at the fletcher's. Can you show us to Nina's room?"

He nodded. "We share a room, but I can show it to you." He stepped back, making space for us to come inside.

I led the way ahead of Steifan and Tholdri. A peculiar sensation shivered across my skin. Almost the sensation that struck when vampires were near, but there were no vampires in this place. The sun was full in the sky. If they were somewhere in the house, they'd be utterly defenseless.

Nothing seemed amiss within the small home. A few dirty wooden bowls sat beside the washbasin, but the rest of the corner comprising the kitchen was clean. The hearth was cold, making the cushioned chairs before it seem sad and uncomfortable. There were two doors within the home, one for the parents' room, and one for Nina and her brother, whose name I kept forgetting to ask. They were more well-off than the girl who'd been killed in Bordtham, but not by much.

The boy walked toward a door and opened it, then gestured for us to go inside. "I'd like to hurry if it's alright with you. I don't want my father to come back and find us. He has a temper."

I glanced at Tholdri, but he didn't seem wary. With a shrug, I walked past the boy into the room. That's when I felt it. The prickling sensation I'd only vaguely sensed before erupted on my skin like lightning. A voice echoed in my brain, *danger*.

I stopped dead in my tracks. The Seeing Sword strapped across my back thrummed with energy. Was this the warning the Potentate had described?

I glanced back at the boy, Tholdri and Steifan at his back. There shouldn't have been any danger in this room. The boy was human, and not a human servant either. I would have sensed it if he were.

"What's your name?" I asked abruptly.

The boy seemed taken aback. "Egar, but what does that have to do with anything?"

I shook my head, turning my attention to the small bedroom. The warning still thrummed across my skin, but there wasn't anything I could do about it.

The room was tidy, both beds made.

"Did you make your sister's bed?" I asked. "Or did she not lay in it at all?"

Egar stepped up beside me. "I made it, just in case my father decided to check."

The sense of warning increased with him standing so close to me, but it wasn't just from him. It was the room itself making me uneasy. What in the light was going on?

Tholdri and I looked through the girl's belongings while Steifan observed our every move. I wanted to explain what we were looking for, but not with Egar around. Prize finds were journals that might hint at feelings of being watched, or might reveal meeting a new person. Vampires tended to stalk their prey for several nights before striking. If Nina had a journal, I wanted to have it in hand before Egar knew what I was looking for.

In the end, we found nothing. We should have found at least something, something to hint at who this girl was, but there wasn't a shred of her personality in the room.

Finished looking under the bed, I stood and looked at Egar. "We'll check around outside for tracks, but if we can't find anything, we'll have to wait until nightfall. If a vampire took her, we won't be able to track it until then."

Egar's eyes flicked to Tholdri and Steifan, then back to me. "All three of you will go?"

I furrowed my brow at the odd question, and suddenly didn't want to answer him. This was feeling more and more like a trap, but why would a young human want to trap us?

Egar's cheeks flushed. "Forgive me, that is none of my concern. I'm just anxious to find my sister."

I nodded. "We'll return here tomorrow to tell you the news, either way."

He didn't protest our return to his home for the meeting, which I found odd after how wary he'd been of his father. He escorted us out, seeming relieved when we left.

Tholdri led the way away from the house, turning to speak with us once we were well out of hearing distance. "There's something off about that boy."

I nodded, wondering if I should mention the warning from the Seeing Sword. I decided to keep my mouth shut. The skin-pricking sensation had left me as soon as we were away from Egar, but he couldn't possibly be a threat. Perhaps the Seeing Sword's gifts had gone awry with age.

"Let's look for tracks," I decided. "If we find nothing, we will wait for nightfall."

Steifan followed as Tholdri and I led the way toward

the back of the house. "Would tracks matter here if Nina was taken from the fletcher's?"

I shrugged without turning back to him. "Probably not. I smelled the blood there, that was where she was taken, but there were no tracks. Whoever is covering this up might not have thought to eliminate any evidence around the house."

We reached a small garden and a chicken pen with a few small birds scratching about, and beyond that, an old storage building barely large enough to fit two people. There was a small outhouse near the chicken pen, but the storage building held my attention. It might only contain tools for the garden, but I'd noticed such tools within the home, along with a wooden barrel that might contain chicken feed. If those items were kept in the home, what could possibly be stored out here?

I figured Tholdri had reached the same conclusion, given he didn't question me as I walked to the door and gave it a tug. It was locked, but that wasn't what I found strange. The door moved a bit and seemed to be barred from the inside. Now why would a storage room be barred from the inside?

I walked around the small building, searching the ground for tracks.

"What are you doing?" Steifan asked, like he was genuinely hoping for some fresh wisdom.

Unfortunately, I was all out. I shook my head and looked at Tholdri.

He shrugged. "We could ask Egar to open it, or we could break it open. Might be hard with the bar on the inside."

I gave him a small smile. It was nice working with someone observant enough to notice the same things I did.

"What are you doing in my garden?" a gruff voice asked.

We all whirled around. I stared at the blacksmith, recognizing him though I'd only glimpsed him through the window of his shop. With his bulk he was a hard man to miss. It was rare a human could sneak up on three hunters, especially one so large.

Having no desire to fight the man, nor to get chased out of town for attacking a citizen, I told the truth. "Your son asked us to come. Any answers you need, get them from him."

"Leave my property," the man growled. Though his black hair was streaked white, and his skin weathered from years of sun and smithing, signs of aging stopped there. Muscles bulged beneath the sleeves of his shirt. He looked like he could fight a bear and win.

He'd stand no chance against hunters, but he'd be dangerous enough we might have to cut him down.

I led the way toward him. "Very well."

I felt his eyes on me as I walked past, but no sense of warning like I got from his son. Tholdri and Steifan followed, none of us speaking until we were out on the street.

We gathered together beneath the eave of a vacant shop.

"What do we do now?" Steifan whispered.

Tholdri and I locked gazes.

"We find a way into that storage building," he said.

I nodded. "Something is amiss in all of this. Egar, as innocent as he seems, is hiding something. We won't be hunting vampires until we know what's in that building."

"What about the blacksmith?" Steifan asked.

"He'll need to be distracted, and I know just the man for the job." I smiled wickedly at him.

86

Steifan's jaw gaped. When he finally managed to close it, he asked, "You want me to distract that horrible man? He'll rip my arms off."

I patted his shoulder. "You're a hunter. You'll be fine. We'll give it a few hours to ease his guard, then well go in. For now," I took a deep inhale, "I'd like to find a pastry before they sell out."

I walked away, allowing no room for arguments. Steifan would do as he was told. Perhaps it would have been better to send Tholdri in to distract the smith, but I was feeling wary, and wanted a well-trained hunter guarding my back. The Seeing Sword might hint at danger, but Tholdri would look danger in the eye and cut out its heart.

CHAPTER TWELVE

"Do you think Steifan will be alright?" Tholdri whispered as we snuck back toward the storage building at the edge of sunset. "There's something off about this family. As soon as I saw the smith, I felt the urge to cower. I *never* cower."

"I've seen you cower," I laughed under my breath. "Now shut up before someone hears you."

We'd done a wide circle around the blacksmith shop and the home behind, but there were only so many ways back toward the storage building that wouldn't draw attention. Dressed in our armor with the Helius Order insignia, and with my flaming red hair and Tholdri's golden locks, we stood out even when we weren't trespassing. We could have waited until full dark, but if we were wrong, and there was a vampire to be hunted, I didn't want to risk losing precious time breaking into an old outbuilding.

I glanced at the house as we made our way toward the back. Was it just my nerves, or had I seen a curtain flutter in the window?

I shook my head and hurried on. I'd be breaking into that building whether we were caught again or not. Let the imposing smith and his strange son try to stop me.

We reached the barred door unimpeded. The smith probably wasn't worried about us breaking it down with it barred from the inside, but he had no way of knowing I wasn't quite human. I was a lot stronger than I looked.

Before Tholdri could speak a word, I lifted my boot, braced with my left leg, and kicked the door with all I had. Wood splintered and the door flew inward, wedging halfway open as it slammed against the fallen bar.

Tholdri gawked at me. "You've been able to shatter doors all this time and you never thought to make our hunts any easier?"

I moved past him, intent on searching the storage space before the smith came running out. Hopefully he wouldn't associate the loud crash with someone trying to sneak around his property.

I widened my eyes as I stepped inside, waiting for them to adjust to the near darkness. Tholdri would soon learn that I had improved night vision too.

"I see nothing of interest," he said over my shoulder. "Though I don't see much at all." He'd propped the door so it was only open a crack. I hadn't noticed until he spoke.

I saw something dully glinting on the wooden floor in a sliver of light and hurried toward it. I knelt, grabbing a loop of steel anchored to the floor. "It's a trapdoor." I gave it a tug, and it opened with hardly a sound. A well-oiled hinge on a hidden trapdoor within a building locked from the inside. *Interesting.*

Tholdri stood over the opening and peered downward. "There's light down there. Torches. Mounted along the walls, I think."

I nodded, hesitating as the prickling sensation of

warning nearly overcame me. "Let's take a look before the smith finds us."

"What if he locks us in?"

I shrugged, but he was right. We couldn't exactly trust Steifan to rescue us. "You stay here. I'll have a quick look around."

"I'll go."

I smiled, though he probably couldn't see it in the darkness. "No, I'm the human servant. I'm more hardy than you."

He didn't argue with me, though I almost wished he had. Being underground made me panic, it always had. Plus, I smelled blood. A lot of it.

There was a ladder leading down, not a far drop before reaching an incline leading further under the earth. I quickly descended, keeping my movements silent in case anything waited below.

My boots slid across the hard-packed dirt of a well-worn walkway. I could stand straight, and appreciated the evenly spaced wooden supports holding up the tunnel almost as much as I appreciated the torches mounted on either side. I most certainly did not want to go down in the histories as the hunter slain by dirt.

I didn't have to walk far before I reached the end of the tunnel, and suddenly I wished I'd never come down.

Half-melted white candles illuminated the space in harsh detail. An altar with a sealed urn in the center shone dully with congealed blood, some fresh, and some older. There were . . . parts strewn around. I had to think of them that way. Even with all the death I'd seen, I couldn't think of the bits littering the earth as something that had once been human.

The Seeing Sword thrummed through my mind. *Danger. Danger was coming.*

I whirled around and ran back the way I'd come. I'd seen all I needed. The smith and his son were far from what they appeared to be.

I reached the end of the tunnel and peered up through the opening just as the trapdoor slammed shut. I heard a latch slide into place, trapping me in the tunnel with nothing but the dead.

CHAPTER THIRTEEN

I stared up at the trapdoor, the old wood lightly illuminated by the torches behind me. I could hear a struggle above, so Tholdri wasn't dead . . . yet. I climbed the ladder and braced my arms against the trapdoor, pushing with all I had, but the angle wasn't right. My feet would break the thin rungs of the ladder before I would ever break the latch.

With a frustrated scream, I banged on the trapdoor over and over, but it didn't budge. The sounds of struggle were difficult to hear now. I was pretty sure they'd gone outside.

"Greetings," a voice said from behind me.

I whirled around, tripping, but managed to hop down from the ladder, landing on my feet in a crouch. I drew the Seeing Sword as I straightened.

A young girl, probably eighteen, approached. She wore a long white dress, stark against her free-flowing black hair. Her skin was paler than Egar's, but there was a definite family resemblance. I'd checked the entire cavern. There had been no one down here with me before.

"Nina, I presume?"

Her berry-hued lips curled into a smile. "Yes, and you are one of the hunters."

She had almost reached me. I had the urge to back up, but there was nowhere to go. The Seeing Sword thrummed with energy in my grip, the blade angled down between me and Nina. I'd raise the blade to her heart before I'd ever let her reach me.

"Egar said vampires took you," I commented. "I imagine it was a ruse to lure me here?"

Her smile broadened. "Yes. When we heard there were hunters in the village, we couldn't pass up the opportunity."

She'd stopped walking. Her gaze flicked to my blade. "What an unusual sword. It will be mine, soon."

I lifted the sword, aiming the sharp tip at her heart. "I don't think so."

She laughed, a cheerful sound like tinkling bells. "Oh your blood will be perfect. A true predator, so very hard to find." Her gaze went distant, as if she were looking through me rather than at me. "And not quite human?" she asked as her eyes refocused.

My skin itched with the need to chop off her head. She'd said I was a true predator, but I was feeling more of the prey variety at the moment. "What do you want?"

"Your death. Your blood on my altar."

My gut twisted, but not because of her threat. I'd realized what she was. It shouldn't have been possible, but I knew with sudden surety that it was the truth. There was only one other creature that drank blood like a vampire, but wasn't the undead. A creature that would keep trophies from its victims upon a ritual altar. "You're a Nattmara," I breathed. "But your kind were killed off long ago."

She tilted her head, draping long black hair across her shoulder. "Yes, they were. My mother was the last pure blood left. She died giving birth to me and my brother."

"And your father?" I pressed. I couldn't hear any more sounds of fighting above. Was Tholdri dead? Steifan?

"My father is descended from the Sidhe. His gifts are strong. He tries to control me, but he is not quite strong enough."

My palms began to sweat around my sword hilt. Now it made sense why Egar had asked us to avoid his father. He didn't want his daughter to feed. He would have kept us away, and perhaps we should have let him. I swallowed the lump in my throat. "The Sidhe have been gone for centuries."

"Have they?" she laughed again.

I needed to figure out what to do, and fast. Nattmara drained the life from their victims. Not like vampires, who merely took your blood. The Nattmara would take your essence, your soul, whatever you wanted to call it. It was how they lived unnaturally long lives. If they didn't kill, their power would fade, and they would age like mortals.

I didn't like being backed into a corner, but there wasn't enough room in the tunnel to step around the Nattmara. Part of me wanted to run screaming from the fate looming before me, but there was nowhere to flee. Might as well go down bravely.

"Well, Nina," I began, "your plan was successful. You lured me here. Your predator's blood awaits. But there is one thing you must know about predators."

She took a step toward me. The hem of her dress brushed the point of my blade. "And what is that?"

"That we don't go down without a fight."

She took her cue, lunging toward me with fingers

poised like claws. Her nails had grown black and sharp, like talons. I swung my blade, and she whirled around me like a dancer, easily evading my strike. She was fast, as fast as the oldest of vampires.

The start of our dance had left her near the ladder, and me with my back toward the rest of the tunnel, and the bloody cavern beyond.

I took a few steps back, giving myself room to maneuver. "Is your plan to kill me atop your altar?"

Her laugh, that a moment before had been that of a charming young girl, came out like the hiss of a snake. Her arms seemed longer, the talons doubling the length of each bony finger. Her face had elongated to accommodate sharp teeth, too long for her to fully close her lips. "Hunter blood holds more power than boring mortals." Her words, forced through sharp teeth, were painful to hear. "Your sacrifice will sustain me for years. I will keep your men here during that time, until I need them."

Well at least that meant they weren't dead. "What happened to the fletcher's son?" I was stalling, but I wasn't sure what else to do. She was unnervingly fast, and if she'd been feeding in recent years, she was nearly immortal.

She met me step for step as I backed toward the altar. "He discovered my plan. He'd suspected what I was for some time. Do you know he tried to go to the inn to warn you last night?"

The image of a man outside my window the previous night came to mind. He'd disappeared so quickly I'd thought it was Asher, but I was wrong. I'd watched the fletcher's son, Thom, coming to warn us, and I'd done nothing to prevent his death.

"Why enter a relationship with him to begin with?"

She licked lips gone wide and cracked, her face

contorted into something monstrous . . . and hungry. "I have needs like any other woman."

Without warning, she lunged, swatting the Seeing Sword aside like it was a plaything before knocking me to the ground. She wasn't a large woman, but she pinned me easily. Her hot breath on my cheek stunk of stale blood.

Her head reared back, then she struck, sinking teeth into the base of my neck near my shoulder. I screamed. Her long teeth cut through my flesh like it was nothing.

She gnawed on my neck like a rabid animal, covering me in my own blood. My hands swiped across the floor, searching for something to get her off me before I fainted from blood loss. If I passed out, I was dead.

A voice slithered through my mind. *The urn. The urn is the source of her magic.*

I didn't know where the voice came from, and it didn't matter. I couldn't reach the urn. Nina had stopped tearing my flesh and was now lapping my blood like a cat. My vision swam with stars and spots of gray.

My hand, growing weaker, fell upon a broken bone, one end sharp and brittle. I forced my hand around the bone, lifted it, then with my final burst of strength, I shoved the bone into her back.

She screamed and reared off me, her arms flailing as she tried to reach the bone protruding from her back. The candlelight danced with her movement, making me dizzy. I needed to reach the urn, but I couldn't seem to move.

I blinked rapidly, trying to focus on Nina as she finally grabbed the bone and tore it free from her back. It came out with a spurt of blood, which she hardly seemed to notice. She stalked toward me.

Alright, maybe I could move. I could move if it meant escaping Nina. I rolled onto my stomach and dragged myself across the bloody altar. My hand extended toward the urn.

"No!" she screeched, and was upon me again. Her body pinned me as her teeth sunk into the unscathed side of my neck.

I didn't have the strength to scream. Knowing I was about to die, I swung my opposite arm. My fingertips came into contact with the urn, the ceramic unnaturally hot. I tipped it, but it didn't break.

Nina was off me in a heartbeat and going for the urn. My pained crawl had brought me near my sword. I grasped it in my hand, unsure if I could even lift it, and waited for the next attack.

She must have righted the urn, because suddenly she pounced. I lifted my sword just as she descended, and she landed right on top of it. It pierced through her belly with a satisfying wet thunk, but still she did not die.

Her teeth came down, and this time, there was nothing I could do.

And yet, I wasn't afraid. A calm presence washed over me. One that I recognized. It was Asher. The sun must have fully set outside, and now he was awake, and able to sense my pain.

Just as calmness took me, I was given a burst of strength. As Nina bit a new hole in my shoulder, I twisted the blade, then pulled it upward through her belly, slicing all the way up. A normal human wouldn't have had the strength to drag the sword through her at this angle, but I wasn't a normal human, and Asher was lending me his power. I could feel his presence like a second heartbeat in my chest.

Nina's throat made a gurgling sound as she lifted her head. Blood, both hers and mine, spewed from her mouth, splattering across my face.

I shoved her off of me, dragging the blade through her flesh to do more damage as I staggered to my feet. I knew even with Asher's power, the blood loss would still take me, but for the moment, I could stand.

I stumbled toward the urn, glancing back at Nina as I went.

Even with all the damage she'd sustained, she was getting to her feet.

I lifted the Seeing Sword, poising its tip over the sealed urn.

Nina staggered toward me, hands that had returned to human outstretched. The eyes that pled with me for her life were those of a young innocent girl.

I smiled at her, braced my legs, then slammed the sword downward.

The urn shattered, and Nina fell to the ground like a broken doll. Her chest gave one final heave, then went still.

I fell to my knees, clutching my sword. It wasn't useless after all. If it hadn't told me about the urn, I'd be dead.

And if Asher hadn't woken and lent me his power, the sword would now be in Nina's possession.

Curse it all. At some point I'd slumped over. I could still sense Asher's presence, but the blood loss had pushed it away. I was too weak.

I heard a thunk in the distance, then Tholdri and Steifan barreled into the cavern with swords drawn. The latter looked a bit bruised and bloody, but they were both very much alive. Thank the light.

Tholdri's calm eyes took everything in. He went to Nina, checked her pulse to make sure she was no longer a threat, then hurried toward me, shucking his vambraces and leather armor as he went. He tore off his shirt, then knelt beside me, pushing the fabric against my neck wound. Only there were two other wounds on the other side, and he couldn't quite reach them all.

"Find a healer!" he growled at Steifan.

I didn't see if Steifan left. At some point I closed my eyes. Darkness took me, and it wasn't Tholdri's embrace I sensed as I went.

It was Asher's.

CHAPTER FOURTEEN

I regained consciousness as Tholdri struggled to carry me up the ladder leading out of the tunnel. He held me in his arms like a sleeping child. I could feel thick, coarse bandages on my wounds, anchored awkwardly by strips of fabric crisscrossing my chest. I wore only my underthings on top, but fortunately had maintained my breeches.

"I can lift her up," Steifan's voice said from above. "Just get her high enough for me to grip her arms."

I groaned at the throbbing pain in my neck and shoulder as Tholdri tried to reposition me. "Stop carrying me like a damsel and I'll lift myself up."

Tholdri stepped off the ladder and blinked down at me, his jaw agape. Someone had either lit candles or carried a lantern into the storage building above, because I could see his face clearly in the yellow light. "You left most of your blood back there in the cavern. How are you awake?"

Even swallowing around my dry throat sent stabs of pain through my wounds. "What did the healer say?" I croaked.

"That you should be dead. As soon as she bandaged

your wounds, she fled. This will all be the talk of the village come morning."

I stared at him, letting him know that his answer wasn't helpful.

I must have looked truly terrible, because he relented, "She said if infection doesn't set in, you should live. Even unconscious, your heartbeat was strong, breathing steady." He gave me a poignant lift of the brow. "She found your survival quite peculiar."

"And what of the Nattmara? What did the healer have to say about that?"

"Let's get you out of this cavern, and I'll tell you. You aren't exactly light as a feather."

I scowled, but when he let me to my feet, I was able to stand. Sort of. I had to lean heavily on the ladder, and Tholdri had to boost me up from below. Steifan grabbed me by my arms, hoisting me up, an action that almost made me scream.

We walked over the shattered wood in the storage room and made it outside into the chill night air. Goosebumps marched up my bare arms as a breeze tugged at bloody tendrils of my hair. I leaned on both men for support. The position strained my bandages, but it was better than falling. I was quite sure if that happened, I wouldn't be getting back up. Feeling vulnerable, I thought of my sword. I panicked for a moment, then saw that Steifan carried the sheathed Seeing Sword in his free hand.

We made slow progress through the garden and around the house. Both house and smithy were dark and quiet. "What happened to Egar and his father?"

Tholdri hoisted me up for a better grip around my waist, making my wounds scream. "The smith attacked me when he found me in the outbuilding," he explained. "He locked the trapdoor, said he'd tried to keep us away, and that you were as good as dead. Now he is the one that is dead, thanks to Steifan. Egar is being held to await judgement."

I looked at Steifan, noting his furrowed brow over his sharp features. "You killed the smith?"

He nodded. "I never expected I'd have to kill a human."

"We fought human servants," I said. "You did not seem to mourn their deaths."

"But that was—" he bit his tongue, but I knew what he'd been about to say. Human servants weren't worth sparing.

"There's someone standing ahead," Tholdri interrupted. "I don't think he's one of the villagers."

My eyes searched the darkness, and it was almost as if my gaze was pulled right to him. The moment I sensed him, I knew just where he'd be . . . but then he wasn't there. My pulse hammered in my throat. Only an ancient vampire could move so quickly.

Tholdri cursed. "Where did he go?"

Steifan held me a little tighter, almost as if he'd protect me. "How did he move so quickly?"

I continued scanning the darkness. "Ancient vampires can move like that."

Tholdri's body tensed. "That wasn't Karpov."

I didn't want to admit who it was. I wasn't even sure. I'd only sensed him. He'd fled before I could solidly lay eyes upon him, but the cold surety in my heart let me know it was Asher. I'd nearly died tonight, and he'd lent me his strength. He'd come to find out why.

I licked my cracked, bloody lips. The men were both still staring off into the darkness. "It doesn't matter. He's gone now. Get me to the inn. I need to rest if we're to meet Karpov tomorrow night."

Tholdri shook his head. "You won't be making that meeting. Not in your current condition."

I was too tired to argue. I healed faster than Tholdri knew. We'd see what shape I was in come morning. "Please, just get me to a bed already. I want to hear what happened outside the tunnel before I pass out."

"And I want to hear just what happened within." Tholdri started walking, and with one of my arms around his shoulder, he brought the other two of us with him.

I hung my head as we walked, partially out of exhaustion, and partially to keep myself from looking for Asher. If he didn't want me to see him, I wouldn't see him. That much I knew.

It felt like it took all night to reach the inn, and even longer to ascend the stairs to our rooms. Once I was flat on my back on the soft brown covers of my straw bed, Tholdri set to removing my blood-soaked bandages so he could replace them with new ones. I told them what had happened with the Nattmara, and that she'd wanted our hunter blood to sustain her life longer than a human's ever could. I also voiced that the smith had tried to keep us away from her, and he probably hadn't deserved to die.

Tholdri set the last binding loosely under my armpit, then at Steifan's dejected expression, steered the conversation away from the smith. "I can't believe you claimed the Nattmara on your own. Such a kill will go down in the histories."

I didn't want merit for the kill. I'd only survived because of Asher and the Seeing Sword. I took a shallow breath, testing the bandages. I still wore my blood-soaked underthings and breeches, but I was too tired to change. The blood was mostly dry now, regardless.

Tholdri walked across the room to throw the used bandages into the fire.

I watched his back, glad that he seemed to have no serious injuries. I looked at Steifan. I didn't want to rub salt in his wound, but I had to ask, "What happened when you tried to distract the smith?"

Steifan sat on the foot of the bed, turning his back to me. I suspected to hide his blush. "I wasn't able to distract him for long. He ended up hitting me in the face with a steel bar."

I snuggled my head back against a pillow, cringing at the feel of dried blood in my matted hair. "You're lucky to be alive."

"I didn't expect him to move so quickly."

"He was part Sidhe, according to the Nattmara," I explained. "He probably cast minor glamour to hide his movements."

Tholdri returned to the bed, propping the other pillow against the wall as he took a seat next to me. "That would explain it, then. He easily snuck up behind me."

"And where was Egar in all this?" I pressed.

Tholdri snorted. "Hiding in his house. The Nattmara males are far weaker than the females." He nudged my shoulder. "Apparently, the same goes for hunters, if you're used as an example."

I laughed, but laughing hurt, so I settled on a smile. Then even that wilted around the edges. "The man you saw outside . . . " I trailed off.

"It was Asher, wasn't it."

He didn't say it like it was a question. He really was far too perceptive for his own good. Steifan was watching us from the foot of the bed.

I sighed. "I didn't see him, but I believe it was him. He—" I hesitated, unsure if I wanted to tell them the truth. But . . . it felt good to speak openly. I'd already hidden so long behind lies. "The Nattmara almost killed me. Asher must have sensed it as he woke for the night. He lent me his strength through our bond. I believe he came to see why such a thing was necessary. His territory is not far."

Tholdri was up on his feet in a heartbeat. He circled the bed and looked out the window into the darkness. He spoke with his back to us. "Is he still out there?"

I closed my eyes. The yellow light of the oil lamp was giving me a headache. "Honestly, I don't really care if he is. He saved me, so he doesn't want me dead. And I'm in no condition to slay him, so I won't be trying to find him. Not yet."

"But what if he tries to take you while you're weakened?" Tholdri asked.

My eyes shot open. I hadn't thought of that. He'd left me alone all this time, so I'd just assumed he'd given up.

Tholdri returned to his seat beside me and rested his hand gently on my forearm. "My apologies, I didn't mean to worry you. Try to rest. Steifan and I will take turns keeping watch."

I wanted to argue that they needed rest too, but I knew I'd never be able to sleep without someone watching over me. Not now that I knew Asher was near. "Thank you."

Tholdri said something else, but I was already drifting off to sleep. I silently wished I would dream about the horror that was the Nattmara, because anything was better than another dream of Asher.

Of course, my life wasn't a children's tale. In real stories, wishes rarely came true.

CHAPTER FIFTEEN

I t was well past midday when I woke. I was alone in my inn room with the sunlight cutting a harsh line across my bed. I sat up with a groan. The wounds still hurt, but not as badly. A few days and I'd be back in fighting form, a few more and the wounds would be fresh pink scar tissue. I'd had to hide injuries in the past for fear that others would see how quickly I could heal.

A knock at the door preceded Tholdri's entry. He looked me over. "I thought I heard movement. I was hoping you'd sleep longer."

I rubbed my eyes. "It's daylight. Why are you guarding my door?"

He stepped into the room and shut the door behind him. "Asher could have other human servants."

I raised my brow. "You're still worried he'll come for me?"

"You're not?"

I shook my head as he walked toward the bed. "I'll admit, last night I had a moment of worry, but he has left me alone for years. He knows I'll try to kill him if he comes for me."

Tholdri sat on the foot of the bed. "Be that as it may, I see no reason to be careless. We should return to Castle Helius so you can heal."

I met his concerned gaze. "I cannot return without Karpov's head. Not again."

He opened his mouth to argue, then closed it, because there was no good argument. I'd returned after my uncle's death, and the other hunters had been out for my blood. To return again . . . it simply wasn't an option.

Tholdri hung his head. "What are we going to do? You say we cannot go to the meeting with Karpov, but you are not strong enough to face him on your own."

I thought about it. I had wanted to kill Karpov as soon as he led me to Asher, but now I needed time. Once my wounds healed, then I could kill them both. "I only have to meet with Karpov," I decided. "He wants an answer from me, and I'll give it to him. I will agree to kill Asher, but only after my wounds have healed."

He looked at me from beneath his furrowed brow. "But that still leaves you alone with an ancient vampire while severely wounded."

I tugged at the bandage on my shoulder, shifting the bindings to pull the cotton free from my skin. It came up with a sickening peeling sound that made my vision swim.

When I could see again, I leaned forward, inviting Tholdri to look.

The wound was still horrific, the flesh shredded and gaping, but it wasn't as bad as it had been.

Tholdri's eyes widened. He stared at the wound for a moment longer, then lifted his gaze to mine. "Days' worth of healing in a single night?"

I nodded. "I will still be injured when I meet with Karpov, but I will not be helpless."

"I still don't like it."

"I know you don't, but it's what I have to do. Where is Steifan?"

Tholdri leaned back, bracing himself with arms stretched behind him. "The healer spread word around town about what happened. They're questioning Egar today. He'll be put to death by evening. Steifan is giving our recount of events."

I closed my eyes for a moment. I didn't want to move, but I really wanted to see what Egar had to say for himself. His father and sister were both dead, and it was his fault. If he hadn't tried to ensnare us to feed the Nattmara, they'd both be alive.

The Nattmara being dead was a good thing, but the smith? That I still felt bad about, even though I hadn't been the one to kill him. He'd tried to keep us away from the Nattmara's lair, not for himself, but to save us. As monstrous as she was, she was his daughter. He'd done what he could to make his children live normal village lives, but in the end, it wasn't enough.

Tholdri watched my thoughts flicker across my face. "What are you thinking?"

"I'm thinking that I want to speak to Egar before he's executed."

He shook his head. "You need rest. Egar tried to have us killed. Let him be put to death."

I blinked at him. "Oh, I want him put to death, but doesn't it bother you?"

At his blank expression, I continued, "Doesn't it bother you to not know the full story? A man with Sidhe blood marries a pure-blooded Nattmara, has two children, then spends his life protecting said children despite them being monsters?"

"Well when you put it that way." Tholdri stood and offered me his hand.

I waved him away. Not because I didn't need the help, but because letting him tug on my arm might reopen one of the wounds.

I struggled out of bed, hiding how relieved I was that I could stand. I looked down at my stained underthings and breeches. It was fortunate I'd brought extra clothing, though I didn't see my leather cuirass anywhere.

I'd ask about that later. For now, I washed the remaining dried blood from my skin and hair with ice cold water from the washbasin, then rebraided my damp locks. I didn't ask Tholdri to leave so I could change. There might not be time. If the villagers were quick, Egar might be dead by the time we reached him. Though Tholdri remained, he was polite enough not to stare.

I dressed in a green silk shirt, fresh black breeches, and boots, then strapped my sword across my back.

Tholdri waited for me by the door. I walked toward him, retrieving a set of silver daggers from my satchel of belongings beside my bed. The sheaths strapped around each of my wrists. They weren't convenient to wear with vambraces, but I wasn't wearing those today. They looked odd without my cuirass.

The daggers were a comforting weight at my wrists. Maybe I'd start wearing them instead of the vambraces, though I could only do so when the Potentate wouldn't know. All hunters were required to wear the uniform of the Helius Order while on duty.

"Can you take any longer?" Tholdri asked.

I rolled my eyes. "And here just a moment ago you were prepared to let him die."

"But the story dies with him."

It was hard for me to believe he hadn't thought of it before. This might be our last opportunity to speak with someone of Nattmara blood. Nina might have been the last powerful Nattmara in existence.

We left the room, locking it behind us, then hurried from the inn. Tholdri seemed to know where Egar was being kept, so I let him lead the way. We ended up at a small temple, its exterior not much different from the other whitewashed homes, except for the symbol of a hand holding a hawk painted on the door.

I could hear voices inside, shouting. I opened the door, walking in ahead of Tholdri. It seemed the entire village had crammed into the small temple. No wonder I had seen no one in the street.

I walked down the center aisle, bumping my hips into the arms and shoulders of those seated. At one point I had to turn sideways just to fit. Egar was in shackles at the front of the room, seated in a wooden chair on a raised platform. To his left was a podium, an old man stationed behind it. To Egar's right were four more chairs. One held Steifan, another the fletcher, and the other two I did not recognize.

The old man behind the podium, who had to be the village elder, looked down upon me. It was only because he was on a raised dais, but I had a feeling he looked down at people when he was on even footing too. He was tall, but hunched with age, and his dark eyes seemed predatory, like a hawk's. "The other hunters, I presume?"

I felt Tholdri behind my shoulder, a little to the right. The people we'd been shoving our way through only moments before suddenly seemed able to make space. We had the center of the floor all to ourselves.

I straightened my shoulders, then winced at the sharp

pain. "I am the one who slew the Nattmara, and was nearly killed. I would like to hear the boy's excuse for luring me to her lair."

Thoughts played across the old man's face. "You slew her? You killed Nina?"

I hesitated at his accusing tone, then nodded. "The Nattmara, yes."

He lifted his nose. "Whether she was a monster is yet to be determined. Perhaps you are simply a murderer."

Steifan buried his face in his palms and shook his head as the fletcher leapt from his seat. "The Nattmara killed my son! Don't you dare claim she wasn't a monster!" His face was puffy, eyes red-rimmed, and no one seemed to be listening to him.

Tholdri leaned near my ear as the audience murmured. "Perhaps you should have stayed in bed after all."

I shook my head, turning my attention to Egar, his black swath of bangs nearly covering his eyes. He was grinning at me. Even with the denial of the old man, Egar had to realize he'd die before the day was through.

The only real question was whether I'd die with him. The room had erupted with arguments. I heard more than one mention of my red hair.

"Silence!" the village elder shouted, his voice stronger than his frail body appeared.

Shouts quieted to murmurs, and a few glares drifted my way. Egar was still watching me with that sick smile on his face.

I smiled back, none too sweetly. "I imagine this was your tale? That I murdered your dear sister for no apparent reason?"

He leaned back in his chair, shackled hands resting in his lap. "Not a tale, the truth. You killed my sister and father, and yet I am the one in shackles."

The room had gone eerily quiet, everyone waiting to hear what I would say next.

I sighed. "Where is the healer who tended me? She saw the Nattmara's lair." I looked around the room. "And I don't for a moment believe that others didn't take a peek after we were gone."

A few mutters. A few guilty faces. These people knew the truth, but they didn't want to believe it. They didn't want to believe a monster could masquerade as a young girl, fooling them all so easily.

I looked at Egar, wondering if it was just that, or if there was something else clouding their thoughts. "Do you have Sidhe blood like your father?"

Egar's smile faltered. That was it. He was using glamour on the room, trying to turn the blame onto me. That's why he wasn't afraid.

I'd expected more whispers, but the room was utterly quiet. All eyes were on Egar.

His smile resumed. "I don't know what you're talking about. If I possessed the magics of that long gone race, wouldn't I have already used them to escape?"

I stepped toward him, close enough that he had to tilt his head backward to look at me. The Seeing Sword thrummed at my back with unease as I met Egar's eyes. "Perhaps, or perhaps this is all a game to you. Turn the village on the hunters before you make your escape."

He tilted his head, and his voice erupted not from his lips, but through my mind. *I would have simply thanked you for freeing me from my father, but you killed my sister too. For that, you must pay.*

Tholdri was at my back, speaking to the crowd, but Steifan was watching me like he knew what was going on. Had Egar spoken into his mind too? Or was I going mad?

I decided to give madness a try. I thought, *You sent a*

hunter into her lair. You practically killed her yourself.

Egar's voice replied in my mind, *You think I should spare you?*

I glared at him.

He laughed through my mind. *Perhaps you are right.* He stood, and suddenly his hands were free.

I whirled around, glancing at the room, but no one else seemed to notice.

Egar stood at my back with his breath in my ear. "You freed me from my father, so I shall repay you with what remains of your life. But I want you to know, standing here and now, I could have had these people kill you. You did not escape. I let you go."

My body stiffened at his nearness. It had been foolish of me to turn my back on him. The room had erupted with fresh arguments, but no one seemed to see us. For all I knew, they still saw Egar sitting in his chair with his hands shackled.

"Why didn't you just glamour me from the start?" I asked. "With this much skill, you could have made me enjoy being eaten by your sister."

He laughed right next to my ear, bathing me in his hot breath. "My father was more Sidhe than I. He limited my gifts. Now I am free from my cage." He leaned so close that his lips touched my ear. I couldn't seem to move. "My thanks, dear lady. I'm sure we'll meet again, if you survive your wounds."

Though I didn't sense him leaving, I felt the lack of his presence. I knew when I turned around, he'd be gone. With an almost audible shift, his glamour left the room. All eyes turned toward me, standing dumbly in front of Egar's now empty chair, still wondering what he meant about my wounds.

He was gone.

CHAPTER SIXTEEN

Tholdri, Steifan, and I stumbled out of the temple with the shouts of angry village folk at our backs. Suddenly I was a witch, and I'd helped Egar escape, but when I threatened to curse them all, they'd stopped trying to apprehend me.

Imagine that.

I stomped down the street in my silk shirt and breeches, really wishing I had my armor. I appreciated Tholdri's drawn sword as he guarded my back. We needed to leave the village before anyone got brave enough to face us. Luckily, we had our swords, but most of our supplies were at the inn.

Now to decide whether we risked fetching them, or head straight for the horses.

I turned as the angry shouts made their way out into the street. "Stop the witch!" the village elder shouted over them all.

Straight for the horses then. Trusting Tholdri and Steifan to follow, I ran toward the stables. If we'd been smart, we would have saddled our horses before going to the temple, but there was no way we could have predicted what would happen. Maybe that's what Egar wanted. He'd let himself be taken just so he could cause trouble for us.

We reached the stables to find the horses unguarded. The stable hand must have been back at the temple with everyone else.

"I don't see our saddles," Tholdri huffed.

I shook my head. The shouts were getting closer. "We'll have to leave them. Fetch any bridles you see and let's get out of here."

Steifan ran up behind us with three bridles dangling from his fists. "These will have to do."

They weren't ours, and the Potentate would give us all stable duty for losing our tack, but stable duty was better than being stoned to death by villagers.

We each set to bridling our horses, and by the time the villagers reached the stables, we were mounted and charging out the open paddock. I gripped my horse's sides hard with my legs, keeping myself steady atop its wide back. A few villagers dove out of the way as I dug my heels in, sending my horse barreling down the street.

Tholdri and Steifan's mounts caught up, and together we fled the village of Charmant, knowing we could never return, at least not any time soon.

Not that I'd want to return, I thought as wind whipped my face, and my mount's steady gait tugged at my bandages, but I wouldn't mind having the rest of my belongings. Tholdri and Steifan each wore their full armor. They looked like proper hunters. I felt like anything but a proper hunter. Then again, maybe I never had been. Perhaps I'd been playing dress up in the garb of the Helius Order all along.

We rode until our horses frothed at the mouth, far from Charmant, and civilization in general. As luck had it, we'd escaped northwest, farther from the mires rather than into them. The morning had gone ill enough without us wallowing in muck.

My horse walked a few more paces down the narrow road, then stopped, huffing heavily.

I watched Tholdri as he rode past me, guiding his horse into tall green grass gently swaying in the breeze. Beyond was a dense copse of firs.

"Where are you going?" I asked.

He didn't turn back, but answered with a curt tone, "We'll need to lie low. Give the villagers a chance to have their search. I'm sure they'll return home before nightfall, and we can be on our way."

Something in his tone raised my hackles. I urged my horse to follow just as Steifan reached me. I caught up with Tholdri. "What are you in such a foul mood about?"

His brow furrowed. He was searching the trees for danger, but I could tell his mind was on other things. "I've never been chased out of a village before. It's like they thought *we* were the monsters."

"That's exactly what they thought," I said. "Lot of idiots."

Steifan caught up on my other side. "What happened back there anyway? How did Egar escape?"

"Glamour," Tholdri growled.

I raised my brows, turning my attention back toward him. "How did you know? It seemed like no one else in the room could see Egar taunting me."

"That's exactly it. You were just standing there, staring at him, and none of the villagers seemed to notice. His father was Sidhe. It didn't take much thought to figure out what was happening."

I nodded. "His father was limiting his powers. By

killing the smith, we freed Egar to be his full-fledged evil little self."

"What else did Egar tell you?"

I shook my head. "It doesn't matter. I might have slain one monster, but we loosed another. I'll not be surprised if we run into Egar again." I suppressed a shiver, not liking the idea. In some ways, he was more frightening than his sister had been.

Steifan was particularly silent on my other side. I wagered he didn't comprehend how dangerous Egar could be. Then again, the Sidhe were supposed to be extinct. Couldn't blame a young hunter for knowing nothing about them.

We reached the trees, and the tension between my shoulders eased. The throbbing in my wounds had grown into a dull thrumming beat, echoing my heart.

I dismounted, walking my horse a little further into the shade of the trees. The vibrant green grass nearly reached my knees. I looked up at Tholdri as he climbed down from his horse. "Why did it bother you so much? Being chased, I mean?"

He seemed taken aback. "Why *didn't* it bother you?"

I stared at his face for a moment, trying to come up with an answer that would make sense to him. "You're a hunter, and a strong handsome man with golden locks. I too am a hunter, but I'm a woman, with the hair color of a witch. Any time I enter a village, I half expect to be chased out."

He narrowed his honey brown eyes. "Villagers don't chase hunters. As much as they don't understand us, they also need us."

I couldn't help but laugh. "Dear Tholdri, don't you realize? Villagers chase that which they don't understand the hardest."

Finally he laughed, and the tension of the moment eased between us, though his dark mood quickly resumed. As always, Steifan watched us both without comment.

As we led our horses further into the trees, I tried to decide what to do next. At nightfall I was supposed to meet Karpov, but I was utterly unprepared. Now not only was I injured, but I was missing my crossbow and extra weapons, and I'd likely be going without supper unless Steifan hunted rabbits better than he hunted vampires.

I watched as he tripped on a root hidden by the tall grass. He nearly fell face-first, but righted himself just in time.

"How did you pass the hunter trials with such awkward feet?" I laughed.

He grinned. "I merely stumble to lull you into complacency. I'm a fine fighter when given the chance."

I chuckled. "You'll have to prove it to me someday."

"If we survive the night," Tholdri muttered sourly.

I sighed. If Tholdri's foul mood continued, I might almost long for Karpov's company.

Almost.

NIGHTFALL CAME QUICKLY, the darkness first slithering out from the trees, then fading upward as the sun made its descent. Once the horses were rested, and we were sure we wouldn't run into an angry mob, we'd ridden east toward Bordtham. There, Steifan and Tholdri would wait while I met with Karpov. If morning came and I did not return, they'd search for me.

I could see the warm yellow light of the village in the distance. Part of me dreaded reaching it to leave my companions behind, but the other part, the dark pit of rage in my stomach, had been waiting eagerly for this night to come.

Well, perhaps not *this* night, but the night I would have my vengeance.

Tholdri was watching me. His eyes lightly reflected the moonlight, making him appear almost supernatural. "Are you sure about this, Lyss? I don't feel good about waiting in the village while you meet him."

I nodded. "Karpov will not speak to me if he sees you. I cannot lose this opportunity."

He glanced at the nearing village, then back to me. "You mean the opportunity to slay Karpov, right? Not to face Asher."

"Of course," I answered curtly.

"You're a terrible liar."

I sighed heavily. "When I plan to face Asher, you will know, I swear it." And I meant what I said. He couldn't divert me from my path, but he'd at least not be taken by surprise.

I looked past Tholdri to Steifan, hunched with a pensive expression atop his horse's back. "You seem to be thinking terribly hard about something," I observed.

He startled, then blinked at me. "I'm tired. Nothing more."

I didn't have time to worry about it. Bordtham might be near, but my ride was only just beginning. I had to reach the crypt by midnight.

When it was time to diverge, Tholdri halted his horse and turned toward me. "If you get yourself killed, know this night will haunt me for the rest of my life, Lyss."

I smiled softly. "I'll be careful, I swear it. If Karpov wanted me dead, I'd already be dead." I didn't add that if he suspected me of trickery, he might still kill me. No sense in worrying Tholdri further.

He watched me for a moment longer. "I'll see you soon, then."

I nodded, then turned my horse away before he could start another argument. I would attend this meeting regardless. Karpov was the only one who could lead me to Asher.

I shook my head as I rode out into the darkness, away from the comforting lights of Bordtham. Perhaps that wasn't quite true. I'd nearly died last night, and Asher had come. If I'd been alone, would he have approached me?

It didn't really matter now. Karpov had the key to me catching Asher unawares. Now if only I had the key to doing the same to Karpov. He'd killed my uncle, a highly trained hunter. If I hoped to stand a chance, I'd have to outwit a being that had survived centuries.

The odds were most certainly not in my favor.

CHAPTER SEVENTEEN

It had been a while since I had been truly alone in the night with a vampire, and now I'd managed it twice in a brief span. I couldn't say I missed the feeling. Karpov had been waiting, just like he said he would be. His long, gaunt form looked like a macabre statue leaning against the wall of the crypt. Weather-worn stones melded with his black clothing like they were a part of him.

"I'm surprised you came alone." His rich voice cut through the night.

"You told me to come alone."

He laughed. "Yes, but you don't strike me as someone who likes to be told what to do."

I didn't reply. He was right, but I wasn't about to agree that he knew me. He didn't know me. I knew he'd been watching me, he wouldn't have chosen me otherwise, but you couldn't know someone just from watching them. You had to know their thoughts, their desires. And such things were rarely visible from the outside.

"What have you decided, Lyssandra?"

"I will help you," I answered, hoping he couldn't sense

131

the lie. Not that it was actually a lie, but I wondered if he could sense my hidden intentions. Sometimes it seemed like the really old vampires could read your mind, but they were probably just more perceptive than those with shorter lives.

Still leaning against the crypt, he lifted his nose, as if to scent the air. "You're injured. What happened to you?"

I had the urge to reach for my sword. He hadn't threatened me, but the fact that he knew I was injured from twenty paces away unnerved me. "That's none of your concern."

"It is my concern. You cannot defeat Asher while weakened." I closed my eyes. It was only a normal blink, but when I opened them, he was right in front of me. He moved faster than anything I'd ever seen. No, that wasn't right. I'd seen it before. I'd seen it the night he killed my uncle.

He loomed over me. His hot breath smelled like blood, and suddenly my pulse was in my ears. "You are too weak to kill him. I thought you stronger, or I would not have enlisted you."

I swallowed the lump in my throat. "I will be fully healed in a few days. I will kill him, but you must show me where he is."

"If you were strong enough to kill him, you'd not have sustained your current injuries."

My skin crawled with his nearness. "Just tell me where he is."

"I should kill you now."

I considered reaching for my sword, but I knew if I drew it there would be no going back. The thought made me realize something. The Seeing Sword wasn't whispering a warning into my mind. Karpov was one of the biggest predators around. It should have been warning me.

Unless it didn't warn me of predators. Maybe it just warned me when others meant me harm, and Karpov didn't. Despite his threats, he needed me.

I craned my neck to look up at him. "Tell me where Asher is."

He sighed. "You really are incorrigible, aren't you?" He stepped away, then walked back toward the crypt. "Come with me, Lyssandra. I'll tend your wounds."

Well that was absolutely the last thing I expected. Or wanted. "My wounds are fine. I simply came to tell you I agree to your terms. I'll return to Bordtham for the night."

He stopped in front of the entrance to the crypt. "You'll do no such thing. I won't allow you to return to your other hunters."

"What are you talking about?"

He gave me a tired expression, his hollow cheeks casting dark shadows on his face in the moonlight. "Don't be foolish, Lyssandra. Did you expect me to have no human servants? They have been watching Bordtham for your return."

I was several steps toward him before I even realized I had moved. "If you harm them—"

He opened the aged, brittle wooden door to the crypt, then turned toward me. "Stay true to your word, and no harm will befall them. Betray me, and we'll find out how many human servants it takes to fell two hunters."

I walked toward the crypt. Karpov had already disappeared inside. I paused at the threshold, unwilling to take that last step. Once I took that step, I would be with Karpov until either he or Asher were dead. I had promised Tholdri I wouldn't kill Asher without speaking with him, so that just meant I'd be killing Karpov on my own, or I'd die trying.

I stepped inside, then descended into the crypt. There

were candles below, but Karpov had gone around a bend so I couldn't see him. I waited for the Seeing Sword to hint at danger, but nothing came.

I reached the bottom of the stone steps, then turned the corner, arriving at the entrance of the room where I'd woken in a coffin. I sensed multiple vampires, but still no warning.

I entered the room and instantly regretted it. Karpov was there, yes, but so were three other vampires. Yet, that wasn't what had me worried. These weren't babies, they were ancients. As old as Karpov, or older. I could feel their age like a heavy weight on my shoulders.

Two were male, one with short hair that had probably been red when it knew sunlight, but now it was a russet brown. He was shorter than Karpov, but then again, who wasn't? The other male had jet black hair cascading in a silken curtain down his broad shoulders. His icy blue eyes watched me with interest. The third ancient vampire was female, a full hand shorter than me. Her hair was meant to be honey blonde, but without sunlight, it had become a saturated yellow. Her face was round, her cheeks plump and lovely. If I couldn't sense what she was, I might almost think she was alive. She watched me with thinly veiled disgust.

The coffins and table that had been in the room when I awoke were gone. There were candles set along the walls where they met the floor, and some higher in recesses in the stone.

It took me several tries to find my voice. "Well now I'm confused. With this much power, why do you need me?"

Karpov leaned against the far wall. "It is not your power that we need, Lyssandra, it is your connection to Asher. Your ability to get close to him."

"A human servant with free will is unheard of." The

female's voice was surprisingly deep and sultry. I'd expected a higher pitch with her small frame. "Only you can get close enough to Asher to weaken him. Once that is accomplished, we will finish the task."

I looked at Karpov with eyebrows raised. I almost asked why they thought Asher would even let me close to him, then dismissed it as a bad idea. If these four deemed me less than useful, I wouldn't make it out of the crypt alive. I was strong, but I knew my limits.

I crossed my arms, looking at each of the ancients in the room. "How can I trust you to finish the task? If I'm going to die for my vengeance, I want guarantees that it won't be in vain."

Karpov inclined his chin. "You have my word, little servant. You and your master shall both perish."

I pretended to think over his words. Really, I was trying to figure out what to do. I had hoped Karpov would give me Asher's location, then leave me to defeat him on my own. Once I had his location, I could kill Karpov first— preferably with Tholdri's help.

Now, not only would I not have Tholdri, but I had three other ancients to outsmart. If they intended to stay with me until Asher was dead, Karpov would survive me. Of course, they had to rest come sunrise, but I knew I wouldn't be lucky enough to be left in a room with their vulnerable corpses. These four had survived this long for a reason.

I was looking down at my boots so my eyes would not betray my thoughts, but I could sense Karpov's heavy gaze on me.

"Come, Lyssandra," he said. "I will heal your wounds."

I kept my eyes downcast. "Vampires are not healers, Karpov. You're killers."

His companions echoed his laugh. "We can be healers if

135

we so choose. A taste of my blood will heal your tainted wounds."

My eyes snapped upward. "Tainted?"

"I can smell them from here," he sneered. "Something with dark magic has pierced your flesh."

I shifted my shoulders, frantically searching for any sign the wounds were not normal wounds. They hurt, badly, but it just felt like torn flesh. "What will happen if I don't let you heal them?"

"The corruption will spread through your blood, and you will die. Asher's power can only save you from so much."

The female stepped toward Karpov. It was odd, but as soon as she moved, the Seeing Sword started tingling up my spine. "You've given me an idea," she said. "What if she doesn't taste your blood, but Asher's? We could send her to Asher while she's injured. He will be inclined to heal her himself, and the exchange would give her reason to be close to him."

I glared at the female vampire, knowing by the seeing Sword's warning that she wasn't simply toying with me. She was more intelligent than I'd initially assumed, which was stupid of me. I'd seen someone small and pretty, and deemed her as the least threatening. I'd been spending too much time around male hunters.

Karpov stroked his chin as a wicked smile blossomed across his face, stretching thin skin over sharp bones. "What an interesting idea." He tilted his head, observing me. "I do not know why he made you his servant, but I have always wondered. Perhaps this test will prove if you're actually important to him, or if he gave you this gift on a whim."

I didn't argue about it being a gift. It would fall on deaf ears. "I have no desire to drink your blood, Karpov, but I find the thought of Asher's blood somehow even less appealing."

His eyes glittered with malice. "You will drink his blood, or you will die. Your thirst for vengeance will outweigh your disgust, I'm sure. We will bring you to Asher tonight. Let him heal you, gain his trust. Once he accepts you by his side, we will come for him, and you will deal the first blow."

I blinked at him. He would bring me to Asher tonight? "Won't he wonder how I found him?"

"We will leave you near his lair. He will find you near death, and either he will save you, or he will not care to. If he will not care to, then your death will not be a loss to us."

I stepped back. Near death? Before my mind could register the threat, the Seeing Sword screamed through my mind. It had warned me when the female had decided she meant me harm, and now they all did. I drew the sword, for what little good it would do. The female reached me first, a look of hunger on her lovely face.

Hungry for me. They all were. And there was nothing I could do about it.

CHAPTER EIGHTEEN

My body was cold, unbearably cold. I seemed to float above the ground. I could no longer feel the pain in my shoulder and neck. I had so many wounds that the Nattmara's bites seemed minor. Distantly, I could smell the fetid stench of the mires, but a more relevant smell overwhelmed my senses. I smelled the turned-earth scent of vampire, with an undercurrent of vanilla and sage.

More strange still, I felt *safe*. I hadn't felt so safe since I was a child in my mother's arms.

My mind struggled to make sense of things, but I'd lost too much blood. Karpov and his other ancients had nearly drained me dry, but not with their fangs. They'd sliced me up, tearing the flesh to make the wounds jagged like I'd been attacked by wild animals, or ghouls. I groaned as sudden nausea lanced through my stomach.

"Don't move," a male voice soothed. "You've lost too much blood."

My pulse fluttered, too weak to hammer with panic. My breath rasped in my throat. "Asher?"

"Shh."

Of course it was Asher. They'd left me for him to find. And I wasn't floating, he was carrying me. He was . . . carrying me? It seemed Karpov's test had paid off, though we'd see if he would actually save me.

Or maybe I wouldn't see. The gentle rhythm of Asher's steps faded from my senses. Everything faded. I had definitely lost too much blood, as evidenced by my final emotion—guilt. Guilt that Asher had been lured to save me, when I fully intended his death.

I wasn't sure how long it was before I regained consciousness, but I could sense it was still night. I hoped it was still the same night, and that I hadn't lost an entire day in between. If that was the case, Tholdri and Steifan would be out with freshly saddled horses looking for me, and they might find Karpov and the other ancients instead.

I was lying on a hard, cold surface. My fingertips grazed across carved stone. I jumped as my hand touched something cool, then I relaxed. My fingers wrapped around the hilt of the Seeing Sword. Just touching it calmed my frayed nerves. I wasn't entirely helpless.

I sat up with a groan, but I was feeling better. A little *too* much better. I looked around the small stone space, lit by a single lantern. Another crypt. *Wonderful.*

I had two choices. I could get up and look for the way out, or I could search for Asher. Though my journey to the crypt seemed like a dream, I knew I hadn't imagined him. He had saved me again, and I didn't understand why. Why would a vampire care if a human, even a human servant, lived or died? It made little sense. Monsters cared only for themselves.

I lowered my feet to the ground, wincing as my toes

absorbed the cold through my stockings. I searched around the base of the sarcophagus I'd been lying on, finding my boots placed neatly against one side. Asher had left me my sword and my boots. It was almost as if he wanted me to flee. Maybe he did. Maybe he already knew what I planned.

I laced my boots up to my knees, then tugged down the bloody, tattered fabric of my shirt to look at my wounds. The bandages were missing, and the places where the Nattmara had bitten me were almost healed.

Once I was on my feet, I took the time to assess my other injuries. I was sore, and some puncture wounds still stung, but given a few more days, I'd be fine. I swished my tongue around in my mouth, searching for the taste of blood. Karpov had claimed that was the only way to heal me, which meant Asher had given me his blood. I had the sudden urge to vomit.

I took shallow breaths, waiting for the nausea to pass. I focused on the nearby lantern in the corner of the small stone space on the floor. Had Asher left it there for my benefit, or did he intend to return?

All right, decision time. Should I flee, or follow through with Karpov's plan? I almost wanted to flee just out of spite since he left me nearly dead in the mires, but I knew I couldn't let this opportunity pass. I took a moment to strap my sword across my back, just in case.

"Asher?" I called out.

He wasn't in the room with me, I could tell that much, but he was a vampire. If he was nearby, he'd hear my voice.

Moments crept by. I'd almost begun to doubt myself when I felt the air shift behind me. I turned around, and there he stood, just as I remembered him. His hair was almost an absence of color, pure white like the elderly, but it wasn't from age. It was just his natural tone, slightly more colorless than his pale skin. The strands were pin straight, trailing well below the shoulders of his fitted black coat. His eyes were a deep gray that might look blue in the sun, though I'd never know for sure. In moonlight, they looked silver. I could meet them with impunity since I was his human servant. Charcoal breeches tucked into black boots completed his outfit.

He was handsome in a bone-chilling kind of way, reminding me of a wolf. Stunningly beautiful, but you were always well aware that it might choose to eat you. And you might like it.

Standing before him with only the sarcophagus between us, I was suddenly painfully aware of my bloody clothing, matted hair, and bedraggled appearance.

I squared my shoulders, unwilling to feel like a sad, sickly human in front of him. "It was bold of you to leave me my sword."

He smiled, though it didn't reach his eyes. "I found you lying with it still clutched in your grasp, even as your body neared the brink of death. It would be cruel of me to take something you fought so hard to keep."

Karpov must have placed it that way to make it seem like I'd been attacked by ghouls. They'd have no interest in claiming a mortal's weapon.

"You gave me your blood." I meant it as an observation, but my words came out accusatory.

He nodded. "You might have survived the more recent injuries, but the Nattmara's poison would have killed you."

A fine trembling set into my shoulders. I'd waited for this moment for so long, but now I didn't know what to do with it. "You were there that night. Tholdri saw you."

Again, he nodded. "It took much of my energy to help you. I was curious why you needed it. I saw the slain creature in her lair after you were safe within the inn."

It felt oddly normal talking to him in the ancient crypt, by the light of a lone lantern casting shadows across one side of his face. The entire scene seemed . . . anti-climactic. "Why did you help me, Asher? Why did you help me then, and again tonight? It is the same night, isn't it?"

He stepped toward the sarcophagus, splaying his long fingers across the stone surface. He lowered his head, then looked up at me through a swath of white hair. "Yes, it is the same night. You are my servant, Lyssandra. It comes with certain privileges."

My hands clenched into fists. "Something tells me you do not extend this privilege to all your servants."

"I have no others. Only you. The novelty of someone fawning at your feet fades quickly."

Anger smothered my fear. I wanted to scream at him, for this meeting had been far too civil. I took three long steps forward, pressing the front of my thighs against the sarcophagus. I leaned toward him, close enough to kiss. "I have waited long for this meeting, Asher. Don't you dare lie to my face. I want answers."

A small smile tugged at the corners of his lips, drawing my attention to them. "You are brazen. That was the first thing I noticed about you. I found myself wondering, who was this brazen young hunter, willing to have a conversation with a vampire?"

"Is that why you did this to me?"

He leaned in closer, and suddenly I regretted approaching the sarcophagus. I could feel his breath on my face, not warm like human breath, but cool like the grave. He hadn't fed yet. He had no warmth to give. A chill went down my spine.

"I saved your life, Lyssandra. I saved your life, and you repaid me with threats. The last time we spoke, you claimed you would kill me. Yet here you are with your strange sword yet strapped across your back, ready to pierce my flesh. Do your threats mean so little?"

He was baiting me, but to what end? Maybe he was just baffled that I hadn't attacked him yet, but I couldn't attack him until Karpov came. "I will still kill you," I growled, "but first I want answers."

He pushed away from the sarcophagus, stepping out of reach, though I knew it wasn't from fear. He didn't really believe I could kill him. "Why would I grant answers to someone who wants my death?"

"Asks the madman who has twice saved someone who wants to kill him."

He laughed, then walked around the sarcophagus, approaching me. I stepped back instinctively, my heart suddenly racing. He continued walking toward me, and I continued retreating until my back was against the wall. It was so oddly reminiscent of my dream that I had to close my eyes for a moment. This wasn't a dream. I had to keep my wits about me.

He leaned in close to my ear, his body almost touching mine. "Why did I find you in the mires, Lyssandra? Why were you left for dead in my territory?"

His words felt like a trap. Did he already know? Had he seen Karpov and the others leave me? I opened my eyes and looked past him. I could barely see the outline of the door he'd entered through. It had been hidden from me in the darkness. I debated going for it now, but he was too close.

With my pulse hammering in my head, I met his eyes. "After my fellow hunters and I saw you last night, I decided to find you. I have been searching for you for years, after all. Unfortunately, I was already weakened from my wounds, and I was attacked."

He lifted one arched brow. "And what has become of

your fellow hunters? Why would they let you run off alone while injured?"

I sneered. "You know nothing of the other hunters."

"And you know nothing of me."

His words were like a slap in the face. He was right. I only half remembered our drunken conversation from the night we met, and it had occurred so long ago that even most of that had faded. All I knew was that he was a vampire, and he had taken me against my will. And he had done so tonight too, even if it was to save me.

"Why are you really here, Lyssandra? You may be foolish, but you're not stupid enough to try to kill me on your own, not while injured. Were you aware the Nattmara's poison would have killed you? Is that why you came?"

My breath eased out of me. He didn't know about Karpov. He thought I'd come to save my own skin. "If all I wanted was to be saved, I would have fled while I had the chance."

He spun away, stalking across the crypt. With his back to me, I saw his shoulders rise and fall with a heavy sigh. "You will be safe to rest here until dawn. I suggest you wait until then to leave."

He was giving me another out. A final chance to flee from him, Karpov, and from myself. I stepped away from the wall, toward him. "I'm not leaving."

He let out a bitter laugh. "I'm sure you'll tire of waiting alone in this crypt, eventually." He walked toward the door.

I chased after him. Without his blood, I wouldn't have made it a single step, but I was starting to feel almost normal. Tired and sore, but normal. "Where do you think you're going? We are not done." I followed him outside into the darkness.

His expression when he turned back toward me was *not* friendly. "I do not know what you're planning, Lyssandra, but I am not a fool. I do not intend to wait around to find out. I know you didn't just come here for answers, nor for my blood."

He turned away from me, and I put my hand on his shoulder to stop him. I froze. Did I really think I was going to physically *stop* a vampire? The only way to stop a vampire was with a sword through the heart, and I wasn't quite ready to do that.

And yet, he turned back toward me, looking at my hand on his shoulder like it was some strange creature.

I licked my dry, cracked lips. "I do want answers," I assured.

"I offered them to you long ago. You chose not to hear me. I will not give you the choice again."

I forced myself to keep my hand on his shoulder, though I wanted nothing more than to pull it away. No, that wasn't true, but I *should* have wanted it. "Then you will have to live for the rest of eternity with me haunting your every step. I'm not going away."

His laugh echoed across the quiet night, startling me. "Who could have guessed that granting a beautiful woman eternal life could end with such misery?"

I couldn't tell if he was complementing me, or insulting me, so I moved past it. "Does that mean you'll give me my answers?"

He watched me for a moment longer. "Rest here until morning, then start walking. Walk far from this place, and tomorrow night I will find you."

That would not work. Karpov was supposed to find us here, or at least that was what I assumed. "Why not just meet me back here?"

"You still intend my death, Lyssandra. I will not walk into your trap. Do as I say, or you will never see me again."

I finally removed my hand from his shoulder. "Fine, but how will you find me?"

He smiled an eerie smile. "Dear Lyssandra, you are my human servant. I could find you anywhere."

And with that, he was gone. I flexed the hand I had used to grip his shoulder, realizing it was the first time I had ever touched him willingly. The few other times we had met, I had kept my distance.

I had gone from running from him, to chasing him, and now I had him. So why did I want nothing more than to run away again? I wasn't sure, but the irony of the situation wasn't lost on me. All I knew was that tomorrow night I had yet another meeting set up with a vampire. With multiple vampires, if Karpov could find us. If I had my way, we'd all end up dead. But something told me I wasn't going to get my way. Something told me that the only one who'd end up dead, was me.

CHAPTER NINETEEN

I took Asher's advice and stayed in the crypt until dawn, but I didn't rest. I was hungry, thirsty, and annoyed. I had made the mistake of trusting a vampire, and Karpov had left me near death in the mires. Now I had to trust Asher too.

At first light I started walking, squinting my eyes against the harsh sun. There were swamps to the east, and west would lead me out of the mires. South, by my estimations, I wouldn't reach a village by sundown. So north it was. A crypt wouldn't have been constructed far from civilization, so there had to be something nearby. Though the crypt was old enough, whatever village it belonged to might be long since deserted.

Regardless, I saw no other choice. I'd be a weak puddle by nightfall without food, though even if I found a village, I might not be welcome. I had to look awful. My green silken shirt was torn and massively blood stained, and my breeches were no better. My hair had pulled fully free from its braid and was matted to one side of my head with blood.

At least I was alive, for now, and still possessed the sword strapped across my back. My wrist sheaths hadn't survived the attack. They were probably resting somewhere in a puddle of my blood.

I walked until the sun was high overhead, until finally I saw smoke from a village. I still had my coin pouch at my belt, so I could buy something to eat if someone would actually sell it to me. They might take one look at me and chase me away. I no longer had any insignia marking me as a hunter. All I had was my strange sword, and flaming red hair that to some, marked me as a witch.

Each step felt labored by the time I reached the small village. I had hoped for something larger, because people stared less in the cities, but I could smell fresh baked bread and my stomach was painfully hungry.

A few villagers glanced my way as I walked down the main street, but their gazes quickly averted. I headed straight for a small cart selling fresh loaves of bread. I would find food, then water, then hurry on my way. I wanted to be far from civilization before Asher came looking for me.

The girl selling bread widened her eyes at my approach. She glanced around, probably looking for a route of escape. She was young, around fifteen I'd guess, with long brown hair cascading over a willowy frame. Her dress ended well above her ankles, a common style in the mires where crops grew in fields of water.

I quickly fished in my pouch and withdrew a copper, gesturing toward her with it.

She bravely waited for me to reach her, though I caught her eyeing the dried blood on my shirt. She probably wouldn't react well if I asked her where we were. A bloody stranger wandering through the mires was never a good sign.

She watched me as I picked my loaf. At first I thought her too frightened to speak, but then she whispered, "I'd find different clothes if I were you, or at least wash up in the spring north of town. With so many being killed lately, some might think you a vampire, even in the daylight."

Clutching the largest loaf I could find, I raised a brow at her. "Killings?"

She nodded, her expression serious. "Two killed last night, one the night before. Three others missing."

Perhaps this village was where Karpov was getting his baby vampires, though I didn't think so. He'd more likely do that in his own territory, which meant there were other vampires around. "Thank you for warning me," I whispered, handing her the copper.

I hurried onward to find the spring she had mentioned. I had no water skin, but I would drink my fill and clean my shirt and hair as best I could. I caught a few more glances as I continued on, but no one tried to question me. These people were obviously terrified, and they had good reason to be. If the vampires really were going to war, humans would surely suffer most of the casualties.

Reaching the spring was a relief. Other than a lone man filling a water pail, there was no one else around. I moved further down the stream from where it fed into the main pool, stopping where I'd be blocked from view from the main street. I huddled behind some shrubs to remove my sword and shirt. The green silk was ruined, which was unfortunate as it was one of my favorite shirts. I really hoped I could pay Karpov back for ruining it.

Once my hair and clothing were sopping wet, but relatively clean, I sat in the grass beside the stream to eat my bread. The thick crust was the finest thing my teeth had torn into in a while. I wished there were some way I could send word to Steifan and Tholdri, to warn them not to look for me. Even if they could find me, they couldn't pull me out of the mess I'd gotten myself into. They'd likely just get killed, and it would be all my fault. I regretted telling them the truth.

It was about midday by the time I was ready to leave the peaceful spot. My shirt and hair had started to dry, and walking would help finish the task. With the Seeing Sword quiet at my back, I felt relatively calm. I had the rest of the day to myself. A single day to choose whether I would live or die tonight, if I'd even have a choice.

I stood to start walking, then tensed, sensing a presence at my back. I turned, finding the girl who'd sold me the bread, standing just a few paces away.

I felt embarrassed that she'd snuck up on me. "You move quietly for a village girl," I observed.

She wrung her hands. "Forgive me, but I noticed your sword. I wondered if you knew how I could get one."

I looked her up and down. She was a scrawny thing. I doubted she could even lift a sword. "I believe your small hands would be better suited to a dagger. But I fear I have none to spare at the moment. Why do you want one?"

She glanced around warily. "The killings. No one knows how to stop them, and the hunters are yet to arrive. I live only with my older sister. We have no one to protect us."

I didn't want to tell her she would stand no chance of wielding a dagger against a vampire. It would be like telling her to look death in the eye and accept her fate. No one should have to accept that, save those passing from old age. I could tell her to leave the village, but she'd probably be no better off anywhere else in the mires.

All I could do was kill the monster hunting from her village. In fact, I was sworn to do so. It was my solemn vow to protect innocents like her. But I needed to meet Asher. I had to make him trust me.

Karpov and the others would be waiting.

The girl watched me, waiting for me to speak, fear clear in her wide eyes.

I let out a heavy sigh, knowing I'd regret what I was about to say. Fortunately, if I died tonight, I wouldn't have to regret it for long. "I'll need to speak to the families of those who were killed. I want to know how many vampires we're dealing with before night falls."

Her jaw went slack. When she finally managed to close it, she opened it again to stammer, "Y-you're a hunter?"

I nodded. "I'll do my best to protect you and your sister, and once the vampires plaguing your village are dead, I'll see about finding you a dagger."

She smiled at that, and hope glittered in her eyes. I wasn't sure if it was at the idea of me killing the vampires, or at her getting a dagger. I suspected the latter. I was liking this girl better by the moment.

OUR FIRST STOP was the girl's home. Her name was Elizabeth, and she was intent on finding me new clothes. I'd been skeptical of her size, but she claimed her sister was taller, and would have something more suitable for me.

The home was larger than I expected, more suited to a family of five or six than to just two girls. I assumed they had inherited it, but didn't ask the details. If the rest of their family was gone, it was probably a painful story. And I was better at killing things than I was at offering comfort.

As soon as the door was shut behind us, Elizabeth hurried into a bedroom. I glanced around the home. It was clean, if a little cluttered. Rocks and little bits of nature littered every window sill. Some larger pieces had built up on the room's sole table. I didn't think her sister was home, but that wasn't unusual since it was the middle of the day. They would both need to work to support themselves.

Elizabeth returned with a bundle of clothing. She seemed more excited than frightened now, and proudly offered me the garments. I looked through them, handing back a dress and a long skirt, but keeping a tan colored long sleeve shirt, and a loose coat two shades darker.

"No pants?" I asked.

She shook her head, swishing her long brown hair from side to side. "My father passed away many years ago. We finally gave away his clothing."

And here I was thinking I could avoid the sad story. While I dressed and braided my hair, she told me of how her father had died in a carriage accident, and her mother a few years later from illness. There'd been an older brother, but he left shortly after the father died. He'd been intent on making a life for himself in Silgard, the Capital to the south, and had never been heard from again.

I didn't tell her that her brother had probably died before he made it. In that, perhaps I could offer at least small comfort, or just not make things worse.

I caught her eyeing my sword longingly as I strapped it back over my shoulders on top of the new shirt and coat.

"You truly want to learn to fight?" I asked.

She hesitated, then nodded, wringing her small hands. "I'm grateful that the other villagers want to buy my bread. We need the extra coin to supplement what my sister makes in the rice fields, but my true longing is to become a hunter, like you."

My eyes widened. "You know only certain bloodlines can become hunters, don't you?"

She nodded. "Yes, I'm not foolish enough to think I

154

could actually go out and hunt vampires, but if I can't do that, learning to fight seems like the next best thing. I could at least go out hunting bandits."

I laughed. This girl had lived a hard life, but it was still so much more simple than mine. It made me long for my youth. I wasn't that much older than her, but it felt like decades. "Introduce me to the villagers who have lost loved ones recently, and if there's time, I will teach you a few things before dark."

I smiled at her as she rushed toward the door, but my smile soon faded. I would do my best to protect her, but when dealing with vampires, things rarely went as you hoped. I had to ensure she was nowhere near when Karpov came for Asher. If I could slay the monster plaguing her village before then, all the better.

Tugging down the sleeves of my new coat, I followed her outside. She was waiting for me by the gate of a small front garden. Hardy chard and beet stalks were already well underway to prepare for the colder months. It rarely snowed in the mires, but the moist ground would get cold enough to kill more delicate crops.

As I followed Elizabeth down the dirt street, I thought for a moment that she would enjoy seeing the snow. Castle Helius would be covered in white all winter. It was miserable, but also beautiful. The tall peaks of the mountains beyond would glitter with the dawn, and moonlight would bring with it a shimmering feast for the eyes. Though Castle Helius had been my home from a young age, I never tired of seeing it blanketed in snow.

I cast away my thoughts. Elizabeth might see Castle Helius someday, but I wouldn't be the one to show her. I didn't think I'd be seeing it again.

We reached the first home, but no one answered the door. "This is Sarsa's house," Elizabeth explained. "She lost her grandson." Without further explanation, Elizabeth hurried on toward the back of the house, and I followed.

An old woman tending her chickens gasped as she saw us. She held a bony hand up to her heart. Her frail body trembled beneath a loose brown dress. "Elizabeth, what are you doing here? And who is—" She finally seemed to really look at me, her eyes lingering first on my hair back in its braid, then on my sword.

"This is Lyssandra," Elizabeth explained. "She's a hunter."

The old woman's face drained of color. She took a step back. "No, you cannot hunt her. It will only make it worse."

Her reaction surprised me so much, it took me a moment to respond. "Her?"

The old woman's expression fell. Her bony hand raised back up to her heart. "The vampire who killed my grandson. If you hunt her, she'll bring more of them down upon us."

I looked at Elizabeth, who seemed confused, then back to the old woman. "Not if she's dead."

The old woman backed up another step, shaking her head back and forth. She didn't seem to notice the chickens scurrying around her feet, hoping for feed. "You can't," she rasped. "Please."

I reached a hand out, to do what I wasn't sure, but Elizabeth made it there first, placing a comforting hand on the old woman's shoulder.

"You can't," the old woman said again, but her words were weak. Her hands shook.

I looked at Elizabeth. "You should take her inside. Have her lie down."

Elizabeth nodded, then guided the old woman toward her house. I watched them go, wondering at the old woman's reaction. It would be interesting to see how the families of the other victims reacted. If they were all as strange as the old woman, I might suspect something else was going on. Perhaps something that had nothing to do with vampires.

I just hoped it wasn't another Nattmara. I really didn't want to have to drink Asher's blood a second time.

THE OTHER FAMILIES proved more normal. They provided me with stories I'd heard countless times before. People feeling like they were being watched. Loved ones disappearing, or found lifeless and drained of blood. In one case, it was only the blood that was found. The body was never recovered.

What was most odd, was that all of the stories were different. Vampires tended to have patterns. Either they took the bodies, left them, or lured the victims somewhere far away while still alive. We should have had all the bodies, or none of them, unless some were being made into vampires. But with that, there should have been more killings. According to Elizabeth, the nearest village was Bordtham, and as far as I knew, the only killing there had been claimed by Karpov.

I told Elizabeth as much as we walked back toward her home. I wasn't sure why I was speaking my thoughts out loud. She wasn't a hunter in training. Maybe I just missed Steifan, who had somehow gone from nuisance to friend in a brief span of time.

"I still don't like how that old woman reacted," I muttered as we reached Elizabeth's front door. "How would she know the vampire was a *her*?"

Elizabeth shrugged as she opened the door and gestured for me to go inside. "Sarsa claimed she was there when her grandson was taken. He was the first one to go, and no one believed her tale at first. Her mind started to go a while back, and we all just figured her grandson had run off now that he was of age."

I stopped walking. "And you didn't think to mention this sooner?"

She shrugged casually, but her face burned with a blush. "You didn't ask. Is it somehow important?"

I shook my head and kept walking. So it had all started with the grandson. The vampire took him, but left Sarsa alive. Interesting.

I had just taken a step inside the front door of Elizabeth's home when a woman screamed. She looked just like Elizabeth, but with darker hair and a slightly sharper chin. She was taller too, by at least a head.

I just stood there while Elizabeth rushed around me, waving her hands for her sister to quiet. This had to be her older sister, but I immediately got the impression that Elizabeth had assumed that role. She spoke in soothing whispers, explaining who I was and why I was there, but her sister's panic only seemed to increase.

"She'll hunt the vampires," Elizabeth said. "We'll be safe."

Like a candle being extinguished, the sister's panic slipped away, only to be replaced by anger. She stormed toward me. "How dare you involve my sister in this!" She reached me and had to look upward. As was the case with most women, I was the taller of the two of us. There was a flicker of hesitation in her eyes, then she continued in a more even tone, "If those things come for my sister next because of you—and why are you wearing my clothes!"

"I gave them to her!" Elizabeth blurted. "Hers were ruined."

The sister's nostrils flared. "You'll not lure the vampires near my sister—"

I held up a hand to cut her off, but it was Elizabeth who spoke. "I invited her here, Mira. She would've left the village behind if not for me. She's endangering her life for us, not the other way around."

Funny, I'd never had a villager worried about me endangering my life before. "Perhaps I should give you two a moment alone—"

Mira took a step back and hung her head. "No, forgive me, I've been terribly rude. I've just been so frightened that something will happen to Elizabeth. She's all I have."

Suddenly it became clear why Elizabeth was yet to run off hunting bandits. Whether willingly, or through death, the rest of the family had left Mira behind. Mira didn't strike me as someone who would share her sister's ambitions, which meant Elizabeth was stuck in the small village for the foreseeable future.

Mira gave Elizabeth a meaningful look, then turned to me. "Is it a vampire then? Will you be able to kill it?"

"I believe it's a vampire, yes, but perhaps more than one."

Elizabeth stepped past her sister, toward me. "Will it be too dangerous for you facing more than one?"

"Not if they are newer vampires," I explained, "which I believe these are." I left out that four ancients would be lurking somewhere in the dark tonight, five if you counted Asher. "I'll start tracking them as soon as night falls, and will return to you in the morning if I am able. But if I do not return, do not come looking for me."

I could tell Elizabeth was about to argue that point, but Mira grabbed her arm and shook her head. "She knows what she's doing, Lizzie. Please, obey her."

Elizabeth pouted for a moment, but finally nodded. "At

least let us make you supper before you go. You'll need your strength."

"You have no idea," I muttered as I followed the sisters into the kitchen. I wouldn't turn down a nice meal, considering it might be my last.

I watched them while they cooked, each always knowing where the other would be. I'd always wanted a sister, but was born an only child. The closest thing I had to a sibling was Tholdri. At the thought, a shiver of guilt snaked up my spine. I sincerely hoped I could kill Karpov by myself. I would slay Asher eventually too, but I wanted to keep my promise to Tholdri. Of course, if Asher and I didn't die tonight, I might not be able to find him again. I'd gotten myself into this mess with Karpov trying to find Asher. Could I really let him go now that I'd found him?

Something startled me out of my thoughts. I blinked, realizing Elizabeth had been speaking to me.

She extended a wooden cup of water my way. "I asked if you were thirsty," she said with a small smile.

I returned the smile and took the water gratefully. Enough with thinking about what would happen tonight. There was no use dwelling on it. If I died, Tholdri wouldn't be able to find me to punish me, and I wouldn't be around to worry about his sorrow.

I waited while the sisters finished cooking, then we sat around their long wooden table, too long for only three people. It probably would have been better for them to move into a smaller house, more suited to just two people, but it wasn't my place to say anything. Who knew, maybe one of them would marry and have children, and it would fill the house with a better story than the previous one. Something I would never have.

We ate mutton soup with a loaf of Elizabeth's bread while the girls told me more about their lives. Nothing terribly interesting, but I enjoyed the conversation none-theless. I didn't have many opportunities to speak with anyone outside the Order, especially not since the night Asher took me long ago. Since that night, I had been intent on a singular purpose, and human interaction had fallen by the wayside. I had no use for marriage, but it might have been nice to make friends besides Tholdri.

Now I might never have the opportunity again. Light was growing faint through the windows. Darkness was coming. It was time to hunt.

CHAPTER TWENTY

I taught Elizabeth what I could, but it wouldn't be enough. She needed a proper teacher, someone who would work with her for years, not a single night. I probably would have been better off teaching her nothing at all. At least then she wouldn't have any illusions about facing opponents she could never overcome. Or perhaps my thoughts were just dark this night, but it was difficult to think about nice things when one's death loomed.

I walked through the darkness, alone, my senses straining for any hint of vampire or other dangers. I walked east, based mostly on intuition. But it also made more sense for vampires to hide in an area filled with massive crags, rather than the open swampland on the other side of the village.

I walked with near silent steps, wondering when Asher would find me, or if he would keep his word at all. I could very well end up wandering alone in the darkness when Karpov came. He and the other ancients would deem me useless and would kill me. I held no illusions that I could face Karpov with his three ancients and live. I needed him alone to make the kill, but I wasn't sure how to manage it.

I stepped over a fallen log, wandering down a ravine with rocky escarpments climbing up into the darkness on either side. My skin prickled. Someone was watching me. Someone not human.

A moment after I sensed it, the Seeing Sword thrummed at my back. It wasn't Asher watching me. He didn't mean me harm. I was quite sure of that. He'd already inflicted all the harm he intended by making me his human servant. I forced my heartbeat to slow, then kept walking as if nothing was wrong. Didn't want to let them know I was onto them. It could well be the female vampire Sarsa described, deeming me easy prey. If so, I didn't sense great power from her. She was relatively new.

Elizabeth had said Sarsa's grandson was the first to disappear, but I hadn't asked about disappearances in the year prior. Feeling how young and limited in power the vampire I was sensing was, a theory came to mind. Sometimes vampires would haunt certain villages only out of convenience. If there were no other vampires in the area, there would be no competition.

Other times, the reasoning was more personal. A vampire would stalk the people it once knew, killing enemies and trying to convert friends. With young vampires the conversions rarely worked. They just didn't have the power needed to bring someone over, so corpses would turn up, some used only as a source of food, and others as failed conversions. On occasion the conversions could work if the young vampire wanted it badly enough. Few believed in real magic, but sheer force of will could accomplish many impossible things.

I stepped on a fallen branch. The resounding crack echoed through the ravine. I froze instinctively. The Seeing

Sword screamed in my mind, and I dove forward just as something passed over me. Without the warning, I might not have been fast enough, but I had time to roll to my feet and draw my sword as the vampire recovered.

It wasn't the woman Sarsa had seen, but a young man, perhaps not even eighteen when he died.

I held my blade out as he circled. He was young, very young. His movements had none of the grace the old ones possessed, and I sensed hardly any power from him at all . . . though that didn't mean he wasn't strong enough to tear out my throat. That, he could do in the blink of an eye.

Dark hair was cut just above his shoulders, the exact color difficult to distinguish in the limited moonlight. He was of average build, not too tall and not too short, though he might have grown more had he lived long enough. I should have asked Sarsa what her grandson looked like. Although, even if this vampire was her missing grandson, I had to kill him.

Of course, I might miss the opportunity. He had stopped circling and was slowly backing away, his eyes intent on my blade.

"Aren't you hungry?" I asked. "Or do you prefer hunting defenseless villagers?"

His eyes flicked to something behind me, giving me the warning I needed.

The female vampire pounced at me as I spun around, slashing my sword across her belly. She screamed, stumbling back and clutching pale hands to the wound. She wore the dress of a village girl, likely stolen from one of her victims. I stiffened, sensing the male's approach.

"No!" she shouted, reaching out with bloodied hands, but she wasn't reaching for me.

Time seemed to slow. I sensed the male vampire lunging toward my back. He was young enough that I even

165

heard him. It hardly took effort for me to thrust my sword back, running the point through his chest. I tugged my blade free, then spun my body around to cast it downward in a well-practiced arc. The male vampire's head fell from his shoulders. His body stood there for just a moment, then crumpled to the ground.

The female vampire's scream was like the wail of a dying rabbit, an almost unbearable high-pitched keening. I turned toward her, bloody sword raised, but there was no need. Asher had her arms locked behind her back. She struggled against him, fangs snapping toward me like a wild animal. Her abdomen dripped blood. She was too newly dead to heal quickly.

She screamed again, then her body went limp in Asher's arms. Her sobs echoed horribly loud in the otherwise quiet night. "You killed him!" she cried at me.

I stood there in the dark with my bloody sword, unsure of what to do. I was used to vampires trying to kill me. I wasn't used to seeing a vampire cry at the loss of a loved one. Because that's what the male vampire had been, I realized. That's why the female had taken him, but left the grandmother alive. She'd loved him, and he her.

She sagged further in Asher's grip, all the fight gone out of her.

The look he gave me was almost indignant.

I scowled. "He was trying to kill me. It is his own fault he is dead. They've been hunting from their former village, probably trying to convert a few friends, and killing those they disliked."

Asher's expression was no less judgmental as he replied, "You owe me no explanation. You are a hunter, this is your purpose." He lightly shook the female vampire still in a loose arm-lock for emphasis.

He glanced at my blade dripping blood onto the ground.

I lifted my nose. I would not let him make me feel guilty for protecting the village. The two young vampires may have been in love, but they were still murderers. They deserved to die.

Asher watched me closely, like he was trying to read my thoughts. "If I let her go, she will flee. She doesn't have to die."

I felt silly with my blade still dangling from my hand. It offered me no further warnings, so I knew Asher's words were true. Neither of the vampires standing before me intended to attack.

But that wasn't really what mattered. "She has killed many, and for that she must pay."

I didn't say out loud that Asher needed to pay for that too. Eventually, vampires gained enough control to not always kill their victims. They could entrance a human, feed, and leave that human to wake up weak, sick, and with two new puncture marks in their neck or wrist, or sometimes the bend of the arm. It was to their benefit to hunt this way. A living human could supply blood more than once, and hunters mostly busied themselves with slaying vampires who actively killed. It was logical to assume Asher no longer killed every time he fed. But he had killed before. Every ancient vampire started as a fresh hungry baby at some point.

The female vampire hung her head. Asher still held her loosely, but his gaze was all for me. "Your eyes betray your thoughts. If you would execute this girl, then so be it, but you will not claim me so easily."

"I do not want to kill you this night." And it was true. Another night, most certainly, but if I could avoid killing Asher tonight, I would. "But she must die. I do not know who converted her, but they have left her to hunt freely from her village. That will only continue if I let her go."

He tossed her to the ground, then stepped back, crossing his arms. "Then do it. I wish to dally with this no longer."

He was testing me. He wanted to see if I would really slay something that wasn't attacking me. This little test proved that he really didn't know me. I'd spent my day talking to the families of the victims. I'd seen the fierce look in Elizabeth's eyes as she spoke about protecting her sister. It was my job to protect them. Even if I couldn't prevent the deaths that had already happened, I could bring the killer to justice.

I thought of Sarsa as I walked toward the female vampire. She'd started to cry again, huddled on the ground on hands and knees. Sarsa hadn't wanted me to hunt her, because deep down she knew what had become of her grandson. She'd recognized the female vampire that took him as someone who had loved him in life.

She knew that if I hunted the woman, I'd be hunting her grandson too. I couldn't bring back her grandson, but I could grant him justice. I met Asher's eyes as I lifted my blade, then swung it downward. The vampire's head parted from her shoulders with a splash of hot blood on my breeches.

Asher looked at me like I had suddenly just appeared, like he really didn't know me at all.

He was right.

CHAPTER TWENTY-ONE

I stood across from Asher with two dead vampires on the ground between us. I wasn't about to cut out their hearts with the way he was looking at me. They were baby vampires—they weren't coming back. It was against the vows I'd sworn to leave the hearts, but in that moment, I didn't care. If the Potentate wanted the hearts out so badly, he could take them himself.

A lock of Asher's white hair fluttered in the wind. He didn't come any closer, maybe because my bloody sword was still out. I took a moment to clean it on the dead female's dress.

"Will you leave the bodies where they lay?" he asked.

"I cannot build a pyre every time I slay a vampire." I sheathed my sword.

He laughed, but not like it was funny. The sound tugged at something deep in my gut. "No, I suppose you can't. If we are done here, let us walk, and you may ask your questions."

"I thought I'd had my only chance for answers."

A trickle of irritation crept into his voice. "You made it

quite clear you would hunt me until I told you what you wanted to know. So ask, and let us be done with it."

I really didn't want to have this conversation over the bodies, and if Karpov found us, I wanted to be farther from the village. "Not here," I said, then started walking. A moment later, he was at my side.

I wasn't sure where to start, and I didn't know how much time we had, but the question I wanted answered most in that moment was, "Why did you save me?"

I couldn't hear his footsteps on the hard-packed soil. It was like walking with a ghost. "Are you referring to last night, or the first time? Or perhaps you're referring to the night with the Nattmara."

"You've made your point. I meant last night, but I wouldn't mind the answers to all three."

The path ahead narrowed, forcing us to walk closer to one another. His nearness sent an electric chill down my spine. I wasn't helpless against him like a normal human servant, but the bond was still there, like an invisible cord pulling us together.

"Why the sudden curiosity?" he asked.

I pondered his question, shutting out my own thoughts. I'd always been morbidly curious about his motives, and since he had saved me three times, I really didn't want to die without knowing why. "The first night, after what happened . . . I thought perhaps you sought entertainment. Make a hunter your human servant, make my vows worthless, that sort of thing. It was the only explanation that made sense to me." I hesitated, glancing his way before quickly averting my eyes. "But you gained nothing helping me with the Nattmara. That part I don't understand."

He was silent for a time, leaving me with only the sounds of my footsteps and night insects to keep me company. I couldn't even tell if he was breathing, since he didn't really need to breathe. Finally, he spoke, "I fear if I tell you the truth, you will simply call me a liar."

"All vampires are liars," I said automatically.

"And thus, you have made my point."

I stopped walking. We were far enough from the village now, past the crags, at the border of a murky forest. The smell of swamp water was stronger here, the moisture creating a haze around spindly tree trunks.

I turned toward Asher to find him already watching me. "Just answer the question," I demanded. "Or did you just come here to taunt me?"

He stepped closer, and I put a hand on his chest to stop his advance. Then suddenly I remembered I was speaking to a being who had survived centuries. One who could probably crush the bones in my hand with hardly a thought.

I stepped back. "Just tell me why you did this to me."

He watched my hand as I lowered it. "I did it to save your life."

I rolled my eyes. It was the same reasoning he had given me before, just after it happened. I hadn't believed him then, either. "All right, let's pretend I believe you care for the sanctity of life. I will accept that answer, but not that answer alone. There's more to it that you're not telling me. There has to be."

"Or else I wouldn't be here now?" he questioned.

I hesitated, surprised by his response, then nodded.

He turned and started walking into the damp forest. I glanced in the direction we'd come, debating my options. I really didn't want to follow him, but curse it all, he had my attention. I turned to see his broad shoulders and white hair disappearing through the trees. The mist surrounded him like an eerie cloak.

With another internal curse, I hurried after him,

wondering what the Potentate would think if he could see me now. Although maybe I'd rather not know the answer to that.

When I caught up to Asher's side, he asked, "Why did you speak with me that first night?" His gaze remained forward, almost as if he were afraid of the answer, though I knew that couldn't be true.

My boots squelched across soggy earth, loud over his silent movements. Moving quietly on hard, dry earth I understood, but this was getting ridiculous. How had I found myself alone in the woods with him after all this time?

"You expect answers, but will give me none in return?" he asked.

I glanced around the dark trees, feeling uneasy. If Karpov and the others were near, I should sense them, and Asher probably would too . . . I realized I didn't want any of them to hear this conversation. It shouldn't have mattered, but it did. This was private.

I stopped walking, and this time he stopped with me. Despite my better instincts, I stepped closer to him. I lowered my voice. "I had seen my uncle killed before my eyes by one of your kind. I returned to the Order beaten and devastated. It was my home, and I thought I'd be welcomed there." I shook my head, hating how the memory still stung. "The majority of hunters called for my death. If not for the Potentate, I would have been killed. It was the first time I truly understood the vows I'd taken, and part of me hated them for that. Perhaps they were right, and I should have died trying to kill the monster who took my uncle, but I would have died in vain. I'd thought, wouldn't it be better to live and grow stronger? I'd hoped that if I kept training, someday I would avenge my uncle. I couldn't do that if I was dead."

Asher tilted his head, draping long hair across his shoulder. "You were angry with the Order, so you got drunk and had a conversation with a vampire?"

I looked down at my boots. "To put it quite plainly, yes, I believe that is why I let you sit with me. Of course, I was already drunk, and my memories of that night are muddy at best. Maybe part of me wished for death, and that's why I invited you in." I forced myself to meet his eyes. "I've answered your question now. It's time you answer mine, truthfully."

He continued studying my face, leaving me time to glance over the graceful curve of his jaw, the slope of his nose, hair that looked like it would feel like the finest silk. I imagined cupping his jaw, then running my fingers back through his hair. Just the thought of the sensation made me clench my hands into fists. What was I doing? Why was I thinking this way?

Still watching me, he smiled, as if he could read every thought in my mind. "You do feel the bond then, don't you? I was beginning to wonder."

"I have ignored it for years, and I will continue to do so." My voice was breathy, and I hated it, but I could still feel the imaginary sensation of his hair sliding through my fingers. I could feel my body pressing against his ...

I took a step closer, and it wasn't a conscious choice. My body was acting on instinct. There was nothing logical about it. I peered up into his eyes gone bright silver as the moon showed itself above us. "You still owe me answers."

His eyes reflected the same heat I couldn't keep from my expression. Servants were supposed to feel loyal to their masters, but not the other way around. There was no way he was feeling what I was feeling.

He leaned closer. No part of him was touching me, but the offer was there.

No. I pressed my fingernails into my palm, hoping a bit of pain would bring me to my senses. He was an ancient vampire, and I was sworn to kill his kind.

I took a shaky breath, but couldn't move back, frozen with indecision. If he had closed that last space between us, I wouldn't have stopped him. But he didn't. He just stood there, waiting for me to make my choice.

A tree groaned nearby. Asher's eyes remained on me, not acknowledging the sound, though I knew he'd heard it. The noise came from something heavy, not just the wind.

The sound broke whatever spell I was under. I managed a full breath, then lowered my voice to a whisper. "I'm well aware that your hearing is better than mine, yet you do not seem alarmed at the sound of something leaning against a nearby tree. Is this a trap?"

His brows lifted. He was close enough that I could feel his otherworldly energy prickling up and down my skin. "I had thought you aware of the small human following us. Your new coat and shirt smell of her."

I palmed my face, rubbing each of my eyes. My heart still thundered in my chest. I had nearly kissed a vampire. I had *wanted* to kiss a vampire. What was wrong with me?

"Elizabeth?" I called out.

And there she was, skulking out from behind a tree. She was far enough away that she might not have witnessed everything, but the look on her face told me otherwise. Since she'd made it this far, she'd likely witnessed me killing the vampires who had hunted her village as well. A normal girl would have run screaming, and yet she had followed me here, spying on my conversation. Spying on . . . *oh light*, how much had she seen?

As she approached, her eyes moved to Asher, and her terror was clear. She knew to be afraid, and yet she had continued to follow. And now I'd called out to her, so she trusted me to keep her safe. The edge of her dress was tied in a knot above her knees, keeping it free from snagging on any underbrush, and her hair fell in a long braid down her back. She looked terribly small and vulnerable standing amidst the shadowy trees.

I put my hands on my hips as she reached us, then willed the breathiness out of my voice. "What in the light are you doing out here alone? Didn't I tell you to stay inside and lock your door?"

She looked down. "I was worried about you. I thought you might need help."

I didn't have the heart to tell her she could have easily ended up as a hostage, crippling my ability to kill the vampires hunting her village. I was glad, at least, that she'd remained hidden during that altercation. But what must she think now?

Asher was watching her with a bemused expression, but she was still staring at her boots, so she didn't notice.

I turned toward him. "I need to get her back to the village, but this conversation is *not* over."

He nodded once, a small smile playing at his lips. He was finding this all terribly amusing. Finding *me* terribly amusing. Was it all just a game to him? Was he toying with me because he knew how the bond might affect me?

"I will find you tomorrow night," he said, interrupting my thoughts. "Perhaps our next meeting can occur without bloodshed."

And then he was gone.

Elizabeth gawked at the space where he'd stood. "How did he move so quickly?"

I turned and started walking southeast. The path I'd spotted should be shorter than the way I'd come, cutting south around the crags. "Questions like that are why you should have stayed home."

She hurried to catch up with me, her eyes wide. "You mean you could see where he went?"

I didn't answer. I had seen him move, but it happened so quickly I couldn't have said where he went. But better for her to think I could see things she couldn't. She needed to understand what a stupid decision it was for her to come out here.

"Lyssandra?" she asked as we walked, her voice small and childlike.

I sighed, knowing I wasn't going to like whatever she was about to ask. "Yes?"

"Why were you walking alone with a vampire?"

I appreciated her phrasing, considering I had been doing a lot more than walking with him. "It's a long story."

She was quiet for a moment, then said, "We have a long walk."

She had a point, and though I'd only known her for a short time, I trusted her. I cast my senses around us, wanting to be sure no one else was near, then I started from the beginning.

WE WERE ALMOST BACK to the village by the time I finished, and Elizabeth turned to me with a look of wonder. "So you're stronger than any other hunter?"

I stopped walking to stare at her. "That was the primary point you took from my story?"

She shrugged sheepishly. "That's what seems to matter the most. My parent's deaths were painful, but what matters is that I still have my sister in the present. You might not like what you are, but in the present, you are strong, and capable of protecting others. Without your strength, you may have died long ago. And without you, those vampires would still be hunting my village. If you weren't saved by a vampire, I might be dead."

I laughed as I started walking. Elizabeth had already promised me a warm bed, and I was looking forward to it. "You don't need to be a hunter, you need to be a priestess. You have a fine way with words."

"Well now that doesn't sound like any fun at all," she chuckled.

We reached the back side of her house, then walked around to the front. I found myself grateful that I was getting to know Elizabeth. Even if the friendship wouldn't be permanent, it meant something to me. It meant something that she saw just what I was, and still cared without having a long history with me like Tholdri.

Elizabeth's hand was halfway to the door when I yanked her backward. She seemed stunned by my strength and speed, having no time to recover as I shoved her behind me and drew my sword. I sensed vampires in the house, old ones. My sword thrummed lightly, a warning, but not an urgent one. Interesting.

I turned to tell Elizabeth to run and hide, but the female vampire I'd met with Karpov stood behind her. With a taunting grin, the vampire snapped her arm around Elizabeth, pulling her back against her chest.

She was barely taller than Elizabeth, pressing her lips near the young girl's ear. "Scream and I'll tear out your throat."

I held my sword toward her, but it was useless. With how closely she held Elizabeth, I couldn't risk an attack.

Elizabeth squeezed her eyes shut as the vampire stroked her face. "Such a pretty young girl." She lifted her eyes to me, leaning forward to blanket Elizabeth in a curtain of yellow hair. "I'd hate to have to crush her skull. Now open the door and go inside."

I kept my sword out, but obeyed, wondering why the sword wasn't screaming in warning. Maybe because the vampires weren't here to kill me, but that didn't mean they wouldn't kill anyone else. I had no doubt the female vampire would kill Elizabeth. I just hoped Elizabeth knew that too and would do as she asked.

I already knew what I would find inside, even before my eyes adjusted to the darkness. Karpov held Mira, who'd fainted, her body slumped over his arm. I didn't see the other two ancients, but knew they'd be around here somewhere.

I faced Karpov as the female vampire shoved Elizabeth through the doorway. The door creaked shut, leaving us with only the sparse moonlight coming in through the curtained windows. My night vision was keen enough to still see the vampires, but Elizabeth was probably blind. I was glad for that. If she saw her unconscious sister, she might start screaming.

This was my fault. I should have passed through this village and kept walking. "Why are you here? I'm doing what you asked of me. I'm gaining his trust."

Karpov's smile was little more than a glimpse of fangs in the darkness. "Then where is he? You met him tonight. I smell him on you, yet you are not with him. Why did you part ways so quickly?" He shook Mira's limp body. "This girl's home smelled more strongly of you than the others. We thought it a good place to wait."

I tensed at the way he shook Mira, like she was a doll, breakable and easily forgotten. "Am I really supposed to believe that your servants haven't been watching me?"

The female vampire spoke behind me. "Asher will sense us if we're near. We don't need him looking for us."

Karpov's jaw stiffened. The female vampire's words had irritated him, but why? I understood her being afraid of

Asher, as he was more powerful than her, but not Karpov. Feeling Karpov's power, if he faced Asher on his own, he might win.

I stepped to the side, then backed toward the kitchen so I could have both vampires in my sights. "You're both afraid of him. Why?"

"I fear nothing," Karpov hissed, moving Mira to his other arm to hang limply from the waist down. Me moving out of the way had allowed Elizabeth to see her, and she cried out.

The female vampire placed her hand across Elizabeth's mouth, jerking her head violently. "Scream again, and you're dead. I have a feeling we only need one of you to hold as leverage."

She was right. With either sister, the vampires had exactly what they needed to control me. "Harm either of them, and I will gladly take your head." I looked directly at the female vampire as I said it.

The slight widening of her eyes said she believed me. Good. I looked at Karpov. "I've done exactly as you've asked. You know I want him dead. Why do you need leverage?"

"You may be an unusual servant," he answered, "but even you may feel more affinity for your master the longer you're near him. These girls will ensure you don't change your mind about our deal. Our servants will watch them during the day, and we will not release them until Asher is dead. We cannot watch you when you're with him, but now we don't have to."

I shook my head. "No, if you take them, no deal. Killing Asher will kill me, so I won't be around to see if they're alright. For all I'll ever know, you'll kill them as soon as they're out of my sight."

This thought seemed to perplex them both. They hadn't thought this through. They were desperate, but why?

Suddenly, Karpov smiled. I didn't like that smile. He dropped Mira to the floor. "You will keep this one. Two nights from now, you will lure Asher to this place. You will see both girls alive before you die. This is the best offer I can make you, and to give you my word that once you are gone, we will leave them alone."

"Don't—" Elizabeth began to say, but the female vampire threw her like she weighed nothing. Her body crashed into the wall, then slid down to the floorboard. If she hadn't groaned as she fell, I'd worry she was already dead.

Anger washed away my senses. My sword lifted before I realized what I was doing.

Karpov's words cut through my rage like a knife. "Will you do as I say, Lyssandra, or shall we kill them both now?"

My sword drooped. I forced my gaze away from the female vampire. "Your word that you will leave both girls and the village alone, forever."

He inclined his head. "I may be what I am, Lyssandra, but once given, I have never broken my word. I will not kill them."

Oddly, I believed him. If I obeyed him, he wouldn't kill the girls. But this also meant that if I tried to kill him before I killed Asher, Elizabeth would die. I wasn't willing to sacrifice her life, yet how many others would be sacrificed if Karpov was allowed to live?

I hadn't thought my situation could get any more impossible, but somehow it had. The only real choice I could see was to kill Asher and be done with it, and hope other hunters would eventually destroy Karpov. It wasn't a good choice, but the hard ones rarely are.

Karpov smiled. "I can see in your eyes that we have an understanding. We'll see you soon, Lyssandra."

The female vampire lifted Elizabeth, who was still groaning softly.

"She better not be permanently injured," I said.

Karpov opened the door for the other vampire. "We can heal her if she is." He followed the female outside.

They took Elizabeth with them, and there was nothing I could do about it. All I could do was die to save her.

I really hated vampires.

CHAPTER TWENTY-TWO

I stayed the night with Mira until she awoke. I didn't want to stay. I didn't want to be the one to tell her that her sister had been taken, and it was all my fault. But it was my fault, so I'd waited with her until she regained consciousness somewhere near morning.

She remembered little from the previous night, only that she'd woken and realized Elizabeth was missing. She had gone to the door to see if it was locked, and that was the last thing she remembered.

When I told her what happened, she hadn't taken the news very well, but she didn't kick me out. Leaving had been my choice. She knew I was Elizabeth's best chance of survival, but her eyes cast blame. Mira wished I had never come to her village, and I couldn't fault her for it. I wished the same.

As daylight caressed the thatched rooftops of the small village, I'd walked through the mires. I'd found shelter cradled by branches in a tree, my body secure near the trunk with heavy leaves sheltering overhead, and there I had rested with the sun warming my cheeks. If I dreamed, I didn't remember it, but I slept a long time.

When I woke hungry and alone, I headed back toward the village. I would try to find some food, far from Mira, then I would wait for nightfall. My boots hissed through dead, damp grass, and birds sung overhead. No matter who died, nature was always there, unaffected. I'd always found it comforting. Now it was just annoying.

I caught bits of excited chatter in the distance and sped my pace. Something was happening in the village. Had Mira told her neighbors what had occurred?

I didn't approach from the main street, and instead crept behind houses, unsure how welcome my presence would be. I had killed the two vampires who'd cost so many lives, but that deed would be overshadowed by Elizabeth's disappearance. She'd been the one closest to me, and now she was gone. Hopefully not forever.

I leaned around the corner of a vacant home, peering out toward the street where the chatter was the loudest, then had to stifle a groan. Three hunters rode warhorses up the street toward the spring at the northern end of the village. I recognized two of them, Isolde and Markus. The third young man I didn't know, but he was likely a new hunter in the care of the other two. All three wore full hunter garb. It was clear to everyone what they were.

I pressed my back against the wall, clenching my fists. I hoped they were just passing through, but I had a feeling I wouldn't be so lucky. I'd been missing for two nights now, enough time for Steifan and Tholdri to return to Castle Helius and petition other hunters to search for me. Though why Isolde and Markus would volunteer was beyond me. Both had wanted my death after my uncle's murder. One might think that Isolde—being another rare female hunter, and only a few years older than me—might have understood, but she'd called for my death the loudest.

I watched as the villagers following them disappeared from sight, then when my breathing had evened, I ran after them. I skirted around the back walls of the next houses, making my way toward the spring. If Isolde and Markus were staying in the village, I needed to know. It would be a complication, but perhaps also a boon.

I reached the far end of the spring just as the trio dismounted. I crouched behind a tangle of brambles to watch.

The youngest hunter, who was beginning to seem vaguely familiar to me, led the horses further downstream to drink. I watched as Isolde stretched her arms over her head. Her black hair was tied tightly back, falling in a long glistening tail nearly to her waist. The style made her sharp features seem severe, but they matched her constant expression of distaste. She'd slain many vampires and was a highly skilled hunter, but I was better. And for that, she hated me. I was only better than her because of Asher's power, but it wasn't like I could explain that, so I just had to deal with her hatred. It wasn't a difficult task. With so many hunters at Castle Helius, I could avoid one or two.

Markus stood, his face dripping wet with stream water. His short brown hair trailed rivulets of liquid down his strong cheekbones. I didn't see a speck of dirt on either of them, but he'd cleaned his face as if he'd been riding for days. Maybe he had been. Maybe they actually weren't here for me.

Isolde glanced around, then turned to Markus. I could barely hear her words over the running water. "Should we give her one more evening? The miller said she went hunting last night. She should have returned by now."

I cringed. Definitely here for me. I cursed Steifan and

Tholdri for not looking for me themselves, but in truth, I knew they were. They'd just enlisted other hunters to cover more ground. I wondered what story they had told Markus and Isolde to get them to come out.

Markus' gaze landed perilously close to my hiding spot. "We'll give her until nightfall. The miller claimed she didn't have a horse, so she might still be walking back." His gaze drifted away from the brambles, and I let out a slow sigh of relief.

Isolde shrugged, then sat near the bank. "The Potentate implied she was in trouble. She might already be dead." The prospect didn't seem to bother her.

My pulse sped. Steifan and Tholdri would have never involved the Potentate. What was going on? How would he even know I was missing when I wasn't supposed to return until Karpov was dead?

Markus glanced in my direction again. "Like I said, we will wait here until nightfall. If she doesn't return, we'll search for her body."

I didn't like how they were both assuming I was already dead. I wanted to know what the Potentate had told them, but I was pressing my luck. I needed to escape before I was discovered. These two weren't here to help me, and if they detained me, it might get Elizabeth killed.

I eased back, escaping the way I'd come. Once I was past the first few houses, I fled back toward the mires. I didn't need any villagers spotting me and telling the other hunters where I'd gone. Come nightfall, they could search for my body all they pleased. All they might find were a few ancient vampires, and I wasn't feeling generous enough to help them out in that regard. I'd let them try their luck with Karpov.

The thought struck me so hard I was glad I was out of sight from the road when it hit me. With three other hunters, I might defeat Karpov without getting Elizabeth killed. Suddenly I was glad they were here. If the ancients were watching the village, they might very well run into the hunters. Maybe they'd pick each other off and solve all of my problems.

Doubtful, but at least there was a chance.

I continued walking, lost in my thoughts. I'd slept enough of the day away that nightfall would come soon. I didn't want to be anywhere near the village and the other hunters when Asher found me. If they saw him, they'd try to kill him, and two experienced hunters like Markus and Isolde might be up to the task.

I stopped walking again. Was I actually worried about Asher's safety? Surely not, at least not beyond me needing to stay alive long enough to ensure Karpov would die.

And yet, the thought of Isolde shoving her sword through Asher's heart made me ill. I recalled Karpov's suspicions that I might develop loyalty toward Asher. Like it or not, we were deeply bonded. I was suddenly nervous to see him, to finally learn why he kept saving me. If I knew the truth, might I want to save him in return?

CHAPTER TWENTY-THREE

Asher found me just as darkness fell, so he must have been resting somewhere nearby for the day. I sat on a rocky cliffside, the open expanse behind me void of trees. I wasn't about to let anyone sneak up on us. The hunters would be out searching for me by now, and while Karpov had claimed Asher would sense him if he came too near, I wasn't stupid enough to trust his word alone.

I didn't turn as Asher approached, though I felt his presence.

"No little human tonight?" he asked.

I shook my head, not trusting my voice. If he sensed something had happened to Elizabeth, he might want to know more. I stared out at the partial moon, hidden mostly by dark clouds. It rained so frequently in the mires, a clear night sky was rare.

He sat beside me on the ground, tucking one knee up toward his chest. The positioning reminded me of the dream I'd had a few days prior.

I observed his face while he looked toward the moon, his pale eyes seeming to absorb the white light.

"Was the dream real?" I asked. "The one a few nights ago?"

He smiled softly. "Perhaps."

His answer let me know the truth. It had been real. He could invade my dreams at will. And yet here I was talking to him, as if he were no longer the object of my fear. "Will you give me my answer now?"

"There are other hunters in the village. Looking for you?"

My jaw fell open, then I shook my head. "You wouldn't have had time to observe the village before coming to find me. It hasn't been dark long enough." Could he actually read my thoughts? Had he been playing me for a fool this entire time?

"I wake at dusk, Lyssandra, well before true dark. It comes with age."

"That isn't possible," I gasped. Ancient vampires could sometimes awaken during the day when danger was near, but to actually leave their lairs at dusk?

He looked at me, his expression unreadable. "If you say so."

Well, he had known about the other hunters, so I couldn't really argue with him. But did that mean Karpov could walk around at dusk too? I'd only ever seen him well after nightfall. I wished I could ask, but that was something I'd probably never know the answer to.

I tucked my knees up to my chest, grinding small pebbles against rocks beneath me. My sword had remained silent, even with Asher sitting so close. "I'm still waiting for my answer."

He sighed. "My, you are persistent."

"And you are evasive."

He inclined his head. "Perhaps. Do the hunters have any clue what's happening in the vampire community?"

"Vampires don't have a community."

He gave me a long look. "Would you like me to give you this information, or not?"

"My apologies, please continue." I waved my hand for him to go on.

"As you likely know," he began, "vampires have families, not in the traditional sense, but for practical purposes that is what they are called. Each family begins with a sire, an ancient who created the first vampires of the lines."

I tilted my head, listening. I didn't know much about vampire lines beyond using those ties to track them. Most hunter training focused only on how to kill them. "But where did the original sires come from?"

He shrugged. "Who can say? All it takes to become a sire in the present times is to be powerful enough to control your flock."

"And are you powerful enough?" I asked.

He nodded. "Yes, but while I have sired other vampires in the past, that is something I lost interest in long ago. We need no more of my kind."

"Why are you telling me all of this?"

"It has to do with why I saved you, but if you are to comprehend, you must listen."

I lifted my hands in surrender. "My apologies, no more interruptions."

"A few centuries ago, the ancients came together," he continued. "With too many new vampires, territory lines had blurred. Some hunted with abandon, slaughtering entire villages. From that came your order, humans who faced vampires and lived. You learned that some of you had natural resistances to bespellment. These resistances were often hereditary, making it possible for you to band together and hone your gifts.

"The ancients saw this threat for what it was, a balance

SARA C. ROETHLE

to the destruction we had caused. While few cared for human well-being, practically speaking, we still needed to tend to our food source."

I instinctively wanted to make a comment about being referred to as a food source, but his story was interesting enough that I kept quiet. I knew how the Order had formed, but I had never heard it from a vampire's point of view.

"We laid down new territory lines, and within those lines we would control younger vampires. If any drew too much attention to themselves, they were put down so as not to lure hunters to our territories. I chose the mires."

My brows lifted. "You *chose* the mires? Why would you choose such an awful place?"

"I simply wanted to be left alone. I thought that if I chose an undesirable territory, vampires would not want to hunt there. It worked for a time, I dealt with few. That was, until some vampires grew dissatisfied with the system. They wanted larger territories, and no repercussions for their actions. They started small, making more young vampires than they were allowed, killing in ways that drew attention."

I thought of Karpov, his baby vampires, and his theatric style of murder.

Asher stared off for a long moment. "Many of the ancients who drew the original territory lines have perished. Some killed by hunters, some by flocks of other vampires, and some simply tired of their long existences. Those flouting our laws would like to see the rest of us gone. If this happens, humans will be slaughtered."

I shook my head slowly, waiting for my mind to catch up with processing it all. "You expect me to believe that the oldest of vampires are actually protecting humans?"

He blinked at me, his mouth for a moment forming a grim line. "Have you forgotten that we were once human too? The oldest of us have had a long time to live with our actions. Some enjoy the violence, and crave more. While others, once in control of their bloodlust, have nothing but time to sit and think about the havoc they have wrought."

I took a deep breath and let it out slowly. Realistically, I knew Asher had once been human, but it was difficult to fathom. I'd never really considered the fact that he'd had a father and a mother. Perhaps he'd even been married and had children before he died. Had he killed them once he'd become a monster, or had he lingered in the shadows watching them slowly age and die? Neither option seemed terribly appealing.

"I still don't understand what this has to do with you saving me."

He had gone still. Not that he wasn't still before, but all small movements had ceased. You only notice little things like breathing and blinking once they're not there.

I tensed, listening for whatever he might be hearing.

Asher grabbed my hand, making me jump, then I went still, which was probably what he wanted. I suspected he wouldn't touch me without good reason. He hadn't intentionally touched me since he had saved me the other night.

I stayed still and listened, searching for whatever had him holding my hand so rigidly. *There.* Soft footsteps. The person was obviously well trained, almost as quiet as a vampire.

"You should get back to the village," Asher said evenly. He stood, using my hand in his to guide me to my feet.

"I don't think you'll be going anywhere," a voice said from behind us.

Asher kept my hand as he turned us around, though I

already knew what I would see. Isolde and Markus aimed crossbows our way. I wasn't sure where their young hunter friend was. I assumed they hadn't heard much of our conversation. Asher would have sensed them as soon as they got close. Or maybe he simply smelled their scent on the breeze.

Isolde lifted her nose smugly. "I've never really liked you, Lyssandra, but I honestly never expected to find you holding hands with the undead."

I tore my hand away from Asher's. "What are you doing here?" I didn't know why I asked it. I already knew why they were here, but I wasn't sure what else to say.

Markus stood near Isolde's shoulder, a menacing presence, but it was Isolde who answered, "We were sent here to find you, Lyssandra. The Potentate seemed to think you were in trouble." Her gaze darted to Asher. "Now step aside, and we will *save* you. We will let the Order determine the punishment for your crimes."

I realized in that moment that it was over for me. If she returned to Castle Helius and told the Potentate that she caught me with a vampire, I couldn't deny it. He would know if I lied. But why had he really sent her here?

My thoughts made me realize one other thing. I wasn't fully intending to die if I was worried about returning to the Order. I had thought I was ready, but now faced directly with the prospect, I wasn't so sure. What Elizabeth had said had gotten to me.

Isolde and Markus were waiting for me to make my choice. Either step aside and let them kill Asher, or turn against them here and now. I could tell by Isolde's hungry expression that she preferred the latter.

I stepped in front of Asher, blocking him with my body. "I will kill him when I am ready, and it is none of your concern. You can return to Castle Helius and tell the Potentate I don't need saving."

Isolde's eyes bulged, but her crossbow did not waver. It was now aimed directly at my heart. "You would protect a vampire from your fellow hunters?"

I wasn't about to tell her that killing him would kill me too. That wasn't even why I was protecting him, at least not entirely. "It would seem so. Now you must make your choice. Do you think the two of you could defeat both me and a vampire?"

"This is absurd," Markus growled, his eyes darting around the clearing. "Come with us, Lyssandra, and I will petition for your punishment to be lenient."

I could almost make myself agree. If I went with them now, no one present had to die. It was a long way back to Castle Helius. I could find a way to escape. But in the end, I couldn't go with them. I couldn't abandon Elizabeth.

Asher waited quietly for a decision to be made. If it turned into a fight, would he kill them? Did I want him to?

No. I might not like Isolde, but I didn't want her dead. I wanted her alive more than I wanted answers from Asher. "There are four ancients in this territory. They took a young girl from the village. If I do not comply with their wishes, they will kill her. That is why I am here talking with a vampire."

Isolde snorted and rolled her eyes, but Markus finally seemed interested in what I had to say. He lowered his crossbow to a one-handed grip. Isolde opened her mouth to speak, but he put a hand on her shoulder. Her mouth snapped shut as he stepped in front of her, addressing me. "You were sent to hunt Karpov. Is it him? What does this other vampire have to do with it?" He gestured to Asher.

I dared a glance back at Asher. His expression was

unreadable. I had no idea what he thought of what I'd said, but I imagined I had just lost the answers I had worked so hard to claim. He now knew I had sought him out because of Karpov.

I returned my attention to Markus. I had already started telling the truth. I might as well continue. "Yes, Karpov is among them. Had he been alone, I would have tried to kill him myself, but I know my limitations. I cannot face them all and win."

I turned back to Asher, hoping this admission wouldn't get Elizabeth killed. "The other ancients have interest in Asher. They sent me to find him and gain his trust."

Just a hint of emotion flickered in his pale eyes, then was gone. Though I spoke to Markus, my gaze remained on Asher. "I could not let them kill the girl."

"This is ridiculous," Isolde cut in.

I turned to see her lifting her crossbow back in our direction. Markus moved to stop her, then I sensed movement at my back. I heard a bolt being released and dove to the ground. I rolled over to the sound of Markus cursing and looked up.

Asher was gone. He now knew why I'd become so intent on answers, and he knew it hadn't started with Elizabeth. It had started before I'd even met her. I had tried to trap him willingly.

He was the undead. He stole my life. So why did I feel guilty about that?

Markus stomped toward me with Isolde's crossbow in hand, and his under the same arm. He glared down at me as I sat up. I almost thought for a moment he'd kill me, then he growled, "Get up, I want to know everything you've learned about these ancients before the night is through, including the one who just left us."

I stared up at him. There was nothing about Asher's

appearance that would hint at his age. Could Markus actually sense it? Tholdri couldn't do it, so I'd thought it was just me. But honestly, I knew little about Markus. I suspected I was about to find out just what sort of man he really was.

CHAPTER TWENTY-FOUR

Markus dragged me to my feet by my arm, hauling me past Isolde. She was on her butt in the dirt. A line of blood trickled from the corner of her lip. Markus must have hit her to get the crossbow, but Asher's departure had distracted me.

"Get up," Markus said as we passed.

I glanced back at Isolde, stumbling as Markus continued to drag me. I tore my arm free of his grip. "If you want my cooperation, you'd be wise to stop manhandling me."

He stood rigidly. A muscle ticked in his strong jaw. "Just be glad you're still alive. It was foolish of you to involve yourself in this way. You cannot trust vampires, *any* of them."

I crossed my arms, sensing Isolde as she approached my back. "Who says I trust any vampires?"

"You were *holding his hand.* It seems you do even more than trust them."

My cheeks were suddenly on fire, partially from embarrassment, but anger was my ruling emotion. "He heard your lumbering footsteps and was trying to warn me, you bumbling ox."

Markus narrowed his eyes. "And you trusted his warning, and allowed him to touch you. You were alone with him. You let him near you willingly."

There wasn't much I could say to that. I was grateful when Isolde shoved her way between us, then started down the incline.

Ignoring Isolde, Markus watched me a moment longer. "Will we be running into any other ancient vampires tonight?" His words were clipped, brimming with irritation.

I shrugged, the picture of nonchalance, though inside my stomach was churning. "Probably not, but once they learn I failed at what they wanted me to do, they will come to kill me."

"Good. If they come, it will save us the trouble of hunting them." He turned and walked in the direction Isolde had gone.

I debated for a moment, then hurried after him. "No, not *good*. If they learn what has happened here, they'll kill the girl they took."

I stepped back as he spun on me. "Are you implying that we should continue this ruse? Would you like more time alone with that vampire?" His words dripped with sarcasm.

Isolde had turned back to watch us both. She had wiped the blood from her mouth and now glared daggers at me. It seemed she blamed me for her humiliation, not Markus.

I lowered my voice—not that I sensed any vampires nearby, but this just didn't seem like a conversation to be shouted from the cliff tops. "I have to deliver that vampire to the other ancients to get Elizabeth back. Once she is safe, I will help you kill them all."

His eyes searched my face. "Even your lover?"

"He's not my lover," I hissed. "And him, I want dead most of all."

His thoughtful expression said he believed me, which was surprising, because I didn't really believe myself. I held no love for Asher, but Elizabeth's words kept ringing in my mind. Was death really the best answer, when by living I could save lives? If Asher's words were true, and this new regime of vampires overthrew the old, I'd be needed. I wasn't bold enough to think I could stop the bloodshed from happening, but saving even one life was reason enough to live, at least for a time.

Or maybe I simply wasn't ready to die.

Markus was still watching me, but not like he suspected anything. There was nothing to suspect. I would help him kill the other ancients, and after that . . . well, that was yet to be determined.

"Useless," Isolde muttered, shaking her head as she continued walking.

The moment between Markus and I broke, and he gestured for me to walk ahead of him.

I started forward. I might have worried that Isolde would put a dagger in my back, but not Markus. No, Markus wasn't a back-stabber. His issue would be much more difficult to handle. I needed him to follow my lead if we were going to save Elizabeth, but Markus was a man accustomed to giving orders, not taking them, unless they came from the Potentate.

Once we reached the bottom of the hill, I found out what had become of the third hunter. He was waiting with their horses.

I scowled at Markus. "You know, he's not going to learn anything tending to your horses all the time."

He narrowed his eyes at me. "You were watching us earlier by the spring. I knew you were there."

I put my hands on my hips. "And just how did you know that? You didn't see me."

"It doesn't matter." He walked past me to retrieve his horse, then looked back at me, reins in hand. "You'll ride with me."

I didn't like the idea, but I understood. He was afraid I'd try to slip away. He could watch me all he wanted. I wasn't going anywhere. If these three could help me save Elizabeth, I could share a horse for a night.

Once we were mounted, we rode toward the village. I ignored the feel of Markus at my back and focused on my thoughts. After tonight, I'd probably never see Asher again, so I needed to come up with a new plan. I had to lure Karpov and the others in without endangering Elizabeth.

My thoughts lingered on Asher. Why was Karpov afraid of him? He was making new vampires and had the other ancients to aid him. He should have been able to kill Asher without issue.

The scent of smoke hit my nostrils a moment before Markus said, "Fire."

The village came into view, hazed in a yellow glow. Several structures had to be ablaze to create so much light and smoke. Markus tapped our horse's sides with his heels and the beast lurched forward, its hooves pounding down the narrow dirt path.

Isolde and the other young hunter, who'd been introduced as Niall, followed close behind.

I gripped the saddle, leaning forward. The smell of smoke intensified, making my eyes water more than the whipping wind already had. My throat grew tight. At first I was sure it would be Mira and Elizabeth's home on fire, but as we neared I realized the flames consumed a different part of the village.

Markus slowed our horse as we reached the main street, and I slipped out of the saddle before he could stop me. I ran full out down the street, toward the fire.

I stopped behind the growing crowd. Many carried pails of water—not to put out the burning buildings, but to keep the fire from spreading further—while others stood and stared.

It was clear which home started the blaze. Sarsa's cottage was nothing more than smoldering blackened sticks and rubble.

My knees buckled, but someone caught me. I turned my gaze to Markus, who held me steady, but he was staring at the fire.

"Is this where the girl lived?" he asked. "The one who was taken?"

I shook my head, pushing away from him to stand on my own. "No, this home belonged to the grandmother of one who was made into a vampire. I killed him last night. Someone must have found the body and told her." I swallowed the lump in my throat, then forced myself to stand straight.

"She killed herself," he said.

I nodded, stepping back to make room as a few villagers came through with more pails of water. Maybe the fire had been an accident, but I didn't think so. I flashed on the old woman begging me not to hunt the vampires. Maybe no one had even found the bodies. Maybe he'd still visited her, and when he didn't return, she knew what had happened.

"It was her choice," Markus said. "You couldn't have stopped her."

I had no reply to give him. I knew it wasn't really my

fault, but if I hadn't been so consumed with my own worries, I might have delivered the news to Sarsa myself. She deserved at least that much.

Markus gripped my shoulder, pulling me away from the crowd. Away from the crowd sounded good, even if I didn't appreciate my present company. Isolde and Niall waited in the darkness beyond with the horses. Isolde looked as sour as ever. Niall just looked confused.

"We'll camp outside of the village tonight," Markus said as we reached them.

I stepped back. "I can't stay with you. If the vampires see me with you, they'll assume I betrayed them. They'll kill Elizabeth."

Isolde snorted. "You expect us to trust you not to run off? You'll flee the first chance you get."

"I need your help. I'm not going to run." I gave her my best bored expression, hoping that my eyes watering from the smoke didn't make it look like I was crying. I felt guilty about Sarsa, but if I cried over every death, I'd never stop.

Isolde looked at Markus for support, but his eyes were on me. "Where will you rest?"

Isolde's jaw fell open, and mine nearly did the same. While I knew I needed to stick to my plan, I hadn't expected it to be so easy to get him to agree. "I slept in a tree this morning. That will do just fine."

Markus nodded. "Stay in the village until dawn."

He wouldn't leave until I agreed, so I didn't argue. I almost wanted to do as he asked, to not venture out into the night again, but there was Elizabeth. Elizabeth was spending the night with vampires. I couldn't leave her with their servants for another day without a promise that things would end the next night. If Asher wasn't coming back, I had to plan a trap for Karpov. I would convince him that Asher trusted me, and that I would bring him to Elizabeth's home tomorrow night. Once he was there, Markus, Isolde, and I could face the ancients, while Niall got Elizabeth and Mira to safety.

That still left only three hunters to face four ancient vampires, but what plan is ever perfect? Most vampires relied on strength and speed alone, they didn't need battle training. Training was all hunters ever did.

We stood a chance of prevailing, or I would have run rather than bringing Markus and Isolde into it. Now that I had somehow managed to convince them to help me, I might actually see Karpov dead. I could figure out what to do about Asher later.

Things were working out so much better than I expected, I almost felt excited. Then I glanced back at the smoldering remains of Sarsa's house. I met the gazes of the few villagers glancing my way. I wasn't sure what they saw in my expression, but they hurried along toward their homes.

I took one last look at the burning buildings, the flames now ebbing with the villager's efforts. If the fire was the worst thing the villagers saw going forward, then I'd done my job.

Vampires dead, innocents safe. That's how things were supposed to be. But why was it never that simple?

CHAPTER TWENTY-FIVE

Before leaving the village, I stopped to check on Mira. It was too late to disturb her, and she wouldn't want to see me regardless, but I had to make sure she was still well and that Karpov was keeping his word. I snuck to her bedroom window and peered through her sheer curtains. I could see her, just barely, lying on her bed. The rise and fall of her chest told me she was alive. If we survived this, I'd tell her to get thicker curtains.

I crept away from the house. Since I wasn't with Asher, hopefully Karpov would find me so I could set my trap to have him slain the following night. I couldn't be sure it would work, but with the other hunters, there was at least half a chance to avenge my uncle's death, and kill the other ancients in the process.

I stepped lightly, venturing away from the village, flinching at every sound. Had Karpov seen me with Markus and the other hunters? If he had, I might not survive the night. He wouldn't wait to find out if they had come to hunt him.

I reached the tree where I had rested most of the day.

The hum of marsh insects was a comforting din around me, keeping away the silence. I leaned my back against the tree and waited, straining my senses for any hint of vampire.

I'd almost resigned myself to climbing up into the branches to rest when I felt it—the power of the ancients.

No, just one particular ancient.

I sensed him approaching from behind the tree, but suppressed my urge to look. "I didn't expect to see you again."

Suddenly, he was standing by my shoulder, though I hadn't heard his footsteps. If not for my keen senses, I'd have thought he appeared out of thin air.

His white hair blew forward, partially obscuring his face as he gazed in the direction of the village. "The girl you were with last night, she is the one who was taken?"

I stared at him. It was the last thing I'd expected him to say. "Did you not hear me earlier? I was planning on setting you up to die."

He tucked a strand of hair behind his ear, revealing his soft smile. "Lyssandra, you have threatened to kill me multiple times. Did you expect me to be surprised that you would enlist others?"

"I didn't enlist them. They enlisted me."

Finally, he looked at me. Standing so close, I could see flecks of pure silver in his irises. He was like something out of a fairy tale—too handsome—not real. "Does it matter?" he asked.

I crossed my arms, pressing my back more firmly against the tree trunk. I used the rough wood to anchor myself in reality. He was a bloodthirsty monster. I couldn't trust him. I couldn't give in to the draw of our bond. It was an illusion, nothing more. "I wouldn't willingly ask others to enact my vengeance, and I would never work with vampires if given an option."

"And it is important to you that I know this?"

I glowered. "No." But I'd obviously already given myself away. Why did I care what he thought? "Why are you here?"

"We didn't finish our conversation earlier."

I shook my head slowly, letting my disbelief trickle into my tone. "You found out I was tricking you, and you fled. I didn't think there was any conversation left to finish."

He gave me a look like I was being quite silly. "I smelled Karpov on you from the start, Lyssandra. He bloodied you so severely to cover his scent. A lesser vampire would have been overwhelmed by the smell of fresh blood, and wouldn't have noticed the scent of other ancients on your skin."

My jaw fell open. He knew? He knew the entire time I was working with Karpov? "Why did you save me?"

He laughed. "You really enjoy asking that question, don't you?"

"You know what I mean. You knew it was a trap from the start."

He shrugged. "Trap or not, you would have died without my blood."

I hunched my shoulders, hands falling to my sides. How humiliating, all this time thinking I could actually outwit a vampire. This was why we were supposed to kill first and ask questions later. "I don't understand why you keep coming back. If I were you, I would've left me to die."

"Perhaps I just find you entertaining."

I frowned. "If you weren't surprised, then why did you run when I admitted the truth?"

"Would you rather I had killed the other hunters? If I

had stayed, they would have attacked. In my absence, were you able to come to terms with them?"

I looked down at my boots. It made perfect sense when he put it that way.

"Would you finally like your answer, Lyssandra? Even if you may find it difficult to understand?"

I searched his face for any sign that he was teasing me, but his expression gave nothing away. "Yes, I still want my answer. I didn't think I would care this much, but the longer I go without it, the more I want to know."

He leaned his back against the tree, his shoulder almost touching mine, but not quite.

I didn't move away. If I was going to finally have my answer, I could stand a little closeness. And . . . it didn't feel bad to have him near. It was like the bond was snapping more firmly into place, just like Karpov said. Would more time together only increase what I was feeling? That thought alone made me want to move away, but then, Asher spoke.

"The night we first met," he began, "I thought would be the last night of my life . . . if you could call my existence a life. I had grown tired of vampire politics, always striving for power and territory, but to what end? I know us to be monsters, and that is what I still believe. For a time, human servants dulled my misery, but even that relationship grew tiresome. I was truly alone, and saw little point in continuing. When I saw a hunter in a tavern, I thought, what a perfect opportunity."

My brow furrowed as I watched him. "You thought I would kill you. Instead I invited you to drink with me."

He laughed, as if at some private joke. "Did you know that was the first conversation I'd had in eight years? And it didn't come from a human hoping to become my servant. It didn't come from someone begging for immortality, nor did it come from a vampire wanting protection or territory. It came from you, a hunter, someone sworn to eliminate my kind. Have you any idea what that meant to me?"

All I could do for several long seconds was stare at him. He met my gaze unwaveringly, and I was the first to look away.

"I was drunk," I muttered, sure I was misunderstanding, though his words had been quite clear. "It meant nothing. It was a foolish mistake."

He laughed, the sound which a moment ago was pleasant, now sharp like shattered glass. "To you, but not to me. You asked me once why I would save someone who wanted to kill me. Perhaps you are right. Perhaps I long for death. Or perhaps I had finally just found someone worth saving."

I stepped away from the tree, shaking my head. My cheeks felt hot despite the cool breeze tugging at my hair. "Do you really expect me to believe this?"

He shrugged, still leaning against the trunk. "Believe what you wish. If you'd rather believe I simply find you entertaining, that is up to you. I told you I would answer, and now I have."

This was a trick. I knew it was a trick, but what was his goal? Did he want to mess with my mind after I had tried to trap him? I stared at him, waiting for further explanation, but he simply leaned against the tree, gazing at the sky like he had all the time in the world.

Of course, he did have all the time in the world, but I didn't. Morning was coming, and I needed a plan to save Elizabeth. "Why does Karpov want to kill you?"

"He wants to slaughter humans freely, and I will not allow it."

I shook my head. "He kills as he pleases. He murdered a woman in Bordtham just a few nights ago."

"I cannot prevent another from feeding, but he knows if a larger scale killing takes place, I will slay him."

I crossed my arms and walked closer. "Why? Why would you kill him? Why do you care?"

He lifted a brow. "Did he not tell you why he needs your help to kill me?"

"No, and it hasn't made sense to me from the start. His strength matches yours, and he has enlisted other ancients."

Asher pushed away from the tree, stepping close to me. He leaned his neck forward so we were eye to eye, draping his white hair down both sides of his face. "I am Karpov's sire. I created one of the worst monsters among us. All of his victims suffered because of me."

I stumbled back like he'd struck me. "No, that can't be true. You are not old enough to have created something so powerful."

He tilted his head. Amusement danced in his eyes. "Mortals always think age makes such a difference. Young vampires can be strong, and the oldest amongst us can be weak. I created Karpov when I was young, and though he has grown in power, I have always maintained the strength to control him. The other ancients aren't as powerful if they follow him willingly. This is why they have asked for your help."

I glanced past him to the distant horizon, spotting the first hint of light. "You need to go."

"Worried for my safety?"

I returned my gaze to find his smile mocking. "If you die, I die. That cannot happen until Karpov is gone, and Elizabeth is safe."

He lifted a brow. "And after that?"

"I won't remain a human servant for the rest of eternity."

He stopped smiling, but his eyes were still terribly amused. "You are right, I must go."

"Will I see you again at nightfall?" But I was talking to empty air.

With a curse, I climbed up into my tree to rest, but I didn't close my eyes until the sun was shining strong in the sky. I had missed my chance to tell Karpov I would bring Asher to Elizabeth's house, but there was nothing I could do about that now. Either he'd show up, or he wouldn't. Either Asher would show up, or he wouldn't. But I would be there, and the other hunters would be there.

There was no predicting how the night would end up. I only knew one thing.

There would be blood.

MY TREE SHOOK with a mighty thud. With my mind still spiraling up from a dream, I cast my arms out, searching for a hold. I grabbed nothing but air, then toppled to the ground below. Now fully awake, I rolled across the soggy earth, drawing my sword as I hopped to my feet.

I had its tip aimed at Tholdri's throat before I realized what had happened.

He smiled at me, not worried about my blade in the slightest, though Steifan standing a few steps behind him seemed alarmed.

My sword-arm sagged in relief, leaving the blade's tip to scrape across the earth. "You have no idea how glad I am to see you." I looked past Tholdri to Steifan. "Both of you. How did you find me?"

"We came across Markus and Isolde camped to the

south of the village," Tholdri explained. "Markus said you were sleeping in a tree somewhere. There aren't many trees big enough to hold a person in the mires." He watched as I sheathed my sword and dusted myself off. "Aren't you always claiming to be a light sleeper? I'm surprised we were able to sneak up on you."

I finished straightening my borrowed coat, then glared at him. "It's been a long few days."

He grinned. "Yes, Markus mentioned something about several ancient vampires and a village girl you're trying to save."

My stomach growled. It really had been a long few days, and I hadn't been eating enough. I glanced around. "I'm starving. Where are your horses?"

"That's my Lyss," Tholdri laughed, "always looking for a free meal. We left the horses just over the rise so we could sneak up and knock you from your tree. We even found your mount outside of a crypt . . . " his expression darkened, and he shook his head. "All of that blood, Lyss. I thought for sure you were dead."

I lifted a brow. "Yet you kept looking?"

He clapped me on the shoulder. "No body, no death. Now let's get you fed so we can meet up with Markus."

I didn't argue. It seemed to be a theme as of late, which was new for me. Most who knew me knew that I would argue to the death just on principle.

Steifan fell into step at my other side as Tholdri led me toward the horses. His nervous energy made me twitch.

"Ask it," I sighed.

He blinked innocent hazel eyes at me, but I wasn't fooled. "You're hopping around like a lad with his first bow. You're dying to ask me something, so ask it."

The horses came into view, and I started salivating at

thoughts of what might be in the saddlebags. Even a hunk of stale bread would feel like a feast.

"Have you seen Asher?" Steifan blurted.

I stopped walking, turning to fully face him. "Out of all the questions you could've asked, that's what you want to know?"

He nodded.

I rolled my eyes and continued walking. "Yes, I've seen him."

Tholdri and Steifan hurried to catch up on either side of me. "And?" Tholdri asked.

"It's complicated."

Tholdri turned to me as we reached the horses. "Lyss, we have been tracking you for days after finding a crypt full of blood, *your blood*, I'm assuming. You're going to have to give us more than that." He reached out and tugged at the sleeve of my borrowed coat. "You've been busy."

I pulled away from him, crossed my arms, and jutted out my hip. "Give me my horse and something to eat, and I'll tell you everything on the ride back to the village. You'll need to know it all if we are to be prepared for tonight."

"Prepared for hunting the ancients?" he asked. I could hear the excitement in his voice, and wasn't surprised.

I smiled. It was good to have him back. "Indeed. Tonight we will find out if four experienced hunters are a match for four ancient vampires." I glanced over my shoulder at Steifan. "No offense meant, but you and Niall don't really count."

Steifan snorted. "Get me through tonight alive, and no offense taken."

Tholdri handed me some cured venison wrapped in waxed parchment from his saddlebag. I snatched it greedily, then we mounted and started the ride back toward the village.

SARA C. ROETHLE

I refused to show it outwardly, but Steifan's words had started a snake of guilt slithering up and down my spine. He trusted me to keep him alive. Elizabeth trusted me to keep her alive.

Please, I thought to myself, let me keep them all alive.

CHAPTER TWENTY-SIX

The night was heavy with anticipation, or maybe it was just me. Maybe I didn't enjoy waiting alone with Mira for Karpov to arrive. He would quickly realize I hadn't brought Asher. I could only hope he'd want to know why before he killed me. I needed to stall him long enough for the other hunters to arrive.

Unfortunately, they couldn't wait nearby because Karpov might notice. Instead, they hid around the quiet village, and would listen for my screams. I'd never been much of a screamer, but to bring in the hunters, I could try.

Mira's eyes were too wide, her breathing heavy. She wore a thick tan coat, similar to the one I'd borrowed from her, and a mud-stained dress. Even knowing that tonight would be the night Elizabeth was supposed to be returned to her, she'd spent the day harvesting. She hadn't gotten home until after I arrived, just before dark. She should have been resting after a long day, instead she was cowering in her home, waiting for vampires.

I hadn't told her the plan. I couldn't be sure of what she

might do. She might give us away as a trade for her sister, and I wouldn't blame her. If Elizabeth had been my sister, and I didn't personally know the hunters, I might give us away too.

I waited with my back to the wall, feeling naked without my armor as I watched the front door and peeked through the larger windows. My sword was quiet, and I hoped that meant an ambush wasn't coming. Just in case, I had made Mira stand to my left in the corner, where I could block any vampires from reaching her. Wouldn't do to have her get snatched up as a second hostage.

I sensed when Karpov arrived. The others were with him. The Seeing Sword thrummed in my mind like a second heartbeat. Karpov wasn't here to negotiate, he was here to kill. He knew I had failed him.

The door exploded, raining shards of wood across the floorboards. Mira screamed, lunging forward to clutch my arm. I shoved her aside none too gently to draw my sword.

In the open doorway stood Karpov, the ancient female behind him. If they cared about drawing the attention of the villagers, they wouldn't have broken the door. Any who came to help us would be killed. The other two ancients were probably waiting outside to prevent interruptions.

Karpov's head nearly brushed the top of the doorway as he stepped inside. His dramatic entrance had blown out a few candles, but there was still enough light for me to see his face clearly.

He watched me with hungry eyes. "So he would not trust you enough to come? Or have you decided to protect him?"

"I didn't have enough time to convince him," I lied. I stepped in front of Mira, who'd fallen into a trembling heap on the floor. "Where is Elizabeth?"

Karpov sneered. "You have failed. The girl will die."

Mira started crying. Karpov stepped further inside to make room for the female vampire. The night beyond the doorway was still and silent. Where were the other hunters? Had they not heard the door shattering? The sound should have alerted them just as well as a scream.

The female stepped up beside Karpov, her eyes on Mira. "Who gets the sniveling girl?"

"She is hardly worth killing," Karpov answered, "but if you must."

I held my sword out, stepping directly in front of Mira. "I have not yet failed. I just need more time." *Time enough for the hunters to arrive,* I thought silently.

Karpov's gaze flicked around the room. If I didn't know any better, I'd guess he was nervous. "You have had three nights with him, three nights where he came to find you, and yet he is not here. He has left you at my mercy. You have failed."

I didn't ask how he knew I had seen Asher last night. He already knew about the other two, so maybe he just guessed at the third. The female was edging around us, her attention on Mira.

I pointed my sword at her. "You will have to go through me first."

The female started forward, but Karpov's hand snapped out, grabbing her upper arm. It was almost too fast to see. "No, not yet. I want to witness her surprise before she dies."

I didn't like the sound of that. Where in the light was Elizabeth? Was she already dead?

He looked back toward the doorway, then froze. We all froze. A man stood outside the opening, not close enough for the remaining candlelight to reveal his features. By Karpov's stance, I assumed it was not one of his allies.

Asher stepped inside, into the sparse light. My heart fell, and I realized I'd been hoping he wouldn't come.

Though Asher spoke to Karpov, his eyes were on me. "Kindly step away from my servant, and I will not have to kill you."

Karpov stepped aside, tugging the female vampire along with him. "By all means, if you are capable of claiming her, then do so. Though I do not believe she will want to leave until she sees her human friend to safety." He looked at me, his eyes sparkling with mischief. He was giving me one last chance to help him slay Asher.

I watched as Asher walked across the room. He knew Karpov wanted me to kill him. It was the only way to save Elizabeth. So why was he approaching me?

My palms were sweating around my sword hilt, forcing me to grip the ancient leather even tighter. My muscles ached to put an end to things, but not in the way I had originally planned. I might have started out blinded by my hatred for Asher, but that hatred wasn't enough to die over, at least not yet. First, I had to beat Karpov. I had to get Elizabeth back. If she was already dead, Karpov had to pay for that.

Asher had reached me. He held out his hand. "Come, Lyssandra."

Keeping my sword between myself and all three vampires, I shook my head. If the other hunters would hurry up and arrive, we might stand a chance. But they should have been here by now. Had they fallen to the other ancients? Were there more than the ones I had met?

If I had led them all into a trap . . . I shook my head again, both at my thoughts and Asher's request. "I'm not going anywhere until he returns Elizabeth."

Mira's sobs renewed at the mention of her sister. She

still sat huddled on the floor behind me as far as I could tell, though I didn't dare glance back.

Karpov watched me steadily, waiting for me to make my decision. "You know how to get her back, Lyssandra. I have kept my word. She is still alive. But if I die, she dies."

"There is truth to his words," Asher said.

I looked at Asher. Why was he helping Karpov? I was more confused by his presence now than ever. I looked up and down his tall body, my eyes lingering on his white hair. For just for a moment, I imagined driving my sword through his chest. A single impulsive decision to end both our lives, but maybe spare Elizabeth's.

I took a slow step toward him.

I could feel Karpov's excitement. The female ancient watched everything quietly, standing closer to me than Karpov. Did she hope to feed on my corpse after Asher and I were both dead? Would Asher trust me enough to let me past his defenses?

I took another stiff step toward Asher. It was like everything had slowed down. The three vampires were waiting, as still and silent as the dead. I thought of my uncle, the man who had raised me, and wondered what he would do in this situation. Would he free himself from servitude, or avenge a loved one's death?

My wonder was brief. The answer was clear. In a way, my uncle had spoken from the grave, and I would obey. I owed him that much. I lunged forward with my blade aimed at Asher's heart, then pivoted at the last moment, swiping my sword in a perfect circle around me. My blade's tip sliced across Karpov's throat. He stumbled backwards, but he wasn't dead.

The female vampire launched past me, tackling Asher to the floor. Mira screamed and scrambled away.

Karpov backed up, clutching his bleeding throat. I had

missed anything vital, barely slicing his flesh. "Elizabeth!" he shouted. "Come to me!"

I sensed her in the doorway, and that very fact let me know something was wrong. I shouldn't have been able to sense her.

"Elizabeth!" Mira screamed, running for the doorway.

Karpov laughed, a rich throaty sound that seemed to echo from the walls. I could hear Asher and the female vampire struggling behind me, but I couldn't tell who was winning. If Asher died, I would die too, leaving no one to avenge Elizabeth.

Because she needed avenging. She wasn't Elizabeth anymore. She stared at me blankly from the doorway, while her sister shook her shoulders, trying to get her to run.

Stillness came over me as I looked at Karpov. "You made her your human servant to make sure I couldn't kill you."

He nodded. "I had hoped you'd keep your word, but I know better than to trust a hunter. She is still alive, as promised. I will even leave her here with her sister, though she may prove rather useless."

My shoulders shook with laughter, and it sounded cruel, even to me. He'd been counting on my sentimentality, and though yes, that was there, above that was practicality. Elizabeth wouldn't be like me, able to think and act on her own. She'd be like any other human servant, fawning over her master, and that was a fate worse than death.

Karpov could see his own peril in my eyes. He removed his hand from his throat, showing the bloody skin almost healed. I heard a crash behind us as Asher and the female fell atop the kitchen table, still struggling. The other hunters had not arrived, meaning it was just me and Karpov.

Perhaps that was how it was always meant to be.

With a growl, I swung my sword.

Almost too fast to see, Karpov drew a sword from across his back. I hadn't noticed it until then. It was smaller than mine, but met my blade with a deafening clang. He shoved his blade against mine, sending me stumbling backward.

I tripped over a chair and went down, catching a glance of the sisters watching me from the doorway. Mira looked horrified. Elizabeth just looked blank.

The moment I hit the floor, Karpov was on top of me. I managed to maintain my grip on my blade, but couldn't fend him off as his fangs sunk into my neck.

My sword fell from my grip as I screamed. Karpov tore at the bend between my shoulder and throat like a rabid animal. Pain seared through me, and beyond it, I could sense Asher's panic. He was hurt. So was the female, but she wasn't dead yet. I could sense the Seeing Sword distantly, thrumming with power, but it didn't echo through my mind like usual. It was too far away.

I swiped my hands across the floor, searching for something, *anything*, to use against Karpov.

My vision began to go gray as Karpov reared back, his face dripping with my blood. Mira came into view, holding my sword. She lifted it over her shoulder with two hands, then swung, screaming, "This is for my sister!"

Karpov tried to roll off me, and that was all that saved me from getting hit by the swinging blade. It sliced through his neck, severing his head before embedding into the floor right next to my shoulder.

Karpov's body landed on top of me, gushing blood over my chest, but I was too weak to push him away.

Mira stood over me, swaying slightly on her feet.

"Your sister," I croaked, clutching my hand to my bleeding neck.

Mira blinked past her tears. "She wasn't my sister anymore." She fell to her knees, then despite her words, crawled toward her sister. She gathered Elizabeth into her lap and rocked her like a child. I could just barely hear her words, though I wished I couldn't. "Find mother and father, Lizzie. I will count the days until I see you all again."

She waited, almost as if hoping for an answer from the dead girl, then her expression fell into harsh resolve. She cradled her sister and stood, staggering as she found her balance, then carried her back toward one of the bedrooms. She never even glanced at me, or Karpov's body still pinning me.

My vision went foggy. She wasn't going to help me. She was going to leave me to die on her floor. I heard a door shutting as she sealed herself and her dead sister away.

I closed my eyes, for how long I wasn't sure, but when I opened them Asher had moved into view. He was beaten and bloody, but he was still alive. And so was I. He knelt and helped me push Karpov's body aside, then sat me up, pulling me into his lap to cradle me against his chest.

His arm was bleeding heavily from an injury, the coat and shirt torn up to his elbow. He held his bloody forearm in front of my mouth.

"No," I said weakly, my cheek resting against his chest.

"You will die without it." He pressed his bleeding arm to my lips.

I didn't want to drink his blood again, but I could feel my life slipping away. The feeling of being so close to death while still picturing Mira cradling Elizabeth affirmed something to me that I had been unsure of until this point. I wanted to live. Even with Elizabeth gone, I wanted to do right by her. I knew she'd urge me to continue on saving others.

So I clutched Asher's wounded arm to my mouth and drank. I pushed past my revulsion and swallowed his salty blood, letting it heal me.

My heart calmed as I drank. The pain ebbed. I could feel my flesh knitting together.

I pulled my mouth away from his arm with a gasp, then looked up at him, panting. His face was closer than I'd thought. I took several ragged breaths. I wanted to ask him why he had come, but all I could do was stare at him, because I had realized something. Drinking his blood had made the bond stronger. Whether it was temporary or permanent, I could not say, but my flesh longed for his.

I tilted my head further up as my body grew warm. "This bond," I breathed, "is a curse." Every fiber of my being was urging me to kiss him, to somehow get closer than I already was.

His mouth hovered near mine. "Only if you make it so."

Was that true? Was my resistance what made it feel like a torturous curse? A vampire was holding me in his arms, and I wasn't repulsed. I wasn't even repulsed by his blood on my lips.

I did what I had been wanting to do since I'd first envisioned it. I cupped one side of his face, then pushed my fingers back through his hair. It was just as soft as I had imagined.

He watched me with hooded eyes, leaning slightly against my hand. "Lyssandra." My name on his lips tickled a thrill from the pit of my stomach.

I felt like I was in a trance. I knew there was something I was supposed to be doing, but I couldn't quite remember what. All I could focus on were his lips, so close to mine.

He looked almost stunned, like he hadn't expected me

to react in such a way. Maybe I really was the only one who felt the bond so strongly. And yet, he lowered his mouth toward mine.

My heart thundered as our lips met. I knew it wasn't right. I was a hunter, sworn to kill his kind, but my body resisted any logic. I pushed my other hand up through his hair, pulling him closer.

His arms circled me, lifting me like I weighed nothing.

My entire body came alive. I straddled him, placing my head slightly higher than his. He tilted his head back for me to kiss him more deeply, his hands exploring the slopes of my waist. Every thought of betraying the Order flitted away. The bond was like a pulsing, living thing between us.

I explored his mouth, hesitating for a moment as I felt one of his fangs with my tongue.

"Lyssandra!" a masculine voice called from behind me.

I pulled away from Asher with a loud gasp. My blood surged, making me dizzy. I looked over my shoulder toward the open doorway.

Markus and Tholdri both stood just inside with blades drawn. It was clear they had seen a fight outside, and they'd charged in here ready for another one.

Now they both stared at a scene from their worst nightmares. A hunter, sworn to slay the undead, straddling a vampire with his blood still staining her lips.

It would've been funny if it wasn't so utterly horrifying.

CHAPTER TWENTY-SEVEN

I pushed away from Asher, then scrambled to my feet, wiping my mouth with my sleeve. My wounds ached with fresh scar tissue, clearly visible above my torn shirt and coat. I shrugged the fabric up to cover as much as I could, swishing my tongue around to lessen the tang of blood in my mouth. I realized with a start that there was some fresh blood. I had nicked my tongue on Asher's fang.

Markus and Tholdri just stood there staring at me with jaws dropped. They were dirty and bloody, but safe.

My cheeks burned. I should have come up with something to say, but my thoughts were all jumbled. How had I been so careless? How had I let it go that far at all?

Markus and Tholdri seemed equally at a loss for words. Tholdri's sword drooped as he looked between me and Asher, who was still somewhere behind me.

Steifan stumbled into the doorway next. He gave Markus and Tholdri an odd look, then turned toward me. "I assume this is the only vampire we're not supposed to kill, right?" He gestured to Asher as he moved forward to stand like a tall silent statue at my side, beaten and bloody as he was.

I stepped away from him and crossed my arms.

Markus finally composed himself enough to snap his jaw shut, then he strode forward. "What in the light is wrong with you? Have you lost your mind?"

I opened my mouth and shut it. I felt so uncomfortable I wanted to cry, but I wouldn't give Markus the satisfaction. "Asher gave me blood to heal me. It made me get . . . a little carried away."

"You were drinking that creature's blood?" he hissed. His tone made it seem like he deemed that worse than kissing him.

"She would have died otherwise," Asher said before I could answer.

Markus tightened his grip on his sword. "Do not speak to me, vampire. I have spent this night slaying many of your kind."

I stepped between Asher and Markus as Isolde and Niall reached the doorway. I stifled my groan. Isolde was the last person I wanted filled in on what the others had witnessed.

She took a long look around the room, clearly dismissed the situation, then said, "All of the young vampires have been put down, and we removed the hearts of the two ancients." Her dark eyes landed on me, still standing between Asher and Markus. "I'm choosing to believe you knew nothing of the ambush."

I lifted my brows in surprise, shocked she hadn't commented on Asher's presence.

"She didn't know," Tholdri said, though he was still giving me an uneasy look. "She didn't plan any of this. I swear it."

We all went still as a door opened further in the house,

then Mira came out into the hall. She approached slowly, moving like a sleepwalker. When she finally lifted her gaze, it wasn't to look at any of us. She was looking at my bloody sword, still on the ground near Karpov's body.

"It spoke to me," she muttered. "It told me what to do. It told me that Elizabeth was gone, but that I could give her peace." She lifted her eyes, searching until she found me. "Did I give her peace?"

I wasn't sure what to say. It had been a quick death, a kind mercy to save her from what she had become. Immortal, yes, but not herself. Never again. "Yes, you gave her peace. She was already gone, but you freed her."

Mira watched me for a moment longer, nodded, then hung her head.

I turned my attention to Markus to see if I was done protecting Asher.

His spine was stiff, but he had relaxed his sword arm. "We will discuss this elsewhere. Someone help the girl with her sister. Everyone else, there are bodies to be burned, both human and vampire."

My breath sighed out of my lungs. I had hoped the other villagers wouldn't get involved. I wondered for a moment who had died, then decided I didn't want to know. I also didn't want to see Elizabeth's body being prepared for its rites. I just . . . couldn't. It was cowardly of me, but I simply had nothing left to give this night.

Markus took one last long look at me, then left through the broken doorway. Isolde and Niall followed.

My shoulders relaxed. The fight was over. We had survived, but my life was forever changed. With what Markus had seen, I could never return to the Order. I was tainted now—unclean. The other hunters, many of whom I'd grown up with, would execute me.

Steifan went to help Mira, and suddenly I was left

standing in the moonlit darkness with just Asher and Tholdri. Tholdri was staring at Asher, but not quite meeting his eyes.

"Tholdri," I said, trying to get his attention. "Tholdri, what happened outside?"

He stepped far out of Asher's reach before he turned his attention to me, then shook his head. "Either Karpov knew we were waiting to help you, or he just wanted to destroy the village. There had to be at least six young vampires, led by the two ancients. They descended at once and started breaking down doors, murdering innocents. The young ones were easy to kill, but the two ancients—" he shook his head. "I knew Markus and Isolde were good, but I didn't know they could fight like that. If they hadn't been there, we all might have died. Markus defeated one ancient on his own. It was amazing."

He glanced back toward Karpov's body. "It seems you and Markus are on even footing."

"No," I answered. "Karpov would have killed me. Mira cut off his head."

Tholdri's expression turned dark as he looked at the blood staining my shirt. I could feel the skin on my neck almost healed. "And where was *your master* while Karpov was nearly tearing out your throat?"

Asher lifted a brow. "You told him about me?"

"Don't read anything into it," I grumbled, my thoughts still lingering on Markus. "There was a fourth ancient," I explained, looking around for her body. I had a moment of shock where I thought Asher might have let her go, then I spotted her crumpled near the kitchen with her head nearly torn off.

Tholdri followed my gaze. "He killed her?"

"Yes," I answered. "And he risked himself coming here

tonight. He didn't have to come." I didn't look at Asher as I said it. I wasn't sure I wanted to know his reaction.

Tholdri let out a heavy sigh. "We should go help the others."

"I need a moment to speak with Asher," I said. "I'll be out soon."

It was only as Tholdri looked him up and down that I realized how much blood covered Asher's hands and face. He looked like the monster that he was. I knew I had to look worse, covered in both mine and Karpov's blood, but I wasn't a vampire. I would never be so . . . terrifying.

I put a hand on Tholdri's shoulder. "I'll be alright. He won't harm me."

He shook his head and let out a long breath. "I'm not worried about him harming you, Lyss. What were you—" He looked at Asher again and shook his head. "Never mind. This is all just terribly . . . unnerving."

I knew exactly how he felt. I forced a tight-lipped smile. "It's unnerving for me too."

He hesitated for a moment longer. "I'm glad you're still alive, Lyss, no matter the circumstances that keep you that way." He turned and walked out of the open doorway.

As soon as Asher and I were alone, I walked toward Karpov's body. It seemed almost unreal that he was dead, and that I hadn't been the one to kill him. I didn't care that it wasn't me, all that mattered was that he was dead. He wouldn't be claiming any more victims. Elizabeth had been his last.

I sensed Asher at my shoulder, but didn't look back. Instead, I looked down at Karpov, part of me blaming Asher for making him. "You should have killed him long ago. Why didn't you?"

Asher stepped closer to my shoulder, making my skin prickle. The bond felt even stronger now, like smoldering flames burning within me the closer he got. "The very laws he wished to abolish were the same laws that kept me from killing him, but I'm glad you finally have justice for your uncle."

I shook my head, still staring at Karpov as I tried to ignore the bond. Foolish, I'd been so foolish sharing my vendetta against one vampire with another all those years ago. For all I could have known at the time, Asher might have been part of Karpov's flock. I still didn't know why I had told him. I'd been drunk, yes, but it was no excuse.

"You'll need to burn his corpse," Asher said, "just in case."

"I know." I knew there was a long night ahead still, and I needed to help the others, but something was still bothering me. I turned to fully face him. "Why did you come tonight? You knew I might set you up. Why did you come?"

His expression was blank, unreadable. Even with fresh bloodstains on his face, he seemed unreal and distant, like a dream. "I wanted Karpov dead. While I could not outright slay him, if he attacked me, I'd be within my rights to kill him. You presented an opportunity to force the issue."

My breath caught. I wasn't sure what I had expected him to say. No, that wasn't right, I knew what I had expected. I expected him to say he came to protect me, though why that would be his motive was anyone's guess.

I brushed it off. It didn't matter. Our shared moment was a fluke. It wouldn't be happening again. "What do we do now?" I asked.

He looked toward the open doorway. "I should probably leave before one of your hunter friends decides to kill me."

I joined him in looking out at the night. I could smell smoke as the first corpses burned. After tonight, he could just leave, go back to doing whatever he had been doing. Nothing had really changed for him. *Everything* had changed for me. If it had just been Tholdri and Steifan who'd seen me with Asher, I might be able to return to the Order, but Markus and Isolde would never let that happen. That part of my life was over.

Asher had stepped around me to retrieve my sword. He started cleaning it with the edge of a bloodstained rug, then froze mid-motion. He was staring down at the eye on the sword hilt, which had opened.

Still kneeling, he stared at it a moment longer, then handed it to me. "Where did you get that sword?"

I saw no reason not to tell the truth. "The Potentate gave it to me. It awoke for me." More surprising, it had awoken for Asher too. But why?

He stood, looking down at me as I sheathed the sword over my shoulder. "You should be careful with that. You never know how strong the will is of a sentient object."

My brows lifted. "How did you know it was a sentient object? Could you hear it?"

He shook his head. "The girl said it spoke to her and told her to kill Karpov. It knew Karpov was Elizabeth's master, and how to free her. Does it speak to you this way?"

"It warns me when someone intends me harm. Just a feeling and not words. That's it." I thought about it for a moment. "It might have spoken into my mind when I faced the Nattmara."

He nodded, his expression thoughtful. "Tell me if it speaks to you again."

That sounded a little bit too much like an order to me. I put my hands on my hips. "You speak as if you're going to be in my life going forward. I may have decided against killing you, for now anyway, but only because I wish to live."

He smiled, a soft, knowing smile. "I'm sure you'll be in trouble again soon enough, and what kind of *master* would I be if I didn't protect my servant?"

I narrowed my eyes. "You did come here to protect me, you liar. It wasn't just about Karpov."

He laughed and turned away. "I'll see you soon, Lyssandra. What Karpov started is far from over. The other vampires will continue their work, and they will not rest until the opposing ancients are dead, and the Helius Order is nothing more than a name in a history book."

I opened my mouth to argue, but he was already going for the door. I chased after him, but when I stepped outside, he was gone.

I stared out into the smoke-filled darkness. It was far from over, he'd said. The other vampires who shared in Karpov's thinking needed to be stopped.

And even if I could not return to my order, even though I had sullied my vows by kissing a vampire, I intended to be the one to stop them.

CHAPTER TWENTY-EIGHT

I found Tholdri and the others as they were piling the last few bodies. Pyres burned in the open spaces, blotting out the stars with smoke. No one spoke. Though the bodies had been moved away from the village, a few villagers watched on with hollow eyes. I wondered briefly what would have happened if I had ignored Elizabeth's plea when I first arrived. If I'd just kept on walking, leaving the village behind.

I supposed there was no use thinking about it. There would have been deaths either way, but Elizabeth might have been spared. I realized I would have chosen it, to let others die in her place. It wasn't how we were trained to think. We were trained to make the decisions that would spare the most lives. I didn't know if my way of thinking made me better or worse than other hunters. And I would never know. I was a hunter no longer.

Though my limbs ached, I helped with the bodies where I could, toiling long into the night and wondering if Elizabeth's body had already been burned. I hadn't been able to deal with it before, and now I was feeling like a coward.

I distracted myself by watching Markus. If he felt me watching him, he didn't show it. Or maybe since he'd seen me with Asher, I simply no longer existed to him. I cared little about what he thought, not him specifically, but for some reason, it still hurt.

When most of the bodies were burned, I turned as Steifan approached my back. The small torch he held lit up the dark circles beneath his eyes. His skin and clothing were covered in blood and soot, the stains all a similar black in the yellow light. He had seen a lot for a young hunter, and I wasn't sure if it was a good thing or a bad thing. At least he would have no illusions going forward. He knew the type of work that was required of us. Well, required of *him*. There would no longer be an us.

"I thought you might want to say goodbye," he said.

He didn't have to explain any further. Elizabeth's body had not yet been burned. They were waiting for me. I wanted nothing more than to turn and run away. Sensing the coming dawn, I looked up at the sky, watching particles of ash as they danced in the air.

"Take me to her," I sighed.

He turned and led the way, holding the torch before him. I thought I felt Markus watching my back, but I didn't turn around. I followed Steifan toward Elizabeth. It was the bravest thing I'd done since I'd first traveled into the night hunting Karpov.

We didn't have to walk far. To the east of the village, Mira and Steifan had found an empty expanse between the crags. They had built a humble pyre, and atop it lay Elizabeth. I probably should have chastised Steifan for spending so much time on a pyre for a single girl, but I was far too grateful for what he had done. She looked peaceful. The only victim not covered in blood. Her sister stood to one side, her gaze blank. She was no longer seeing the scene before her, her mind had taken her somewhere else. I hoped it was better than here.

Steifan went to stand by Mira as I approached the pyre. I thought about why Elizabeth's death was different from all the others, and I couldn't come up with an answer. It bothered me that I couldn't come up with an answer. I had only known her a short time, it shouldn't hurt so much.

I stared at her peaceful face as the first hints of dawn filled the alcove with blue light. Maybe it just hurt so much because she had trusted me to save her. Maybe when Karpov had made her his human servant, she'd hoped she'd end up like me. I had given her too much hope, and that was what hurt.

I realized with a painful ache in my heart that she had given me hope too. She had given me hope that people could still be kind, and that I could have friends who might one day become family. I would not let her gift go to waste. Even if I could no longer be part of the Helius Order, I would continue fighting. Elizabeth would have wanted me to keep fighting.

Steifan approached my side with the torch, his expression questioning.

I nodded and stepped back.

He lit the pyre while I said a silent prayer that I wouldn't let Elizabeth down.

While I watched the flames, Steifan guided Mira away. I didn't offer to help. Saying goodbye to Elizabeth had stolen the last of my bravery.

I stood alone watching the flames until I heard footsteps approaching. I had expected Tholdri, but I turned to find Markus and Isolde entering the clearing. Markus was finally looking at me, and it was not a friendly look. Isolde's look wasn't friendly either, but then again, it never was.

They stopped before me, and I awaited my judgment. I half-expected them to try to kill me after what Markus had seen.

"Tell her," Isolde said.

Markus looked like he tasted something sour.

Isolde kicked the side of his leg with her boot, not a hard kick, but it was enough to make him speak, grudgingly.

"We will not tell the Potentate about you and the vampire," Markus growled.

I stepped away, looking back and forth between them. "What?"

Markus darted a glare toward Isolde. "We will not tell," he repeated.

Isolde rolled her eyes. "Tell her why."

Markus focused his glare on me. I was more confused now than ever. "You're that vampire's human servant," he stated. It wasn't a question.

I was so shocked my face went numb. "How did you figure it out?" I knew Steifan and Tholdri wouldn't have told him. No one would assume I was a human servant on their own because I had free will.

"Tell her or I will," Isolde hissed.

Markus clenched his fists, and I wondered if he was about to hit me, though the Seeing Sword had been silent since they arrived. "I am—" he hesitated, glancing at Isolde. "I too am a vampire's human servant, though I would never drink that creature's blood."

My jaw gaped, and it took me a moment to reply, "How is that possible?"

"That is a story I am not willing to tell," he said. "The only relevant matter to you is that we will not tell the

Potentate. You may return to the Order without repercussion." He turned on his heel and walked away.

Isolde watched me like she might still want to kill me. "If you tell anyone—"

I held up my hand. "If his secret is truly the same as mine, you know I won't tell. The Potentate would kill me."

"*I* would kill you."

"I believe you," I said, "though I don't understand why you made him tell me."

She watched me for a long, considering moment before speaking. "Until now, I was the only one who knew his secret. We live dangerous lives, and I have little doubt he will outlive me. When I am gone, someone will need to prevent him from going after his master."

I laughed. I couldn't help it.

"What is so funny?" she snapped.

"Nothing. Absolutely nothing. I just never realized how much Markus and I have in common. Tholdri placed the same conditions upon me. I wanted to kill Asher."

For the first time, she seemed truly interested in what I had to say. "Your master? You wanted to kill him too?"

I nodded.

"You seem . . . *close* to him now."

I cringed. I thought about explaining the bond to her, but it would only make her trust me even less. And I most certainly wouldn't be telling her that Asher intended to see me again. I settled on a vague truth. "He has saved my life many times. I still hate him for what he did to me . . . " I trailed off, unsure of what else to say.

She watched me for a heartbeat longer, then nodded. "Do not share Markus' secret with Tholdri. He has told you, and you alone. It will remain that way." She turned to leave.

"Wait," I said.

She turned back to me.

"Thank you for making him tell me. It helps that I'm not alone in this."

She shook her head. "He wanted to tell you, Lyssandra. He just lacked the nerve. I don't like you, I never have, and I never will. But Markus needs someone who understands his experience. As much as I try, I cannot know what it means to be bonded with a vampire. I'll see you back at Castle Helius."

This time I let her go, and was left alone to watch Elizabeth's pyre turning to ash. As I peered into the blaze, I was consumed by the idea that I wasn't the only hunter turned human servant. In a way, it was comforting, but it also made me suspicious. Asher had made me his servant, and had been content to cut me loose. I thought I was special, but whatever vampire claimed Markus had done the same.

It was too big a coincidence to ignore, and I wondered if Asher actually gained something from having me as a servant, and that led me to wonder if there were other human servants within the Helius Order. I hadn't been able to sense what Markus was. Maybe our hunter blood helped disguise the taint of vampire within us.

Too many questions, and they wouldn't have answers now. Not as the sun slowly crept up into the sky.

I left the pyre behind to find Steifan and Tholdri. We needed to report to the Potentate and let him know what Karpov had been trying to do, what other vampires might still accomplish. And when I happened upon Asher again, he had some serious explaining to do.

CHAPTER TWENTY-NINE

Markus and Isolde stayed behind for another night to ensure all of Karpov's baby vampires were gone, while Tholdri, Steifan, and I rode ahead to report to the Potentate. It took two days of riding to reach Castle Helius, just two days. Funny how Elizabeth's village and everything that happened seemed so far away from home, one hundred days instead of two. The last three days felt like I'd been living another life entirely, and I wasn't sure I could return to how things used to be.

I wasn't sure I wanted to.

When I had presented the Potentate with Karpov's head, he hadn't seemed surprised. Pleased, but not at all surprised. He said nothing about sending Markus and Isolde to help me. I still didn't understand how he had known where I was, but I intended to find out, somehow.

Steifan and Tholdri didn't seem to share my worries about the Potentate. Things went back to normal once we were within the castle walls. Steifan continued his training, and Tholdri sauntered around being a pain in the rear wherever he could. They were both able to focus on the present, yet my thoughts dwelled on what was ahead.

The Potentate had believed our story, most of which was the truth, and that had been good enough for him. All we had really left out was Asher. If the Potentate knew we'd left a vampire alive, we'd all be put to death, or at the very least exiled. If he knew what else I'd done with that vampire . . . I didn't even want to think about it.

After our report, and a few days of rest, the three of us were sent out on another hunt. Vampire activity had increased, and moving forward, no hunter was to venture off alone.

We spent our time tracking and traveling. I listened to my senses, and to the Seeing Sword, feeling like both of us were waiting for a sign of a particular vampire. Asher didn't show himself, but I knew he watched us. Not only could I sense him out in the darkness, but it didn't take a scholar to figure out who left a yellow daisy on my pillow one night while I was sleeping. Either he was trying to romance me, or he had a twisted sense of humor. I was betting on the latter.

For the time being, at the end of the day, I only knew three things. One, perhaps not all vampires were absolute monsters. Two, I might not die for my friends, but I would kill for them. And three, not all humans were what they seemed. Steifan was a valuable friend, Markus was a vampire's human servant, and the Potentate, the man we were supposed to trust and respect above all others, was hiding something.

Maybe I'd become so adept at hiding my own secrets that I was just looking for them in others, but I didn't think that was it. Something had changed within the Order, and it was too big of a coincidence to think that it had nothing to do with the brewing vampire war. I would figure it out sooner or later. I had to. Elizabeth's spirit might be watching, and I'd sooner die than let her down.

PART TWO

CHAPTER THIRTY

Two weeks later...

My boots tapped lightly across the smooth stones leading to the main keep. A messenger had found me that morning with word that the Potentate desired an audience with me. The Seeing Sword rode my shoulder, silent since the night Karpov was killed.

I tossed my red braid behind my back as I opened the heavy oak and iron door. I had acquired new armor since my old set was lost in Charmant. My leather cuirass forced my back straight, though my shoulders wanted to hunch. I'd been waiting for the moment the Potentate told me he knew everything. That he knew I was a vampire's human servant. The way he'd been watching me in the dining hall told me he at least knew more than he was letting on. He watched me like I was a strange new creature, and he was trying to figure out my use.

I walked past an older hunter as I made my way up the

staircase. Surely I was just imagining that he looked at me strangely. I'd heard no whispers behind my back. No one had questioned how such a small band of hunters had managed to kill four ancient vampires, along with a slew of young ones. Steifan and Tholdri had been listening closely for such talk, but whenever the event was mentioned, it was not with an air of skepticism. Markus, Tholdri, Isolde, and I were highly capable, and Steifan and Niall had told the tale of our bravery. Never mind that none of us would have survived the night if Markus and I weren't both human servants, and if Asher had not been fighting on our side.

I reached the Potentate's door, which swung inward before I could knock. My eyes landed on the Potentate as I stepped inside.

He stood leaning against his desk, arms crossed. His short silver hair and beard were neatly combed, fitting well with his starchy white shirt and tan breeches. "You appear ready for battle, Lyssandra." The lines around his eyes wrinkled with a small smile. "Do you have a mission I am unaware of?"

I stopped gnawing the inside of my cheek and lifted my chin, moving further into the room. "My only mission is to serve the Helius Order."

His bony shoulders drooped. If I didn't know any better, I'd say he was tired, but men like the Potentate rarely showed weakness, even in old age.

His intelligent blue eyes glanced me over, eventually settling on the hilt of the Seeing Sword peeking over my shoulder. "How has the Voir L'épée been serving you?"

I shifted my weight to the other foot, feeling uncomfortable standing in the center of the room, but he hadn't invited me to sit. Three chairs sat empty near the cold hearth, and another behind his desk. The wide-open door was my only comfort. If we were discussing something important, he would have closed it.

"It is a fine sword," I said. "Finely honed."

He pushed away from his desk, stepping near. Though he had grown thin with age, he was still a head taller than me. His eyes seemed to bore into my skull. "And has it warned you of dangers? Tholdri told me of the Nattmara you slew."

Was he trying to get me to admit that the sword had spoken to me? It had been his sword, he knew of its gifts, yet he'd never mentioned it.

"It thrums through my mind any time someone means me harm," I said. "If I had realized that's what it did, not just warning me of predators but of any who meant me harm, I might not have come so close to becoming the Nattmara's meal."

His frown let me know I'd misspoke. "I suppose that is my fault for not being clearer?"

My jaw hung open for a moment. "Not at all. It is my fault for misunderstanding. But I learned quickly enough, and it is a fine sword."

He turned away, pacing back toward his desk. I wished he would hurry up and tell me what he wanted with me. I was so nervous it felt like there were sun ants marching up and down my back.

He moved his palm across the worn surface of his desk, keeping his back to me. "You will go to Silgard. A duchess has been found drained of blood. Two of her ladies are missing." He glanced over his shoulder at me. "You will bring Steifan."

"What about Tholdri?"

Suddenly his eyes held a hard glint. "What of him? You may have required aid in defeating Karpov, but this should be a simple task. Slay the monster responsible for killing the duchess, and bring its head to the Archduke. Make sure Steifan learns something this time."

I swallowed my next remark, hiding my blush with a bow. "We will depart at once."

He dismissed me with the wave of a hand.

I counted my steps as I retreated to the door. Mustn't look too eager to escape.

When I was out in the hall, I heaved a sigh of relief, then focused my thoughts on the task ahead as I walked. Silgard was the largest city in the Ebon Province. Hunting in such a populous location might prove difficult, especially if the vampire had human servants living within the city walls. The vampire could have any number of well-guarded hiding places.

I walked down the final set of stairs, reaching the main entry, then stepped outside. I needed to gather my belongings, but first I had to find Steifan to ensure he'd be ready to depart. I almost hated to take him into more danger, though he usually fared better than I . . . which I was sure was just pure dumb luck.

I had only taken a few steps down the stone walkway when a shadow crossed my path. A tall, female shadow. I lifted my eyes, already knowing who it was.

Isolde braced her hands on her hips. She wore a plain cream-colored shirt and dark breeches, no armor, so she wasn't going anywhere outside the castle. Her black hair hung in a dark ponytail, leaving her severe features unadorned.

She looked at me as she might a stain on her clean shirt. "What did the Potentate want with you?"

I crossed my arms, jutting my hip out to one side. "And what business is that of yours?"

Her hawk-like eyes narrowed to mere slits. "You know why—"

I lifted a hand to cut her off. "It's nothing that concerns you or Markus. Simply a mission in Silgard."

Her brows lifted. "In Silgard? And the Potentate is sending *you*?"

I couldn't help my slightly mocking smile. Isolde was my senior. If anyone got to go to Silgard, it honestly should have been her. That thought alone stopped me. Why *had* the Potentate chosen me? Steifan made sense, he would know how to charm the dukes and duchesses, but so would Isolde. Finally, I shrugged in reply, not knowing what else to say.

She didn't seem to notice my sudden worry. With a flick of her ponytail, she gave me a final glare, then turned and walked off.

I glanced at the hilt of the Seeing Sword peeking over my shoulder. "You could've warned me an enemy was nearby," I scoffed, then started walking.

I pushed thoughts of the Potentate and Isolde from my mind. There would be real enemies on the road. And come nightfall, there would probably be vampires. I hoped it wouldn't be anyone I knew.

I searched through my weapons trunk, ensuring I had everything I might need. I already wore my armor and my sword, and had packed two spare sets of clothing. I hoped the mission would take no more than a week, but there really was no saying. It would take several days to ride to Silgard, and hunting the vampire might take more than one night. If the creature was killing high-ranking nobles whose deaths would be immediately noticed, it was either extremely intelligent, or extremely stupid. If we killed it in one night it was just stupid, and probably new dead.

But if the creature eluded us, it was older dead, perhaps even ancient and another proponent of Karpov's new order.

I lifted my head at a knock on the door. I'd be leaving soon, so I hadn't locked it. It opened before I could invite the knocker inside. Steifan was the first to enter, followed closely by Tholdri. Steifan was expected, and Tholdri, well I supposed I expected him too, even though he had no reason to delay our mission.

Watching me still kneeling by my trunk, Tholdri walked across the small room and sat on my cream coverlet. He raked a hand through his impressive golden locks, then aimed his speculative gaze at me.

"Don't look at me like that," I sniffed. "The Potentate gave me a mission, and it has nothing to do with Asher."

Tholdri lifted a brow. He wore a pale blue tunic that emphasized his honey brown eyes, no sword or armor like Steifan. He knew he wasn't coming, so he also knew that if I happened upon Asher, he wouldn't be there to stop me from doing anything stupid. "How did you know that's what I was thinking?"

Steifan leaned against the wall near the closed door, watching us.

Clutching two spare daggers and a bundle of crossbow bolts, I stood. "Because you've asked me about him every single time I've left the castle. I already promised you I wouldn't kill him."

He shrugged, giving me a charming smile that would melt lesser women in their boots. "I'm no longer worried about you killing him. I don't think that's likely considering the position you were in the last time I saw you two together. Can vampires make babies?"

I wrinkled my nose. "*That* will also not be happening again."

"Are you sure? You didn't think it would happen the first time."

I set the weapons on my bed beside him. "I have been working on my self control," I said caustically. "Now is there anything else? I want to put good distance between us and the castle before dark."

"Eager to be away from the Potentate's watchful eye?" he asked.

I shook my head, though in truth that was part of it. "The duchess cannot be given her rites until we examine her. It's warm enough in the South that she will grow riper by the day. I would not delay our arrival."

I walked across the room to my stuffed saddlebags, wondering how I would fit any more weapons within. Steifan watched my movements silently, and I realized he was paying attention to what I was bringing on our journey so he could alter his own belongings to fit mine.

I could feel Tholdri's eyes on my back. "Don't you think it's odd that the Potentate is sending you away so quickly after we told him of the vampire war? You would think he would want one of his best hunters close at hand."

"He has you, and Markus and Isolde. *Someone* has to go to Silgard."

He stood and moved in front of me, preventing me from avoiding his gaze. "And if you see Asher along the way?"

I did better than meeting his gaze, I affixed him with an icy glare. "Then I ignore him. Unless he has news on the vampire situation, I have no use of him."

"I'll be with her," Steifan said from behind my back.

Tholdri and I both looked at him, but Tholdri beat me to saying what we'd both been thinking. "And what difference does that make? She's going to do as she wishes regardless."

Steifan shrugged, tucking a lock of chin-length black hair behind his ear. "Whatever you say. I just meant I could be there as a voice of reason."

I glared. "I do not need a voice of reason."

"Yes you do," Tholdri and Steifan said in unison.

I sighed and shook my head. "I won't do anything stupid, and I'm anxious to take to the road." I looked at Tholdri. "And I'm just as anxious as you to discover why the Potentate is sending me."

Dismissing Tholdri with a final meaningful look, I turned to Steifan. "Go ready the horses. I'll meet you at the gate shortly." I looked him up and down. He wore his armor and his sword, but . . . "You do have everything you need ready, don't you? I'd hate to delay further."

His hazel eyes darted, giving away his sudden worry. We were around the same age, but he seemed so very young. "I'll meet you at the gates shortly. I have only a few more things to attend."

Tholdri walked toward the door and clapped Steifan on the shoulder. "Go gather your belongings, I'll have the stable hand ready your horses."

Steifan's eyes shimmered with relief. "You have my thanks." He opened the door and hurried outside before I could make comment, shutting it quietly behind him.

"Am I really that scary?" I asked Tholdri.

"He doesn't want to disappoint you. I think it's quite sweet." He went for the door, then turned with his hand on the knob. "Promise me you won't do anything stupid, Lyss."

"I've already decided I won't be breaking my vows again," I explained. "Not with a vampire war in the works. The Order needs me."

"I need you too. Remember that."

I smiled, and despite my irritation, it was genuine. "You're a good friend, Tholdri."

He snorted. "And you're a terrible one," he joked. He opened the door. "I'll see you soon then, and don't get Steifan killed."

Whatever clever retort I might have thought up was cut off by him exiting and shutting the door behind him. I stared at the door for a minute, then went back to my preparations, sparing the occasional glance for my bookshelf. In a secret cubby behind it was all of my research done to find Asher. So much time wasted, when all I had to do was nearly die to draw him out.

Now I had him, but I wasn't quite sure what to do with him. Part of me still wanted to kill him, to end my existence as a vampire's human servant. But another part of me, a dark hidden part I would never admit to, wasn't sure if I could.

I ARRIVED at the gates before Steifan, and couldn't quite contain my irritation. The stable hand—a young male hunter whose name I didn't know—quickly handed me my reins with eyes averted. Maybe I was scary, or maybe my nerves painted everything in a dark light. Perhaps the stable hand was just distracted and not frightened of me at all.

I stood outside the wooden wall of the stable with my horse and waited. I'd been given a well-muscled brown mare, which I'd ridden many times before. While the horses were not assigned to individual hunters, most of us had our preferences, and the young stable hands tended to remember. For eventually, if they trained well, they would climb up the ranks. And any young hunter would do well to be liked by whatever mentor was assigned to them. Anything less might get them killed.

Steifan had never had to remember horses to earn favor. Because of his wealthy family, he'd skipped many steps. And I could cast no judgment his way. With my uncle Isaac as my mentor, my training had started early, and I was a full-fledged hunter by the time I'd turned sixteen.

I petted my mare's forehead as the sun shifted high enough in the sky to project our shadows across the dirt road leading toward the gates. Steifan had wasted so much time we wouldn't make it far before dark. Normally I would travel through the night, but that might not be wise given the state of things. If vampires wanted to kill freely, they'd be keen to eliminate vulnerable hunters. We would try to reach a village, somewhere safe and easily defended, and rest there.

I watched as another shadow was added to mine and the horse's, but didn't react.

"Isolde told me of your mission," Markus' voice said to my back.

I shifted my stance, bringing him into sight. "Yes? What of it?"

He pushed a short lock of brown hair away from his strong-jawed face. He wore a simple white shirt with pearl buttons, and gray woolen breeches, no armor. So like Isolde, he was not on assignment and could have been sent to Silgard instead of me. "I just think it's odd that you're being sent so far away under the circumstances. If it is a simple killing, one of the lesser ranking hunters could have been sent."

I sucked my teeth and lowered my voice. "Yes, it has been established that it is quite odd, but I'm not sure what anyone expects me to do about that. The Potentate orders and I obey." My horse tugged at its reins, upset that I'd turned my attention away without offering any treats. I gave her the rein's full length so she could snuffle at the ground, even though there was no grass to be found.

Markus' playful smirk made his face seem a little less harsh. His expression surprised me. As far as I knew, I disgusted him. "*You* follow orders?" he joked. "You could have had me fooled."

I narrowed my eyes. "I obey where it matters, and I have an inkling you do the same. Why are you being nice to me?"

"Yes we are similar in that way, I suppose," he agreed. "As for the rest . . . it is not my business. I shouldn't have reacted."

"You were right to react the way you did." I scanned the road to the cobblestoned courtyard beyond for any sign of Steifan.

"Was it really the blood that made you do it?"

"Yes. I feel a certain . . . draw to him, but I had resisted it until that point. I plan to resist it henceforth."

He considered my words. "Perhaps we should just look at it like you had too much wine. One drunken night of bad decisions."

I laughed, relaxing. I wasn't used to having any sort of repartee with Markus, but he was at least slightly less sour toward me than Isolde. Perhaps it was because we shared the same secret, though this was the first time we had discussed it any further.

He spotted Steifan jogging toward us at the same time I did, carrying two heavy saddlebags brimming with who knew what. "This is goodbye then. Do take care you return to us."

I looked to see if he was being sarcastic, but he had already turned to walk away, and Steifan was nearly upon me. His black hair fell forward over his reddened face, flushed either with the effort of hauling the heavy bags, or out of embarrassment.

The stable hand spotted him and approached with a second horse, a white and gray dappled mare.

I nodded a greeting to Steifan as he reached my side, then looked up at the sky. The sun had moved again. We'd be lucky to make it to a village before dark. While Bordtham and Charmant could both be reached in a day's ride to the north, villages were more spread out to the south and east until you got closer to Silgard.

Once Steifan's saddlebags were strapped to his horse, he turned to me. "It really wasn't my fault. My father happened to arrive just as I was getting ready to depart. Now I have an entire list of nobles I am supposed to endear myself to in Silgard, including Duke Auclair, the victim's husband."

I pursed my lips. "Well I don't envy you that, but let us first focus on making it to a village before nightfall. I have an eerie feeling in my bones, and I'd rather not rest without a locked door between us and vampires."

The stable hand glanced between us with wide eyes, then scurried away.

Steifan watched him go. "You do have a habit of scaring people, don't you?"

I scowled. "Hurry up and mount, or I'll be forced to scare you too."

Steifan did as he was asked while I climbed into own saddle, then angled my horse toward the nearby gates, which were already opening for us. A few hunters stopped in the nearby courtyard to watch us depart, and I startled, recognizing a face well behind them near the door to the main keep.

The Potentate stood alone, tall and wiry, but still

strong. He watched me go, that same strange expression on his face, like I was a creature entirely new to him. He'd never watched me like that previously, only since I had returned with Karpov's head.

I wasn't sure what had changed, and it was debatable whether I really wanted to know. I knew better than most that some secrets were best left buried.

CHAPTER THIRTY-ONE

We reached Silgard on the evening of the third day after leaving Castle Helius. We'd made camp near villages too small to have inns the first two nights, and stayed at an inn the third night closer to the city. There had been no vampires, nor Nattmara, nor anything else. I almost felt foolish for being so worried, but I knew all too well that being bold would get you killed. For a hunter, worry was a virtue, even when unwarranted.

Steifan and I were both deep in our own thoughts as our horses plodded down the wide dirt road leading up to the city built atop a hill. We passed farms and peasant dwellings, the chimneys leaking smoke to flavor the air. It was a nicer thing to notice than the underlying scent of manure tightening my throat. My sharp senses were a blessing at times, but could also prove a curse.

As we started up the incline, farms shifted to more homes, and a few merchants with carts. My stomach growled as we passed a cart with honey rolls, but we could not in good conscience delay any further. The duchess' body probably smelled far worse than the manure.

"What do we do once we reach the city?" Steifan asked, his eyes wide with excitement.

I gazed at the distant metropolis, its walls twice as high as those of Castle Helius and made from pale gray stone. "We seek out Duke Auclair. We'll need to observe the duchess so she can be given her rites. If we are lucky, the duke will offer us a meal and a place to stay, as is customary, but I have not come to expect it. Few want a red-haired witch within their estate."

He straightened in his saddle and blinked at me. "Truly, you were not offered lodgings on those grounds?"

I shrugged. "Old tales tend to linger." In truth I could have changed my hair color, there were many ways to stain or lighten one's hair, but I'd never tried. I knew the color had to have been passed down by one of my ancestors, and with so few of my relations still living, I clung to that small connection.

Steifan turned his attention to the city gates as we approached. The portcullis stood open with just two city guards posted to question visitors. It didn't seem a good way to protect the city to me, but then again, Silgard, the Capital of the Ebon Province, had not suffered siege in over a century. Between the Capital and the other provinces lay the mires, desolate forests, vampires, and ghouls. Further south was the Merriden Sea, an impassible expanse. If the vampires weren't enough to scare away conquerors, the lack of motivation to acquire such cursed lands would do the trick. Though Silgard was as large as any great city, the rest of the province left much to be desired.

We dismounted as we reached the wide bridge leading to the gates, and I wondered how many vampires were lurking within the walls. Other provinces had them too, but none could rival the Ebon Province in number of undead. Maybe it was the lack of sunlight that drew them, or perhaps many of the lines simply originated in my homeland and never branched out.

The guards standing to one side of the entryway were both older men wearing polished breastplates over midnight blue livery. They looked at our hardened leather armor skeptically as we approached, as if unaware Steifan and I could probably throw them into the open canal below with little effort.

"We weren't told to expect the Helius Order," one said.

I furrowed my brow, holding my mare's reins taught to keep her close behind me. "Were you not informed of Duchess Auclair's murder?"

They locked gazes for a moment, then the one who'd spoken shrugged. "Many believe the murder wasn't actually committed by a vampire. I did not think the Order had been contacted."

"We were told there was no question to the murder," Steifan cut in. "What do you mean, it wasn't committed by a vampire?"

Another knowing glance between the guards. "Forget we said anything," the more vocal guard continued. "The duke's estate is on the northern end of the city, further up the hill. Head that way then ask around. Most anyone can point you in the right direction. Duke Auclair is a well-known man."

They both turned their attention forward, making it clear we were dismissed.

I shrugged to Steifan, then led my horse into the city. Past the barracks, the wide stones transitioned into a hard-packed dirt road. Eventually the dirt turned to cobbles, spreading before us to form a central court. Merchants gathered there, backed by stables and an inn on one side, and short wooden homes on the other. Beyond the inn, I could see the tall arched roof of the guild hall.

The chatter of voices as we walked further into the square was both comforting and unnerving. I couldn't pick out any specific conversations, but surely some were remarking on our arrival. I supposed I would never know what was said, but it was still nice being in a city outside Castle Helius.

I received curious glances from market goers on all sides as I led the way toward the stables. I was sure there would be separate stables near the duke's estate, but after the strange words of the guards, I wasn't keen on leaving my horse there.

We didn't make it far before a courier in green and gold livery stopped us. He was young, probably only twelve or thirteen, with sandy hair and freckles that made him look even younger.

He shifted his eyes between me and Steifan, finally settling firmly on Steifan. "Duke Auclair tasked me with waiting here every day for your arrival. He'll be pleased to see you shortly. You can stable your horses within the White Quarter."

I appreciated Steifan looking to me for instruction.

I clutched my reins protectively. "We will stable our horses here, then you will lead us to the duke's estate."

The courier opened his mouth like he wanted to argue, then his eyes flicked to the sword visible over my shoulder and his mouth snapped shut. He bowed his head. "As you wish. The White Quarter is not far."

I had already deduced as much. In the distance, a cobbled path led upward from the square, lined with a secondary inner wall. Tall roofs towered beyond that wall, their white shingles glaring in the sun. I was betting the duke lived somewhere behind those walls. Curious, that the vampire would risk the well-guarded area instead of preying on the peasants outside the city walls. Maybe the guards were right and it wasn't a vampire. Either way, the murder was probably personal. Not a random killing. If the only need was blood or death, a duchess was not necessary.

The courier and Steifan were both watching me, and I realized I'd gotten lost in my thoughts.

I cleared my throat, then tugged my mare's reins, continuing toward the stables. I gave the courier the choice of either moving out of my way, or getting trampled by my horse. He moved.

We stabled our horses, then rented a room at the inn to store our belongings. Once we were ready, we followed the courier toward the duke's estate. I noticed the market goers sparing more glances for the courier than they did for Steifan and me. His livery made it clear to which noble he belonged. Just what type of duke was this man who made city guards nervous, and whose courier drew more curiosity than a red-haired hunter?

I could feel eyes on my back as we started up the cobblestone expanse toward the wealthy estates. The path wound upward, bordering the tall wall guarding the homes to our left. To the right of the path were shops and more modest wooden homes.

Eventually we reached wrought-iron gates and two more city guards, this pair younger and more alert than those outside the main wall. They wore the same navy livery as the gate guards, though the similarities ended there. Both were tall and fit, but one was pale and freckled, the other with black hair and a neatly trimmed mustache.

The wide gates rose up behind them, tipped with sharp posts that would make them difficult to scale.

Both guards wordlessly observed the courier, then looked us up and down. "You'll need to leave your swords," the dark-haired one said.

Standing straight I was taller than the pale guard and Steifan was taller than both, but I didn't think these two men would be intimidated by size. Regardless, they were fools if they thought they would part me from my sword.

"We are here to hunt a vampire," I said. "We will not be without our swords."

"It's daylight," the dark-haired guard said tiredly.

He had a point, but I still wasn't giving up my sword. I was tired from our travels, and ready for a hot meal and a pint of ale. As I saw it, these two guards were the only thing standing between me and that end.

"Lyss—" Steifan began, likely noting the change in my expression. The young courier watched us both warily.

But I was already stepping forward past the courier toward the guard who'd spoken. "Look, you can try to physically take my sword from me, which I do not recommend, or you can explain to Duke Auclair why his wife will spend another day rotting in her bedroom waiting for us to avenge her murder."

The guard to my right audibly swallowed. The one I was eyeing paled.

Finally, he gave a curt nod. "I suppose if I escort you, and the duke accepts your presence with weapons, then we can allow you to pass."

I wanted to say, *There, was that so hard?* But I knew better than to press my luck. I accepted his offer with a nod. "Lead the way."

I stepped back as the pale guard who would remain

behind opened the ornate gate, letting the rest of us pass through before shutting it behind us. The other led the way past a grouping of stables, down a wide expanse between estates. He walked with stiff shoulders, nose lifted, mustache bristling.

As we walked, Steifan gave me a look that told me I should behave.

I wrinkled my nose, but nodded. He was likely worried that word of my rude actions would make it back to his father. I felt sympathy for his position, but he was the one here to charm nobles. I was just here to solve a murder.

More confident now that he was within the secondary walls, the courier scurried forward to lead the way while the guard seemed to think better of keeping his back to us and fell into step beside Steifan.

I smiled to myself. The guard had deemed Steifan the greater threat, the one who needed to be watched more closely. *Amateur.*

My grin faded as I glimpsed an oddly familiar face beyond the wrought-iron fence of one estate's expansive garden. I blinked, and the face was gone. Had I just imagined it? I didn't have time to consider it further as the courier stopped before the tall wooden door of a particularly grand estate.

We waited at the base of three wide stone steps leading up to the door while the courier knocked. Almost immediately the door swung inward, revealing a servant in the duke's green and gold livery, an older man who seemed relieved to see us.

He gave the guard a quick, questioning glance, but waved us in, stepping back and holding the door wide.

Steifan and I stepped inside and glanced around. The floor beneath our boots was pristine marble, matching white walls rising tall overhead. Bookshelves lined the sitting room, though they held few books and even fewer trinkets. While the home was grand, the decor was oddly sparse. The smell of a rotting corpse hung in the air.

A man came down the adjoining stairs to greet us, presumably the duke. He looked us over with small eyes set in a ruddy face. At our backs, the servant who'd opened the door was arguing with the guard on whether or not he would be allowed inside.

The duke straightened his stiff crimson lapels, ignoring the arguing men in favor of regarding us. "You are late. It's preposterous how long I have been asked to hold my wife's body. She deserves her rites." With jerky movements, he swept his hand over his thinning silver hair, then his fingers fluttered down to flatten his well-oiled beard.

Steifan swooped into a ridiculous bow. "My apologies, Duke Auclair. We have ridden many nights from Castle Helius to reach you. I am Steifan Syvise, son to Gregor Syvise. My father sends his greetings, and his condolences."

I snapped my jaw shut. I knew Steifan was practically nobility, but I'd never seen him act the part. His words seemed to placate the duke.

We turned at the sound of commotion as the guard pushed past the door servant, charging inside. The courier followed, reaching out helplessly to stop him. The servant stood stiff-spined near his post.

"Duke Auclair." The guard bowed his head, then quickly raised it. "The hunters would not relinquish their weapons. I wanted to ensure they were welcome in your presence."

The duke's face grew ruddier. "They are hunters, you fool!" He waved his hands. "What good are they to us without their weapons? They must find the creature who killed my wife!"

At that point I would've interjected to calm the flustered men, but I was too busy trying not to breathe in the stench of rotting corpse coming from upstairs. Could the men not smell it? It was only comfortably warm outside, but I had a feeling the upper rooms must amplify the heat to produce such a smell.

The guard and courier were muttering apologies while the servant watched the duke to see how he would react. Steifan seemed unsure if it was his place to intervene. What I wouldn't give to be hunting in a small village away from such ridiculous men.

The duke's body grew stiff as the guard continued to convince him that he had done the right thing in escorting us. "Silence!" the duke snapped. "Everyone away except the hunters. Make sure we are not disturbed."

I'd never seen two men and a boy move so fast. In mere moments, Steifan and I were alone with the duke.

"This way," the duke said blandly, gesturing up the stairs.

It made me wary that his anger could disappear so quickly. I wondered what other emotions lurked just below the surface. But that was a worry for later. I led the way up the stairs, overly conscious of the sound of my boots on the painted wood. The rest of the house was utterly silent.

I reached the top and stepped aside to wait for the duke, pretending I didn't know which direction to go. Steifan came up last, and I fell into step beside him as the duke led us down a wide hall adorned with the longest rug I'd ever seen. Following the putrid smell, my eyes landed on the door before the duke stepped in front of it. It wasn't as hot up here as I'd imagined. A few oil lamps provided minimal warmth, but there wasn't much sunlight. It should have taken the body longer to stink.

"I'd rather not see her like this," the duke said as he opened the door. "I'll wait out here."

I nodded, then stepped inside the room. As soon as the duke shut the door behind us, I lifted my sleeve to cover my nose and mouth. There were no candles in the room, and the window was covered with a sheer curtain, providing just enough light to see by. It wasn't warm, but the smell was horrific.

Steifan moved to my side, already looking green. Together, we looked down at the bed.

The duchess wore nothing but a night shift, the fabric thin enough to clearly show her wilted shape beneath. She had probably been stripped when the corpse was examined. Graying ringlets were plastered back from her snow white face. As reported, there were two small puncture wounds in the side of her neck, but that wasn't what held my interest. The way her curls dried made it seem like they'd been sopping wet when she'd been laid upon the bed. Parts of her shift were stained brownish yellow, like blood had been washed away. I wanted to speak my observations out loud to Steifan, but had little doubt the duke would be listening from outside the door. I didn't want him to hear me, because no one had mentioned the body being tampered with. I'd guess she was moved long after her death. It explained the lack of blood on the wound, and the water stains. Just how long had the duchess been missing before her death was finally reported?

I leaned closer, my nose and mouth still covered by my sleeve, for what good it did against the stench. Judging by her skin, I didn't think the rotting had occurred while she'd been submerged in water, more like she'd died, rotted, then had gotten wet far after the fact.

I straightened, giving the rest of the room a quick glance. Nothing stood out—other than Steifan looking close to retching in the corner. The dresser was tidy, with only a few visible trinkets, just like in the sitting room. I would have liked to peruse the drawers, but had a feeling the duke would intervene if he heard me rifling through things. I didn't want to let him know I suspected anything. Not just yet.

I motioned for Steifan to exit the room ahead of me. The duke still waited for us in the hall. He didn't look our way until the door was closed behind us.

I searched his expression, looking for hints of guilt. If the guards at the main gate didn't think the duchess was killed by a vampire, did they perhaps suspect her husband? The bites on her neck were real, but they might not have been what killed her. Either way, something was very wrong here.

"I was informed she was found in her bed, deceased," I said simply.

The duke puffed up his cheeks. "That is correct. This is where I found her. Her body was damp, but I do not know why."

I cleared my throat, trying to rid myself of the clinging smell of death. Perhaps he was telling the truth. Maybe someone else had put her there. "Do you have any enemies? Anyone who would do this to your wife to horrify you?"

Sweat shone on his brow as he shook his head. He removed a white handkerchief from his breast pocket, using it to sop up the sweat. "Wealth breeds enemies, but I can think of no one in particular."

I sighed. It wasn't warm in here and he was sweating like he had been running in the sun. He was definitely hiding something, but what was yet to be determined. "I'll need a list of all of her friends," I explained, "and any places she frequented. If she kept a journal, seeing that would be helpful."

The duke's tiny eyes went so wide they bulged. "Questioning her friends, I understand, but what use would you have for her journal? Is she not deserving of her privacy?"

Steifan stepped closer. "Often vampires will stalk their prey for days or weeks before attacking. Sometimes journals can reveal if the victim noticed anyone watching them, or if they recently met someone new. It might even provide a physical description."

I gave him an approving look. He was learning.

The duke's already thin lips thinned further, disappearing into his short beard. "Well I," he paused, "I don't know where Charlotte kept her journal. I'll search for it."

I bet you will, I thought. *And once you find it, you'll burn it.* Outwardly, I smiled. He wasn't going to let me search his house, of that I was sure. If he burned the journal, there was nothing I could do about it. "That will be very helpful. In the meantime we'll get started questioning her close friends. When did her two ladies go missing?"

The duke seemed to calm himself. "The first left us weeks before my wife's death, the other shortly after. Their bodies were never found, so I don't know if the vampire took them, or if they simply fled."

I nodded, taking in his words. "And Charlotte's friends?"

"My courier should be able to provide you with a list. He ran all of Charlotte's errands and scheduled her outings. Now if you don't mind, I'd like to prepare my wife for her rites."

Steifan and I both bowed. Steifan because it was the proper etiquette, and me to hide my calculating expression. There was something wildly off about Charlotte's murder, and her husband's behavior, and I fully intended to find out what that was.

For while my purpose was to hunt vampires, it was also to avenge innocent lives. I wasn't sure what type of monster had caused Charlotte's demise, but I would see that monster brought to justice, even if it was the man standing before me.

CHAPTER THIRTY-TWO

The older servant held the door for us as we walked outside, duteously avoiding eye contact. The young courier waited below the three steps leading down to the street. The guard who had escorted us was gone. Apparently he'd done his duty.

I looked down at the courier as the door shut behind us. "You are to give us a list of all of the duchess' friends and places she frequented," I explained. "If you know what her schedule was a few days before she was killed, that would also be helpful."

The courier stepped back, looking to Steifan as if expecting him to dispute my words. When he didn't, the courier nodded quickly, splaying short hair across his freckled forehead. "I can escort you. The duchess had few friends. I can show you where they live."

What was this, I thought, *someone actually being helpful?* "What's your name?" I asked.

His flush hid his freckles. "Bastien Goddard, my lady." He dipped his sandy head in a bow.

I realized then that he didn't keep looking to Steifan

because he was male and therefore in charge. I just made him nervous in the way many women make young boys nervous.

I smiled. "Pleasure to meet you, Bastien. We will follow your lead."

Bastien lifted his head and was off like a colt.

Steifan leaned near my shoulder as we hurried after him. "That's the nicest I've ever seen you be to, well, anyone."

"Oh shut up," I said, not wanting to embarrass Bastien.

My grin faded as we followed him into another square, much smaller than the one near the entrance of the city. I'd realized why I found the boy's demeanor charming. He reminded me of Elizabeth, the last person to find me worth interest. She hadn't been frightened spending time with a hunter either, and it had gotten her killed. *I* had gotten her killed.

Bastien stopped walking at the edge of the square and turned to us. "Lady Montrant lives over there." He pointed past gilded carts bearing pastries, cakes, and meat pies toward a massive estate bordering the square. "But she should be out here soon. Most of the noble ladies take tea at this hour."

I followed his finger as it moved to point at a gathering of wrought-iron tables. Many ladies gathered there, and my first thought was how did they move in all that fabric? And how did their heads remain upright with such tall hair? I'd seen such garb on rare occasions growing up, but I was far more used to village girls in simple dresses, with their hair hanging in practical plaits.

A woman emerged from the home Bastien had pointed out. Her lilac dress looked like it weighed more than three other ladies' dresses put together. Her hair was pure silver with age, but appeared silken in texture, piled into artificial ringlets atop her head. Purple jewels embellished her bodice and her throat.

"That's her?" I asked Bastien, keeping my voice low.

"Yes, Lady Montrant. She and the duchess were close friends for many years."

I looked at Steifan. "Find a place with Bastien to look inconspicuous. I want to know if anyone watches me questioning the lady with too much interest. Don't question anyone. Just note who might be watching and ask Bastien for their names."

Steifan seemed hesitant. "Do you want to question her yourself? Are you sure you know how to speak properly?"

I scowled. "They will understand my words well enough."

Bastien tugged Steifan's sleeve. "Come, I know just the place. No one will notice us watching."

Steifan gave me one last hesitant look, then allowed Bastien to guide him away.

I turned my attention to Lady Montrant, now seated at a table with two other ladies while a servant poured them tea. I started walking toward them, then froze mid-step, sensing a dull thrum of energy from the Seeing Sword. It was the first time it had awoken since the night of Karpov's death.

I looked around, but no one was watching me, let alone threatening me. Perhaps it was nothing, though it did make me realize the sword had been quiet around the duke. If he was trying to cover up his wife's murder, surely the sword would have seen him as a threat?

I shook my head minutely and kept walking, stopping in front of Lady Montrant's table.

"My ladies," I said, encompassing the two younger women with Lady Montrant in my gaze. "Do you mind if I join you?" I gestured to the empty chair at their table.

The two younger women seemed to shrink as they looked up at me, while Lady Montrant seemed to grow. Her spine stiffened and her narrow nose raised. "I imagine this is about Charlotte? I can see no other reason for a hunter to be in this part of the city."

I ignored the subtle insult, not bothering to argue that many hunters came from noble families and could fit in well amongst the wealthy. No matter that I wasn't one of them. "Yes, this is about Charlotte. I'm told you and she were close friends. I'd like to ask you a few questions."

"*Close friends.*" She snorted. "Very well, have a seat."

I pulled out the remaining seat and lowered myself less than gracefully, snatching a pastry from the table on my way down. Lady Montrant already didn't like me, so I might as well skip the niceties.

I took a bite of the pastry, chewed, and swallowed. "Were Duke and Duchess Auclair struggling with coin?"

The lady's jaw fell open, showing healthy teeth, a rarity in someone her age. Or at least a rarity in the small villages. I imagined many in this part of the city still had all their teeth. She shut her jaw with a click. "Why would you think such a thing?"

"I was just at their home. It is a grand estate, but there are few grand treasures within." I took another bite of pastry, enjoying the sweet, flaky crust.

The lady seemed to think about her answer while her two companions pretended they were not in the middle of our conversation, politely sipping their tea.

She started to reach for her own tea, then pulled her gloved hand away. The jewels at her throat caught the sunlight, a dazzling display. There had been no such jewels in Charlotte's room. They could have been in her dresser drawers, but I doubted it. "Very well. Yes, Charlotte was struggling with coin. I grew tired of sponsoring her every time we were out. I told her as much roughly two weeks ago. I now feel great remorse for what I said to her."

She didn't look like she felt great remorse. She looked like she didn't really care at all that her friend was gone.

I decided on another tactic. "Do you know if Charlotte felt like anyone was watching her? Had she met anyone new?"

The Lady Montrant smiled a secretive smile, deepening the furrows around her thin lips. "Charlotte met many new people, many new *men*, if you understand my meaning."

Was she implying that Charlotte was less than faithful in her marriage? Perhaps to earn extra coin? I couldn't think of any way to ask my questions that wouldn't have the lady calling for guards to escort me away, but I would remember the implication.

"Do you know if Charlotte kept a journal?" I asked.

The Lady Montrant stood, her movements quickly echoed by the two younger ladies. The lady looked down at me. "If Charlotte had a journal, it would be filled with the blatherings of a simpleton. Now if we're quite finished, I have things to do."

I nodded. "If I have further questions, I'll visit your home."

Her eyes went wide for just a heartbeat, but I didn't miss it, and I would remember it. "Very well," she snapped, then turned and walked away. Her two ladies curtsied, then followed Lady Montrant across the square.

I watched them go, then looked down at the platter of uneaten pastries, and the three mostly full cups of tea. I highly doubted the lady had anywhere urgent to be. She had planned on a long teatime.

I took another pastry for myself, and two more, one for Steifan and one for Bastien. We now had two suspects in the crime, the duke, and the Lady Montrant. I was eager to see if Steifan and Bastien had spotted any more to add to the list.

I stood and looked around, remembering the slight warning from the Seeing Sword. While a few ladies watched me curiously, none watched threateningly.

But the threat was another thing to remember. Just because I was around civilized folk, didn't mean I could lower my guard. If anything, it meant I should raise it.

BASTIEN AND STEIFAN found me as I meandered back in the direction of the duke's estate. Bastien's hiding place had indeed been a good one, because I hadn't been able to pick them out from the growing crowd. The three of us walked down a small side street, and I handed each of them a pastry.

Bastien looked at me like I was his new favorite person.

I wiped away my smile, then turned my attention to Steifan. Mustn't get too attached. "Did you notice anyone?"

Steifan tucked a lock of black hair behind his ear, glancing out toward the main street warily. "Everyone was watching you, but most just glanced your way curiously. We did see the servant we met at the duke's estate, but he never looked your way. Perhaps he tried *too* hard to not look your way."

I turned to Bastien, who had devoured his entire pastry in three bites, leaving behind crumbs all around his mouth. "What do you know of him? Have you worked with him for long?"

Bastien wiped frosting from his upper lip, missing half the crumbs. "His name is Vannier, I am not sure of his surname. As far as I know, he has always served the duke. He speaks to me little, except to relay my tasks for the day.

He trained me when I first came into the duke's service, but has always maintained his distance."

I stroked my chin in thought. Vannier might have just been out running the duke's errands, but he also seemed to be one of the only other members of the household. He had likely been present when Charlotte's body showed up, and he was keeping the duke's secrets about it. "Three suspects for our list then. The duke, whose motives are yet unclear. The Lady Montrant, because her former friend borrowed too much coin. And Vannier." I looked down at Bastien. "Was Duchess Auclair a cruel mistress?"

Bastien shrugged. "She was nicer than the duke. She looked down her nose at everyone, but at least she didn't have a temper."

Steifan watched me intently, seeming to absorb every word.

"Questions?" I asked.

"I'm just wondering why you haven't mentioned the vampire. We saw the bite. Do you think it was staged?"

I shook my head. "No, I don't think it was staged. I'm just not sure it's what killed her. Lady Montrant implied that Charlotte spent time with men for coin. I don't think a vampire would be beyond paying for blood if he was trying to remain well hidden within the city. It would explain why he would bite a duchess rather than taking a peasant."

Steifan stared at me wide-eyed. "You mean she willingly let a vampire bite her?"

I shrugged. "If she was desperate enough, it's a possibility. Whatever is going on here is dire enough to have resulted in a murder. We cannot afford to ignore any possibilities." I snapped my mouth shut, realizing I probably shouldn't be saying all of this in front of Bastien. He did, after all, work for the duke. He could be a spy.

I observed his intrigued and somewhat excited expression. I really didn't think he was a spy, he seemed to be having too much fun. But you never knew. I needed to be more careful around him.

Steifan looked back toward the main street again as a well-dressed couple passed by. We had all gone silent, so they didn't notice us.

"What now?" Steifan asked once the couple was out of hearing range.

I looked up at the sun. "We still have a few hours until evening. I want to question some of the common folk in the city before dark. Their lips might be a bit looser about things concerning the Duchess and Duke Auclair." I didn't think we'd be hunting any vampires tonight, but we would still search. I wanted to know as much as possible before we went out into the dark.

I turned to Bastien. "This is where we leave you, for now. Do you think you can meet us again tomorrow? I may want to question more of Charlotte's friends."

He grinned and nodded excitedly. "I can wake up early to take care of any tasks the duke might have for me. I could meet you an hour after dawn."

I nodded. "Meet us in the main market square. We'll be waiting."

With that, he hurried off.

"So you really didn't see anyone else watching with interest?" I asked Steifan.

He shook his head. "No one that stood out, though I had an uneasy feeling, like someone was watching me that I couldn't see."

I once again thought of the warning from my sword, and of the face I had glimpsed when we'd first entered the White Quarter. "Be on your guard, Steifan. I have a feeling we have fallen into something much bigger than the

Potentate could have known. We'll stay at the inn near the market tonight. I don't want to be anywhere near the duke's estate while we sleep."

"Agreed," he said as we started walking. "I'll have nightmares enough about Charlotte's corpse tonight."

I smirked. "Stay with me, and you'll eventually collect enough nightmares to last a lifetime."

His black hair lifted in the breeze as he glanced at me. "You know Lyss, I don't doubt that at all."

"Then you're learning," I said more somberly as we headed toward the gate.

And he would continue to learn. Someday he would kill just as easily as I did, and part of me would mourn that day. My life was not something I would wish upon anyone, let alone a friend.

CHAPTER THIRTY-THREE

We learned little more that evening, except that there were more people missing than just the duchess' ladies. It wasn't uncommon for people to go missing in such a large city, but it did seem an unusual amount. We ended up at the inn where we had rented a room upon our arrival. There had only been one room available, which was well enough, as it saved coin. If Steifan was uncomfortable with the impropriety of the situation, well, he'd just have to deal with it.

We had a meal of smoked trout and honeyed ale, then returned to our room. We would rest a short while, then go out into the night to see if I could sense any vampires.

I unlocked the door and entered first, observing the lone bed, washbasin, and our belongings in the corner. My eyes darted back to the bed, realizing there was a yellow daisy there. Steifan pushed into the room behind me and I lunged toward the bed, snatching the flower and crushing it in my palm behind my back. I whipped around as Steifan shut the door.

Steifan narrowed his eyes at me. "Why are you standing like that?"

I relaxed my shoulders, still hiding the crushed daisy. "I just realized I had wanted to check on the horses one last time before we rested. I'll be right back."

His continued gaze said he didn't believe me, but after a moment, he nodded.

When he turned his back to fetch something from the saddlebags, I hurried out of the room, shutting the door quickly behind me. I looked at the crushed flower in my hand, fueling my budding anger, because I knew exactly who it was from. What right had Asher to follow me here? And to know which room I rented? He'd probably bespelled the innkeep into telling him while Steifan and I had been busy with our evening meal.

I hurried through the hall and down the stairs before Steifan could think to follow me. Once I was outside, I dropped the daisy on the ground, then headed for the stables. If Asher was around, he would find me.

The stable gate was locked for the night, but it was easily vaulted over, and soon I was surrounded by the warmth of horses and the comforting smell of fresh hay. The stables were large enough that I assumed they did not solely belong to the inn, and were likely used by traveling merchants and farmers bringing goods from distant villages. There was a large pasture beyond the sheltered stalls, housing a few more horses who were likely long-term residents.

I passed a pair of massive draft horses, even larger than our warhorses. They stretched their furry snouts toward me, hoping for treats, and making me feel guilty that I hadn't brought any. I stroked their soft fur, then continued on until I reached our horses in their individual stalls.

I ran a hand over my mare's silky neck. The stable hand

had done a fine job with grooming her. I would have to remember to tip him extra coin the next time I saw him— even if he had only shown so much care because we'd frightened him.

I froze as I sensed a presence at my back. I had been too busy enjoying the horses to sense him sooner. Careless of me. I turned to find Asher leaning against a thick wooden post, one of many supporting the roof of the stable. He stood in profile, his face partially obscured by his long white hair draped over his black coat. I could admit that he was lovely to look at, like a painting.

"You should know by now I'm not impressed by dramatic entrances," I chided.

He turned his face toward me and smiled. "Yes, you are impressed by very little." The moonlight hit his face just right, cutting across one gray eye and one high cheekbone.

I crossed my arms and leaned my back against my horse's pen. "Why are you here? We are a long way from the mires."

He pushed away from the post and closed the distance between us. My skin prickled as he neared, my mind flashing through thoughts of our last meeting. "I wanted to ensure you wouldn't get into any more trouble. You seem to attract it from all directions."

I wanted to back up, but I had effectively trapped myself with the pen behind me. My horse nudged my shoulder, reminding me that she was there. I found myself breathless, my cheeks hot. Nothing but a mouse cornered by a vicious cat. "You didn't come all this way just to keep me out of trouble. Why are you really here?"

"Are you truly so displeased to see me?"

I thought of the night in Elizabeth's house. The taste of his blood in my mouth, his lips pressed against mine. His hands running over—

No, I couldn't let my mind go there again. I was still a hunter of the Helius Order. Hunters did not sleep with vampires. "Tell me why you're here," I said through gritted teeth.

If I didn't know any better, I'd say my reaction disappointed him. Maybe I wasn't the only one who couldn't stop thinking about that night. "One of the ancients who maintained the old order was killed recently," he explained. "I had hoped you could help me hunt the culprits. When I searched for you, I could hardly sense you. I didn't expect you to travel so far."

My breath caught at his words. If an ancient had been killed, that meant there were indeed other vampires carrying forth Karpov's plan. I exhaled, then sucked in a sharp breath. "When did it happen?"

"Two nights ago. Quite the coincidence that you were sent to a far off city not long before, if my estimations of your travel time are accurate."

Finally managing to calm myself, I narrowed my eyes. "The Potentate sent me here. There was no way he could have known one of the ancients was to be killed. I imagine you have ruled out the possibility of the kill being claimed by a hunter?"

He nodded slightly, his gaze intent on my face. "I smelled no humans around the corpse, nor did I recognize the scent of the vampires."

"So what does this mean?" I pressed. "How close are we to a vampire war?"

He arched a white brow. "Dear Lyssandra, we are already at war, just a more subtle war than those waged by mortals."

I wasn't bold enough to believe that me being sent away could have anything to do with the ancient's murder. Was I actually thinking of the slaying of a vampire as a murder?

I scowled. "So you are at war then. We knew this was coming. Why travel all the way to Silgard to tell me? There's nothing I can do to help you until I solve the murder here. Even once I return to Castle Helius, I may not want to help you."

He splayed one palm against my horse's pen near my shoulder, leaning forward but not quite touching me. He never seemed to touch me unless I was dying and needed to be saved . . . or when I was crawling into his lap, kissing him. My lips parted at the thought, then I frowned.

Watching my expression, Asher smiled. "For now, we are on the same side. We both want to prevent the slaughter of mortals. So I believe you will help me, if only to achieve your own ends."

I tucked my arms in tightly against my body to keep from being too close to his hand. Physical contact was bad. It made the bond more difficult to control. "You are insufferable."

He ignored my discomfort, but still didn't touch me. "Is that how you truly feel?"

"Yes." And it was the truth. I did find him insufferable. The fact that I couldn't stop watching his mouth only made it worse.

"You spoke of a murder here," he continued like I hadn't spoken. "Perhaps if I help you solve it, you can return to aid me more quickly."

I stiffened. "I don't need your help. You know nothing about being a hunter."

"You are training that other hunter, the one you seem to be *sharing a bed* with tonight. Surely you can tell me enough that I may be of use."

I ignored the subtle insinuation. If he wanted to think something was going on with Steifan, then so be it. It made no difference. I wanted to tell him to go drown in a swamp, then I realized he might actually be useful.

"You have thought of something," he said, watching my expression.

"There is something you could do to help, but you will do it only to help solve a murder, because it is the right thing to do. Not as a favor where I will owe you something in return."

He leaned a little closer and lowered his voice. "Name it, and it will be done."

His words shivered down to my core like a lover's caress. I rolled my eyes to hide my discomfort, ignoring his cool breath on my skin. "I would like to find the murdered woman's journal, but my worry is that if her husband finds it first, he will burn it, if he hasn't burned it already. If he has, search her room for anything suspicious."

His brows raised as he leaned back. "You would like me to break into a mortal's home?"

I nodded. "It's one of the large estates up the hill. You should be able to follow the smell of rotting corpse. I imagine her body will not be burned until tomorrow."

He smiled tightlipped, hiding his fangs. "Very well, I will fetch it shortly. Where will you meet me once the task is done?"

"Steifan and I will be out searching the city for vampires. I imagine you'll be able to find me."

His palm still braced beside me, he leaned forward again. "There are many vampires within the city, Lyssandra. Be careful what you dig up."

"Would a vampire ever pay a mortal woman for blood?" I asked abruptly.

My question seemed to catch him off guard. He took a moment to think about it. "Perhaps, if one was in jeopardy of being discovered, and did not want to flee their territory."

"Have you ever paid for blood?" I regretted the question as soon as I asked it.

The edges of his mouth ticked up. "Dear Lyssandra, I would never pay for something I can easily get for free."

With that, he was gone, leaving me alone with my thoughts and my blood coursing loudly through my veins. I had hoped with some distance the bond would lessen, but it seemed as strong as ever. I would have to find some other way to deal with it, because I couldn't continue on like I was, especially not if he was staying in Silgard. I had a feeling if I spent much more time around him, I would be ripping his clothes off whether I liked it or not. And *that* was unacceptable. Something I could never let happen.

I shook my head at my thoughts, then noticed something caught in my hair near my ear. I pulled it free, then looked at the yellow daisy in my hand.

Utterly insufferable vampire.

I dropped the daisy at my feet, patted my horse's cheek, then left to find Steifan. I didn't know how long it would be until Asher returned with the journal, so I'd just have to drum up trouble as quickly as I could.

CHAPTER THIRTY-FOUR

A few hours later, Steifan and I walked down the quiet nighttime street. I had relented and told him about my meeting with Asher. Better to explain it while we were alone, rather than explaining it once Asher showed up with the journal. *If* he showed up with the journal. It might already be gone, leaving us no other clues.

"I can't believe he followed you all the way here," Steifan said, breaking the silence as we meandered down an alleyway. I had sensed vampires a few times, but we were yet to come close enough to seek them out.

If it weren't for the deaths weighing heavily on my mind, it might have actually been a pleasant stroll. "He didn't follow me," I snapped. "He only sought me out after the ancient was killed."

"Yes, because a young huntress will surely be able to figure out a vampire murder. He probably just wanted an excuse to see why you were in the city."

"We were apart for years. I see no reason for him to care what I do now. Nothing has changed."

Steifan grinned, knowing all too well that things

weren't exactly the same as they were before. "And yet, he is here, stealing a journal for you."

"Only because he wants my help." I held out my hand, sensing a familiar vampire coming near, and I wished Steifan had not chosen now to start this conversation. Asher had probably heard every word.

I truly did not wish to know if any of Steifan's implications were correct. I waited, keeping one hand on his arm.

Steifan slowly reached for his sword, not understanding my silent warning.

I turned and looked back the way we'd come. Asher now stood roughly twenty paces away, having approached us as silent as only the dead can manage.

Steifan visibly relaxed, which was unnerving. One should never relax around a vampire.

"Did you find it?" I asked as Asher moved near us at human speed.

He produced a small, leather-bound journal from within his coat pocket.

My heart skipped a beat. Could it possibly be this easy? Would we find the answers to Charlotte's murder tonight?

Asher reached us, but did not offer the journal.

"Was it difficult to find?" I asked.

"No, the husband had already found it. He was preparing to burn it when I arrived."

"Did you kill him?" Steifan blurted.

Asher glared, and Steifan stepped back. I found myself glad to not be on the other end of that silver glare.

The vampire turned back to me. "I was forced to bespell the man. I tried to question him, but his mind proved surprisingly strong. I hope this will hold the answers you seek." He lifted the journal in his hand.

I reached for it, but he pulled it away.

"Give it to me," I demanded.

"Promise me that after this murder is solved, you will help me discover who killed the ancient."

I lowered my hand. There was no use trying to snatch anything from a vampire. "I can make no such promises. I follow the Potentate's orders, and he may have another mission for me."

He dangled the journal just out of reach above my head. "I don't think you follow anyone's orders, Lyssandra."

I put my hands on my hips, refusing to jump for the journal like a fool. "You know, people keep saying that to me."

"Promise me," he repeated, "and the journal is yours."

I frowned. I didn't like promising him anything, but I was already planning on looking into the murder. How could I not? "Fine," I hissed. "I promise."

He extended the journal to me, and I snatched it away, clutching it against my chest. "I would thank you, but I don't want to, so for tonight, we are done. Where will I find you when I am ready to look into your murder?"

He looked up at the stars visible between the roofs on either side of the alley. "I believe I will spend some time in the city. I see no reason to waste such a long journey." He turned and strolled back down the alley.

Steifan moved to my side as I watched Asher fade into the darkness. "Yeah, he definitely came here just to see you."

"You don't know what you're talking about."

He snorted. "You know, when the two of you are together, it's like I don't even exist. Neither of you seem able to tear your eyes away from each other."

I wrinkled my nose. "Shut up, Steifan."

His laughter followed me as I retreated down the alley, making my way back toward the inn. As annoyed as I was, I was also excited to read the journal. When you needed to solve a murder, the mind of the victim was usually the best place to start.

I SAT on the wooden floorboards of our inn room, a flickering lantern near my curled up knee. On my other side sat Steifan, leaning over to peer at the journal in my lap. No, not a journal, a ledger. In rows were scrawled names, locations, and numerical amounts. Unfortunately, most of the names and locations were abbreviated, but at least the dates at the start of each new page were clear. We had taken off our armor to sit more comfortably, and had flipped through every page.

The ledger went back months, the final day taking place two weeks ago.

"Do you think this is a record of her," Steifan hesitated, "*trade contacts?*"

I smirked. "That's a pleasant way of putting it, but we don't even know if that rumor is true. What we do know is that this ledger was filled out nearly to the day she died." I pulled my braid from being trapped between my back and the edge of the bed we leaned against. "And her husband didn't want us to have it."

"How do you know which day she died? I assumed it was not as the duke claimed judging by the smell . . . "

I smiled, glad he'd noticed. "I know mostly from the smell, and the fact that she was moved. Lady Montrant claims she ended her friendship with Charlotte two weeks ago. That is about as long as it would take for a body to reach that stage of decomposition if it was left in a place warmer than the duke's estate."

"Why do you think the duke is lying about her death?" he asked.

I shrugged, still looking down at the abbreviated names in the ledger. "Who can say? I think he saw the bites on her neck and figured calling us here would be a good way to cover up what really happened. We would see the bites, hunt down the vampire, and the murder would be solved."

"So he didn't count on us actually having brains," Steifan said caustically.

I laughed. "It is not an uncommon assumption. We are warriors, not scholars."

Grinning, he gestured down to the ledger. "So what do we do with this?"

I lifted the book and flipped to the final filled-out page. "Just two names on this page. If she made these meetings, they might have been the last two people to see her alive. Tomorrow, we try to find them."

Steifan read the page. "Well I'm not sure how we will locate S.D., but I recognize the second name, J. DeRose. At least I recognize the surname."

I tilted my head. "Odd, that she would mention a surname when most other names are abbreviated. Do you know any DeRoses in Silgard?"

He cringed. "The DeRose family probably has around one hundred living members, fifty or so of which dwell in the city. Ignoring the children, maybe twenty-five."

"And how many with the first initial J?" I asked.

"I could not say, but I imagine Bastien will know. The DeRoses are a prominent family."

I gave the ledger one last look, then shut it. "So tomorrow we will search for J. DeRose. We should get some rest now while we can."

He lifted a brow. "No more hunting vampires? I assumed you would want to go back out."

I stood. "Asher claims there are many vampires within the city. We may find one or two, but the chances of finding the one who bit Charlotte are slim. Now that the ledger has provided us with more to go on, I would rather rest, then pursue more likely angles tomorrow."

Still seated leaning against the bed, Steifan looked up at me. "Do you think Asher could figure out which vampire bit her?"

I tossed the ledger on the foot of the bed, then retrieved the sheathed Seeing Sword where I had left it on the ground beside me. "Even if he could, I would not ask him."

"But you asked him to steal the ledger."

I leaned the sword against the head of the bed, where I could easily reach it if we were awakened. "He wouldn't be able to find the vampire," I sighed. "A bite on a dead woman is not much to go on. Normally when a body turns up, we can hunt the area and find the vampire's flock. But there are no territory lines here. We cannot pin a death to a certain flock just judging by the location. And like I said, I'm not sure the bite is what killed her."

He stood and straightened his shirt. "But if Asher could help, you would ask him?"

I narrowed my eyes. "I asked him tonight, did I not? His presence may vex me, but I would not put that above solving this murder."

He held up his hands in surrender. "My apologies, I did not mean to imply as such."

"And you will do well to not trust him either," I forged on. "I may be his human servant, but to him, you are just food. Do not let down your guard around him, nor any vampire."

Steifan fetched the lantern from the ground, then moved around the bed to set it on the windowsill. "Believe as you like, but I'm quite sure he won't harm me, because I am important to you."

I flopped down on the bed, nestling the back of my

head against a pillow. "Every part of that sentence is irritating to me."

He walked to his side of the bed and plopped down beside me. "Are you more irritated that I am important to you, or that Asher so obviously cares?"

There was no way I was answering either of those questions. "Remember when I told you to be careful around Asher?" I asked evenly.

"Yes, that was only moments ago."

I smiled sourly up at the ceiling. "Well you should be even more careful around *me*. I'm just as likely to tear your heart out."

He laughed, then got up to extinguish the lantern.

I shook my head, smiling in the sudden darkness. Steifan really believed I wouldn't tear out his heart. Maybe I was going soft.

CHAPTER THIRTY-FIVE

As promised, Bastien met us in the square an hour after dawn. I almost didn't recognize him without the duke's showy livery. He looked like any other merchant's son running across the Square.

I said as much as he approached where we stood just outside the inn.

Looking down at his boots, he tugged the hem of his tan tunic. "I reckoned you'd not like me drawing any extra stares," he panted. He had probably run the entire way to the square.

I realized I'd embarrassed him, and it really was smart for him to dress in less conspicuous clothing. His tunic and breeches, while well-made, were unremarkable. He did not stand out in the markets, nor would he be noticeable amongst peasants. He would obviously still be recognized in the White Quarter, but there, it would not matter as much. There everyone already knew what we were looking for.

"You did good," I said. I glanced at Steifan, wondering where to begin.

We'd both had similar thoughts to Bastien on our clothing. I wore a midnight blue silk shirt and black leggings, and Steifan wore clothing nearly the twin of Bastien's. While we were supposed to wear our armor with its insignia at all times on a mission, we were far from Castle Helius, and we might gain more answers if people didn't realize we were hunters.

Our swords and extra weaponry might still stand out, but most would think us mercenaries.

I turned back to Bastien. "How much time can you spare us today?"

He grinned. "I have the rest of the day off. Vannier requested I do whatever it takes to help you find the monster who killed Duchess Auclair."

My eyebrows shot up. Odd, that it was the servant pushing for justice rather than the husband.

I glanced around the market, making sure no one paid us too much attention as I wondered how to broach the subject of J. DeRose with Bastien. By now the duke would have realized the ledger was missing, unless he simply woke up thinking he'd already burned it. Regardless, it was better to exercise caution and not let Bastien know we had the ledger.

Seeming to realize my predicament, Steifan looked around me at Bastien. "For our first task, can you guide us to the DeRoses? My father requested we pay several notable families a visit, and I'm not sure where this particular family dwells."

Bastien's expression fell. "I fear the DeRoses have gone out of favor. They fell victim to criminal activities and went destitute."

Steifan and I locked gazes for a moment. Why would Charlotte be meeting with a family that had fallen out of favor?

"Is there a particular member of the family you were tasked to approach?" Bastien asked hopefully.

Steifan's bashful expression was almost believable. "My father only gave me a list, and did not fully explain the names. At the top of the list was J. DeRose."

Bastien nodded, easily accepting the explanation. "That would be Jeramy DeRose. I know the general area of where he now lives," he paused, his eyes darting to me. "It is not an area for a proper lady to be seen."

Steifan snorted, earning him a deathly glare. I turned back to Bastien before I could ensure I had wiped the grin off Steifan's face. "I will be fine. Can you take us there?"

Bastien glanced at the Seeing Sword. "Yes, I do suppose you can take care of yourself. This way."

We followed as he cut across the square, opposite the direction of the stables. Eventually, the din of the city faded at our backs. He led us down a narrow dirt street bisecting small wooden homes, modest, but well-kept. Occasionally we heard voices from within the homes, most seeming to belong to mothers and children, though sometimes a man's voice was thrown in. These were probably the families of smiths, tailors, tavern workers, and the like. Farmers and peasants would live outside the city walls.

We followed the interior curve of those walls now, as the homes slowly fell to disrepair. Many windows had broken glass, while some had never had glass to begin with. Eventually, the homes were little more than shacks, the planks oddly spaced enough to barely keep out the elements. Thatched roofs were mostly rotted, with some gone entirely, showing the wooden supports beneath.

There were more people out in the street here, some sleeping in the open beneath ragged piles of bedding. Two dirty, but healthy-looking young men watched us closely as we passed. I didn't miss the way their eyes lingered on mine and Steifan's weapons, probably wondering if they could take them from us. It was a much different atmosphere from the main square, and not one I was accustomed to. The smaller villages took care of their own. There was no place for something like this, where people were . . . forgotten. That Jeramy had ended up here let me know he had fallen quite far indeed. I wondered if Charlotte had walked these streets alone to meet him, or if they had gone somewhere else.

Bastien stuck close to my shoulder as we continued on. "We will need to ask someone. I don't know exactly where Jeramy ended up."

My nose wrinkled at a familiar odor amidst the bouquet of unwashed bodies and excrement. "Perhaps, but let's check this way first."

I veered right after passing a vacant home, with Bastien and Steifan close behind. The smell grew worse. I was getting a bad feeling.

Just as I thought it, the Seeing Sword thrummed at my back.

I increased my pace.

Realizing something was wrong, Steifan jogged to keep up at my side, but didn't ask questions.

We came to a small cul-de-sac of homes. A young mother watched us from across the way, her children playing in the dirt at her feet. Her eyes lifted to a house directly across from hers, which seemed to be the one harboring the horrid stench.

Bastien and Steifan each lifted a sleeve to cover their noses, so it must have been strong enough now for them to smell it too.

"I really don't like the smell of this," Steifan groaned.

"It might have nothing to do with J. DeRose," I said, already walking toward the home. The young mother had gathered her children and retreated through her door.

I reached the odor harboring door with the Seeing Sword thrumming steadily at my back. I listened for a moment, then braced my right leg, flicking out the other to kick the door in.

It flew back with a loud *thwack*, then fell partially off its hinges. The smell was overwhelming. I covered my nose and mouth with my sleeve and walked inside.

A man lay sprawled in the middle of the floor, his body ripe with the hot sunlight streaming in through the damaged roof. Rusty brown stains had soaked into the hard-packed dirt floor. The straw mat and few belongings within the home had been tossed about, some things torn to shreds.

I sensed Steifan and Bastien at my back as I knelt near the putrid corpse. It was difficult to tell with the mottled skin, but it seemed like he had been badly beaten before being killed. I picked up a fallen quill to move light brown hair away from his neck. No vampire bites, though that didn't mean they weren't elsewhere on his body.

"I think that's Jeramy," Bastien croaked behind me.

I turned to see him staring wide-eyed at the corpse. His skin had gone so pale, his freckles stood out like ink stains.

"Are you sure?" I asked.

Bastien's body convulsed like he might vomit. He clamped a hand over his mouth and nodded.

"Wait for us outside," I instructed. "Do not go far. Yell if anyone bothers you."

He rushed back outside, and a moment later I could hear him retching.

I looked at Steifan. "What do you think?" I asked it like I already knew what he should think, but in truth I hadn't a clue.

While he looked a little green, Steifan maintained his composure. "I think that our only lead is dead, though I cannot tell the cause of death."

I stood and took a step away from the corpse. "The patterns on his flesh would suggest strangling after a long period of physical violence. Yet the stains on the floor suggest a large amount of blood was spilled here."

Steifan observed the darker stains on the dirt floor. "Do you think . . . Charlotte?"

I looked back down at the corpse, willing it to tell me its secrets. "Perhaps. Her neck wound wouldn't have been enough for so much blood, and that would mean a vampire didn't drink it. We should have checked the back of her body for other wounds." I shook my head, feeling like the idiot that I was. "I don't go into situations considering that mortals would actually fake a vampire kill. Perhaps I should start. Our carelessness has deprived us of answers."

"But if she was here . . . "

I nodded. "If she was killed here, she was moved. The question is, by whom? Either her husband is complicit, or she was moved into their estate right under his nose."

"But how do we figure out which it is?"

It was a good question, and not one easily answered. "We start by figuring out why she was meeting with Jeramy. If she really did come all the way out here, she was desperate to keep the meeting secret."

Bastien's raised voice caught my ear, interrupting my thoughts. "It would be unwise of you to quarrel with my associates!"

I was rushing outside before I could even think about it. Once I saw the four men surrounding Bastien, and they saw me, the Seeing Sword echoed a warning. As if I couldn't already tell that these criminals meant us harm. They were ragged and dirty, but fit, none of them too old.

Even if they didn't know how to use their weapons, two of them looked strong enough to easily break Bastien's neck.

Then I realized how careless I'd been. The sword had warned me while we were walking. These thugs had been watching us from the start.

Steifan guarded my back in case we were being surrounded, both of us yet to draw our swords.

Our would-be assailants took measure of us. They hardly merited the same in return, but the one with a crudely made blade was too close to Bastien. He could slit Bastien's throat before we could reach him.

I took a few slow steps toward the group, and the men did not react. *Good.* If I could get close enough, I could eliminate the threat before Bastien could be harmed.

"We probably don't want to kill them," Steifan whispered behind me.

"I'm not an idiot," I hissed, then more loudly asked, "What do you want?"

The man with the blade spun it like he knew how to use it. "Your swords, and perhaps a taste of your lovely flesh, witch."

Bastien seemed frozen beside him, unsure of what to do. Two of the other men had swords riding their shoulders. Muscles corded down their tanned arms, with white scars standing in stark relief. The older of the pair had a wicked scar across one eye.

I took another step closer. "Well you can't have my sword, and my flesh is out of the question, so I might just take a slice of yours instead."

The man closest to Bastien laughed. "Come and get it, witch."

I drew the Seeing Sword, but Steifan was right. We needed to avoid killing them. Wouldn't do to have word spread that hunters were killing innocent people, because that's exactly what witnesses would say if they figured out what we were.

The men eyed my sword hungrily. I heard Steifan's sword hiss from its sheath.

With all eyes on our swords, I swiftly moved one hand from my hilt and drew a dagger from my belt, sending it sailing toward the man near Bastien.

It sliced across his arm, as intended, missing anything vital. But his momentary surprise gave me the time I needed to lunge forward and shove Bastien out of the way. As Bastien hit the dirt, I turned, lifting my sword to parry a strike from the scar-faced swordsman. I spun my sword in a small circle, catching his blade and tossing it aside.

He looked at me in shock, like he'd never had someone disarm him before, and maybe he hadn't. He preyed on the weak. I would have loved to kill him.

He saw his own death in my eyes, and slowly backed away, hands raised.

Steifan had disarmed the other swordsman, and the man who had originally threatened Bastien clutched his bleeding arm, his blade nowhere to be seen. The fourth man, who had never shown a weapon, was backing away, on the edge of fleeing and leaving his partners behind.

With the situation fully assessed, I whipped my blade back toward the scar-faced swordsman, aiming the tip at his throat.

He lifted his hands again. "You win, no amount of coin is worth this."

I edged my blade's tip a little closer to his throat. My sword was quiet. He meant what he said, yet his words confused me. "What do you mean? What coin?"

His voice came out strained. "A stranger approached me with a lot of coin. Said to gather some of my boys and keep an eye out for a red-haired witch."

I pressed my sword against his flesh. "Did the stranger tell you to kill me?"

He gulped, drawing a pinprick of blood on his throat. "Yes, and anyone with you. But it's not worth the coin to me anymore, I swear it."

"What did the stranger look like?"

He shook his head minutely. "Don't know. It was dark, he wore a hood. He gave me half the coin upfront and said he would find me with the rest once you were dead."

I smiled wickedly, debating killing him regardless of the consequences. Anyone who would take coin to kill an innocent stranger deserved to die.

"Please don't kill me," he rasped.

"Lyss," Steifan's voice was low with warning.

I lowered my blade, my attention still on the man before me. "You will leave the city, and you will never look back. If I ever catch a glimpse of you again, you will become the hunted. For I am of the Helius Order. Hunting is what I do best."

His bulging eyes and gaping jaw told me the stranger had not informed him we were hunters. Now that he knew, he would not be bothering us again. But still, if I ever saw him outside of the city, somewhere private, I would finish what I had started. Because I knew he would go on to harm someone else. I usually shied away from killing humans, but for this man, I'd make an exception.

He took two steps back, then turned and ran, leaving his sword in the dirt.

Steifan brandished his blade at the other three men, and they all turned tail and scurried away, leaving us in a faint cloud of dust.

Once we were alone, Bastien brushed himself off and ran toward me. "That was amazing! You saved my life!"

"No," I said, my gaze on Jeramy's broken door, "I nearly

got you killed. I want you to go back to the duke's estate. Do not approach us again."

"But—"

"Go!" I shouted.

Bastien aimed the full weight of his hurt expression at me for a heartbeat, then turned and ran away.

Steifan moved to my side, watching him go as the dust began to settle. "You didn't have to be so harsh."

I sheathed my sword, then picked up my dagger from the dirt. "There have been two murders, and someone wants them to go unsolved enough to hire mercenaries to kill us. They could have killed Bastien before we even stepped outside. If anything, I was not harsh enough. He needs to stay away."

He glanced back toward Jeramy's door. "I suppose you're right."

I turned away from him, not wanting him to see my pained expression. I *was* right. If I had refused to go to Elizabeth's home, if I had spent less time with her, Karpov would not have caught my scent on her. He wouldn't have targeted her as someone to use against me, just as Bastien had just been targeted. I could not make friends. I would only be signing their death warrants.

Steifan sighed at my back and sheathed his sword. I jumped at the dull sound of steel sliding within leather.

"What do we do now?" he asked to my back.

I steadied my breathing. If I could not be a friend, I would be a blade. "We find anyone involved in Charlotte's murder, and we cut off their heads." I started walking. If I wasn't on a warpath before, I most certainly was now.

CHAPTER THIRTY-SIX

We headed back toward the inn in silence. I wanted to make sure our few belongings and horses were safe before venturing back toward the White Quarter. If someone had been hired to kill us, someone else might have been hired to make off with our horses and goods to cover up our disappearance.

The Seeing Sword was steadily making my spine itch with its energy as we walked, but it was hard to tell who was pondering attacking me. Many eyes watched us from within hovels and out on the street. Word of our altercation had spread quickly.

I took another step, then nearly stumbled as a strange sensation passed over me, like walking through quicksand. I tried to continue on, but my feet slowed until each step was a battle of wills against my own body.

I tried to speak to Steifan, but my mouth wouldn't work. He continued walking, not noticing as he left me further and further behind.

I could no longer lift my feet. I couldn't even move my

arms. The eyes on either side of the street followed Steifan, none looking my way, like I was suddenly invisible.

Panic tickled my throat. I felt oddly *not real*, and it was a sensation I recognized. It was broad daylight, so it wasn't vampire mind tricks. It was glamour. Glamour so strong it made my mind believe I couldn't move. It made everyone around me believe I wasn't there. Even though I knew it was happening, I couldn't fight it.

I wasn't surprised when I heard the Nattmara's voice behind me. "Hello hunter, I did not expect to see you this far from Castle Helius."

I turned to face Egar, the male Nattmara who'd escaped us in Charmant. He was casting a glamour powered by his Sidhe blood, which was why no one in the streets could see us. He looked the same as I remembered. Black hair, dark eyes, a face that still held the plumpness of youth.

Now that Steifan was out of sight, the people who had been watching us retreated to their homes. I wondered if they had seen an illusion of me departing with him, and when he would notice that I wasn't really there.

Egar freed my mouth enough for me to speak. "I saw you yesterday, didn't I?" I asked. "I saw you beyond a fence in a garden."

The face I had seen was clear to me now. Me not recognizing him had been no illusion. I simply hadn't wanted to believe it was him.

Egar inclined his clean-shaven chin. He looked young and harmless, friendly even, though I knew he was anything but. He stood too close, but I could not step away. "I smelled a corpse among those fancy estates. I wanted to collect it, but you beat me there."

I nearly gagged at the thought of Egar eating Charlotte's rotted corpse. "I thought Nattmara preferred fresh victims."

He licked his lips. "Yes, but any will do. All I need is flesh and blood to sustain me. I like to get to know my environment before I hunt, and I only just arrived here yesterday."

I considered the possibility of Egar being Charlotte's killer, and perhaps seeking her corpse to finish feeding, but it didn't add up. If he'd had her and maybe even Jeramy freshly dead, we would have found little more than bones and globs of flesh.

"What do you want from me, Egar? You know now that I've found you, I will have to kill you."

He laughed, a young, charming sound that fit his exterior. The worst of monsters were usually just dark on the inside. "You are trying to solve a murder. I could tell you what you're missing."

He was standing so close he could reach out and strangle me, and I would be powerless to stop him. Every muscle in my body strained to move, but it was hopeless. "You claim to have just arrived yesterday. What could you possibly know?"

His satisfied grin told me he hadn't just arrived, and he had lied about what he'd been doing among the wealthy estates. "I know a lot of things, hunter. I know that there is powerful blood within the city, far more delicious than yours. Help me find it, and I will help you solve your murder."

"You know I would not sacrifice another human to you. Now free me from this glamour. I have much to do."

He tilted his head. "I thought you wanted to kill me. Now you simply want to escape?"

I sucked my teeth. That, and moving my mouth was all I could manage. I was lucky he was allowing air into my lungs. I *did* want to kill him, he deserved to die, but I knew I wasn't capable. I wanted to draw my sword, but my arms didn't budge. If he wanted to kill me right then, he could just cloud my mind, and I'd be dead before I realized what was happening.

He watched the thoughts play across my face, his intelligent eyes noting every small facet of my expression. "I see you understand. My sister was powerful, but she inherited mostly my mother's blood. I have the glamour of the Sidhe, and no mortal can stand against it. I believe you will be drawn to the powerful blood in this city like a moth to the flame, or else it will be drawn to you." He stepped closer. "I will be watching you, hunter. You will lead me to what I want, and if you don't, I'll take you instead. You should have let me help you solve your murder while you had the chance."

Reality seemed to shift, sending me reeling backward. When I righted myself, I was alone in the street.

"Lyss!" Steifan shouted.

I turned to see him running toward me.

He grabbed my arms as he reached me. "Where did you go? I was nearly back to the inn when I realized you weren't beside me."

I took a moment to catch my breath. "The Nattmara was here," I panted. I shook my head. What were the chances that I would run into that creature again so soon? "It is hunting something here."

Steifan let me go. "Egar? Egar is here?"

"Yes." I felt badly shaken. I had faced powerful beings, but not like Egar. How could you kill something that could warp your mind so completely? The death of Egar's father, the one who had kept him contained, was going to be the death of us all.

Steifan looked me over, slowly shaking his head. "I've never seen you like this, Lyss."

"Like what?" I asked distantly.

"Scared."

A few people had come out into the street to watch us. Despite the sun shining overhead, my skin felt cold. "Let's get out of here. We need a pint of ale and a new plan. We must figure out how to kill the Nattmara."

As we started walking, I noticed Steifan glancing around warily, as if he expected the Nattmara to still be watching us. Maybe he was, but as long as I wasn't under the creature's glamour, the Seeing Sword should warn me. In fact, Egar was probably the reason the sword had whispered a few warnings while we were in the wealthy district. And maybe even the reason Steifan thought he felt eyes on him.

"How can we kill it, Lyss?" Steifan asked, breaking the drawn out silence.

"I don't know. Most of what is known about Nattmara is little more than myth. We are probably some of the only people alive today to have faced one."

Steifan was quiet for a moment, but I could tell he had something to say.

I kept my attention trained on the street around us as we neared the nicer homes leading back to the market square. "What is it?"

"Asher is an ancient. He might know something about Nattmara. He might even be able to kill it. Does glamour work on vampires?"

I sighed. Now that the shock had worn off, I was getting angry. We were here to solve a murder—two murders now—I did *not* need the issue of the Nattmara added to the list. "I don't know. I don't know anything anymore, but the Nattmara is not the only thing in the city that wants our blood. We must move forward with caution."

"Should we leave the inn?"

It wasn't a bad idea. Surely once the mysterious stranger realized we were still alive, someone else would be hired. We might be attacked in a more public place where we would be forced to kill someone. "I don't know where we would go." I stopped walking and turned toward him. We were nearly at the square. "Do you have any connections you could use? Find us a place to stay, and a place to stable the horses?"

His hazel eyes danced with worry. "I might be able to find us somewhere, but we would be endangering any who would take us in."

He was right. We could not ask innocent people to harbor us. "We'll have to find somewhere on our own. There are plenty of warehouses in the city. If you could find someone to stable our horses, that should be safe enough. We will move them in the night. I will ensure no one sees us."

"Consider it done."

We were drawing a few eyes, so we continued walking. I didn't like feeling so vulnerable, far away from Castle Helius and other hunters. I knew Steifan would watch my back, but it might not be enough. I might just have to take his suggestion and ask a certain vampire for help.

Did glamour work on vampires? We would soon find out.

CHAPTER THIRTY-SEVEN

By nightfall, Steifan had found a place to stable our horses with our few extra belongings, and I had learned some interesting information. Talk of the tavern was that there was a witch practicing within the city. Real witches were extremely rare, so she probably wasn't genuine . . . but if she was real, she might know how to break Egar's glamour.

It was worth investigating, mostly because we didn't have any other options. Maybe she would even have insight on the missing people. Of course, she could also be the murderer. According to the histories, the most powerful spells often required sacrifices, the closer to human, the better. Even if she wasn't a witch, she might be a different malevolent being. Another problem added to our list.

As the city went still for the night, we moved our horses and our belongings, depending on the Seeing Sword to alert us if any of our enemies saw our movements. Once everything was stashed away, Steifan and I walked north, passing the wrought-iron gates to the wealthy estates without stopping. We had provided enough pints of ale to learn that the witch could be found in the old part of the city where the former keep once stood, long abandoned since a new keep had been erected within the White Quarter.

The road we walked wound ever upward toward the apex of the hill upon which the city was built. We left the light of torches and lamps behind for the more subtle glow of occasional candles in windows and a few distant fires. These darker streets were the perfect haunt for pickpockets, yet somehow I felt safer in the darkness. More hidden and at peace.

The old wall came into view, casting deeper shadows in the darkness. Parts of the wall had been toppled during the siege that had taken place well before the borders of the Ebon Province had been drawn.

There were fewer people in this part of the city, but we still caught occasional glances from beyond open shutters, evidenced only by a shadow darting away as soon as it caught our attention. A young couple hurried down the road toward us, giving us a wary glance as they passed by. Judging by their clothing, they were rushing back to a rich estate, and judging by their pace, they were fearful of being robbed now that darkness had fallen. I briefly wondered what they were doing in this part of the city to begin with, then cast the thought aside as we neared the old keep and the small nomadic civilization that had sprung up around it.

My eyes searched across flickering lanterns and small fires. Clusters of people shared pots of soup and loaves of bread while sitting near covered wagons and stacks of crates.

"This must be where traveling merchants and caravans come to stay," I said to Steifan as we stopped walking.

"And other sorts," he added, eyeing a pair leaning against a nearby wall in dark cloaks, their faces lost in shadow. They had no visible weapons, but instinct alone told me they were not to be trifled with.

We kept walking, observing the small camps while keeping our ears open for mention of the witch.

A young woman hurried out of the gaping doorway of an ancient stone home. She clutched a wrapped bundle against her chest, her eyes shifting around nervously. Scented smoke wafted from within the home, which glowed with flickering firelight.

I stopped across the street from the home as the nervous young woman scurried off into the night. "Something tells me we've found what we're looking for."

An old merchant sitting near a fire to our right looked up at us, the firelight emphasizing the deep lines etched into his face. "If you're searching for the witch, you have found the place. But be wary. Those dwelling in these parts are protective of her."

I nodded my thanks. "I assure you, we mean her no harm."

A little thrill of excitement trickled up my spine. If these people would protect her, maybe she was a real witch, and a helpful one at that. Just as witches could curse and maim, they could also heal. This might very well be the only chance Steifan and I would have to meet one. If she could help us with the Nattmara, then all the better.

I led the way across the street and looked into the open doorway.

The woman sitting cross-legged in front of the fire was already looking up at me. Her dark eyes, like flecks of onyx set into a pale face, matched her long black hair. She appeared young, I would guess around twenty, and wore a long white dress that looked almost like a night shift.

She watched me warily. "I sensed someone coming, but I did not expect a hunter. Why are you here?"

I stepped through the doorway, making room for Steifan. The feel of magic made me catch my breath. Her dwelling was strongly warded, and I knew instantly I had only stepped inside because she let me.

I swallowed the lump in my throat, wondering why in the light I had been *excited* to meet a witch. "How could you tell I was a hunter?" We had intentionally left our armor with our horses, not wanting the witch to believe we had come to kill her.

She seemed small huddled behind her fire, the yellow light giving her an ethereal look. "I can sense what you are, just as much as I can sense what he is not." She bobbed her chin toward Steifan.

Did that mean she could sense that I was a vampire's human servant? I didn't have the nerve to ask. "Are you really a witch?"

She bared her teeth. "Some say I am. What is it to you?"

It seemed I had angered her. *Wonderful.* A witch cursing me on top of everything else was all I needed. "We are here to ask for your help. Something hunts us, and we do not know how to defeat it."

She stood, and she was just as small standing up as I had imagined. "The hunters are the hunted? How poetic."

I was getting the feeling that she wasn't fond of hunters. If she was a real witch, I couldn't blame her. While we had stopped hunting witches decades ago, there was a time when we killed them as indiscriminately as vampires.

I glanced at Steifan, who shrugged. He wasn't quite sure what to make of this woman either. Staying any longer was a risk, but . . .

"Look," I said, stepping toward the fire, "I have never

harmed a witch, in fact I have never met one. Any quarrel we might have is between our ancestors, not us."

She stepped up opposite me on the other side of the fire, so that we mirrored each other over the flames, though I stood a full head taller. "Does our ancestors' blood not run through our veins? Have hunters ever paid us reparations?"

She had me there. Hunters did not apologize to their prey. We never had. "If you cannot help us, we will leave you in peace." I stepped back. If she wouldn't help us, I'd rather not make her angry. There was no telling how powerful she might be.

Her brows lifted. "You will truly leave? You will not threaten me into helping you?"

I hesitated. "Forced allies are no true allies at all."

She smiled at my words, and it lit her entire face. She was suddenly a different woman. Someone kind. Someone you would want to share stories around a fire with. "A hunter willing to back down, how refreshing. What is your name?"

I watched her cautiously, wondering if my fear of her had been an illusion. "Lyssandra."

"I am Ryllae. What is it you would like help with?"

Her sudden change in mood had me grasping for words. Finally, I managed to ask, "You were testing me, weren't you?"

"Can you blame me?"

I shrugged, glancing at Steifan. "I suppose one cannot be too careful. Does this mean you'll answer my questions now?"

"It means we will trade information. You have many secrets, Lyssandra."

"Lyss," Steifan interrupted. "Some secrets might not be worth sharing."

He was right. She had already implied that I was different from Steifan. If she wanted to know what I was, I would be a fool to tell her. If she sold me out to the wrong person, it could get me killed.

Of course, it wouldn't matter much if Egar killed me first. I recalled the sensation of him clouding my mind, how helpless I was standing before him, and my decision was made.

I stared into Ryllae's dark eyes across the fire. "Fine, if you tell me what I need to know, I will share whatever secret you wish, but *only* if you have the answers I seek."

She inclined her head, draping long hair across her shoulder. "A fair trade. Now ask your question."

I glanced at Steifan again, buying time. If I was only going to get one question, I needed to make it count. And when it came to Egar, only one question really mattered. I turned my attention back to Ryllae. "Do you know anything of glamour? How to break it?"

"You are hoping to slay the Nattmara," she observed.

"You know of it?" Steifan asked, stepping up beside me.

She crossed her arms and shivered, though the fire in the small space had me sweating. "It hunts me too. It has not managed to find me yet, but I fear it will eventually."

Could she be the powerful blood the Nattmara had mentioned? It would make sense. "You're afraid of it," I observed.

"I have been hiding since it arrived in the city, watching it when I can. It seeks me tirelessly."

"You were not so difficult to find, you do realize that?"

She smiled. "You found me because I wished you to find me. I knew it was a risk, but I needed to see if you could be trusted."

"And can I?"

"You were prepared to leave me when I would not

cooperate," she explained. "That alone lets me know I can trust you. You are not working with the creature. Anyone working with that thing would have tried to force answers from me."

"Do you know how to break his glamour?"

Her arms still wrapped tightly around her, she raised dark brows. "If I knew, do you believe you could kill it?"

"I slew the creature's sister in a small village in the North. She had hoped to feast on my blood."

She finally lowered her arms, her surprise clear. "Did the sister not share in his glamour?"

"Their father was part Sidhe, and the mother pure-blooded Nattmara. The sister took after their mother, but Egar strongly inherited his father's gifts. The father was keeping them both contained until he was killed."

She looked down into the fire. "This explains much. The creature has nearly broken through my glamour many times. I hadn't previously understood how he would possess such gifts."

"Do witches really know glamour?" Steifan asked.

Her lips curled into the barest of smiles. "No child, I never said I was a witch, only that others believe it to be so."

I blinked at her as realization threatened. Suddenly, it made sense how a magic user could survive in the middle of the city. How she could only be found by those she chose. If she could do glamour, she could hide in plain sight. But witches couldn't do real glamour. Only one type of creature could. "You're Sidhe, aren't you?"

Steifan balked at me, but I was pretty sure I was right. It was why the Nattmara wanted her blood so badly. Such powerful blood could potentially sustain him for centuries.

She watched me for a moment, then nodded.

"So you know how to break his glamour?" I pressed,

stepping close enough to the fire that my toes grew hot through the leather of my boots.

"Yes, but there is one problem. You are hunters, and you may someday hunt me. If I tell you how to break the Nattmara's glamour, you may be able to break mine as well."

I shook my head. "We have no reason to harm you. The people of this area protect you. It seems you live a life of peace."

She watched me for a long moment, and I almost thought our slim chance of defeating Egar was slipping through my fingers. Seeming to come to a decision, she said, "I will tell you, but my price still stands. There is a secret to you, something you hide. It makes you different from him." She gestured to Steifan. "Tell me what it is, then I will decide whether or not I will help you with the Nattmara."

My stomach seemed to turn over completely within me. I had spoken this secret three times now, but no time had been any easier than the prior.

"Ask something else," Steifan interjected. "Anything else."

I turned to him.

"We have only just met her," he pleaded. "This secret can be a danger to you. If she tells anyone . . . "

"I am well aware of the danger, but we cannot leave Egar alive. He will kill many, and he will eventually kill us." My mind made up, I turned back to the woman who had already shared a dangerous secret with us. I had to trust her. "I am a vampire's human servant. If the Helius Order were to find out, I would be executed. If you can tell us how to break the Nattmara's glamour, I will take your secret to the grave."

Her dark eyes scrutinized me. She took a long slow

breath, then exhaled. "I will teach you, and only you. You will share this with no one, not even him." Her eyes flicked to Steifan, then back to me. "And we will swear an oath. We will take each other's secrets to the grave. As a hunter, you should know what it means to swear an oath to one of the Sidhe."

I did know. I knew if I betrayed her, the spirits of her ancestors would haunt me for eternity. But I would take the risk if it meant slaying the Nattmara. "I will take your oath, and together we will defeat our enemy."

She smiled then, another real smile that lit up her face. "Send your companion outside and we will get started."

"Lyss, think about this," Steifan cautioned. "She has glamour too, just like Egar. She's dangerous."

I placed my hand on his shoulder and gave an encouraging squeeze. "Egar intends to kill me eventually. I cannot wait around for that to happen. I must learn to break his glamour."

He looked at Ryllae. "If you harm her—"

She smiled indulgently, like one would at a child. It made me wonder just how old she was. Pure blooded Sidhe were immortal. She could be twenty, or she could be two hundred. "I will only harm her if she harms me. If her intentions are pure, she is safe. Do not fear."

He didn't look like he quite believed her, but he squeezed my hand on his shoulder, then turned away. He walked out into the night, leaving us alone in the small stone space.

I watched him go, suddenly worried that he wouldn't be safe out there.

"I will sense if danger is near," Ryllae said to my back. "He will be fine."

I tore my eyes away from the door, scrutinizing her across the fire.

"You really killed a Nattmara?" she asked.

I nodded.

"And if you can break his glamour, you will kill the one in this city?"

I smiled and answered honestly. "It would be my pleasure."

CHAPTER THIRTY-EIGHT

I guessed it was sometime around midnight when I finally emerged from Ryllae's home. I had already sensed what I would find outside, and my eyes confirmed it. Asher waited with Steifan, both leaning against a portion of wall near a merchant camp. Seeing me, they headed in my direction, looking like perfect opposites, one with black hair, one with white. A few merchants cast wary glances at Asher's back.

Ryllae walked out and stood beside me, following my gaze. "*Oh*, now I see why you don't want to kill him." Her mischievous smile said she knew exactly who Asher was to me, and she approved of what she saw, at least physically. I knew from our conversation she held no love for vampires, especially ancient ones. She believed all vampires were monsters. I agreed with her . . . mostly.

"I never said I didn't want to kill him," I grumbled as the men neared. "Just that I'm not going to kill him quite yet."

"You are an honest woman, Lyssandra. It would be a shame if you continued to go against your nature by lying to yourself."

I frowned as Asher and Steifan reached us, wishing I had been a little less honest with the woman at my side. I'd felt I had owed it to her to answer her seemingly harmless questions when she was sharing with me the most closely guarded secret of her people.

Said secret wasn't as complex as I had thought it would be. All it required was a resilient mind, an ancient chant, and enough power to back it up, which she swore I had, though I was doubtful. The jar of ointment she had given me would be supplementary. I could put it on my eyes and ears to block out visual and auditory glamour. The ointment was for Steifan too, but the bit of chanting and magic was just for me.

"What are you doing here?" I asked Asher.

But he was looking at Ryllae. "Not a witch after all," he said. "How interesting."

Ryllae's eyes flared at his words. Suddenly, she seemed bigger than the tiny woman she was. She took a step toward Steifan. "You told him."

Steifan held up his hands. "I did no such thing!"

A few onlookers still awake sitting around fires glanced our way like they might interfere.

"I can smell your blood," Asher said lowly. "I have known your kind before. No one has betrayed your secret, nor will I."

Ryllae stepped back like he had struck her. "My kind? Where? When?"

Sorrow stabbed my gut. I looked at Asher and saw that sorrow echoed in his expression. I stared at him, unsure where my sudden emotions had come from.

"It was many centuries ago," he said to Ryllae. "I apologize if I gave you false hope."

I moved to stand closer to Steifan, further from the vampire. Had I actually just felt his emotions? Once again,

Karpov's warning about me growing closer to Asher the more time we spent together reared its ugly head. Was that happening now? Would I feel even more of his emotions soon?

I didn't have time to ask questions, and now wasn't the time for it regardless.

Ryllae took a moment to process Asher's words. I wondered how long ago she had become separated from the last of her kin, and if any could possibly be alive.

"I am sorry," Asher reiterated.

Ryllae waved him off. "Unless you killed them, you have nothing to apologize for." She met my waiting gaze. "Remember what we discussed. Return to me when the Nattmara is dead." With that, she turned and went back into her home.

I looked at Asher. "You never answered my question. Why are you here?"

"I will tell you, but not here." He gestured subtly to the men still watching us.

I met their waiting eyes, then nodded. The Seeing Sword had offered no warnings. The men meant us no harm, but it was best not to discuss anything near listening ears. The shock of feeling Asher's emotions had made me careless. I wouldn't let it happen again.

I looked around, then led the way toward the dark remains of the original keep. There were a few other fires in that direction, but more spread out. We should be able to find a private place to speak.

When the three of us were crowded into an alcove, far from any fires, I looked at Asher expectantly, angling my shoulder back so it wouldn't be touching his. The partially ruined alcove was dark save a sliver of moonlight, and felt far too intimate.

There was just enough light for me to see Asher smile at my obvious discomfort.

"Why are you here?" I asked yet again. I sidled closer to Steifan, pushing my shoulder against his.

Asher continued to smile. "You act as if my touch brings illness."

Was that why he was always so careful about touching me? Because I made it so obvious how unappealing it was? "Why are you here?" I demanded for what I hoped would be the final time.

"I believe I may have learned something that will help in solving your murder. I began my evening near the home of the man you had me steal the journal from. I witnessed a servant exchanging coin with an unsavory type in the dark shadows of the gardens."

I crossed my arms, growing colder the longer I was away from Ryllae's fire. "What sort of unsavory type?"

"The type that carries a sword, has many scars, and bathes little. I followed him as far as I could, then picked up his scent later on near the inn. I attempted to check on your belongings, but it seems someone else now occupies your room."

I mulled over this new information before looking to Steifan. "You didn't tell him?"

Steifan shrugged, looking a little embarrassed. "I wasn't sure how much you wanted him to know."

I smiled, appreciating the gesture. "I suppose we were wise to move the horses."

Asher looked back and forth between us. "Would one of you mind telling me what you're talking about?"

I almost didn't want to tell him just to be petty, but he *had* brought us the information about the duke's servant, presumably Vannier, paying someone who looked like a mercenary. "We were attacked this morning," I explained. "A group of men was hired to kill us."

He went utterly still. Only the tendrils of his white hair slightly shifting broke the illusion that he was suddenly a statue. "Someone was paid to kill you?" he asked slowly.

"Why do you seem so surprised?"

His expression returned in the form of a scowl. "I am not surprised. I am outraged. For someone to not only mean you harm, but to be cowardly enough to not enact it himself? If the man I robbed of the journal is responsible, I will put an end to him."

I grabbed his arm, just in case he was thinking about going anywhere. "We don't know that it was him. Vannier, the duke's servant, could have been paying that man for any number of reasons. The duke wanted us here to investigate his wife's murder. I don't know why he would try to kill us."

"Unless we were getting too close," Steifan said. "He probably expected us just to come in and hunt a vampire."

"You're right," I conceded, letting go of Asher's arm. "He seemed surprised that we wanted to question her friends and read her journals, but that doesn't mean he tried to have us killed. Still, he is covering up something larger than his wife's murder, and we need to find out what that is."

Asher shifted a little closer to me as voices came near our alcove, then faded away. "The Sidhe mentioned a Nattmara earlier. How is that related?"

Steifan really didn't tell him *anything*. I was so proud. "The Nattmara I slew in Charmant had a brother. Their father was Sidhe."

Asher's brow furrowed. "That is an unfortunate combination. A predator with gifts only a peaceful race like the Sidhe should possess."

I nodded. "And possess them he does. I encountered him earlier, and he clouded my mind to the point where I could not move. No one around could see us, and not even my sword could mutter a warning."

"And why have you only just encountered this creature recently?" Asher asked. "I imagine it would have been killing often."

I gave Steifan an apologetic look, knowing it was a sore subject for him, then answered, "His father had limited his powers, but unfortunately was killed."

"By me," Steifan added. "I freed the beast."

Asher barely acknowledged Steifan. He was still staring at me. "And you approached the Sidhe hoping for a way to limit the effects of glamour."

"You do catch on fast," I said. "And my hopes were answered. She taught me how to overcome the Nattmara's glamour. I can only hope I am strong enough."

"I would give much to learn what she told you. Yet because you're my servant, your mind is closed to me."

I snorted. "Well that is fortunate, isn't it? Because if I told you, I'd have to kill you. And that would kill me too."

I noticed Steifan watching us with amusement and my mood soured. "Let's get out of here. I think it's time we paid Vannier a visit."

Both men nodded their agreement, and we left the alcove, heading back toward the newer part of the city.

In truth, the servant was probably the least of our worries, but we would focus on him while we could. I had no idea how to hunt down the Nattmara, but I knew soon enough, the Nattmara would be hunting *me*.

CHAPTER THIRTY-NINE

We walked along the wall bordering the estates in silence, with Asher on my left, and Steifan on my right. It seemed Asher would be joining us for the rest of the evening. I wasn't sure how I felt about that. At least there were no other hunters around to see me walking with a vampire.

It was late enough now that few people were out, so we were alone as we rounded a bend and the two guards posted in front of the wrought-iron gates came into view. I stopped walking, then retreated out of sight, pressing my back against the wall. Steifan followed my movements like a normal human being, but Asher was like a shadow. As I moved, he moved, needing no time to catch up. It was horribly unnerving.

Steifan didn't seem to notice. He stood at my shoulder, leaning near to keep his voice low. "How are we going to get in? I doubt they'll believe we are going to visit the duke at this late hour."

I didn't want to admit that I hadn't even thought about

the guards. Between the mercenaries, Egar, and Ryllae, it had been a long day.

Asher's silver eyes sparkled with moonlight as he leaned close to me and lowered his voice. "The man who met with the servant went through the canal beneath the wall. That is perhaps an option you would like to consider."

I blinked at him, too stunned to demand he give me space. "You followed him through an underground canal?"

"No, only to the entrance, as I wanted to keep an eye on the servant. I picked up the unsavory man's scent again after leaving the inn. There is a canal entrance behind the guild hall."

"And what were you doing at the inn?" I pressed.

"Looking for you. After that, I followed your trail to where you stabled your horses, then to the Sidhe."

"My, you've been busy," I said tersely.

"We should take to the canals then," Steifan interrupted pointedly, giving me a look which implied I should behave myself.

I would have argued, but he was right. If there was an underground way into the White Quarter, we should explore it. "Yes, back to the subject of the canals," I sighed, turning to Asher. Then my mind caught up with my mouth and my jaw fell open.

"You've had a realization," Asher observed.

I just shook my head, not in response to his question, but to my own stupidity. I knew the canals existed, but I hadn't considered them. "That's how they must have moved Charlotte's body. That's why it was wet."

Asher tilted his head. "Charlotte is the murdered woman? If one wanted to move a body through the canal, one might do so without getting wet."

Steifan nodded along. "But if she was killed with

Jeramy, that would have been a long way to carry a body, especially if it was just one person carrying her. It would be easier to float the body through the water."

I looked back at Asher. "Can you show us the way into the canal?"

He gave a small bow. "As *my lady* wishes."

Steifan let out a soft chortle at my indignant expression, lifting a hand to his mouth to suppress the sound.

I glared at him as I turned to follow Asher.

The vampire led us away from the wall and out of sight from the guards, then south toward the guild hall not far from the inn. As we walked, I pictured the canals beneath us. They would have been expanded as the city grew, with the oldest tunnels being near the old keep. By now, it was probably a maze down there. We could get lost just as easily as finding anything important.

The guild hall came into view, its tall spires seeming to pierce the partial moon. We circled the towering building, heading into a dead-end alcove with walls lending privacy on all sides. If Asher hadn't been looking for me at the inn, he might not have caught the man's scent in this out-of-the-way place.

Asher stopped walking and gestured toward a set of cellar doors. A steel chain wound several times between the handles, held in place by a padlock.

"I found the man's scent again here," he explained. "The padlock also smells strongly of him. I imagine he had a set of keys."

I stared down at the thick steel chain. "Was the other end of the canal locked?"

He shook his head. "The man did not lock it upon his departure, but I cannot guarantee someone else did not lock it after I was gone."

"Couldn't you just have bespelled him or the servant?"

Steifan asked. "It seems an awful lot of work to do things this way."

Asher gave him a less than friendly look. "You would be surprised how resilient the minds of some mortals can be. If I would have attempted to bespell the servant, there's a chance it would not have worked, then I would have needed to kill him. That seemed unnecessary."

Unnecessary, I thought. That was one way of putting it.

"But you bespelled the duke," Steifan pressed. "If it hadn't worked, would you have killed him?"

"Yes."

I gaped at him.

Asher lifted his nose. "Judge me if you will, Lyssandra. But I was only in such a situation because *you* asked me to go. It is not my fault you did not consider the possibilities."

I let out a long breath through my clenched teeth. "I suppose you're right." I had to be more careful what I asked for in the future. Turning away to hide my flushed cheeks, I gestured to the cellar doors. "Can you break the lock?"

Asher stepped up beside me. "As could you, I imagine."

"I might be able to break down doors, but I cannot bend steel."

"If you believe it to be so, then it must be so." With that annoyingly cryptic reply, he knelt, wrapped one pale hand around the chain, then tore it free with a loud groan of metal.

The handles on the cellar doors gave before the chain did, but it got the job done. Asher lifted one door open, revealing stairs leading down into darkness.

"What's that term . . . " Steifan said at my opposite shoulder. "Ah yes, ladies first."

With a smug look, I marched down into the darkness. The Seeing Sword would warn me if there was any danger . . . I hoped. I reached the bottom of the short stone staircase, then could go no further. It was pitch black. I could feel the stone wall to my right, and could hear water flowing to my left. The cellar door creaked shut above as footsteps echoed down the stairs behind me.

I heard the distinct sound of flint grating on fire steel, then a lantern flared to life.

Asher shielded the lantern with one hand so as not to blind me. "I could smell the oil," he said, bobbing the lantern in his hand. Once my eyes had adjusted, he extended it toward me.

"My thanks," I said through gritted teeth, finding it difficult to muster my gratitude. I took the lantern handle, brushing his long, cool fingers with my skin. I suppressed a shiver. "Let's go."

We walked one by one down the narrow canal. Asher walked directly behind me, making me uneasy. I had been trained my entire life to never turn my back on a vampire, now here I was, willingly working with one. If only my uncle could see me now.

The strangest part was that I trusted him. In a fight, I would rather have him at my back than Steifan. I hated that I had become such a traitor to the Helius Order.

I strained my fingers around the lantern handle until my knuckles turned white. *Just keep walking,* I told myself. *Solve the murder. Slay the Nattmara. Simple.*

"Right," Asher said as we reached a juncture.

I stopped and glanced back at him. "I thought you said you hadn't been down here."

"That man's scent lingers," was his only explanation.

I shook my head and turned right.

Supposedly following the man's scent, Asher spoke directions as we continued to wind our way through the canals. As I'd suspected, they were like a maze. Anyone traveling this route would have to know the way well. It made me wonder just who had transported Charlotte's body.

"It is here," Asher said as we rounded a bend.

I extended the lantern to light the way ahead. Sure enough, a rickety metal ladder led up to a closed hatch.

I approached the ladder, then set the lantern on the stones near its base before climbing the bottom rung. "Is it just me, or is it odd for the canals to have these random entrances?"

Asher answered at my back. "After the siege where the old keep was destroyed, new canals were built. The nobles wanted a way to escape should the city fall under siege once again. Some of the outlets lead all the way outside the main wall. The easy access to water was a secondary concern."

I looped one elbow on a ladder rung, then leaned to look back at him. "So if the city were to fall under siege, the nobles could escape, leaving everyone else to die?"

"Something like that."

Humans truly could be as bad as vampires, I thought, then finished climbing the ladder. The closed hatch had a long metal handle. I grabbed it and pulled it toward me, and was able to push the hatch open. No locks after all. I supposed they were more worried about people getting in, than getting out.

I peeked my head up, glancing around. We were in the back of someone's garden.

The night was utterly silent, and my sword issued no warning, so I climbed the rest of the way out of the hatch. I crouched in the shadows of a meticulously trimmed shrubbery while I waited for the men to ascend.

Asher came up next. He stood out in the open, raising a brow at me crouching near a shrubbery

I looked up at him.

He shrugged. "There is no one here to see us. I would hear them breathing."

Feeling a little foolish, I stood as Steifan climbed out of the hatch, then shut it gently behind him, sealing the light of the lantern within.

"Your duke's estate is that way." Asher pointed. "Three gardens down."

I glanced around at the surrounding shrubs, having an odd feeling of noticing them before. I took a few steps toward the fence separating the garden from the street, then froze. I recalled black hair framing dark eyes, watching me from just this spot.

"This is where I saw Egar," I breathed. I turned back to the men. "The Nattmara knows about the canals." I thought about it. "If he *did* kill Charlotte, he could have moved her body. Maybe he noticed the vampire bite on her neck and thought it might be a way to lure hunters to the city. The female Nattmara told me our blood has more power than other mortals."

"But why kill Jeramy?" Steifan asked.

My elation abated. Perhaps I was just grasping at threads. "I don't know. I suppose that doesn't really make sense. Why kill Jeramy, and not feed?"

Asher watched us, silently absorbing our words. Or maybe he was just waiting for us to shut up and get on with things, who knew?

"Let's find Vannier," I decided. "Maybe he can answer these questions."

As we started walking, I wondered how I planned to pull the servant out of his bed. I most certainly did not want to be caught breaking into the duke's estate in the middle of the night. At the very least, we would be thrown out of the city. At the most, we would be imprisoned indefinitely, or killed by guards.

We cut across the gardens, scaling fences where necessary, until we reached the duke's estate. I leaned against a tree with Steifan on the other side, both of us hiding in its shadows. Asher stood close behind me, and I couldn't exactly tell him to back up because it would put him out in the open. The back windows of the estate were within view. Someone might glance outside and see us.

Trying to ignore Asher's nearness, and the accompanying tingling sensation in my gut, I focused my full attention on the back side of the estate. Usually servants' quarters were either in the back, or in a separate building. Since I didn't see any separate buildings, I imagined Vannier's chamber was behind one of the three windows on the bottom floor.

"Wait here," I whispered to Steifan. I didn't bother saying anything to Asher. He would do as he liked regardless, and I wasn't worried about him getting caught.

With my next step in mind, I crept forward, skirting around a garish white fountain with two scantily clad maidens pouring water from pitchers. I barely breathed as I reached the first of the windows and peeked inside. I could see a bed and small nightstand through gauzy white curtains, but the room appeared to be unoccupied.

I sensed Asher behind me and briefly glanced back at him, then crept to the next window. There was a blanket covered lump on the bed. I couldn't be sure that it was Vannier, but I was pretty sure I could see a tuft of gray hair poking out near the pillow.

I looked back at Asher now peering over my shoulder. *Is that who you saw?* I mouthed, though we would be judging solely on the hair.

Perhaps, he mouthed back.

I nodded, then turned back to the window. Now to get him out of there so we could question him privately.

A tap on my shoulder almost made me scream, but it was only Asher. I was just surprised because he so rarely touched me. He would stand close, yes, but there was always a hair's breadth between us.

He gestured to the sleeping man, then gestured to himself.

Was he offering to fetch Vannier for me? I supposed that would solve a few problems. *Don't hurt him,* I mouthed.

Asher rolled his eyes, then shooed me away.

I retreated to wait with Steifan back by the tree.

I watched as the shadow of a shape that was Asher disappeared around the side of the house. Not but a few moments later, a stifled shout emanated from within.

I leaned forward, peering around the tree at Steifan.

He shrugged. No more sounds came from within the house.

"There," Steifan whispered.

I followed the direction of his outstretched finger, spotting Asher returning the way he'd come. He clutched Vannier in front of him, one hand covering the old man's mouth while making him walk forward. Vannier wore an old-fashioned sleeping gown, a style now uncommon amongst younger folk.

I caught the wide-eyed look of fear on his face as Asher forced him near, then recognition dawned, and that fear turned into confusion.

Asher maintained his grip over Vannier's mouth, but I suspected the old man wouldn't scream if he let him go. Not without first finding out why two hunters had him pulled from his bed in the middle of the night. We were supposed to be on his side, after all.

I stepped around the tree, facing Vannier. "Earlier

tonight," I whispered, "you paid a scarred man. What was his task?"

Vannier's eyes shifted from side to side. He mumbled words, but they were muffled by Asher's hand.

My eyes lifted to Asher. "Let him go. If he shouts, break his neck." I hoped my raised brows conveyed that I didn't actually want him to break the poor man's neck. I didn't think Asher would kill on my command regardless.

He freed Vannier, then stepped aside to stand beside Steifan.

I glanced around the dark garden, wishing we had somewhere better to question Vannier, but this would have to do. "Answer the question," I ordered.

Vannier wiped his mouth, then cast a quick glare at Asher before turning back to me. "How do I know I can trust you?"

I shrugged. "If you killed Charlotte, then you can't. But if you want to find the murderer as badly as we do, we are perhaps your only true allies."

His eyes narrowed. "What do you mean?"

"I mean, I know the duke is hiding something. The guards are hiding something. And Lady Montrant is most *certainly* hiding something. I suspect that none of them truly wish Charlotte's murder solved. I'm hoping that you do." I was also hoping that his next words would either prove his guilt or innocence. If he shared with me what he knew, he was probably innocent. One suspect to cross off our list.

He glanced at Asher and Steifan again, then back to me. "Fine. The man you saw is an old friend. I needed someone I could trust."

I was sure my disbelief showed clearly. "A duke's servant, friends with a mercenary?"

Vannier's shoulders slumped as he sighed. "I was not always a duke's servant."

Now that, I actually believed. He had wiped away his fear quickly. "And what did you pay this *friend* to do?"

He searched my face, as if my deadpan expression could provide the answers he sought. Finding nothing, he sighed again. "I suppose if I must trust someone, it might as well be hunters with few connections in this city."

I didn't correct him in thinking Asher was another hunter. Better than him realizing what he really was.

Vannier eyed each of us before speaking. "The boy, Bastien, is missing. The duke did not seem surprised by this revelation, so I can only assume he is involved. I contacted an old friend to find out what happened to the boy."

I crossed my arms casually, belying the sudden tension radiating through my body. Bastien was missing. Could he have been taken when I sent him running after our encounter with the mercenaries? "Bastien seemed to think you held little regard for him."

Vannier's wrinkles deepened with a sour expression. "The boy is my grandson. His mother was a drunk, and I was forced to disown her early on. When I learned she had perished, I secured a life for the boy."

He couldn't have shocked me more if he admitted to being the duchess' murderer. When I could find the words, I asked, "Bastien doesn't know?"

"What good is a grandfather who abandons his kin? I deserve no relationship with him, but I can at least make sure he is all right."

I met Steifan's waiting gaze, knowing we were both thinking the same thing. He had been apprehended, and maybe killed, because of us.

I turned back to Vannier. "Tell us everything you know

about the duke and duchess, and about why anyone might not want the duchess' murder solved. I will do everything within my power to find Bastien."

Vannier licked his thin lips, considering my offer. He wrung his wizened hands. "All right, I'll tell you everything, but not here. This information could get me killed. You know of the canals leading out into the city?"

I nodded.

"Good. Meet me at the entrance behind the guild hall at first light. I'll tell you everything, but for now, I must not be found missing."

"We will see you at dawn," I said, gesturing for him to retreat.

Sparing a final glance for us all, he hurried back toward the estate.

Steifan moved to my side as we watched him go. "Do you think we can trust him?"

I sucked my teeth. Bastien was missing, and the duke knew about it. "We're going to have to. Now let's get out of here."

We retreated through the canals the way we'd come. We would seek a place to rest, perhaps back near the old keep, then we would meet Vannier at first light. I didn't ask Asher where he was staying, or if we would see him tomorrow night. Despite how much he had helped us, I really didn't want to know.

CHAPTER FORTY

Vannier awaited us behind the guild hall at first light, as promised. Even hidden near the cellar doors, he stuck out like a red flycatcher standing stiff-backed in his showy livery.

His shoulders relaxed as he spotted us coming toward him. "It's about time. I must get back before I'm missed."

I glanced up at the first hint of sunlight just now showing over the rooftops. We were precisely on time, but I didn't bother pointing that out. He didn't have to meet us. I could be patient with a bit of bluster . . . but only a bit.

"Stand guard," I said to Steifan. "I don't want anyone sneaking up on us."

I tugged the hood of my brown traveling cloak forward a little further, making sure it covered all of my hair. Steifan wore a similar cloak. After one attempt on our lives, we couldn't be too careful. I had belted my sword around my waist instead of across my shoulders to make it less conspicuous. The blade was a bit too long for comfort, and it would take me a few moments longer to draw it, but no compromise was perfect. A woman with a greatsword would stand out. At least around my waist, someone searching for me wouldn't spot it from a distance.

I watched as Steifan walked out to the narrow intersection and disappeared around the corner. We both had Ryllae's ointment smeared across our eyelids and over our ears, so hopefully even if someone with glamour came, Steifan would be all right.

I turned my attention to Vannier. "Tell me everything you know."

His eyes couldn't seem to settle on a particular part of my face. He wrung his hands, finally meeting my gaze. "You swear to me you will find the boy?"

"I will not give up until he has been found, one way or another."

Vannier rubbed his tired eyes. It looked like he hadn't gone back to sleep after we left him. "Lady Charlotte had many secrets, and I was sworn to keep them, but if telling you will help solve her murder and bring back the boy, I will break my oath."

I anxiously waited for him to continue.

He let out a long breath. "Lady Charlotte had a . . . business. She had suitors other than her husband." His lined face grew redder as he spoke.

"If you are trying to tell me she was selling her womanly charms for coin, you can save your breath. Lady Montrant already hinted at as much."

His eyes flew wide for a moment, then he seemed to settle himself. "I suppose that makes this explanation a little easier. Lady Charlotte kept to a regular schedule, and while her business was less than proper, it seemed she was staying safe. Her husband pretended not to notice, but he was well aware of the coin coming in. I believe he knew precisely what his wife was doing."

I agreed, though I didn't say so out loud. Duke Auclair

had known exactly what her ledger was when he tried to burn it.

"Do you believe one of her clients killed her?"

He shook his head. "I know you were called here to hunt a vampire, and I saw the bite, but it was already there before she died. She had many others."

I raised my brows. "She didn't try to hide them?"

He swiped a palm over his sweaty face. "She did at first. The first time, I caught just a glimpse of a fresh wound when her sleeve pulled up too far, revealing her wrist. She noticed me staring and quickly covered it. Eventually, she seemed to care less if they were covered."

"So the bite on her neck wasn't anything unusual." *And the duke knew that*, I added silently. He had known for a fact the bite wasn't what killed her. "How long was this going on?"

"It started a few weeks before she went missing," he explained. "At least that is when I noticed the first bite. It was confusing, to say the least. I had believed that vampires could not feed without killing their victims, yet she always returned home, a little pale, but she never took long to recover."

That vampires couldn't feed without killing was a common misconception. "The old ones have more control," I explained. "An older vampire could feed from her roughly once a week without weakening her. If they were meeting more frequently, he could take little enough that she would hardly be affected . . . " I trailed off at a sudden thought, realizing this was the first time anyone actually admitted she had gone missing before she was killed. "Vannier, how long was she actually missing before her body was found, and why did no one report it?"

He'd nodded along to my explanation, though I didn't think he was really listening until I asked the question. His eyes searched my face before he answered, "She was missing for eight or nine days before her body suddenly just showed up in her bed."

"Why didn't the duke tell us she had been missing? Why wouldn't he report it the first night she didn't come home?"

Vannier shook his head. "I don't know, and he made me swear up-and-down that I would not tell you about her business."

If I hadn't suspected the duke before, I most certainly did now. "So he knew about her business. And he must have known about the bites too, if she was making little effort to hide them."

He glanced around warily, though there was no one near us. "I cannot say for sure, but he had to know. I wasn't the only one who noticed them. When Lady Montrant noticed, she stopped speaking with Charlotte entirely."

So Lady Montrant knew. She had mentioned the business, and the lack of coin, so why not the bites? "What can you tell me about the Montrants?"

His eyes narrowed and went distant as he seemed to really consider his answer. "They came into a lot of coin this year, but I know little of the circumstances. They are well respected. Lady Montrant was previously one of Charlotte's best friends." He hung his head for a moment. "I fear that is all I can think to tell you. I hope it will be useful."

"You gave us a place to start, at least. We will not leave this city until we figure out what's going on."

He nodded, but I had the feeling once again he wasn't listening to me. If I had to guess, I would say he was genuinely distraught over Charlotte's murder and Bastien's disappearance.

"Wait." I held up a hand as a thought came to me. "We heard rumors of other missing people."

He furrowed his brow. "Peasants and vagrants. I don't see how it could be connected to Bastien and Charlotte."

"No other nobles have gone missing besides Charlotte and her ladies?"

"Her ladies fled because of the vampire bites. They were afraid."

I rubbed at the ache beginning in my temple. "Likely not connected then," I sighed, though I didn't like it. I had been sent to Silgard to solve Charlotte's murder, but I didn't like leaving the other disappearances unaccounted for.

He glanced around. "I must go. I've been absent too long already."

"I will find you again if I have more questions."

"If you must." He met my gaze, giving me the full force of his gaunt face and the purple marks beneath his eyes. "I would appreciate it if I could leave first. I'd rather avoid being seen with you."

"My, aren't you a charmer?"

He didn't seem to get the joke. With a final nod, he hurried past me, then down the adjoining street.

Steifan peeked around the corner. "Learn anything new?"

"A bit. How would you like to take another trip underground?"

He stepped fully around the corner and walked toward me, flapping the hem of his cloak behind him. "I wouldn't like that at all, but I imagine I don't have a choice."

"Well at least you're realistic." I moved toward the cellar doors.

The chain and padlock were still on the ground, and one handle barely hung onto the door. If anyone had been here since we had ventured through, they had made no effort to re-seal the entrance.

I hoped it meant no one had been here at all, and we wouldn't be confronted with a knife in the dark, or something far worse.

"Isn't this it?" Steifan questioned, extending the lantern we'd left the previous night toward the ladder. His hushed words were barely audible over the sound of running water.

I peered down the corridor going in the other direction. We could go up to the White Quarter the same way we went before, but it would be difficult to spy from the sunny gardens. "Shine the light down this way. I'm wondering if there are other ways up."

Steifan squeezed past me, heading slowly down the corridor. I could see why someone would need to float Charlotte's body. It would be difficult to carry with how narrow the walkways were on either side of the water.

I considered the layout of the estates above as we walked, wishing I had spent more time in the area. I could roughly judge where we were, but I wasn't sure where we would come up, and we would be doing it in broad daylight.

We stopped as the corridor forked off in two directions, with a metal grate leading over the water to our right.

I glanced one way, then the other. "Would you say we are somewhere near the square where I questioned the illustrious Lady Montrant?"

"I believe we are almost directly beneath it," Steifan answered.

I turned to him, surprised at the surety in his tone.

He shrugged, bobbing the lantern in one hand. "I'm good with directions and distances."

"All right, cartographer, which direction do we go to put us near the Montrant estate?"

He smirked, the expression eerie in the lantern light. "While I do not appreciate your sarcasm, I believe we should go left. If there is an exit within the next forty paces, it should lead to the Montrant's garden."

"Remind me to bring you if I ever go caving." I gestured for him to walk ahead with the lantern.

We got lucky, finding another ladder up not forty-five paces away.

Steifan held the lantern while I went up first, pausing with my ear near the hatch. I heard nothing above, so I turned the handle and opened the hatch a crack. I had expected daylight, but I couldn't see a thing.

"Lantern," I whispered, extending one hand down toward Steifan.

The handle pressed into my palm, and I wrapped my fingers around it, lifting it slowly. When I had enough light to see by, I opened the hatch just a touch more and peered through the crack.

I looked down the length of a wooden floor stretching out into the darkness. The space was still and musty. I was quite sure we'd found our way into someone's cellar. If we were lucky, it was the Montrant's.

I listened for any footsteps or voices, but the rooms above were silent. I opened the hatch the rest of the way and climbed into the cellar, shining the lantern around the space. Along one wall were several barrels next to shelves lined with cheeses, ceramic crockeries, and baskets of goods.

I turned a slow circle as Steifan poked his head up into

the room. The lantern cast odd shadows across metal grating.

My mouth went dry. "Something tells me those cages aren't used to hold dogs."

Steifan climbed into the room, and we both stared at the empty cages lining the far wall. Dirty, tattered rags were scattered within the enclosures, some stained dark reddish brown with dried blood.

"Do you think—" Steifan choked on his own words, lifting a hand to cover his mouth.

I could smell it too. Blood, excrement, and fear. "The missing people. I think they might have been held here, maybe transported through the canals."

His hand still clasped over his mouth, Steifan shook his head. "But for what purpose?" he muttered against his fingers.

I walked closer to the cages, not sure what I hoped to find. "People are stolen away for all sorts of reasons. Judging by the cages, their captors wanted them kept alive." I glanced at the low ceiling above us. "We need to find out where we are. If this is the Montrant's estate, it may help us piece together what happened to Charlotte. Maybe her death is connected to the other missing people after all."

Footsteps echoed across the floor above us, drawing near.

"Down!" I hissed. "Go back down!"

Steifan hopped back through the hatch, barely catching a ladder rung to slow his fall.

My descent was no more graceful, and I nearly lost the lantern on my way down. I had just eased the hatch shut when footsteps hurried down the cellar stairs. I descended the last few steps of the ladder, then waited shoulder to shoulder with Steifan at the bottom.

"Get her in the cage," a man's voice strained.

Muffled cries, then the sound of a cage door slamming shut.

One moment Steifan was standing beside me, and the next he was lunging for the ladder.

I grabbed his shoulder and yanked him back, giving him a demonstration of my unnatural strength. He stumbled, and would have fallen into the water if I hadn't maintained my grip on his cloak.

I jerked his collar, bringing him to face me, then lifted a finger in front of my lips. While his outrage was admirable, we weren't going to stupidly rush into things. The girl was in a cage now. She wasn't going anywhere without us noticing. And if we could follow her, we might find the other missing people, including Bastien.

Steifan's eyes finally focused on me. His jaw was tight, but he nodded.

We both went still as two sets of footsteps echoed up the stairs, leaving behind only the sound of soft crying.

Steifan met my gaze solidly. "We have to get her out of there," he hissed.

I gripped his wrist, just in case. "It's broad daylight up there, so she was already being kept somewhere else in the house. They probably moved her once the servants were sent out for the day. If we leave her long enough to be transported, we may find the other missing people."

His eyes flew wide. "I don't care how long she's been held captive. We can't leave her in a cage. She must be terrified."

I kept my voice low. "Think, Steifan. Her being scared now could save many lives. If the missing people are still in the city, we have to find them. We have to find Bastien."

His expression fell. "We at least have to tell her that we intend to save her."

This was one of those moments where working with

someone so new to hunting was a massive detriment. Being a hunter required practicality above all else. We couldn't let one girl's fear risk an unknown number of lives. "If we go up there, she might start screaming, and the missing people could all end up dead. Do you want their blood on your hands?"

It was the first time Steifan had ever looked at me with hatred. My gut clenched, but I knew I was right. He had to see reason, whether he liked that reason or not.

"We will wait right here until she is moved," he said slowly. "We will ensure she comes to no harm."

"Agreed."

He relaxed his stance, probably thinking he had won the battle. In truth, I had planned on waiting here until the girl was moved regardless. I wasn't about to let her slip through our fingers.

I didn't know if this was all related to Charlotte's murder, but it would be a pretty big coincidence if it wasn't. If Charlotte and the duke knew people were being taken, it could've been the reason Charlotte was killed. I needed to figure out who else was involved, and not just to solve a murder. Anyone involved in stealing people away needed to be brought to justice.

My sword felt heavy at my hip, longing to protect the weak from these monsters. For although a sword was perhaps the most brutal form of justice, it was my favorite kind.

CHAPTER FORTY-ONE

I could sense the sky growing dark outside as we waited down in the canal. Eventually, the girl above had stopped crying. I genuinely hoped she had fallen asleep to spare herself from waiting in fear.

Steifan sat with his back against the damp stone wall, his shoulders hunched and knees pulled up to his chest. The lantern sat on the ground beside him, the wick pulled low to dampen the flame and preserve oil.

I waited on the other side of the ladder, leaning one shoulder against the stones. I had moved my sword from my hip to my back, pinning my cloak behind my shoulders. If we were to fight, I didn't want to waste the few extra seconds it would take to draw it from my hip.

Steifan looked up toward the ladder at the sound of footsteps. The girl started crying again, her sobs accompanied by the metal creak of the cage door opening.

Steifan stood, and we both waited, looking up at the ladder. We locked eyes as the footsteps and the sound of crying stopped right above us. Steifan grabbed the lantern, and we both fled around the corner in the direction we'd come.

I peeked around the corner as the hatch door opened, letting a pool of light down into the canal.

"Climb," a man's voice ordered, the same one who had ordered the girl put in the cage.

I saw the hem of a dark-colored dress billowing around two small feet coming down the ladder. She wasn't a child, but she most certainly wasn't an adult either. It was difficult to judge for sure in the low lighting.

I pulled myself back around the corner. If they came this way, we would have to run, but I didn't think they would. They weren't bringing this girl to another hatch among the estates, and I doubted they were bringing her to the guild hall, which meant they were going in the other direction we were yet to explore.

By the sounds of it, two more people came down behind the girl, but I didn't dare look in case any of them were peering my way. I held the lantern at my other side, shielding the small light with my cloak.

My shoulders relaxed as footsteps headed off in the other direction. I held one arm out, preventing Steifan from trying to follow too closely. They weren't going anywhere in these canals that would prevent us from following at a safe distance.

Once the footsteps had almost faded entirely, I crept forward, peering around the corner before venturing that way. The straightaway ahead was empty, so I held the lantern out in front of us to keep from falling in the water. It would be a shame if one of us splashing around undid all of our patient waiting.

Steifan followed behind me. Though his steps were light for a normal mortal, they seemed deafeningly loud to my ears, even with the rushing water. I could only hope the girl and her captors would not expect anyone following them, and so would not be listening for sounds of pursuit.

We reached another fork in the canal, and I peeked out, glancing both ways. Both directions were empty, but I had heard footsteps going across the metal grate to our right, so that was the way I chose.

As we reached the end of the next corridor, I noticed the soft glow of firelight. I handed Steifan the lantern, gesturing for him to stay back. A few more steps and I could tell where the light was coming from. There was a small room built off the side of the canal, probably originally for maintenance supplies, but the girl and her captors were in there now, and it didn't seem they planned on leaving any time soon.

The two men conversed casually, nothing about their current task, while the girl wept. Smoke from torches trickled out into the corridor.

I crept back to Steifan, debating what to do next. Did we confront the men and hope we could beat enough information out of them to find the other victims? Or did we wait to see who was coming to meet them, because I saw no other reason for them to dally.

I quickly decided on the latter and gestured for Steifan to go back around the nearest corner. There, we waited, hoping whoever else was coming would not be venturing from this direction.

Before long, we heard a fourth voice, though I hadn't noticed any footsteps.

I peered around the corner. I didn't dare go close enough to look inside the room, but the smell let me know who had arrived. I smelled rich, turned earth, and a prickling sensation danced up and down my skin. The new addition was a vampire. That's why we hadn't heard any

SARA C. ROETHLE

footsteps, and that's why the men had waited until nightfall to move the girl.

If the vampire was here for her, we could wait no longer.

I nodded to Steifan in the near darkness, then drew my blade and started forward, leaving our lantern where I had set it. It would be out of oil soon regardless.

I listened for my sword's warning as I tiptoed toward the doorway, but none came. They hadn't noticed us yet, so they didn't mean us harm.

That would soon change.

I tugged my hood forward, then stepped into the open doorway, not bothering to sneak in as the vampire would hear me coming long before he spotted me.

He was the first one to turn toward me. He must have only been sixteen when he died, but he was so old his presence felt heavy in my mind. These stupid men were working with an ancient, one who had amassed much coin judging by his fine brocade tunic and velvet pants. Black boots encased his legs up to his knees.

Beyond him were two men I didn't recognize, but judging by their soft bellies and oiled beards, they were middle-aged nobility. They were both near the girl's new cage, one on either side, about to open it.

She trembled in the corner, her face obscured by long, strawberry-blonde hair.

I held my sword at the ready. "You may as well finish opening that cage. I'll be taking her with me."

The vampire's dark eyes seemed to sparkle with amusement, or maybe it was just the torchlight. He pushed a strand of chin length brown hair away from his soft-featured face. "Where is your master, girl? Why has he let you so far off your leash?"

"I needed enough length in my cord to use it to strangle

you," I snarled. I stepped further into the room. "Take care of the men," I said to Steifan. "The monster is mine."

"So bold," the vampire said as Steifan moved past my back with his sword drawn. Neither of the men had visible weapons, so he should be fine.

"Where are the other missing people?" I asked the vampire.

The vampire splayed his hands. "I do not require the death of my food. If you cannot find them, it has nothing to do with me."

I edged closer. If I could catch him off guard, I might be able to remove his head before he could attack. If Markus was capable of slaying ancients, then so was I. "You're paying these men to bring you victims so you can live unnoticed within the city. I can hardly believe you would let them go."

"Oh there's more to it than that. My purchases fit my physical preferences. It's oh so convenient."

Oh yuck. That I did not need to know. Steifan had cornered the two men, both lifting their hands in surren-der. "Many have disappeared," I said. "Too many to become your servants, and you wouldn't waste the coin on a simple meal."

The vampire shrugged. "Some become my servants, but others have disappeared. If you could help me find them, I'd be most grateful." He smiled at his own jest.

He obviously hadn't realized that Steifan and I were both hunters, but he knew I was a human servant. He probably thought I'd been sent here by my master to obtain information. I would use that to my advantage.

I stepped closer. The men behind me were muttering to Steifan that none of this was their fault. That they were just doing the vampire's will so he wouldn't kill them.

"Too many have gone missing for just your needs, even

if some were taken from you," I said to the vampire. "How many others are involved?"

"That is a question you should ask our friends." He lifted one hand toward the men behind me. "It is none of *my* concern."

So it wasn't just him involved, and it probably wasn't just these two men. I could kill them all, and the operation might continue.

I tightened my grip on my sword. At least it would be a start.

He narrowed his eyes. "Who is your master, girl?"

I smiled coldly. "I have no master."

He glanced down at my sword, then stepped back into a defensive stance. "That is not possible. I can smell what you are."

I lifted my sword. "If you don't believe me, I'll just have to prove it to you." I launched myself at the vampire, swinging my sword through the air. He evaded me, just barely, and my sword came to life, singing through my mind.

The vampire grabbed for me, and I whirled away, slashing at his belly as I went, but missing again.

"You do not fight like a mercenary," he said, dodging another strike.

Our movements had put me in the corner, with the vampire's back to Steifan and the two men. Steifan had his sword aimed one-handed at the men while he tried to open the girl's cage with the other, but his eyes were on me, a silent question.

"He's mine," I said, keeping my sword between me and the vampire.

The vampire grabbed for me again, regaining my full attention. "You don't fight like a soldier, either. You are something else."

I slashed at him again. He now knew my skills, I may as well tell him. "I am a hunter of the Helius Order, and I have come here for your head."

My hood fell back as I evaded his next lunge. My braid whipped out, following my movements.

"Such red hair," he said, taking a step back. Recognition dawned. "I have heard of a red-haired hunter being servant to another of my status. To what master do you belong?"

I slashed toward his belly again, and he hopped back. It was more difficult to get close when he wasn't attacking me. All he had to do was stay out of reach. "What does it matter?" I growled.

He took another step back, placing himself near the doorway. "If you are who I think you are, you belong to an ancient. I would not kill the servant of another ancient, lest I bring the rest down upon me. I know our laws."

Curse it all, he was about to run. The Seeing Sword echoed through my mind, urging me to throw it. I obeyed before I could even register the vampire's movements. If I was wrong, and he still intended to attack, he could easily end me.

My sword sailed true, landing with a meaty thunk in the middle of his back. He *had* been turning to run. It was a good thing. I hated to be wrong.

Not sparing a glance for Steifan and the others, I hurried toward the vampire. The wound would not be enough to kill him, not if he was truly ancient. I pulled my sword from his back as his hands swept across the stone. He was halfway up as my sword came down.

Blood splattered across my cheeks, then his head rolled across the stones. I lifted my sword, then turned toward the men. Steifan had managed to get the cage open, but the girl was still in it. She appeared to have fainted.

I took a slow step toward the men, depending on my

bloody sword and splattered clothing to scare them. Scared men would tell a multitude of secrets.

"Who are you working for?" I asked. "How many others are there?"

Both men lifted their hands, pressing their backs against the wall. "It wasn't our fault. The vampire bespelled us. We had to do what he wanted."

I neared the men, then extended my bloody sword, poking at the fat coin pouch on one man's belt. "If he bespelled you. Why did he feel the need to pay you?"

The man's eyes bulged.

I shifted my sword beneath his belt, pointing the tip at his groin. "If I were you, I would not lie again."

He gasped, plastering himself against the wall. "Please, I'll tell you everything. I'm not the man in charge. I'll give you the man in charge."

I smiled. "Now that's more like it."

I lowered my sword a fraction, then my smile faded. I sensed something else down here, something near. My thoughts went muddy, and I nearly dropped my sword as the glamour closed in around my mind like an iron trap.

CHAPTER FORTY-TWO

I pushed against the magic cloud in my mind, maintaining my tenuous grasp on reality. Steifan's blank expression let me know Ryllae's ointment wasn't strong enough to withstand Egar's magic. The two men we had been questioning stared off at nothing, and the girl was still unconscious. I was on my own. Perhaps I should have waited a little longer to kill the vampire.

I sensed Egar as he moved through the entryway at my back. I chanted the ancient words Ryllae had taught me in my head, and visualized myself pulling free of Egar's glamour. Claws ripped across my mind as I pulled away enough to take two steps, turning around to face him, but that was it. Sweat beaded across my brow. Just that small act of rebellion had cost me too much. I still held my sword, but couldn't lift it.

Egar lifted his eyes from the vampire's corpse to observe me. "I see you have learned a new trick. Does this mean you have located the one I hunt?"

The force of his magic lessened, allowing me to speak.

"Even if I had, I would not give you what you want. How did you find me down here?"

The corner of his mouth ticked up. "These canals begin in the highlands, bringing water down throughout the entire city. I kept sensing fresh blood beneath my feet, and eventually I found an entrance. It is so easy to find a meal when your prey is already locked up in a cage."

I remembered the ancient saying some of his victims had disappeared. Now I knew the reason. "This was your clue on how to solve my murder. This was what you refused to tell me. How long have you been stealing the vampire's victims?"

He shrugged, stepping around the vampire's corpse to approach me. "Not long. Weak mortals are not my preferred prey, but the vampires will eat anything."

I thought he would come to stand before me, but instead he stepped around me. I was able to shuffle my feet enough to follow him with my eyes. He stood before one of the men, looking him up and down.

Faster than I could follow, he shoved his hand through the man's chest, then ripped out his still-beating heart, cradling it in fingers turned to black claws. The man slumped to the ground, dead. He never even screamed.

My heart pounded in my head as I willed myself to move. I chanted Ryllae's words and imagined myself lifting my sword. At the thought of my sword, I finally sensed its presence.

Egar tossed the heart onto the ground, then stepped toward the second man.

"No!" I gasped, but I still couldn't move.

Egar smiled back at me. "You wish me to spare him?"

I managed to nod.

"Then give me what I seek. Tell me how to find her."

Cast away your fear, a voice said in my mind. At first I

thought I had imagined it, but then it spoke again. *Your fear feeds the creature's magic. Cast it aside.*

I closed my eyes, trying to push away my fear, then a wet sound hit my ears. I opened my eyes to find Egar had killed the second man the same way as the first. He stepped toward Steifan, watching me with a cruel smile. "I think you will tell me what I want to know now." He extended one clawed, bloody hand toward Steifan's chest.

I chanted Ryllae's words over and over again in my head, but beneath them were my own words. Or maybe they came from the Seeing Sword. *I am a hunter of the Helius Order. I am not afraid.*

The words melded in my mind, the ancient words giving strength to the new, which were no less powerful.

Egar's nostrils flared. He stepped closer to Steifan, but his eyes were all for me. "What are you doing?"

I chanted the words again in my head. *I am a hunter of the Helius Order, and I am not afraid.* Slowly, I lifted my sword, wrapping my other hand around the hilt. The moment both of my hands touched the weapon, it gave me strength. I steadied my blade, then stepped toward the Nattmara. "Touch him and you die."

Egar sneered at my sword, then let out a bitter laugh, stepping away from Steifan. "Do you truly believe you have the strength of will to best me? I have proven time and again that I can crush your mind with a single thought."

My confidence wavered, and fear came crashing through. My grip loosened on my sword hilt.

"I am not afraid," I spoke out loud, echoing my sword's voice in my mind.

My words wiped the grin from Egar's face. "You will bring me to the Sidhe. She cannot hide forever."

So he knew what Ryllae was. I tightened my grip on my

sword and took a step toward him. "She will not have to hide once you are dead."

Egar licked lips thinner than they were just a moment before. His face elongated, making room for rows of pin-sharp teeth. He held up one bloody hand as his black-tipped claws grew even longer. He clicked those long claws together, then charged me.

My lingering fear fell away as long-honed battle instinct kicked in. All that I knew were his movements and mine. I swung my sword, slashing across his belly.

He reared away with an unearthly shriek, clutching at the deep gash.

I advanced, sword at the ready.

He staggered away from me, his chest heaving, clawed hands gripping at his wound. He was terrifying, but he didn't know how to fight. He had never needed to. His words came out warped by his long teeth, "Once I find the Sidhe, I will come for you."

"No," I said. "We finish this now."

He stumbled toward the doorway.

I charged after him, but his glamour hit me like a warhorse, making my mind go momentarily black. When I recovered my senses, he was gone.

Trembling, I turned to Steifan.

He blinked a few times, looked down at the two dead men, then back to me. "What in the light just happened, Lyss?"

I fell to my knees, maintaining my grip on my sword. Without its help, I would have been dead. "The Nattmara. We cannot let him find Ryllae. If he drinks her blood, he will kill us all."

"He was here? How did you escape?"

I shook my head, unable to answer. I had broken

through his glamour enough to fight him. I could do it again.

Sensing another presence, I looked back toward the doorway to find Asher standing there. "Took you long enough," I muttered, feeling like I might be sick.

He stepped into the room, taking in the scene. He was the only one of us not covered in blood, though it would hardly show up on his black coat and black suede breeches. Steifan had the worst of it. He'd been standing close to the two men when they were killed.

Asher walked toward us, then offered me a hand up. "What happened here?"

I ignored his hand and stood on my own. "We figured out what has been happening to the missing people. They are being sold to vampires for blood, or to be turned into human servants. We followed the two men bringing the girl down here, then the Nattmara came."

Asher looked me over, lingering on the blood staining my shirt and cloak. "And the dead vampire? He was here to buy the girl?"

I nodded, then frowned, remembering the vampire's words. "He said he had heard of me, and that he couldn't kill me because I belong to another ancient. He tried to run."

Asher's expression gave nothing away, but his words were enough. "He surrendered, and you killed him as he fled."

If he wanted an apology, he wasn't getting one from me. "He was buying this girl. He would have kept her like a slave."

"I did not ask for justification."

I sighed, feeling like my knees were about to give out. I had just faced the Nattmara, and here we were discussing a vampire's death. "You may not have asked for justification, but you wanted me to know that you disapproved. Well, I know it, and I stand by what I did."

Asher lowered his chin, draping his white hair across his high cheekbones. "I would expect no less from you."

There were one-hundred different ways to interpret his words, so I didn't try. I turned to Steifan as he retrieved his fallen sword and sheathed it. "Can you carry the girl? I want to get out of here before Egar decides to come back."

Steifan nodded, then knelt by the cage, gently pulling the unconscious girl into his arms.

I was ready to go, but Asher was still looking at the two dead men.

"Hungry?" I asked, then instantly regretted it. I had used all of my energy breaking the Nattmara's glamour. I was getting cranky.

"The Nattmara killed them where they stood," he observed, ignoring my foulness. "They did not struggle." He looked at me. "His glamour is this strong, and you managed to break it?"

Suddenly I was uncomfortable. In truth, I was just as surprised as he. "My sword helped," I muttered.

He observed me closely, probably wondering if I was joking, though he knew the sword was sentient. Whatever conclusion he reached, he did not question me further. "I found another entrance near the old keep. Perhaps we should go that way."

"Lead on." I gestured toward the doorway with my bloody sword. Even though the danger was gone, I didn't feel quite ready to put it away.

I followed behind Asher, and Steifan behind me. We found our lantern with just enough oil to see us out. The girl never woke as we walked, and I hoped she would not until morning. I didn't want her to wake screaming in the night. Better to wake when she could see her surroundings and know that she was safe.

We would take her back to where she belonged, and she would be safe. It was more than I could say for the rest of us.

CHAPTER FORTY-THREE

The entrance Asher had found let out just south of the old keep. It was another old cellar, like the one behind the guild hall. As we climbed out into the moonlight, I wondered if there was another entrance near where we had found Jeramy's body. If I could find it, it would confirm some of my theories about Charlotte's death.

With Steifan still carrying the unconscious girl, we searched for a private area in the keep. We would need to watch her until she woke. Unfortunately, dawn was still well off. I was hungry and cold, more cold than the weather permitted. It was like pushing Egar out of my mind had taken the very warmth from my veins.

Asher found a small alcove, protected on three sides by ruined walls still tall enough to conceal us. There was no covering over our heads, giving a clear view of the calm stars.

I helped Steifan remove his cloak, then spread it on the ground for him to set the girl upon it. We tugged the edges of the cloak around her, leaving her to rest.

Asher watched us silently.

I glanced at him as I stood. "I appreciate you escorting us out of the canals, but there is no reason for you to stay here any longer."

He didn't move. He just stood there like a tall, brooding statue. "We need to speak about the ancient you killed, and the Nattmara."

Steifan looked back and forth between the two of us. "I think I'll go see if I can find a bit of wood for a fire." He retreated from the alcove, though he probably wanted sleep even worse than I did.

I bundled my cloak around me, suppressing a shiver. My sword had remained silent at my back after it helped me with the Nattmara. It obviously didn't mind Asher being near. "What else is there to talk about?"

Asher stepped close, looming over me. If he was bothered by the blood on my face and clothing, he didn't show it. "You are my servant, and you killed an ancient."

I hiked one shoulder in a small half shrug. "Three other ancients were killed the night Karpov died. Why is this one any different?"

Ire pinched his eyes, making me suddenly nervous. I couldn't recall if I had ever seen him truly angry. Annoyed, yes, but not the wrath I was sensing from him now. "Those who had joined Karpov had turned against us. They signed their own death warrants. The vampire you killed tonight tried to leave you in peace. He respected our laws."

Anger prickled my skin. "He was trying to *buy* that girl." I gestured to the small, cloak-wrapped bundle behind me. "And he had bought others. If I left him alive, more would be kidnapped. I can only hope his death will set an example for the other vampires in the city."

Asher lifted his chin. "My kind must feed, Lyssandra, it is what we are. Many are not strong enough to bespell victims and not take too much blood."

I stepped closer, my indignance making me bold. "If vampires kill, I hunt them. That is what *I* am."

He leaned in toward my face and lowered his voice. "I am well aware of your oaths, but your self-righteous attitude has furthered Karpov's plan. One ancient was already killed several nights ago. And now another has perished. Soon there will be too few of us to control the young ones. And what will you do then? What will be the cost of your actions this night?"

My back hunched. He was right, I had helped Karpov from beyond the grave. But it could have been no other way. The kidnappings had to stop.

Asher watched me. "Your expression hints that you have seen reason, though experience tells me that cannot be the case."

I rubbed my eyes, slowly shaking my head. "I do see the reason behind your words, but you cannot ask me to forsake my oaths. I am sworn to protect innocents. Every life is valuable. I could not sacrifice that girl and others like her just to keep one ancient alive."

"If you're going to help me discover who killed the other ancient, you will need to be amongst more of my kind. I cannot bring you near them if you plan to personally dole out justice for their crimes."

I tried to call back my anger, but it was no use. I was just too tired. "The dead deserve justice."

"Perhaps, but it does not always have to be dealt by your hand."

I looked up at him. "How about this? If I am to meet a vampire, forewarn them to commit no crimes in front of me. If I do not personally see them attacking or killing someone, I will have no need to hunt them."

A smile tugged at the corner of his lips. "My, what a generous compromise."

I glared, tugging my cloak more tightly around me. "My advice to you would be to accept what you can get."

His smile broadened. "Dear Lyssandra, that is what I have been doing with you from the start."

I wasn't sure why I asked my next question. Call it exhaustion-induced delirium. "Is that why you never touch me? You take only what is offered?"

"Would you *like* me to touch you?"

I frowned and stepped back. "Absolutely not. I was just curious." I tensed as he moved a hand toward his coat pocket.

He stopped for a moment, noting my reaction, then slowly tugged a white handkerchief from his pocket. He stepped toward me.

Feeling like a hare cornered by a snake, I watched him wide-eyed as he dabbed the handkerchief against my cheek, then down across my chin, ending just below my mouth. When he pulled the fabric away, it was stained with drying blood.

My throat went tight at his closeness, my mouth dry. "I thought you wouldn't touch me unless I offered."

"You said that, not I."

I sneered. "Way to prove a point."

I wasn't sure what triggered the thought, but suddenly I was thinking about his sorrow when he told Ryllae he didn't know if any of her kind were still alive. He had a heart, unless the emotions were a ruse to trick me into thinking as such.

"Why did you really come to Silgard?" I asked quietly. "And don't say it was only to ask for my help. I won't believe you."

He tucked the stained handkerchief back into his pocket. "I do not believe you actually want the answer to that question."

He was right. If he came here just to see me, I didn't want to know. "Never mind. Steifan and I can watch over the girl. There is no reason for you to stay with us."

"Do you find my company so distasteful?"

He knew I didn't. I never would have kissed him if I did. "I must focus on the tasks before me."

He smiled. "And I'm too . . . *distracting?*"

"Too annoying is more like it."

He laughed, not offended in the slightest.

I rolled my eyes and turned as Steifan peeked into the alcove. But he wasn't looking at me. He was staring at Asher, who was grinning wide enough to show fangs. Steifan seemed to take it as a sign that it was safe to return, and stepped the rest of the way into the space, a few small jagged pieces of wood bundled under one arm.

He walked past me and tossed the wood into the dirt. "I begged a flint and steel from a merchant caravan. They didn't seem to want to ask questions once they noticed the blood on my clothes."

I used the distraction to step away from Asher. It was time to get back to business. "We need to discuss the Nattmara. We must seek his lair and weaken him before he can find—" I hesitated, not wanting to speak Ryllae's name out loud. "What he seeks," I finished.

Asher followed me to stand in front of the fire Steifan was attempting to build. "It nearly killed you tonight. Now you want to find its lair?"

Steifan and Asher both looked at me as I explained, "The Nattmara's lair is its place of power, a site for ritual magic. When I slew Egar's sister, I weakened her by destroying a ritual urn."

"But Egar is as much Sidhe as he is Nattmara," Steifan countered. "His magic may not be the same."

He was right, but I didn't know what else to do. I

couldn't just wait around for Egar to find us again. "He travels the canals. If he does have a lair, I think it is somewhere down there. It is the only way I can think of to weaken him."

Smoke billowed up from Steifan's small wood pile. "And what about everything else we discovered tonight?" Steifan asked. "We must remember we are here to solve Duchess Auclair's murder."

I sat in the dirt, extending my cold hands toward the first small flames. "Tomorrow we will go to Duke Auclair and tell him what we know. He can either admit his role in things, or we will take our findings to the Archduke."

"What about the Montrants?"

I stared down into the flames, wondering if the Potentate had known what he was sending us into. "Let us start with the duke. We don't actually have any solid evidence, so having his testimony will help. If he is frightened enough, he may tell us if the Montrants are in charge, or simply just involved."

My shoulders began to relax from the fire's warmth. I longed for my comfortable bed at Castle Helius, with four safe walls and a locked door . . . and no vampires.

Asher loomed over the fire, but did not sit. I was pretty sure vampires never got cold. "You should rest," he said to me. "I will keep watch."

I gave him an incredulous look. "You expect me to trust you enough to sleep in front of you?"

He stared at me, his face impassive.

I chewed the inside of my cheek. I didn't need a vampire watching over me. I didn't *want* a vampire watching over me. But Steifan and I were alone in this city. The Nattmara was out there, and I couldn't forget that someone had been hired to kill us. So maybe I just didn't *want* a vampire watching over me, but the need would have to outweigh my pride, if only to keep Steifan and the girl safe for the night.

"Fine," I acquiesced.

Steifan gave me a shooing gesture with his hands across the fire, urging me to say more.

I gritted my teeth. "You have my thanks."

Asher shrugged and walked toward the opening of the alcove. "Consider it pre-payment for the aid you will give me once we are back in the mires."

I stared at his back for a moment, then shook my head. Usually, I found men easy to understand, but the vampire perplexed even me.

Steifan had already laid on his back in the dirt and closed his eyes. *He* didn't seem perplexed by the vampire.

I tugged my hood up, then curled on my side near the fire, wrapping my cloak around me. I left my sword on, just in case. Maybe I didn't understand men as well as I thought, though I really hated being wrong.

I closed my eyes, willing myself to rest. While I could have gone another night or two without sleep, there was no saying what morning might bring, and I needed to restore my energy if I was to hunt the Nattmara.

As I fell in and out of wakefulness, I sensed Asher's eyes on me from time to time, and I noticed when he added a bit more wood to the fire. When he came near, my body naturally relaxed, like my instincts were telling me I was safe. And when he retreated . . . I felt the loss of him, even though I knew he wasn't going far.

I was beginning to regret my years of hunting him. I should have stayed far away, where the bond between us was nothing but a flimsy thread. Now it was an iron chain, binding us together. Only it didn't feel like cold iron. It felt like warm silk rubbing across my bare skin.

Eventually, I forced myself to sleep. After all, Asher

401

could only watch us until dawn. For as human as he sometimes seemed, he was still a creature of the night. And that was a fact I would never forget.

MORNING CAME TOO SOON, and my stomach was painfully empty. I sat up to find Steifan already awake, speaking with the girl, who seemed calm.

"Why didn't you wake me?" I groaned.

Steifan and the girl both looked at me. She seemed older now than I had originally thought, just small-boned, but lovely. Her reddish hair puffed up around her face, and I wondered if the color gave her any trouble, though it was not a true ruby shade like mine.

"Asher woke me when he had to leave," Steifan explained. "He said you spent too much energy last night . . . *dealing* with things. He asked that I let you rest."

I pinched my brow as a dull ache started between my eyes. "I would like to argue, but I cannot. I don't usually sleep so deeply."

"Perhaps he knows what's best for you." Steifan winked.

I rubbed my sore head as the ache progressed. "I really wish I had something to throw at you right now." I turned my attention to the girl. "Are you alright?"

She nodded, though her eyes were a touch wary.

"She lives not far from here," Steifan explained. "She didn't know the man who took her from the square, nor did she at any time see anyone she recognized."

Though I felt like a sack of manure, I forced myself to stand. "We will walk you home then," I said to the girl. "I would ask that you hide away for the next few days until we make sure we find everyone involved in kidnapping you."

As she stood, I looked her up and down, ending with her bare feet. "What happened to your shoes?" I asked.

"They took them when I tried to run away. They said if I tried again, they would cut off my feet. Steifan says you don't yet know who took me."

I sighed. "We have a few ideas. Are you acquainted with any of the nobility?"

Frowning, she shook her head.

I believed her. She had probably just been randomly chosen based on her appearance. Like the Nattmara said, vampires will eat just about anything.

I tugged up my hood, covering my hair and shadowing the blood likely still staining my face, then moved the Seeing Sword back to my belt. "Let's go. I need something to eat."

I turned away, heading out of the alcove. Steifan and the girl followed. It was an effort to keep my dizziness at bay. I hadn't realized how much I had pushed myself to break the Nattmara's glamour.

While I was reluctant to visit Ryllae again, I might just have to find her after we visited the duke. I needed to be better prepared to break Egar's glamour, or else next time I faced him—with him ready for my new skills—I would lose.

CHAPTER FORTY-FOUR

Mid-morning found us back at the wrought-iron gates leading to the wealthy district, arguing with the two guards, *again*. At least the girl's husband had insisted he provide us with a meal when we brought her home, else I would not have been able to maintain my temper.

I was barely maintaining it as it was.

The guard arguing fervently with us was the same one who had escorted us to the duke's estate. "Come back in proper attire, and I will let you through," he said for the hundredth time.

Steifan and I were both still in our traveling cloaks. The fabric was dark enough to hide the bloodstains, and we used them to cover the more obvious stains on our clothing underneath. I almost wished I hadn't washed the blood from my face. Maybe then the guard would be frightened enough to let us through without argument.

I crossed my arms. "We are not leaving to simply change into our armor and return. Just the other day, you didn't want us passing with armor and weapons. Now you want us to have them?"

He glanced at the sword, still obvious at my hip even though it was mostly covered by my cloak. "You still have weapons, and now you don't even look like hunters of the Helius Order. I won't be up on charges of letting mercenaries past my guard."

"But we're *not* mercenaries," I growled.

"But you *look* like mercenaries."

I wanted to argue that we could just go through the canals and bypass them, but one, I didn't want him to know we knew about them, and two, I didn't want to risk running into Egar again before we could confront the duke. It pained me though to not point out to the guard how silly his argument was.

Steifan and I both turned at footsteps approaching our backs. It was the duke himself, looking disheveled and flustered. Surprisingly, he seemed relieved to see us. "I've been looking for you two everywhere. Come with me." His beady eyes scorned the guards yet blocking our way. "What are you waiting for? Open the gate."

The guards hurried to obey, and I couldn't help my smug smile as Steifan and I followed the duke through the entrance.

Not saying a word, the duke led the way toward his estate.

I glanced at Steifan as we followed the duke's podgy, brocade-clad form, my brows lifted in question.

Steifan shrugged. So we both didn't know why the duke had sought us out personally, rather than sending Vannier or another servant. Nor why he had been out in the city searching for us alone.

We reached the estate, then waited while the duke ascended the short exterior stairs, opening the door himself. No sign of Vannier within. We went inside, and the duke shut and locked the door behind us.

"Upstairs," he said. "I don't want to risk someone listening at any of the windows."

We followed him across the sitting room, then up the stairs. The situation was getting stranger and stranger, but my sword hadn't warned me. We weren't being lured into a trap.

Once we were upstairs, the duke gestured for us to go through the first doorway, which led into a large office. Open shutters let in a cool breeze. There were two chairs on the far side of the desk, opposite the over-cushioned monstrosity meant for the duke.

I decided against either chair, opting to lean my back lightly against the wall just inside the doorway.

The duke didn't seem to take offense. He hurried around Steifan, then stood facing us both. He tugged a handkerchief from his vest pocket, wiping the sheen of sweat from his forehead. "I have something I must admit to both of you. My life is in danger."

I crossed my arms, waiting for him to continue. If he was about to tell us everything, there was no need to threaten him yet with the information we had discovered.

He glanced around the office, as if someone else had followed us up the stairs, but we were entirely alone. I heard nary a sound from the rest of the house.

"I didn't find Charlotte's body here," he breathed. "I found her rotting in the slums."

He seemed to expect surprise from us, but neither of our faces gave anything away. I nodded for him to continue.

He licked his lips, considering his next words. "I knew she wasn't killed by the vampire who bit her, but I needed a reason to bring in outside help. I wanted hunters to investigate her murder because too many of the city guard are involved."

I lifted my brows. He had finally surprised me. "You wanted us to investigate, even though you knew she wasn't killed by a vampire?"

He nodded quickly, his eyes wide. "I can trust no one within the city. I needed outside help. I . . . I wanted out, and they killed her as a warning to me."

I decided to put him out of his misery, if only to speed the conversation along. "You were involved in the kidnappings, and you knew they were being sold to vampires."

He paled. "How did you—"

"You wanted us to investigate, did you not? We could tell Charlotte had been moved here through the canals after her death, and we found Jeramy DeRose. And you obviously know that two men and a vampire were killed in the canals last night, or else you wouldn't have so desperately sought us out this morning."

The duke hung his head, shuffling around the desk to slump down into his chair. He rubbed his eyes with one plump hand. "They think I sent you down into the canals. They've realized why I really called you here."

I stepped toward the desk. "Who are they? Who is in charge?"

"So you haven't figured out everything then," he muttered, slouching further down in his seat. "Bellamy Montrant. He is the one who made the deal with the vampires. Charlotte had started a . . . business, else we would have gone destitute. When Bellamy approached me with an opportunity, I jumped at it. I would have done anything so that Charlotte could . . . "

Steifan moved forward and took one of the chairs across the desk from the duke. "We know of Charlotte's business. You can speak freely."

I blinked at them both, realizing something. The duke was a terrible man, but he did have an ounce of honor to him after all. "That's why you didn't want us to have Charlotte's ledger. You didn't want anyone else knowing her secret. You hoped we could solve her murder without uncovering that aspect."

His face pinched and grew red. "So you knew about the ledger, then. I did want to keep her secret buried. She deserved that much consideration, at least. When she started coming home with the vampire bites, I worried she was going to get herself killed. I think—" he shook his head. "I think she was actually in love with the creature, and she never would have met him had I not involved us in Montrant's scheme."

I nodded along. "You tried to pull out to get her away from the vampire, and you think Montrant killed her to send you a message. But why was she meeting with Jeramy DeRose?"

He rubbed his face and shook his head. "That was my fault too. I knew Montrant was watching me, so I sent Charlotte there instead. Jeramy was the first person Bellamy approached about his scheme. When he refused, the Montrants ruined him. I thought if we went to Jeramy, we might have enough evidence to approach the Archduke."

"And you think Montrant killed them both," I finished for him. "When Charlotte never returned, you went looking for her body, and knowing she had vampire bites, you devised your plan. But why wait so long to bring her body home? The rot would suggest she was in Jeramy's home for quite some time."

He grimaced. "I had to figure out a way to bring her body back without anyone seeing it, but I didn't know who to trust. I knew she was supposed to meet with the vampire at the end of the following week. She always met him on the same night, so I went in her stead. I think the creature loved her too, as much as he was able. He helped me move her body."

I stared at him. "If the vampire really loved her, why didn't he avenge her?"

The duke looked like he was trying to swallow something sharp. "He said there was an ancient vampire involved, and he could not stand against him. After he helped me move Charlotte's body, he fled the city. He agreed that I should contact the Helius Order, but wanted to be nowhere near once you arrived."

"Smart vampire," Steifan muttered.

I considered all the duke had told us. It made sense. If he would repeat the story to the Archduke, and we could provide validity by backing up his claims, we might just get permission to launch a full investigation. No more sneaking through canals or having our way barred by guards.

"We will go to the Archduke immediately," I decided. "You will repeat everything you have told us."

His eyes went wide. He stood, staggering backwards with palms outstretched. "No, you don't understand. I'll be killed before I can utter a word. Too many guards are involved." He backed away until he was near the open window. "You'll have to go to the Archduke yourselves."

I heard the bolt release outside and opened my mouth to shout a warning, but I was too late. The duke's body lurched forward as an arc of blood erupted from his neck.

Steifan hopped over the desk to land beside the fallen duke while I rushed to the window. I peered out just in time to see a figure in the duke's garden, hiding a crossbow in the folds of his loose cloak. A hood shadowed his face.

I rushed past Steifan and out into the hall, then took the

stairs down two by two. I exited the estate, then practically flew back to the garden, vaulting over the tall fence. I whipped around, scanning the manicured shrubs and the garish fountain.

I cursed under my breath. I hadn't been fast enough. The garden was empty, and I had seen the duke's wound. He would not survive to tell his tale again.

"Lyss!" a voice I recognized called out.

It was almost too much to hope for, but when I turned I spotted Tholdri's golden hair out on the street beyond the fence. He wore his full armor, with a sword at his shoulder.

I cast a final glance around the garden, then ran toward him. "What in the light are you doing here?"

He gave me a smug smile and leaned his hands against the fence. "I convinced the Potentate to let me come. I told him I was worried you would get into trouble amongst the nobles. I was just coming to Duke Auclair's to look for you."

I shook my head, overwhelmingly grateful to see him, but too busy to express it. "We need to get back inside. Someone just hit the duke with a crossbow through the window. I ran out here looking for them, but they're gone."

His eyes widened. "Why wasn't that the first thing out of your mouth when you saw me?"

He turned away from the fence, leaving me to vault over it and catch up to his back as he walked toward the door. We both hurried inside and up the stairs, finding Steifan just about to come down them.

His grim expression and bloody hands told me what I already knew. "He's dead." He looked at me. "Did you find who shot the bolt?"

I stepped next to him and shook my head. "I wasn't fast enough. Tholdri found me as I was searching the garden."

Steifan looked at Tholdri. "I must say, I'm glad to see

you. We have found ourselves in quite the mess. Has Lyss told you about the Nattmara?"

Tholdri blinked at me, his jaw slack. "Now *that's* what you should have started with. The one from Charmant?"

I sighed. "We have much to catch you up on, but first we need to fetch the guards and let them know the duke is dead. If we are lucky, they'll believe we didn't do it."

"Perhaps it was unwise of me to come after all," Tholdri said.

I started down the stairs. "You have no idea."

"Asher is here," I heard Steifan whisper to Tholdri at my back.

Tholdri chuckled. "A fresh murder, an ancient vampire, and a Nattmara? Traveling with Lyss is never dull, is it?"

I reached the foot of the stairs and went for the door. "We will add two more murders to the list if you two don't shut up."

Masculine laughter followed me out the door.

Tholdri was right. My life was a lot of things. Dull was not one of them.

CHAPTER FORTY-FIVE

The guards didn't blame us. Imagine that. It was clear that the bolt came from outside, and someone on the street had seen the cloaked man running away and confirmed that it wasn't Tholdri. Though that still left us with knowing everything, but having no evidence or reliable testimony. With the duke dead, it would be our word against the Montrants, and we would lose.

We explained everything to Tholdri as we headed back toward the old keep, since I wasn't sure where else to go. I didn't think the duke's death would cancel out the contract on our heads. In fact, it would be safe to assume things had escalated. The duke had been killed for what he had to tell us, and now we knew highly dangerous information.

Tholdri glanced around the ruins of the old keep. Many of the camps had cleared out by the light of day with most of the traveling merchants down at the main square, though a few lone souls remained behind to watch over wagons and horses.

"We have to go back to the canals," I said to Steifan.

"We'll find proof to take to the Archduke." I leaned my back against a crumbling stone wall and looked up at the gray sky. Rain would come by midday.

"What about the Nattmara?" Steifan asked, leaning against the wall beside me.

I shook my head. "I don't know. I'm not sure if I could break his glamour again now that he would be ready for me. I wounded him, but there's no saying how fast he might heal."

"Should we go back to Ryllae?" he asked.

Finished looking around, Tholdri stood in front of us. "Who is Ryllae?"

I winced at the second mention of her name. I doubted Egar was watching us—my sword would warn me—but just in case, it was best not to speak her name if he didn't know it. I didn't want to give him any more information on her if I could help it. "She is someone whose name we should not say out loud. She taught me how to break the Nattmara's glamour, but we can't risk returning to her now when her blood could make him practically immortal. If he hadn't wanted to toy with us down in the canals, Steifan and I would both be dead. We must attack before he can lay a trap."

"She taught you to break glamour?" Tholdri asked. "Is she a witch?"

I relaxed my stance. Tholdri was far too adept at telling when I was lying. "Yes. She has studied every aspect of magic, and taught me some of what she learned."

I figured since Ryllae was already masquerading as a witch, it was the best lie I could tell to cover up her heritage. Technically the oath I had sworn was in regard to breaking glamour, but I thought it prudent to keep all of Ryllae's secrets, just in case.

Tholdri stroked his chin in thought. I thought for a moment he had caught my lie, but then he asked, "So the Nattmara wants to eat her? Poor woman."

Steifan moved away from the wall to look at me. "Lyss, if Egar kills us, there will be nothing to stop him from finding her. I think it might be worth the risk to speak with her first."

"He has a point," Tholdri said, always one to catch on quickly.

"She has strong magic," Steifan added. "She can protect herself."

I mulled it over, easily recalling the feel of Egar's glamour scraping across my mind. He'd almost had me. My breathing felt too shallow. Could I face Egar again without further preparation? Could I risk Steifan and Tholdri in the process?

"Be smart about this, Lyss," Tholdri pressed.

He was right. I hated endangering Ryllae further, but I would not exchange her life for Steifan's or Tholdri's. "Fine," I decided, "we will go to her. *I* will go to her. You two will hang back and make sure no one is watching."

Tholdri looked at Steifan. "She has become far more reasonable since she started spending time with you."

"Or far more stupid," I muttered, pushing away from the wall.

Tholdri laughed, and both men turned to follow me.

I kept my eyes trained on my surroundings as I walked, ignoring the presence of Tholdri and Steifan behind me. If I led Egar to Ryllae . . .

I could not think of that now. Steifan and Tholdri were right. I needed the tools to defeat the Nattmara. If I could not kill him, he would find Ryllae eventually, with or without my help.

We reached the small structure Ryllae called home. A few men and women stood around, eating their midday meals and lounging by the smoldering embers of their campfires. Steifan lingered near one of the larger camps. Tholdri had diverted. I didn't see him, but I knew he would be watching.

An older woman dressed in bright foreign silks eyed me as I neared Ryllae's doorway. "She's not there. I heard a struggle near dawn."

My breath left my body, and I was frozen for a moment. Then I took an aching inhale and rushed through Ryllae's doorway, taking in the signs one by one. Blood on the hard-packed earth. Ashes from the fire scattered. A few belongings strewn about.

My heart thundered in my ears. No mortal could take one of the Sidhe on their own. Egar had found her.

I ran back outside, spotting Steifan.

He met me halfway. "What happened?"

I shook my head over and over. This was my fault. I hadn't been able to finish Egar off, and now he had found Ryllae. "He has her. He has Ryllae. We need to search the canals, we have to find his lair."

Steifan's eyes went wide. "But what if his lair isn't in the canals?"

I reached out and gripped his arms. "It has to be."

Tholdri appeared at my side. I turned to explain things to him, but he shook his head. "I heard, let's go."

I nodded. "There is an entrance to the canals near here. We'll start with that. If Ryllae is still alive—"

"We will find her," Tholdri cut me off. "I promise."

With another nod, I turned and led the way, not speaking my final thought. *Don't make promises you can't keep.*

WE CREATED a makeshift torch to light our way. Fortunately, Steifan still had his borrowed flint, and I still had Ryllae's ointment. We smeared it on our eyes and ears, for what good it would do.

I led us deep into the damp darkness, praying we could find Ryllae in time. If she was already dead, Egar would kill us all. My heart pounded loudly in my ears as we crept down one long stretch of canal. I held the torch out to light our path, wondering if Asher would feel it when I died, then I pushed the thought away. Dying wasn't an option, not when Steifan and Tholdri would go with me.

We passed the tunnel that would eventually take us to the trapdoor in the estate cellar. I knew that direction led to other trapdoors among the estates, then farther along would be the exit behind the guild hall. I didn't think Egar would be in that direction, else we would have seen signs of him. If he was stealing the vampire's victims, he was probably somewhere close to where they were held, but far enough to not be discovered.

We reached the place where the two men and ancient vampire fell. I held the torch inside, taking a quick glance around. The bodies were gone, the cage empty. I moved on. Steifan and Tholdri followed silently at my back.

Fear made my hand clammy around the torch. Cold sweat dripped down my brow. I could not recall being so frightened since the night Karpov killed my uncle, so many years ago. But I couldn't let that fear get the better of me. Egar would only use it against us.

We reached another intersection, and I had to make a choice, because there was no way we were splitting up. I closed my eyes, reaching out with my senses. I could usually sense vampires when they were near, and I knew the feel of Egar's magic. I had to try.

Steifan and Tholdri didn't speak a word. They trusted me. It was nice to know I had good friends, especially since we all might die before nightfall.

My senses found nothing but darkness. The running water seemed impossibly loud. I cursed under my breath. I didn't know which way to go.

I was about to take my chances and head left when I felt a prickling at my back. It didn't feel like Egar, it felt like Ryllae. Was she still alive? Had she sensed me and managed to reach out?

"This way," I whispered to the men. "Be prepared."

I turned right, breaking into a jog with the torch's flame wavering wildly. I focused on that distant little flicker of magic, ignoring my other senses. I took countless turns, and knew if I managed to survive, I might have trouble finding my way back out. Tholdri and Steifan's footfalls echoed at my heels. Just as my lungs started burning, I sensed it. Great, concentrated magic. Egar's lair was near.

My sword awoke, sensing the magic too, but I didn't slow. Egar would already know I was coming.

I reached another bend and turned with Tholdri and Steifan breathing hard behind me. I turned again, running down a more narrow passage with no water flowing through it. Parts of the walls had crumbled, strewing rubble across my path. If I couldn't sense the magic so strongly, I would have passed the entrance. But I did sense it, so strong it was nearly overwhelming. What had once been a doorway was now half-filled with debris.

I halted so abruptly Tholdri had to reach out his arms, bracing on either side of the narrow tunnel to stop himself from running into me.

I drew my sword in one hand with the torch in the

other, then squeezed through the narrow opening. Jagged stone scraped across my skin through my clothing. Then I was out on the other side, looking both ways down a vacant tunnel with a long-dry canal. The tunnel must have been part of the original canal system, long since replaced with newer passageways.

Further down, soft light emanated from a doorway.

I waited for Steifan and Tholdri to make it through the opening, the latter having trouble squeezing his broad shoulders through the narrow space. I gave myself one last moment to observe both of them, to treasure them, knowing it might be the last moment we would ever have.

I am a hunter of the Helius Order, I said in my mind. *And I am not afraid.*

I crept toward the light with Steifan and Tholdri following close behind, slowing as I neared the doorway. The smell of blood was so overwhelming for a moment I thought we were too late, but then I realized I could still feel Ryllae's magic urging me forward.

"Greetings, hunters," a distorted voice echoed from within the chamber.

I handed the torch back to Steifan, gripped my sword in two hands, then walked through the doorway.

My stomach lurched. The floor was coated in blood, both old and new, with body parts strewn about. I didn't let my eyes linger long enough to figure out exactly what they were. In the center of the room was Ryllae, lying eerily still on her back.

Egar hunched over her, clutching her small body with long claws. He lifted his face, catching the candlelight in the room to show rows of sharp teeth dripping with Ryllae's blood. I took a step closer to see a wound at her neck.

The Seeing Sword's magic flowed through me, eager to slay the monster before us.

Egar's glistening eyes looked past me. "I see you have brought me a feast."

He meant Steifan and Tholdri, but I didn't dare look back at them. "Step away from her," I ordered. "It is time we end this." The reek of decay in the chamber made it difficult to regain my breath, but I held my sword steady.

Egar stood, and if I didn't know any better, I'd say he'd grown taller. His monstrous claws were half the length of his forearms. He flicked the blood off of them, sending tiny crimson droplets across the floor, then used his sleeve to wipe the blood from his malformed mouth. "It is too late. The Sidhe's blood has strengthened me. I will cut off your legs and keep you here to feed from in the future."

His glamour slammed into me. Everything went gray, then I felt a sharp stinging pain at my throat. I staggered back, clutching the hilt of my sword for dear life. I couldn't see, I couldn't hear. I didn't know where Steifan and Tholdri were.

The Seeing Sword came alive, pushing back a small measure of the glamour. I felt blood trickling down my throat, but the wounds caused by Egar's claws seemed shallow. He could have killed me in that first rush, but either his desire to draw things out—or to keep me alive for later—had stopped him.

I still couldn't see, but I could sense Egar's movements. He circled me, and I was able to move my feet to follow his pacing, keeping my sword between us.

Egar stopped moving. "Tricky girl with your strange sword. But can you sense your companions? Are they already dead?"

My hands trembled so violently that I nearly dropped my sword. It urged me to remain calm, but my fear was winning. Why could I sense Egar, but not Steifan and Tholdri? Had he killed them as soon as he blinded me?

No. I had to shut the thoughts out. I wouldn't let him manipulate me. My sword in my hands was the only thing that felt truly real, so I focused on that. I gripped the hilt so tightly that the leather dug into my calloused skin.

My sword echoed a warning in my mind and I spun, but I was too slow. My arm stung with four fresh cuts from Egar's claws. His glamour swirled around me.

"Open your eyes. See what you have done to your friends."

I blinked, and my vision came swimming back. Blood, so much more blood than there was before. Steifan was on the ground, face down. I couldn't see his injuries. And Tholdri—

Tholdri lay on his back, a gaping hole right where his heart should have been. Killed, just like my uncle Isaac had been killed.

The tip of my sword dragged across the ground as my grip on it weakened. Bile crept up the back of my throat. I shook my head, still staring at Tholdri. He had been a part of my life from the start. He was my dearest friend. And I had done this to him. I brought him down here, knowing we couldn't win.

The Nattmara approached my back, but I couldn't move. "Do you see what you have done?"

There was a roaring in my mind, drowning out everything else. He had killed them. He had killed my two dearest friends. My *only* two friends.

The roaring in my head grew louder, so loud I couldn't hear Egar's next words. I screamed, then tore free of his invisible hold on my body. I spun my sword, slashing it across his chest.

He screeched and staggered back, then his glamour slammed into me again. Everything went black.

Focus, I told myself, or maybe it was my sword speaking to me. With Steifan and Tholdri gone, I did not care if I died. I would die right then and there, but I would be taking Egar with me. He did not get to kill them and live. I tried to feel the presence of my blade, but a different kind of magic seeped into my consciousness. *Ryllae*. She was still alive. Her old words coursed through my mind. I had forgotten to use them, but she was using them for me now. The gray began to lift from my vision.

Egar's shriek of rage was the only warning I had. My sword moved, but I didn't remember moving it. It was as if it guided my arms and not the other way around. I felt it slide into Egar's flesh.

He shrieked again, but more importantly, his glamour lessened. I was finally able to see the room. The *real* room. Tholdri still stood in the doorway, staring blankly. Next to him, Steifan blinked, as if trying to focus his eyes on me. The fresh wounds on my arm were steadily dripping blood onto the ground. My eyes welled with tears. It had been an illusion. He hadn't really killed them.

I tore my gaze away from Steifan and Tholdri, searching instead for the Nattmara.

I found him pressing his back into the far corner, clutching his torn abdomen. His glamour scraped against my mind, trying to find a way back in.

"How?" he rasped. "How are you keeping me out? The Sidhe couldn't even keep me out."

I didn't bother to explain that my sword and Ryllae had helped me. Together, we were strong enough. I lunged forward, shoving my blade up through his chest. He grunted, and I pulled it out in a wash of blood. He fell to his knees, but still he did not die.

"How?" he gasped again. "With her blood, I should have been immortal."

I raised my sword over my shoulder. "Ask me how many *immortals* I have killed, and maybe it will make sense to you."

I didn't give him time to ask. I swung my sword, parting his head from his shoulders. I watched his head rolling across the floor, and could have sworn it blinked before the eyes finally went distant with death.

CHAPTER FORTY-SIX

Panting, I lowered my sword, glancing back toward Steifan and Tholdri.

Steifan was the first to regain his senses. He looked at me, his eyes registering the death of the Nattmara, then he rushed to Ryllae.

I was at her other side in an instant, placing my bloody sword on the stone floor beside me. I knelt over her, checking her blood-slick neck for a pulse. Her bleeding had slowed, but there was a big pool on the ground and who knew how much had gone in Egar's mouth.

I nearly jumped out of my skin when her eyes fluttered open. She lifted a hand to her throat, her fingers fluttering like butterfly wings. "You came." Her words gurgled, letting me know she had blood in her airway, but she seemed to be healing. Even now, I could see her torn skin slowly beginning to reknit.

If she healed faster than a vampire, could Egar do the same? I whipped my gaze back toward his body, then calmed myself. His head remained fully parted from his shoulders. But seeing how well Ryllae could heal, I knew I'd be burning his body before I'd be able to sleep at night.

Tholdri had finally regained his senses and came to stand over us. "What in the light just happened?"

I looked up at him. "Glamour. Steifan seems to have more of a resistance to it than you." My mind flashed across the image of Steifan on the ground, of Tholdri with his heart torn out. My tears threatened again.

Steifan stayed kneeling at Ryllae's other side, not noticing the look in my eyes. "I could hear what was going on, but I couldn't see nor move." Ryllae reached out for his hand, and he helped her sit up.

Steifan might not have noticed, but Tholdri had always been the most perceptive man I'd ever known. He stepped toward me. "Lyss, what happened while we were gone?"

His choice of words made a fist clench around my heart. *Gone*, I had thought they were both gone. I shook my head. "Egar was messing with my mind, showing me things that weren't real."

"What things?"

I shook my head again. "It doesn't matter." I turned back to Ryllae. "Can you walk?"

She still clutched her throat, but the color was returning to her cheeks. She nodded.

Tholdri watched her, wide-eyed. "How is she healing?"

Ryllae looked at me, managing a pained smile through the blood coating her face. "You really know how to keep a secret, don't you?"

"That she does," Steifan said from her other side.

Tholdri put his hands on his hips, looming over us. "Would someone please tell me what's really going on? Witches are only so powerful. Why did Egar want her?"

I stood with my hands coated in Ryllae's blood. "The

Nattmara is dead, and his victim will survive. Does it matter how she manages to heal?"

"You're infuriating."

With Steifan's help, Ryllae stood. "It is not her secret to tell. Just be grateful that she shares her own with you."

I raised a brow at her. "How do you know that?"

She shrugged, then winced. "They are both important to you. Egar tried to use them to destroy you. When I helped you overcome the glamour, I could sense that your greatest need was to protect them."

Though he still didn't fully know what was going on, Tholdri grinned and put an arm around my shoulder. "That's our Lyss. Just a big softy."

I shoved his arm away with a laugh, though it cost me. I wanted nothing more than to stay wrapped up in his arms, assuring myself that he was real. Instead, I glanced once more at the Nattmara. It was hard to believe he was actually dead. I searched for the torch, finding it had rolled against the wall right next to the doorway.

"Let's burn the body here," I said. "I don't want to risk him ever coming back, and we still need to bring justice to Duke and Duchess Auclair before the day is through. Maybe if we approach the Montrants covered in blood, we can scare them into confessing." I meant my words in jest, but thinking about it, maybe it wasn't such a bad idea.

"They are the culprits of your murder investigation?" Ryllae asked.

"Yes," I answered, "and they have been kidnapping people to sell them to vampires. The Nattmara was stealing some of the victims."

"And you would like to scare them into confessing?" she asked.

"I meant it half-joking," I explained. "I don't know how we would scare them enough to confess."

Seeming more steady on her feet, Ryllae smiled. "I believe I can help with that."

I found her smile unsettling, but I wouldn't turn down the help.

Just how frightening could one of the Sidhe be? We were about to find out.

WE BURNED the Nattmara where he lay. The task would have been near impossible without Ryllae's magic to help the flames along. She could not create the elements herself, but if they already existed, she could feed power into them.

By the time we were ready to flee the smoke-filled chamber, Tholdri was staring at Ryllae with a hint of realization. He hadn't heard Egar saying she was Sidhe, but he knew she'd taught me to break glamours, and that her blood was powerful. I was pretty sure he had figured it out. Thankfully, he said nothing of his findings.

As we fled the smoke, I filled Ryllae in on the rest of the details of the murders, learning that she had actually met Charlotte before. She knew her face well, and believed she could help.

Our first step was to leave a bloody piece of parchment in the Montrant's cellar, and I was quite sure after the duke's confession that it had been their cellar where we had first found the kidnapped girl.

That first step was easy, the next, more difficult. We had decided to wait until nightfall, which would give us time to make ourselves more presentable. Of the three of us, I was the most grotesque, covered in blood both old and new, with three scratches already healing at my throat and a collection of deeper ones across my arm.

Seeing no other option, I bathed in the cold dark water

of the canal. I ended up with sopping wet hair and clothing, trudging back toward the canal entrance near the old
keep. Once we were above ground, I hung my outer layers
of clothing to dry. Ryllae stayed with us, prepared to
protect us with her glamour if need be.

Yet, there was no need. We waited out the rest of
the day, which stretched on impossibly long, and eventually my clothes had dried enough to wear. Now that
Egar was dead, my mind was consumed with
providing justice for the Auclairs, and for all the
missing people. We had never found Bastien, so I
could only guess that he was dead. Maybe once the
Montrants confessed, they could tell us where to find
his body.

Ryllae stood beside me as I watched the sun making its
slow descent. Steifan and Tholdri had gone to buy food
and a new lantern, and it was the first time we had been
alone since she had first taught me about glamour.

"Your sword is special," she said, tucking a lock of dark
hair behind her ear. Her throat was fully healed, though
blood still stained her clothing.

I startled. "How do you know?"

"I've been alive a long time. I've seen something like it
before. It speaks to you."

"Could you hear it?" I hesitated, surprised at how easily
I admitted the secret.

She shook her head. "No, I would need to touch it to
hear it, and I would rather not. Such magic can sometimes
leave a residue. Where did you find it?"

There were few secrets between us now, so I saw no
reason not to tell her. "The Potentate of the Helius Order
gave it to me. It woke to my touch."

"I imagine it did," she said. "That blade was made by a
witch for a vampire. It is only meant to wake to the touch

of the undead, but it seems the bond you share with the vampire is enough."

I stared at her. That couldn't be right. "What do you mean?"

Her dark eyes held too many secrets. "I mean exactly as I say. Your sword was made for a vampire. Curious, that your Potentate would have it in his possession."

I shook my head, tossing my loose, drying locks over my shoulder. "No, you're wrong. The sword woke for the Potentate too. He was the last one to wield it. But he is not a vampire's human servant. He has aged at a normal rate."

She shrugged. "I do not know the man, but he has lied to you in one way or another. Either he did not actually wield the sword, or he is something other than what he seems. Considering he gave it to you with the expectancy for it to wake, he suspected what you are."

My mouth went dry. If the Potentate knew what the sword would do, and had suspected what I was, having the sword wake for me would have confirmed it.

And yet here I was, still alive and free.

"He claimed he tested it on others too," I said. "But it only woke for me."

"Perhaps it is a test he places upon the most skilled hunters."

I thought over her words, but it didn't make sense. Why would he need to test us? Hunters becoming human servants could not be a common thing. As far as I knew, Markus was the only other one. Of course, I hadn't known what he was before. There could easily be others hiding amongst our ranks.

"I would be careful around this man," Ryllae said.

I nodded, my gaze distant. "I'm always careful."

I fell silent with too many thoughts coursing through my mind to articulate. And I wasn't sure I wanted to. I had known the Potentate nearly my entire life. I had trusted all of his orders blindly. My uncle Isaac had trusted him too.

The sun disappeared over the ruins of the old keep, letting the darkness slowly seep in from the ground up. I had always found it strange that darkness fell that way, not from the sky, but from the ground. I gasped, feeling it the moment Asher woke.

Ryllae put a hand on my arm. "Are you well?"

I let my breath out slowly as the sensation faded. "I think I just felt Asher waking. He will be here soon." I turned wide eyes to her. "I don't know why I am feeling so much. It was never like this before. I've even felt his emotions. It was just for a moment, and it quickly went away, but it was so strong for a moment I thought the emotions were my own."

She glanced me over, as if there was something *else* I couldn't see. "I am not well-versed in the bond between vampire and servant, and even less so when the servant is a hunter, but I imagine it is similar to other types of magical bonds. They tend to strengthen with proximity, and time."

I licked my lips, considering her words. "Someone else told me that too, but I hadn't realized it would get this bad. Do you think it will get worse?"

"If it comes and goes, I'd say it already has. He's probably protecting you from much of it."

My stomach clenched, making me feel ill. If the bond would keep growing . . . Would I eventually become like any other servant? Would I lose my free will and identity?

I would kill us both before that happened.

Ryllae patted my arm. "I do not think it the most of your worries at the present."

I leaned against the wall and went quiet. I wasn't sure if that was true. It would be more true to say it wasn't my *only* worry. If the Potentate knew what I was, why hadn't he confronted me? I remembered his watchful gaze as Steifan and I departed Castle Helius. Why was he watching me? What was he waiting for?

The sword at my back, which had helped me many times, suddenly felt like a mighty weight.

I stood in silence as darkness took full hold of the night.

Just when I would have started to worry, I heard Steifan and Tholdri approaching, and could sense Asher with them.

The three men rounded the corner and came into view. Steifan and Tholdri both seemed to blend into the darkness, but Asher's white hair and pale skin stood out like the moon. With his black clothing, his pale skin was even more apparent. I shivered as I watched him approach, wondering if he really was blocking the bond between us to spare me.

His eyes were only for me as he reached us. He lifted a hand as if to touch me, then let it fall. "You defeated the Nattmara," he said.

I watched his hand as it returned to his side, imagining his long fingers caressing my cheek. If he really was protecting me from the bond, and it was still this intense . . . Hidden places in my body went tight just at the thought of it, contrasting with the nervous feeling in my gut.

I mustered a glare for Steifan and Tholdri, then turned my attention back to Asher. "I see *someone* filled you in."

He continued on as if my tenuous hostility did not exist, "And you have a plan for bringing your investigation to a close?"

I glanced at Ryllae, not sure how much she would want me to tell him.

She nodded once, her eyes wary. "Yes, we have a plan."

I realized Ryllae wasn't just protective of her secret. She

was actually frightened of Asher. At least someone was. It made me like her even more.

Asher watched me as Steifan unwrapped a piece of waxed parchment, then provided an enormous pastry.

The smell of cinnamon and pumpkin made my mouth water. I took the pastry with a lifted brow.

He grinned. "I thought you deserved a treat."

My laughter seemed to dissipate some of the tension. We had survived the Nattmara, and we had all but solved the murders. And Steifan knew the true way to my heart.

"We should go," Ryllae said with a mischievous smile. "We do not want to keep the Montrants waiting."

I grinned. I was actually excited to see what Ryllae could do, and to witness the utter terror on Lord and Lady Montrant's faces. Frightening a confession out of them was far better than just killing them. I wanted to see the pair utterly disgraced before they went to the executioner's block. Not to mention, they could provide the names of any others involved.

Asher watched the entire exchange impassively, not asking to come, but also not excusing himself. I needed distance from him, but . . . he had helped us along this far. He was just as involved as any of us.

I pursed my lips. It was only one night. One final task before I would run in the other direction. And he might be useful. "Do you want to come?" I glanced at Ryllae. "If it's all right with you?"

She considered for a moment, then nodded.

Asher seemed genuinely surprised. "An invitation from *my lady*? My, I thought this day would never come."

I narrowed my eyes. "Don't push it." I looked past him to Steifan and Tholdri. "Are you both ready?"

Tholdri grinned. "We were born ready."

I rolled my eyes, then led the way out toward the street.

Tholdri and Steifan would be going through the gates, while Ryllae and I would take back to the canals. I thought it best if Asher came with us and not the men. I might trust him more than I wanted, but I still didn't trust him not to eat my friends. What did that say about our relationship? What did it say that I actually thought of it as a relationship?

As usual, too many questions, not enough answers. Best just to focus on bringing justice. After all, it's what I did best.

CHAPTER FORTY-SEVEN

Ryllae, Asher, and I waited at the ladder leading up into the Montrant's cellar. I tried to keep my breathing quiet as Asher listened for sounds coming from above.

After a moment, his gray eyes turned down to me, glinting in the light of my new lantern. "There are four people in the house, none in the cellar. We should be safe to go up."

Ryllae huddled close to me, her eyes a bit wide.

I turned toward her. Still in her tattered dress, she looked ready to frighten the Montrants on appearance alone. She had washed away most of the blood, but there was no mistaking the stains for anything but what they were. "Are you sure you can do this?"

She stood a little straighter. Next to Asher, she looked like a doll. "They won't be able to break through my glamour. They won't see any of us." She looked at Asher again. "But I will not lead them to their deaths, only to justice."

I finally realized what she was worried about. "Asher won't eat them. He can control himself."

439

Surprisingly, I believed my words. Asher would not be consumed by simple bloodlust.

Ryllae considered for a moment, then nodded and started up the ladder. She reached the top, then tugged the handle. "It won't budge. I think it's locked. They must have found the note."

She climbed back down, then Asher climbed up. He tugged the handle until metal groaned and wood splintered. He descended, then gestured for Ryllae to try again.

I watched her go up, then she opened the hatch and crawled into the cellar. I hoped her glamour would be enough. Now that the Montrants had seen the bloody note, simply stating *I know what you did*, they would be wary. But that's why we had Asher. If Ryllae's glamour failed, he could try to bespell them long enough for us to escape. The note would be proof for them that whatever they saw was real.

Tossing my cloak behind my shoulders, I ascended the ladder, setting my lantern on the wood floor above so I could climb out. The Seeing Sword was silent, just as silent as Ryllae as she waited in the cellar.

Asher came up next while I looked around with my lantern. The cages were gone, as were the bloody rags and any other signs the cellar had contained captives. They had already been gone when we delivered the note. The Montrants had likely cleared them away once Duke Auclair had been killed.

Asher listened again, one ear tilted toward the rooms above us. He nodded, signaling we were clear to venture up the stairs. Once we had the Montrants in our sights, Ryllae's glamour would take over. She would conceal us, and frighten the Montrants into confessing.

If things went wrong . . . Asher and I would be there to clean up the mess. The Montrants would be brought to justice one way or another. If things went right, however, Steifan and Tholdri would be waiting outside in full hunter garb, ready to escort the criminals to make their confession to the Archduke.

We went up the stairs and opened the door leading into the estate. We were in the kitchen. A cast iron pot burbled over hot coals in the hearth, and smoked trout was already arranged on a wooden platter on the nearby table, but the cook was nowhere to be seen. It seemed the Montrants appreciated a late supper, which was convenient. They would be easier to frighten if they were both there to witness the phantoms.

Asher gestured for us to step back into an alcove at the sound of footsteps. I didn't like it, but I knew Ryllae would prefer if I were the one with my back pushed up against the vampire instead of her. My skin tingled at his nearness, even though he'd gone as utterly still as only the dead can manage. If I didn't know any better, I'd say my nearness made *him* uncomfortable. But I really didn't know any better. I had no idea what he was thinking. I wondered if he was currently blocking me from his emotions, and what I might feel if he let down that wall.

I didn't have time to consider it further. The footsteps retreated, taking the scent of smoked trout with them.

Ryllae stepped out of the alcove ahead of us, then hurried out of the kitchen.

We followed her down a narrow hall and past the dining room, plastering our backs against the wall just as the female cook emerged and headed back toward the kitchen to fetch the soup. If she saw us, Ryllae should be able to conceal us, but I wasn't sure what would happen if she ran directly into us.

We waited as the cook returned to the dining room with two porcelain bowls of soup. She headed back toward the kitchen again, then veered off without going inside. A moment later, we could hear her feet on the stairs.

I kept my back pressed against the wall. "She must be calling them to supper," I whispered. "Where should we hide?"

Ryllae leaned in close to my ear. "I will need a clear view of them."

Asher had gone around us into the dining room. There were doors on two sides, and large cabinets surrounding the massive table. The far wall was lined with curtains covering tall windows. He opened one door and peeked inside, then motioned us over to peer into a small linen closet.

"Lyssandra and I can hide in here," he said as we approached his back. "We don't need a clear view, only Ryllae."

Ryllae pulled back one of the tall curtains. "I'm small enough. I shouldn't make much of a bulge. It will be easier if I don't have to use part of my magic to conceal myself."

She was right. As soon as she was behind the curtain, I couldn't see her at all, and she could peek out once the Montrants were focused on their food.

"We can all hide in the curtains," I decided, anxious about being alone in the closet with Asher.

Footsteps coming down the stairs preceded murmured voices.

Asher grabbed my arm and shoved me into the closet, turning to close the door so that it was open just a crack.

I resisted the urge to push him out of the way. The voices were too close. A moment later, the Montrants and a third presence entered the room. Asher moved aside for me to peer out the crack so I could watch as a middle-aged male servant seated Lady Montrant. Tonight she wore pink silk, with her hair piled even taller than before. Her husband, a thin man with sharp features, sat across the table from her. Neither seemed to sense anything amiss, both focused on the bowls of soup the servant moved before them. He poured their wine, then went to stand stiff-backed on the side of the room opposite our hiding place.

I felt Asher at my back, peering through the crack above me. I could sense his excitement. It wasn't often one saw glamour from a pure-blooded Sidhe.

Curious, I focused on that trickle of excitement, seeing if I could feel more. I wanted to know if he was actively blocking me out. I soaked in that hint of excitement, feeling it like it was my own emotion, but suddenly it shifted to a feeling of unease.

Asher gripped my shoulder, then leaned in near my ear. "Pay attention, Lyssandra," he whispered.

I shivered. Had he sensed me trying to feel more of his emotions? Would I be able to feel it if he did the same? My stomach dropped as I wondered how much of me he had already felt without me knowing. I wasn't an ancient vampire. I didn't know how to shut him out.

He lowered his hand, and gave no further signs of sensing me, instead focusing his attention on the sliver of dining room visible to us both.

I swallowed the lump in my throat, then leaned my face toward the crack. I could feel Ryllae's magic building. I blinked as the air near the table seemed to ripple, and the glamour began.

It started with a green light swirling at the head of the table, small enough that one could pass it off as a trick of the eye. The servant was the first to notice. He stared at it, blinking rapidly.

The light grew, swirling larger.

Lady Montrant seemed to notice it next, though her

back was to us, so I couldn't judge her reaction. "Bellamy," her voice was barely audible.

Finally, Bellamy Montrant noticed the light. It swirled larger until it formed a feminine figure just a few paces away from him. Charlotte's features became clear. For the first time, I saw her just as she would have looked in life. She was lovely, aged in a graceful way. I could see why her vampire had been drawn to her. Although if he had truly loved her, I wondered why he hadn't changed her. Perhaps he hadn't been strong enough. It was almost sad.

"Charlotte," Lady Montrant gasped. "How?"

Charlotte didn't speak. She gave the Montrants a moment to fully take her in, then she grinned. Her features sagged, growing heavy with fluid. Her eyes bulged for a moment, then sunk into her face.

Lady Montrant screamed.

I searched for the servant, but I couldn't see him anywhere in the room. He must have run while everyone focused on Charlotte.

"A phantom!" Lady Montrant shrieked, standing so abruptly that her chair went skidding across the rug.

Bellamy stumbled to his feet, slowly backing away. He turned to run, but another specter blocked his path, this one looking just like Duke Auclair. Ryllae had done a spectacular job replicating his likeness, for someone who had only spied him a few times from afar.

"You killed me, Bellamy," Duke Auclair's specter moaned, clutching his bleeding neck.

Bellamy staggered back. "W-what do you want?"

Lady Montrant had crawled under the table, cowering in a puddle of pink silk with her hands over her head.

"You killed me," the duke's specter said again.

"You killed me," Charlotte echoed.

A wet stain grew across Bellamy's velvet pants. "Phantoms! What do you want of me?" he rasped. He clutched the back of his vacated chair, trembling.

"Confess!" Charlotte ordered.

The lanterns in the room flickered as an unearthly wind kicked up, tinged with the scent of the grave.

The duke's face began to rot. "Confess," he hissed, "or I will drag you to the underworld here and now."

Bellamy let go of the chair and fell to his knees.

His wife had collapsed under the table, sobbing. "We must confess, Bellamy! Charlotte was my friend!" She started muttering apologies.

I would have almost felt bad if I didn't know what they had done, but I had seen Charlotte's body. I had witnessed the duke's murder. How many victims had ended up enslaved to vampires, or dismembered in the Nattmara's lair?

The phantoms moved closer to Bellamy, trapping him as their bodies continued to rot. The smell of decaying flesh reached my nostrils.

"All right!" Bellamy shrieked, covering his head with his hands. "We will confess, just leave us!"

"*Now*," the duke demanded. "You will go to the Archduke now. We will be watching you. If you fail, I will drag you into eternal torment." Blood flowed freely down his neck, soaking the rug at his feet.

Trembling, Bellamy reached a hand under the table toward his wife. "Come. Come now."

She gripped his hand and allowed him to guide her from underneath the table. Duchess and Duke Auclair watched them both with scornful eyes.

Huddled together, the Montrants scurried out of the room. Steifan and Tholdri would be waiting outside to make sure they followed through.

My breath eased out of me. It was done.

"Do you believe they will actually confess?" Asher said behind me.

I nodded, still staring out the crack. The specters began to fade. "If they don't, we will haunt them until they do."

"Why not just kill them yourself?"

I turned to face him, only able to see a sliver of his face from the light shining through the doorway. "You mean like I would kill a vampire?"

He nodded.

"We need to know who else was involved in their operation. This way, they are alive to share those names, and to keep it from continuing without them."

"And if those other names were not a factor?" he pressed.

"If I could send vampires to the executioner's block instead of killing them myself, I would."

He watched me for a long moment in the dim light coming from the dining room. "There is a part of you that enjoys the bloodshed, Lyssandra. Do not lie to yourself."

I stepped closer to him, which didn't take much effort in the small space. I wasn't sure why he had chosen now to question me. Perhaps he thought he wouldn't get another chance. Perhaps he sensed that I intended to run from him once we were done in Silgard.

I tilted my head back to meet his eyes. I wondered how many people he had bespelled with those eyes. How many people he had killed. "Yes, I enjoy the thrill of battle, but if you think for a second that I enjoy taking lives, the only one lying to themselves is you."

I turned away from him and pushed the door open, then stepped into the dining room. The duke and duchess were gone, and there was no hint of blood on the rug.

Ryllae stepped out from behind the curtains. "Was that adequate?" she said with a smile.

I looked her up and down. She seemed so small and harmless. "It was utterly terrifying."

Asher exited the closet behind me. "We should return to the cellar. I still hear others in the house." His tone was deadpan. If I had angered him with my words, I couldn't tell.

I imagined the servant and the cook would be hiding for the rest of the night, but he was right. I wanted to regroup with Steifan and Tholdri as soon as they were dismissed by the Archduke.

I led the way down the hall, back through the kitchen, and into the cellar. I avoided Asher's gaze all the while. For some reason, what he'd said had bothered me. He really thought I *enjoyed* executing vampires.

In truth, I rarely regretted the deaths when the vampires were attacking me, but the executions . . . cutting off someone's head while they begged for mercy tended to stick with you. I did it because it was the right thing to do. That didn't mean it was easy.

I didn't know how to explain that to him. I didn't know how to explain why I would kill a defenseless vampire without blinking, when I would go to such elaborate lengths to scare humans into a confession.

I couldn't explain it to him, and I couldn't explain it to myself. But what was done, was done. Justice would always be served, one way or another.

CHAPTER FORTY-EIGHT

Asher escorted us back to the old keep where we would wait for Steifan and Tholdri. My body was aching for a proper bath, a hot meal, and a soft bed. Unfortunately, I wouldn't be getting any of those things until the following night, once we were assured that any involved in the Montrants' scheme would be hunted down and questioned. If everything went according to plan, we would depart Silgard within the next few days.

We reached the partially sheltered area where we had spent the previous evening with the moon still shining overhead. The night was only just beginning, and there were no vampires to hunt, no Nattmara to slay, and with the Montrants heading toward the Archduke, I hoped it also meant there would be no more hired swords tracking us. While I had no evidence, I assumed Bellamy or Lady Montrant had hired the thugs. For the first time since we had reached the city, we were relatively safe.

Still, Asher checked the perimeter to make sure no one was lying in wait. Ryllae waited silently by my side.

I looked down at the dirt in distaste, not relishing the

thought of sleeping in it. My body was sore with healing injuries. I would be so stiff in the morning, I would barely be able to move. Perhaps once Steifan and Tholdri returned, we would risk an inn after all.

Asher returned, giving us a nod.

Ryllae let out a heavy sigh, then turned toward me and gripped my arms. "You did a good thing this night. The people who were taken deserve justice."

I managed a weak smile. "You did all of it. I hope you can return to your normal life now that the Nattmara is gone."

Her eyes shuttered as she lowered her hands. "Yes, my life will be much the same."

"You miss your people," I said without thinking, then instantly regretted it. It wasn't any of my business. I had thought before that my life was lonely, but seeing Ryllae, I realized I knew nothing of true loneliness.

She glanced at Asher, who was now pretending he wasn't paying attention to us, then turned back to me. "Yes, you are right, I have never stopped missing them. But it is an old ache."

Selfish. I had been so selfish in not valuing my fellow hunters. As alone as I had often felt, I had never been truly isolated. "The Nattmara's father was Sidhe," I pressed. "He is gone now, but his existence means there could be others in hiding."

She gave me a sad smile. "I spent many years searching. Ultimately, I would rather spend my time helping people, if I can."

"I understand, but I owe you a debt for helping me. I travel a great deal. I will search for others like you when I can."

I tensed as she hugged me. I wasn't used to hugs.

Tholdri was an occasional exception. Most hunters showed little physical affection.

"Visit me before you leave," Ryllae said, still embracing me. "I should like to say goodbye."

I nodded as she released me. I thought I caught the glitter of tears in her eyes, but she had already turned away. She said nothing to Asher as she walked past him, and then I was alone with the vampire.

He watched me quietly as I removed my cloak and spread it across the dirt. If I was lucky, I could get a bit of rest before Tholdri and Steifan returned with their report.

Sensing Asher's eyes still on me, I looked over my shoulder. "What?"

"Your sentimentality surprises me." He gestured in the direction Ryllae had gone.

I scowled. "I don't know what you're talking about."

"Ryllae is not human, yet you feel compassion for her."

"So do you," I sighed. "I felt your remorse when you told her you had not encountered her people in centuries. Is that going to keep happening?"

He only stared at me, long enough to make my skin itch. Finally, he asked, "When can I expect your help with the murdered ancient?"

I sucked my teeth. I didn't want to help him, but I did want to find the killer. If someone was carrying on Karpov's work, I needed to know. "I have to return to Castle Helius first. I will meet with you as soon as I am able." *As soon as the bond fades back to normal*, I added internally, though I wasn't sure it would.

He lifted a brow.

"*What?*" I snapped.

"I did not expect you to agree so easily."

"We made a deal. I uphold my oaths . . . as well as I am able."

I tensed as he stepped closer, but he stopped there, not closing the final space between us. "You're still afraid of me," he observed.

"You're an ancient vampire, of course I'm afraid of you."

"But not as much as you used to be," he pressed.

I glared at him. "If you are feeling my emotions without my permission, I am going to be angry."

He leaned a little closer. "If you do not want me to feel them, then perhaps you should learn to keep me out."

My heartbeat sped. It was as I suspected. He had been able to feel my emotions all along. He had felt how much I truly hated him at first, and now he knew I was beginning to hate him a little less. As infuriating as he was, he had helped me on many occasions. He had saved my life more than once, and at great risk to his own.

I could admit to myself that it was more than just the bond. You could be attracted to someone and still hate them.

Asher smiled at me.

"Don't tell me you can read my thoughts too," I grumbled.

"Would your thoughts make me smile?"

"They would make you run away," I sneered.

He tilted his head, draping his hair across his shoulder.

Suddenly I wanted to touch his hair again. I could remember just how soft it felt running between my fingers. My mouth went dry. "Can you tell what I'm feeling now?"

His brow furrowed. He seemed almost . . . sympathetic. "You are not terribly adept at shielding."

"The Helius Order frowns upon magic. I was never in a position to learn such a thing." I tried to divert my thoughts, but it felt far too intimate standing close together in the darkness.

"It is something you could still learn with time," he soothed.

Great, I thought. *And in the meantime, you can feel just how much I want to touch you.*

I looked up, and suddenly he was even closer than before, but still not quite touching me. The look in his eyes made me catch my breath. "You know it's not fair that you can feel what I'm feeling, but I can't read you at all."

"I would show you, if you would let me. But you might be . . . overwhelmed." His last word was practically a whisper.

His suggestive tone made my body throb with sudden need. I had vowed that I wouldn't go to this place with him again, but I couldn't make myself step away. "It was just the blood before," I rasped. "That's the only reason I lost control."

He leaned his face closer. A single gasp would press our lips together. "Are you trying to convince me, or yourself?" he whispered.

His cool breath against my lips sent a thrill through my body.

"Why did you really come to Silgard?" I asked.

"To see you."

"Why?"

"Because I could think of nothing else. No one else."

His words sent a tug low in my body. I couldn't do this. I had to—

"I will leave you now, if that is your wish."

The thought of him leaving sent panic rippling through me. I didn't *want* him to leave. As wrong as it was, I wanted him to stay with me. *Curse it all.* I pressed my lips to his, inhaling his scent of sage and vanilla, and beneath that, the turned earth of the grave. The scent should have helped me regain my senses, but it only drove me further. I pressed my body against his.

Finally, he reacted. His arms pulled me more firmly against him as he deepened our kiss.

My final shred of good sense flew away into the night as heat erupted through me. I wanted to run my hands up the bare skin of his back, but his coat was in the way. As if reading my thoughts, he removed it, dropping it to the ground.

My hands dove beneath his shirt, smoothing across the skin of his lower back. His body trembled against mine. His mouth moved to my neck and I froze, suddenly worried he would bite me.

Instead, his lips pressed softly against the skin just below my ear. I innately knew he wouldn't bite me unless I asked for it, and I definitely wasn't *that* far gone. He kissed further down my neck, reaching the top of my shirt. My breath heaved in my lungs as his tongue skimmed my collarbone.

I brought my hands to the front of his shirt and ripped it open, sending the buttons flying.

He pulled back, his eyes wide with surprise.

It should have been enough for me to regain my composure, to stop and rethink what I was doing, but the sight of his bare chest sent a ripple of pleasure through my core. I closed the space between us, running my hands up his abdomen. I had to stand on my toes to run my tongue across his collarbone, wondering if he would enjoy it as much as I had.

His answering moan told me all I needed to know.

His hair caressed my cheek as I searched higher up his neck with my mouth. As I went up, his hands went down, smoothing across my hips then curving around my butt.

I pressed my hips against him and tried to lean back,

but my sword got in the way. I couldn't arch up the way I wanted to.

I started undoing the straps as Asher returned to kissing my neck. As soon as I was free of my sword, he pulled me back against him, then slowly lowered us to the ground atop his fallen coat.

I ended up straddling him like I had at Elizabeth's cottage, but this time there was no one to interrupt us. And no blood had been exchanged. It wasn't the blood that had caused me to act in such a way. It was just me—and him. Whatever this thing was between us.

I pushed him down flat on his back, then kissed him deeply. My shirt hiked up, and his long fingers tickled across the bare skin of my waist. His hands slowly traveled up my body beneath my shirt. I broke the kiss and sat upright, making room for him to unbutton my torn and stained shirt. He slid it down my shoulders, leaving me just in my undergarment.

His eyes roved across my bare skin, then across the contours of my chest. His hands curved around my waist, pulling me back down across him. He kissed me again, more gently this time. He kissed me like I was something fragile, like I might break.

The feel of my chest against his bare skin with only my thin undergarment between us made a moan escape my lips. I shifted the position of my knees, bumping my calf against something on the ground. I realized distantly that it was my sword.

My sword. I sat up with a gasp. The thought of the sword gifted by my Potentate brought my thoughts to a screeching halt. Had I really just tossed it in the dirt like it was nothing?

Asher peered up at me, reading my expression. He

lifted his graceful hands to cradle my jaw, then pulled me down for another soft kiss.

I returned his kiss, my body tight with need, but guilt swam through me. "I can't," I gasped, pulling away again.

He gave me a knowing look, but he let his hands fall. "As you wish."

I inhaled sharply, then let out a ragged breath, climbing off of him. I lifted my shirt and sword from the dirt as Asher stood.

I clutched my shirt over my chest, then forced myself to look at him. I could still see his bare skin framed by the black fabric of his shirt. I still wanted nothing more than to touch him.

"Is this only going to get worse?" I managed to ask.

He frowned, then lifted his coat. "I cannot say. I have never experienced something like this before."

"You've had other human servants."

"None that I was romantically involved with. The bond —it has never been like this before."

I wanted to call him a liar, but he had let some of his emotion leak through. I could taste the sincerity of his words.

I looked down at my boots to hide my burning cheeks. "I don't understand," I said. "Why didn't you just kill me as soon as I refused you? I will never be a loyal servant, so why let me live?"

I sensed him stepping toward me, but didn't look up.

He put one finger beneath my chin, lifting my eyes to see his small smile. "You are not the only one who can be sentimental." He took a step back, then donned his coat. "I can hear Steifan and Tholdri approaching. I will see you soon, Lyssandra."

And with that, he was gone, and I was left alone in the dark to wait for Steifan and Tholdri. I quickly put my shirt

456

back on, my fingers fumbling with the buttons. I had more success with my sword, and felt better once it was returned to my back. I wrapped my arms tightly around myself, then leaned against a wall, pinning my sword between the ancient stone and my body. My blood continued to pound in my head as my heart teetered perilously between my vows and the abyss.

The bond with Asher was an issue—a *huge* issue—but he had piqued my curiosity. I had always been taught that vampires were monsters, and they were, I still believed it. But I had also believed I could trust the Potentate, and I had believed it was better to die than to live as a human servant. I had always held firm in my beliefs, and yet now, they scattered around me like the wilting petals of a flower. When the last petal fell away, I wasn't sure what would be left.

But I had come this far. I might as well stick around to find out.

EPILOGUE

The Montrants confessed to everything. The other guards and nobles involved were arrested, and every inch of the canals were scoured for the bodies. Bastien and Vannier were never located, which stung, but I couldn't search forever for a child who might not be found.

Three days after the events in the Montrant's cellar, Steifan, Tholdri, and I visited Ryllae to say our goodbyes. She had cleaned up her home, and the small nomadic civilization around her were back to protecting her, watching us warily as we walked through her doorway.

Within her small home, she embraced me, pulling away with a knowing look. "You be careful, and remember all we discussed."

I stepped back to stand between Steifan and Tholdri, acknowledging her words with a nod. I hadn't told either of the men my suspicions about the Potentate. Such thinking could be dangerous, and I didn't want them involved.

"If you ever find yourself in the North," I said, "come pay us a visit."

Her mouth twisted. "I find that unlikely, but if you run across any of my people in your travels, I will come."

Unfortunately, that was just as unlikely as her coming to visit, but I would try. "We'd better be off," I said. "We have a long ride ahead."

Ryllae's mouth twisted further. "A word alone, Lyssandra, if you would."

Before I could answer, Tholdri patted me on the shoulder. "We'll wait for you outside."

Steifan followed him out, leaving me alone with Ryllae. I found myself nervous about what she might have to say. I already knew I had to worry about the Potentate. I wasn't sure what else she could tell me.

She stepped closer, craning her neck to look up at me. "I think you should ask your vampire about your sword. I believe together you could discover the reason it has found its way to you."

I furrowed my brow. "The Potentate gave it to me intentionally. It didn't find its way to me."

Her smile bordered on condescending. "Dear child, such objects go where they please. The sword would never have made it to you if that was not its wish."

I glanced at my sword hilt over my shoulder, once again thinking it might be more of a burden than a boon. "Whenever I see Asher again, I will ask him."

"You speak so casually," she laughed, "as if you will not be seeing him quite soon."

I narrowed my eyes. "I haven't seen him since the night we haunted the Montrants. How can I say when I will see him again?"

She hugged me again, muttering against my shoulder, "You will be traveling through dangerous lands. I have little doubt that he'll be watching over you."

"I thought you didn't like him," I said as she pulled away.

She shrugged. "I don't like any vampires. They are bloodthirsty monsters, but that does not mean that I cannot see the truth. He will be watching you, and protecting you. Whether that is a good thing or a bad thing is yet to be seen."

I smirked. "Your advice is confusing, as always."

"I fear I have no clear advice on this matter, but you are a clever woman. You will figure it out. *All* of it. Now off with you, the morning wears on."

I hugged her again, then turned to leave, glancing back at her as I reached the doorway. "I promise I will do all I can to find them."

She smiled. "Of that, Lyssandra, I have no doubt."

With a final wave, I walked out to meet Steifan and Tholdri. I found myself sad to leave Ryllae behind. It was nice having another woman around. Maybe when I got back to Castle Helius, Isolde and I could have some girl talk.

But then again, maybe not.

LATER, as we rode toward the city gates, we were approached by two familiar faces.

Bastien grinned when he saw us, and parted from Vannier to run toward us.

I slid down from my horse and met him halfway, scooping him up in a hug. I twirled him once, then set his feet on the ground. "Where in the light have you been?" I gasped.

Vannier approached as Steifan and Tholdri reached us with our horses. "My old friend found him hiding in the slums. Someone had tried to take him, so he thought it best to lay low." Vannier patted Bastien's sandy hair. "He's a smart lad."

Bastien grinned. "When my grandfather found me, we thought it best to hide until you solved Duchess Auclair's murder. Then we heard about the duke." His smile fell.

I looked at Vannier. "Grandfather, eh?"

His wizened cheeks reddened. "When we heard of the duke's death, I thought I might as well tell him. We will both need to search for new employment."

"Well I'm glad to see you both alive," I said. "Truly."

"Not that this isn't touching," Tholdri said to my back, "but we need to get moving."

"We will let you go," Vannier replied. "We just wanted to offer you our thanks. We could have ended up just like the duke and duchess, or the countless victims lost in the canals. We heard the Archduke is still weeding traitors out of the guard."

I nodded. "The Montrants gave many names. It will take time to question them all and punish the guilty."

Vannier placed his hands on Bastien's shoulders. "We can only hope they all get the block. Now we'll let you be on your way. I'm sure you have other innocents to save."

I gave Bastien a pat on the head. "You stay out of trouble now." My throat tight, I climbed back up on my horse, then urged it forward, not looking back. I'd never been good with goodbyes.

Together, Tholdri, Steifan, and I rode through the gates.

"If I didn't know any better," Tholdri said as our horses ambled down the bridge away from the guards, "I'd say Lyssandra has a weakness for children." When I glared at him, he winked. "I've never seen you grin like that. And you almost cried when we left him."

"I was simply relieved he didn't get killed because of us."

"If you say so," Tholdri teased.

The rest of the day's ride was pleasant and without issue. It was good to be on the road again, though I had my fears about returning to Castle Helius. Beyond that, I had promised to help Asher figure out who had killed the other ancient. I wasn't entirely sure I was up to the task, and I wasn't even sure when he would find me again.

Yet that night, Ryllae's words held true. I sensed his presence in the darkness, watching over me. Part of me wanted to find him and chase him off. Yet another part, a small dark part I would never admit to, took comfort in knowing he was there.

NOTE FROM THE AUTHOR

Hello Readers!

I hope you enjoyed the first installment of A Study in Shadows! Please take the time to leave a review, and visit my website to learn more about this and other series.

www.saracroethle.com

ALSO BY SARA C. ROETHLE

TREE OF AGES

A tree's memory is long. Magic's memory is longer, and far more dangerous.

After a century spent as a tree, Finn awakens into a world she barely recognizes. Whispers of the Faie, long thought destroyed, are spreading across the countryside, bringing fears that they are returning to wreak havoc amongst the mortals once again.

Dark shapes lurk just out of sight, watching Finn's every move as she tries to regain the memories of her past. As if by fate, travelers are drawn to her side. Scholars, thieves, and Iseult, a sellsword who seems to know more about her than he's letting on.

When one of Finn's companions is taken by the Faie, she will be forced to make a choice: rescue a woman she barely knows, or leave with Iseult in search of an ancient relic that may hold the answers she so desperately seeks.

Her decision means more than she realizes, for with her return, an ancient evil has been released. In order to survive, Finn must rediscover the hidden magics she doesn't want. She must unearth her deepest roots to expose the phantoms of her past, and to face the ancient prophecy slowly tightening its noose around her neck.

THE MOONSTONE CHRONICLES

When the fate of the elves rests on the shoulders of an antisocial swamp witch, will a common enemy be enough to bring two disparate races together?

The Empire rules with an iron fist. The Valeroot elves have barely managed to survive, but at least they're not Arthali witches like Elmerah. Her people were exiled long ago. Just a child at the time, her only choice was to flee her homeland, or remain among those who'd betrayed their own kind. She was resigned to living out her solitary life in a swamp until pirates kidnap her and throw her in with their other captives, young women destined to be sold into slavery.

With the help of an elven priestess, Elmerah teaches the pirates what happens to men who cross Arthali witches, but she's too late to avoid docking near the Capital. While her only goal is to run far from the political intrigue taking place within, she finds herself pulled mercilessly into a plot to overthrow the Empire, and to save the elven races from meeting a bloody end.

Elmerah will learn of a dark magical threat, and will have to face the thing she fears most: the duplicitous older sister she left behind, far from their home in Shadowmarsh.

THE WILL OF YGGDRASIL

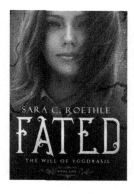

The first time Maddy accidentally killed someone, she passed it off as a freak accident. The second time, a coincidence. But when she's kidnapped and taken to an underground realm where corpses reanimate on their own, she can no longer ignore her dark gift.

The first person she recognizes in this horrifying realm is her old social worker from the foster system, Sophie, but something's not right. She hasn't aged a day. And Sophie's brother, Alaric, has fangs and moves with liquid feline grace.

A normal person would run screaming into the night, but there's something about Alaric that draws Maddy in. Together, they must search for an elusive magical charm, a remnant of the gods themselves. Maddy doesn't know if she can trust Alaric with her life, but with the entire fate of humanity hanging in the balance, she has no choice.

FATED is Norse Mythology meets Lost Girl and the Fever Series.

THE THIEF'S APPRENTICE

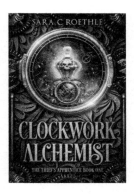

The clock ticks for London...

Liliana is trapped alone in the dark. Her father is dead, and London is very far away. If only she hadn't been locked up in her room, reading a book she wasn't allowed to read, she might have been able to stop her father's killer. Now he's lying dead in the next room, and there's nothing she can do to bring him back.

Arhyen is the self-declared finest thief in London. His mission was simple. Steal a journal from Fairfax Breckinridge, the greatest alchemist of the time. He hadn't expected to find Fairfax himself, with a dagger in his back. Nor had he expected the alchemist's automaton daughter, who claims to have a soul.

Suddenly entrenched in a mystery too great to fully comprehend, Arhyen and Liliana must rely on the help of a wayward detective, and a mysterious masked man, to piece together the clues laid before them. Will they uncover the true source of Liliana's soul in time, or will London plunge into a dark age of nefarious technology, where only the scientific will survive?

Clockwork Alchemist is classified as Gaslamp Fantasy, with elements of magic within alchemy and science, based in Victorian England.

Printed in Great Britain
by Amazon

42359685R00273